Praise for THE

'Reading *Of Saints and Shadows* again, I was amazed how many elements now familiar in the vampire and thriller genres appeared in *Saints* first. Golden's imagination and expert plotting wove these elements into a startlingly original book, as exciting to read now as it was when it first appeared on the rack'
Charlaine Harris

'Christopher Golden has reinvented the vampire myth into non-stop action, suspense and fascinating dark fantasy. [He's] an imaginative and prodigious talent who never lets genre conventions hold him back'
Douglas Clegg, author of the *Vampirycon* series

'Filled with tension, breathtaking action . . . and a convincing depiction of worlds existing unseen within our own'
Science Fiction Chronicle

'Harrowing, humorous, overflowing with character and plot contortions, abundantly entertaining . . . a portent of great things to come'
Douglas E. Winter, *Cemetery Dance*

'Golden combines quiet, dark subtle mood with Super-Giant monster action. Sort of M. R. James meets Godzilla'
Mike Mignola, creator of *Hellboy*

'A breathtaking story that succeeds in marrying gore and romance, sex and sentiment. A brilliant epic'
Dark News (Paris)

30131 05262778 0

LONDON BOROUGH OF BARNET

'The most refreshing books in the vampire genre since Anne Rice wrote *Interview with a Vampire*, [Golden's novels] are completely in a class by themselves'

Pathway to Darkness

'Passionate . . . excellent . . . and a surprise explanation for vampires. Brilliant'

LitNewsOnline

'Wildly entertaining . . . like mixing Laurell K. Hamilton with the dark ambivalence of an H. P. Lovecraft story. The pacing is always pedal-to-the-floor, the main characters are larger than life and the demons and other assorted monstrosities give Lovecraft's *Cthulu* mythos a run for their money'

Barnes & Noble Online

The Shadow Saga

ABOUT THE AUTHOR

CHRISTOPHER GOLDEN is the award-winning, *New York Times* bestselling author of such novels as *Of Saints and Shadows*, *The Myth Hunters*, *The Boys Are Back in Town*, *Strangewood* and, most recently, *Snowblind*. He has also written books for teens and young adults, including *Soulless*, *Poison Ink*, and the *Body of Evidence* series of teen thrillers. His current work-in-progress is a graphic-novel trilogy in collaboration with Charlaine Harris.

A lifelong fan of the 'team-up', Golden frequently collaborates with other writers on books, comics and scripts. He has co-written three illustrated novels with Mike Mignola, the first of which, *Baltimore, or, The Steadfast Tin Soldier and the Vampire*, was the launching pad for the Eisner Award-nominated comic-book series, *Baltimore*. With Amber Benson, he co-created and co-wrote the BBC online animated series, *Ghosts of Albion*.

As an editor, he has worked on the short-story anthologies *The New Dead*, *The Monster's Corner* and *Dark Duets* among others, and has also written and co-written comic books, video games, screenplays, and a network television pilot.

Golden was born and raised in Massachusetts, where he still lives with his family. His original novels have been published in more than fourteen languages in countries around the world.

Please visit him at www.christophergolden.com

KING OF HELL

A Peter Octavian novel

CHRISTOPHER GOLDEN

**SIMON &
SCHUSTER**

London · New York · Sydney · Toronto · New Delhi

A CBS COMPANY

First published in Great Britain by Simon & Schuster UK Ltd, 2014
A CBS COMPANY

Copyright © Christopher Golden 2014

This book is copyright under the Berne Convention.
No reproduction without permission.
All rights reserved.

The right of Christopher Golden to be identified as the author of
this work has been asserted by him in accordance with sections 77
and 78 of the Copyright, Designs and Patents Act , 1988.

1 3 5 7 9 10 8 6 4 2

Simon & Schuster UK Ltd
1st Floor
222 Gray's Inn Road
London WC1X 8HB

www.simonandschuster.co.uk

Simon & Schuster Australia, Sydney
Simon & Schuster India, New Delhi

A CIP catalogue record for this book is available from the British Library

Paperback ISBN: 978-0-85720-967-2
Ebook ISBN: 978-0-85720-968-9

This book is a work of fiction. Names, characters, places and incidents are either
a product of the author's imagination or are used fictitiously. Any resemblance
to actual people living or dead, events or locales, is entirely coincidental.

Typeset by Hewer Text UK Ltd, Edinburgh
Printed and bound by CPI (UK) Ltd, Croydon CR0 4YY

In memory of my dear friend, Rick Hautala.
'In the end, the love you take is equal to the love you make.'

ACKNOWLEDGEMENTS

Thanks to the wonderful Sally Partington. Without you, these last tales of Peter Octavian would never have been told. My deep gratitude, as well, to Maxine Hitchcock, Lynne Hansen, Howard Morhaim, Peter Donaldson, Tom Sniegoski, and Allie Costa. Love and thanks always to Connie and our three crazy kids, Nicholas, Daniel, and Lily.

1

Salem, Massachusetts

The trouble with living as long as Peter Octavian had was that the past waited around every corner, draped in shadow and cobwebbed with forgotten faces and bittersweet memories. A path once teeming with possible offshoots narrowed and became rutted and overgrown, until at last it arrived at a dead end. Octavian had acquired enough magic to make himself nearly immortal, yet in a world of more than seven billion, he felt cast adrift, alone and rudderless.

On the Friday of the first week of October, he drove his grey, second-hand Audi through the gates of Greenlawn Cemetery in Salem, Massachusetts. The wrought-iron gates stood open, but they held an unsettling sort of promise, as if someday they might close and trap him inside, keeping him among the dead. It almost cheered him to think so, to imagine being laid to rest here amidst the evergreens and the sloping grass and the headstones and tombs.

Listen to yourself, he thought. *What an asshole*.

He reached for the radio knob and turned up the music. 92.5 The River was running a Nikki Wydra retrospective – playing her entire catalogue – and it seemed right to him that her voice should accompany him on this errand. The wistfully sad opening chords of 'I Am the Answer' emanated from the car speakers and the music clawed its way into his heart. He could remember the night that Nikki had written the track. Often she had come away from working on a new song with a kind of frenetic buzz and searched the house for him, horny and not shy about it. He could still remember the first time he had seen her, playing her guitar and singing in a dive bar in New Orleans.

An image flashed across Octavian's mind, splashed with crimson: Nikki, in bed as if sleeping peacefully, save for the light spray of blood across the sheet and the spatter upon the carpet. He tapped the Audi's brake, squeezing his eyes shut as he caught his breath. It didn't seem fair that he could remember the scene of her death with better clarity than their first meeting.

'Fair,' he said aloud, scoffing as he drove along the main road that wound through Greenlawn. *No such thing*.

He drove past the duck pond and turned uphill, travelling along a thin lane of broken pavement. The knuckles of tree roots showed through the blacktop in some places. Halfway up the slope he pulled to a stop in a pile of leaves the wind had swept into the gutter between grass and macadam.

The handbrake squeaked as he set it. He popped the door and stepped out, leaving the door hanging ajar. Nikki's voice on the radio followed him as he went around to the front of the Audi. Pine needles crinkled underfoot and then he crunched through the leaf-strewn gutter and onto the lawn. The gravestones were silent as ever, the names of the dead etched on their faces in stark remembrance. Nothing of the spirit remained in these places, Octavian knew. Even when ghosts managed to cling to the flesh-and-blood world, they avoided cemeteries, not wanting to be reminded of their morbid condition. Not wanting to see the evidence that *dead* had no cure.

Haunted by the anguish in Nikki's voice, Octavian stood and stared down at the gravestone in front of him.

MARCOPOULOS.

He let out a long breath and ran a hand over the slick stone, just above the tiny canyons made by the stroke of each engraved letter.

'Hello, old friend,' Octavian said.

He knew that George Marcopoulos was not there, but thought that perhaps somewhere the old man's spirit might still endure and might perk up at the sound of his voice. Peter Octavian had been a warrior, a vampire, a prisoner of Hell, and a sorcerer. He had fought demons and witches and ancient gods and encountered all kinds of spirits – he knew better than to question the existence of ghosts.

The autumn wind blew dry orange leaves across the graves as he walked around to the back of the stone. During the time Octavian had lived in Boston, George had been his closest friend and confidante, a man of quiet wisdom and enormous heart who had never allowed himself to be frightened off by things he did not understand. He had died a quiet death, sitting by the fireplace in his rocking chair – the kind of death so few were granted – and Octavian still missed him terribly.

3

On the back of the stone, two names were carved. *George J. Marcopoulos. Valerie Moustakis Marcopoulos.* Dates provided the parameters of their lives but the only thing that mattered to Octavian that morning was the symbol that separated the two names: ~

It linked them for eternity, husband and wife buried there together. In the centuries Octavian had been upon the Earth, he had been in love many times, but he did not know if he had ever loved a woman so fiercely that he would have chosen eternity with any of them. Death always seemed to come for them before he could find out. Before Nikki, there had been Meaghan Gallagher, whose memory still made him ache with loss. But Meaghan had died a hero in a moment of self-sacrifice, and Nikki . . .

'I miss her, George,' he whispered, glancing up at the grey October sky.

In truth, he missed them all. Over his long life he had lost friends and lovers and fellow warriors, but only weeks ago he had lost nearly all of his remaining friends in a single night. Weakened by supernatural incursions from infernal dimensions, the soul of the Earth – the goddess spirit worshipped by so many under the name Gaea – mustered her strength and channelled it through an avatar, causing the planet to fight back. All over the globe, portals had opened in the ground and dragged every demon and vampire through, shunting them into parallel worlds with no more effort than it would have taken to throw out the trash. It had ended a savage battle between the forces of Hell and those who sought to preserve humanity, and Octavian had been at the very centre of it all.

'I never asked for this,' he said, leaning against the headstone. 'Not any of it. All I ever wanted to do was make my father notice me, and he's been dead almost six hundred years.'

He uttered something halfway between a laugh and a sigh.

You wanted to be a warrior, he reminded himself. *And you got your wish.*

As a young man he had drunk too much wine and listened to the nightingales sing just inside the walls of Constantinople, fighting the invaders side by side with his dearest friends, Gregory and Andronicus, who had teased him mercilessly when they first learned of his claim to be the bastard son of the emperor of Byzantium. *The last emperor*, he thought, now. His name had been Nicephorus Dragases, and his claim had been the truth.

When Karl von Reinman had approached him and offered to make him a better warrior, to give him the power to kill as many Turks as he could ever wish, Octavian had jumped at the opportunity. As a boy, he had been warned that such bargains always came with a price. For him, the price was dear: fear of the sun, the abandonment of all he'd loved, and that hunger. Years had passed since he had evolved beyond vampirism but he could still remember the bloodthirst screaming inside of him.

Von Reinman's coven had been his family for ages – Una, Xin, Rolf Sechs, Alexandra Nueva and the rest. He'd drifted away from them from time to time, gone off to charge into battle with other warriors, newfound brothers and sisters. War called to him. The tiny spark of humanity left inside of him tried as best it could to keep him on the side of the heroes ... whenever a distinction could be made between the two sides in a conflict. He had met Kuromaku, then – a Japanese vampire, a samurai, and now his chosen brother.

Other faces drifted through his mind, like playing cards tossed to the wind. Ted Gardiner. Frank Harris. Meaghan. Will Cody. Allison Vigeant. Rafael Nieto. The priest, Father Jack Devlin. Nikki. George Marcopoulos. The earthwitch, Keomany Shaw. Keomany, whom Gaea had chosen as her avatar, who had helped to heal the Earth and, in doing so, purged it of demons and the demonic, including vampires, among them Kuromaku, Allison, and a girl named Charlotte, a young vampire he had taken under his wing.

His friends.

He knew many people, but over time it had become less common for him to allow someone a place in his heart. When he did, he nurtured a fierce devotion to them. Now they were all dead or gone except for Keomany, and Gaea had changed her so fundamentally that he was not sure his friend still existed inside nature's avatar. There were those who would rush to his aid if he should call, most recently Amber Morrissey and Miles Varick, neither fully human, but Octavian refused to summon them. They had earned the right to live out whatever sort of life they could create.

Once upon a time, Octavian himself had been shunted into Hell, or at least one of the nightmarish dimensions that had informed stories of the netherworld since humanity's earliest imaginings. Though a mere five years passed on Earth, he had spent a millennium in Hell and during that time he had learned a thousand years worth of dark magic and bright sorcery. For the past two weeks, he had searched for some way back, something that would open a passage for him to invade Hell and bring his friends and allies back into the world of their birth. He had consulted other mages, both powerful sorcerers and academic dabblers, and cast a hundred spells, none of which had worked. He could neither open a portal nor transport himself from one dimension to the next. Peter Octavian might have been the most powerful mage in the world, but he had begun to grow desperate. He would not rest until he had freed his friends from Hell or forced Gaea to return them.

No matter what the cost.

'Maybe you're wondering why I've come to see you,' Octavian said, running his hand along the top of the gravestone. He smiled. 'It has been a while, I know.'

Octavian went around to study the engraved letters again. Smile fading, he began to contort his fingers into strange figures, sketching at the air and then tapping at the palm of his left hand. He knelt before the stone and traced his right index finger along the deep contours of each letter, whispering a spell in ancient Chaldean. He knew variations in everything from Latin to Chinese, but he found that with such magic the oldest tongues still worked the best.

'There,' he said, and sat back on his haunches.

Pressing two fingers to his forehead, then his lips, and then to the smooth marble, he whispered a single word – 'ignite' – and the letters burst into flames. For several seconds, he just watched the blue-white fire burning and imagined what it would look like at night, his dearest friend's name blazing brightly even in the darkest hours. It seemed only right.

'You never wanted anyone to think of you as remarkable,' Octavian said. 'But you were, my friend. You really were.'

He stood and brushed grass off the knees of his jeans. His brows knitted as he realized that the music from his radio had stopped, replaced by a commercial. For the moment,

Nikki's voice had left him. But as long as he still had her music, she would always be a part of him. For that matter, so would George.

Octavian exhaled sharply, glanced at the ground, and then spared one final look at the gravestone.

'You were the kindest, wisest, and most humble man I've ever known,' he said. 'I'd like to think I learned a great deal from being your friend. Once, in another life, I wanted my father to be proud of me and he barely knew I existed. Now I just want to be worthy of the faith you put in me. Wherever my path takes me now, it's unlikely to lead me back here. But I will remember you. I swear it.'

With that, he turned and strode back to his car, stepping over the leaves and pine needles. He slid behind the wheel, shut the door, and turned the car around to drive back toward the cemetery gates. The radio advertisements ended and the retrospective of Nikki's music returned. The sound of her guitar filled the car and Octavian opened his window to let it float out across the granite-and-marble fields. Then her raspy, sexy voice rose above the sound of the guitar. The tune was called 'Tell My Sorrows to the Stones', and the serendipity made him shiver.

Driving out of the cemetery, Octavian sang along.

Istanbul, Turkey

The following Wednesday, half a world away, Octavian walked the grounds of the Topkapi Palace and paused to look out over the Bosporus strait. Even with the steamship plying the wind-tossed waters, the sight transported him back in time to a simpler age. Violence still defined the world, but in those days it had not been so muddied with doubt and recrimination. Enemies waged war and to the victor went the spoils, and the reins of control. The consequences of war had been more localized then.

He could remember only fragments of his youth in Constantinople, recalled only vague shadows where the faces of his mother and friends ought to have been. But there on the bank of the Bosporus, in the shade of trees less than half his age, his history seemed close enough to touch if he could only reach a little further, concentrate a little harder. He found himself thinking of the smell of roses.

A woman jogged by, hair in a ponytail and apparently entirely unselfconscious about the lavender hue of her matching zippered sweatshirt and sweatpants. The outfit hugged her tight curves in a way designed to inspire admiration or at least her own pride, but she watched Octavian carefully, perhaps wary of any man who might be strolling the grounds outside the palace on his own. He smiled at her but she averted her eyes and jogged on.

Maybe she senses danger, he thought. *Good for her. Best keep running.*

The massive sprawl of the Topkapi Palace loomed behind him and he turned to study its strange silhouette. Octavian could not deny the grandeur of its towers and chimneys and arches, but still it seemed nothing more than an elaborate, ornate blight on the banks of the Bosporus. The Ottoman Turks had taken Constantinople in the spring of 1453 and renamed it Istanbul. Thirteen years later, the Sultan had completed construction on the Topkapi Palace, and so to Octavian the place was little more than a crumbling monument to the defeat of his people and the deaths of so many he had once loved. He had killed a great many Turks in the months that had followed the conquest of the city, but even he could not kill enough of them to drive them away. The sun still rose and fell. The world still turned. Other empires had come and gone. But he still felt the bitterness that came with defeat.

'Fortune, good night,' he whispered to himself, staring at the palace. 'Smile once more. Turn thy wheel.'

King Lear, he thought. *You can always count on Shakespeare*.

Octavian turned toward Gulhane Park, further along the bank. Its green trees towered overhead and he could see a round fountain jetting water into the air. Children played amongst the trees and several families picnicked. Older couples walked their dogs and athletes rode bicycles or ran along the broad paved path that ran down the middle of the park. Once, there had been a zoo there, just as there had been in New York's Central Park, but the age of such public displays had passed. Now the many acres of greenery had been set aside purely for peace and wonderment. He could see that it was the perfect place for a picnic, set between the water and the palace.

There was harmony here, a quiet joining of nature and human purpose.

Octavian set it on fire.

He summoned the blaze from deep within himself, filtered his anguish through the ancient sorcery he had accumulated during his time in Hell. It burned up from his heart and from his gut, tapping into raw magic that had become a part of him, woven from spells he knew so well they required only a thought. Hands in front of him, Octavian looked down at the green fire that crackled around his fingers and he watched as it turned red, a crimson so dark it seemed nearly black.

A thin, grey-haired woman in a long, brown wool coat was the first to notice him. She held her purse close against her body and froze, then began to back away in fright. Octavian had a long history of inspiring terror, but it had been a long time since the fear he instilled had been warranted. *Today, though*, he thought, *this woman should be afraid.*

He started with the trees, lifted his arms and let the red-black flames unfurl from his palms. Fingers contorted, he thrust his open hands toward the treetops and loosed torrents of occult fire that engulfed them. Half a dozen trees turned to gigantic torches, the fire roaring as it consumed leaf and branch and trunk. Octavian unleashed all of the grief and loneliness and rage that had been building in his heart, and when the people in the park began to scream and set off running, he did not listen.

His breath came in deep, ragged lungfuls and his hands shook as he turned around in search of other targets. An overturned baby stroller drew his attention and he scanned beyond it, saw a young mother racing away with her squalling infant in her arms. *Not that direction,* he thought. *Not yet.* It wasn't the people he'd come here to kill . . . it was the park. The trees. The pure *nature* of it.

Men were shouting to his right and he strode in their direction. A young policeman appeared in his stiff uniform, face rigid with panic but still courageous enough to move toward the crimson fire instead of away. Octavian respected that, though he was unsure if the man had a warrior's heart . . . or a fool's. Off to the left, nearer the water, the fire spread across the grass to ignite abandoned picnic blankets and a football that had been left nearby. For a moment, Octavian felt profound regret, but then the policeman shouted at him and he remembered why he was here. He hadn't been the one to set this in motion; that had been Gaea.

'You!' the policeman shouted in Turkish. 'Put your hands up!'

Octavian complied, raising his arms as he slowly spun around to glare at the cop. Fat droplets of black fire rained down from his hands and melted the paved path at his feet. The policeman gaped at him, tried to form words and failed, and then began to back away.

'Run!' Octavian snapped. 'Get out of here!'

Turning, he lifted his hands and muttered under his breath, feeding the dark flames with more magic. The red-black fire jumped from tree to tree, turned the thickest trunks to cinders and charred the grass down to dead earth.

'Keomany!' Octavian screamed. 'I know you can feel this! And if you feel it, then you can hear me! Show yourself! Come and meet me face to face or I swear to you that I will decimate every wild acre on the face of this planet until you do!'

He fell silent. Sirens wailed in the distance and the fire roared around him, consuming everything that grew in the park at unnatural speed. Patches of ground had already burned down to gleaming embers. The heat seared Octavian's skin but he ignored it and glanced around . . . waiting.

'Keomany Shaw!' he shouted, but there was still no reply. The sirens were getting closer and he did not want to have to defend himself against cops or firefighters who were determined to stop him.

Octavian exhaled. He did not want to do this.

'All right,' he said quietly. 'If that's how it has to be.'

He went to the edge of the cracked and melting pavement and lowered his head, chin almost touching his chest as he let his eyes close. His upper lip twitched, as it always seemed to whenever he prepared to speak the ancient tongues. The spell would be effective in any language, but the Scythians had perfected it in the sixth century BC. Historians believed that the scorched-earth policy they instituted when retreating from battle with the army of Darius the Great had meant merely setting fire to crops and killing livestock so Darius's troops would have nothing to eat, and burning dwellings so they would have no protection from the elements. But the mages employed by the Scythians had one other trick. One spell that made the land useless to all who came after them.

Muttering in that guttural tongue, Octavian felt beads of sweat pop out on his forehead and his stomach roiled with nausea. The blight came into him, the disease, and, for a few moments, he carried it alone. Then he dropped to his knees, feverish and withering until he put his hands into the blackened grass and pushed his fingers into the soil. Scipio had forced his sorcerers to do the same thing to Carthage. The blight came out of him, seeped into the soil, and the burned grass turned from black to a dead grey.

The poison spread, so vile and powerful that it snuffed the remaining fires. The few skeletal trees that still stood crumbled to pale ash like the powder at the end of a cigarette. Nothing would ever grow in the park again; Octavian had effectively killed it. Regret surfaced in the back of his mind and he strangled it, suffocated it, forced it back down.

'Come on, you bitch,' he said quietly to Gaea. 'Send your girl to parley.'

The ground began to shake. A crack appeared in the poisoned soil a dozen feet from where Octavian stood, and then a green shoot appeared from the crack, stretching upward. It darkened and grew bark and within seconds it turned from sapling to fully grown tree, towering thirty feet over his head, the leaves sprouting so quickly that they made a rustling noise that sounded quite like a cluster of whispering children.

Octavian stared at the tree, waiting. His magic had power, but not so much that he could prevent Gaea from making something grow when she wished it. She was the soul of the Earth itself. The spirit of nature. But at least he'd gotten her attention.

On the side of the tree facing him, the bark had formed with a strange curvature, but Octavian recognized it immediately. He had thought that when this moment came he would want to hurt her, but, as the bark cracked and arms and legs pulled away from the tree trunk, he felt only sadness. The crimson fire that had roared around his fists flickered and diminished and died, snuffed out by sorrow.

A slender female figure separated from the trunk of the tree. Some of her skin was bark, while other parts had the smooth sheen of bare wood. She opened her eyes and Octavian saw that they were the green of fresh grass. The air of calm and elegance that lingered around her made him think that she might smile, but those eyes held only contempt and anger.

'You bastard,' she said.

'Hello, Keomany,' Octavian replied.

He wanted to return her anger but now, after all of the destruction he had wreaked upon the park, there in the shadow of the hated palace of the Sultans, he missed her. Once, they had been friends, and Keomany Shaw had been beautiful, kind and brave, caught up in a supernatural maelstrom. She had been an earthwitch of uncommon innate power, possessed of a spiritual rapport with Gaea unlike any Octavian had ever seen. Their bond had been so strong that when Keomany had died in combat against an ancient chaos deity, Gaea had seen fit to resurrect her as . . . this. A creature more of nature – of earth and water and flora – than of flesh. The avatar of nature itself.

'You can't do this,' Keomany said, walking toward him, somehow still beautiful though she had only the shape of a woman. 'She won't allow it.'

Octavian stood his ground. Cocked his head. Felt the crimson fire crackling in his core, burning low but not extinguished.

'And yet, here I am,' he said, staring at those green eyes. The stink of burned vegetation filled the air. 'I'll do it again, Keomany. And again and again. We were friends once—'

'We're still friends, if you'll only see that.'

'No. All of my friends are gone. She took them all from me, dumped them in some parallel world and sealed off all the doors. I don't even know if they're alive or what kind of world they're in now.'

Keomany dropped her gaze and, for a moment, she looked almost human. Her green eyes were moist as if with tears.

'Hell,' she said quietly. 'They're in one Hell or another. We pushed the demons back to where they had come from, and the vampires – all of the vampires – were pushed with them. Wherever those incursions were coming from, that's where Allison and Charlotte and the others have been sent.'

Octavian nodded, jaw tight with anger. It was just as he'd feared.

'Bring them back,' he said.

'You know I can't—'

'Not you,' he snapped, and then he looked up at the branches of the new tree, this impossible growth. 'Her! Bring them back!'

'That's not going to happen, Peter. I'm sorry, it just—'

Octavian took two steps toward her, but Keomany didn't flinch. He scraped the heel of his shoe in the grey ash that had once been Gulhane Park.

'I can do this everywhere,' he said. He felt the crackle around his hands as red-black fire began to ignite on his palms, and now it filled him so completely that a veil of red fell across his eyes, a burning mist that spilled out of him. 'All I need is time.'

Keomany softened and a change came over her. The bark texture of her skin smoothed to a glossy sheen like newly sprouted leaves and, for a moment, her eyes seemed almost human. He remembered how tough she'd been, and how funny, and the way she and Nikki had laughed together in that way only women who'd been friends for a very long time ever managed.

'She'll kill you, Peter,' Keomany said. 'I don't want that to happen.'

Octavian took a step back. 'She can try. I've fought gods before and I'm still here.'

'You're powerful, I know. And you could hurt her; Gaea realizes that. But you're talking about trying to combat nature itself, the earth and the elements. Do you really want to try to exist in a world where the whole planet is against you?'

Octavian almost fell into the trap of thinking the woman who stood before him was his friend. He shook his head and took another step back. Keomany – his friend – had died, and this thing might have her face and her memories and even some of her emotions, but the avatar served Gaea, not itself.

'I understand why Gaea did it,' he said warily, blood-black fire raging around his fists. 'Without her, I don't think we'd have been able to push back the demons. That invasion might have been successful. Hell might've overrun the Earth. But I've been fighting for over a century to prove that there's a difference between Shadows and vampires. Some of the people shunted into Hell – damned, for lack of a better word – are good and decent. They're not monsters, Keomany. They're fucking heroes, and they deserve a chance. I'm not asking for Gaea to reverse what she's done or throw the doors open again. I'm just asking you to let me through. I've tried every spell I can think of to open a portal so I can go and bring them back, but the barriers between worlds are just too strong. So I'm pleading. Let me through, and then let me come back with a handful of Shadows who strive to be worthy of their divine heritage instead of falling victim to the demon side of their nature.'

Keomany closed her eyes for a second, breathing, listening to some inner voice.

'I'm sorry,' she said, opening her green eyes, some of the bark-like ridges returning to her skin. 'This is the world as it is, now, and you've got to accept it.'

The sirens grew louder. A distant noise grew into a roar and Octavian glanced over his shoulder to see a helicopter approaching. Desperation sparked within him. Whatever he was going to do, it had to be now. He did not want to have to defend himself against the Turkish authorities.

The wind blew off the Bosporus, stirring the ash at his feet and shaking the branches in the towering tree that Keomany had caused to grow there in the devastation.

'Just remember that I tried talking,' Octavian said.

With a wave of his left hand, he froze Keomany in ice, her eyes wide with shock. Then he turned and let loose two arcing blasts of blood-black flame that engulfed the massive tree. The fire roared so loudly that for a few seconds it drowned out the noise of the chopper's rotors. An amplified voice shouted warnings or commands in Turkish – someone on board the helicopter trying to take control of the situation – but Octavian did not even turn. He strode toward the burning tree as the blaze rendered it down to that same grey ash.

'I'm not going to stop—' he began.

The ground shook so hard that it threw him sprawling on his hands and knees. Startled, he glanced around and saw green shoots pushing up from the ruined grey soil. Grass grew beneath his hands and a tree emerged so close to him and so swiftly that its rapid growth knocked him aside.

'No!' Octavian shouted.

But his screams would do no good. Trees and bushes and grass and flowering plants went from saplings and seeds and shoots to a lush expanse of wild flora more like a newborn jungle than some city park. The black-red fire still raged inside of him, but, as Octavian stood, he faltered and lowered his hands. The crackling flames around his fists abated.

'Peter,' a voice said, and he spun around to see a newly grown Keomany tearing herself away from another tree, a deep frown on the bark of her forehead. 'Don't do that again.'

Keomany had grown herself up out of the ground, all roots and vines and leaves, now, a creature made from layers of plant life, but her hands were made of stone and there was a flinty edge to her teeth when she spoke. The thing he had frozen in ice had been left behind, an abandoned husk in the shape of a woman.

'I swear I'll—'

'They're not welcome here,' Keomany interrupted. 'Gaea has made that clear.'

'Then send me with them!' Octavian snapped. 'I was a Shadow for hundreds of years. I spent a thousand years in Hell. Isn't there enough of the demonic in me?'

'You're not a demon,' she said.

The amplified voice came again, but the sound of the chopper's rotors had dimmed thanks to the hundreds of trees that were around and above them now. The canopy dulled the noise and hid them away from prying eyes.

'I've got nothing left here, Keomany,' he said. 'I'm alone. An artifact of a different age. Without Kuromaku and Allison and the others, it's like my time has passed.'

'Your time passed around the beginning of the seventeenth century,' she replied. 'But you hung on.'

Octavian shivered. For the first time in ages, he felt human. All too human.

'Then why won't she just let me through?'

Keomany made as if to reply and then halted, closing her eyes, consulting with the goddess.

'I'm not supposed to tell you this,' she said.

'But you're going to?' Octavian asked, surprised.

Keomany opened her eyes. 'Here, in this world, she can keep the barriers strong. But she's worried that you might be able to find a way to break through from the other side.'

Octavian smiled, the tiniest spark of hope igniting within him. He looked up at Keomany, intending to thank her, but the light had gone out of her eyes. Another husk stood before him, little more than a scarecrow. The stone portions of its hands weighed too much for the roots and leaves to support and, after a moment, they broke off and fell to the ground and the whole thing turned dry and desiccated and broke apart with a puff of dust.

'Thank you,' he whispered to a friend he had thought no longer existed.

Then he turned and strode through the new wilderness of Gulhane Park. If he wished to, he could pass by the police unseen, or masquerading beneath a different face, so leaving Turkey would not be difficult. He had more important things on his mind.

If Gaea feared what might happen were he to break through the barrier that separated Earth from other dimensions – if it worried her – then he felt sure there must be something for her to worry about. There was a way after all.

He just had to find it.

2

Salzburg, Austria

Just after eight a.m., two days later, Octavian stood in the shadow of the great cathedral at the heart of the Old City of Salzburg, and watched workers beginning to construct a stage at the other end of Residence Square. Metal piping made up the substructure and a truck had brought in half a dozen palettes of heavy plywood sheets that would be fitted together to comprise the stage. The work went so smoothly that Octavian imagined that these men and women must have done the same job multiple times in the past. He figured the city must be hosting an open-air concert that evening, though he supposed it might be a political rally or something even more unsavory.

The sky hung blue and bright above the city and the breeze brought clean, pure air down out of the mountains. The Hohensalzburg fortress stood sentry on the horizon, looming

CHRISTOPHER GOLDEN

over both old and new parts of the city. In most of the gardens he had seen as he wandered through the narrow roads this morning, there were still flowers in bloom. October had arrived, but only very gently. Soon, the autumn would take full hold, but not yet. The flowers persevered.

Octavian breathed in the air that came down from the mountains and wished that he could enjoy Salzburg the way a new visitor might. It would have pleased him to be able to sit outside at a café and listen to an orchestra playing Mozart in the square – Mozart, in the city that had been his home. The previous afternoon, he had seen a tour bus driving up toward the Nonnberg Abbey and heard the voices of children and adults alike singing 'My Favourite Things'. The *Sound of Music* tour. The film had been based on the true story of a Salzburg family, and it seemed to bring joy to so many, drawing tourists from around the world.

The city had an old-world quaintness and a beauty that spoke of fairy tales and noble ideals. If only Octavian had not witnessed so much death here, he might have been able to enjoy it. After his time in Hell, Meaghan Gallagher, Alexandra Nueva, and Lazarus had descended into the inferno to bring him back to the world. Alex had died down there, dragged into a pit of needle-toothed mouths, and Lazarus had been consumed by living, burning crystal, but Meaghan and Octavian had survived.

They had returned in the midst of war. The sorcerer-priest Mulkerrin had brought the demon lord Beelzebub across dimensions and into the world of man. Shadows – what the world thought of as vampires – could transform themselves on a molecular level, becoming anything they could imagine. To prevent Hell on Earth, Meaghan and John Courage and a handful of others had entered the gigantic demon's body, turned themselves into liquid silver, and solidified around Beelzebub's two hearts, killing themselves along with him.

The acid of Beelzebub's blood had eaten away at the silver even as the purity of the silver had destroyed the flesh of the demon's heart. In the end, all that remained were two small puddles of solid silver in the midst of the wreckage of Residence Square. It amazed him that the fountain of Triton had not been destroyed in the battle, but there it stood, water spouting from the mouths of horses, with dolphins alongside and giants holding up the statue of the god of the sea. He felt sure it must have been damaged, but it looked precisely as it had in the years after Tommaso di Garone had first sculpted it.

Residence Square was a peaceful place.

Here, he thought. *Right here.*

Friends and allies had died out there in the square where people now strolled on their way to offices and cubicles, and where workers built a stage for a night of music yet to come. Octavian, Will Cody, and Allison had been among those who managed to walk away. Now, looking out over the square and remembering it all, he wondered if he was more a survivor than a warrior.

Last man standing, he thought, turning away from the view of the square. *No curse could have been worse.*

Octavian walked west through Cathedral Square, crossing in and out of the cool shadows thrown by bell towers and long roofs, and then onto Franziskanergasse and past the Franciscan church and abbey. Turning right, he strode along Sigmund-Haffner-Gasse, studying the windows of shops and banks until he saw the small, intricately carved marble owl in the window of a shop with doors tall enough that the giants carrying Triton would not have had to bend to enter.

He tried the knob and found it unlocked, despite the early hour. The proprietor of the Museum of Shadows must have been either a very trusting soul or an early riser. Octavian had thought to surprise him, both because Herr Buchleitner liked surprises and because he knew that the stooped, spindly old man might rightly suspect his visit to be something other than a social call and did not want to give him cause to do anything rash.

A bell rang above the door as Octavian entered. The floorboards creaked beneath his boot heels. In blue jeans and a faded brown leather jacket, he hoped that he looked like any other tourist, though he had been inside the Museum of Shadows many times, had even been responsible for donating many of the items on display inside its glass cases.

Herr Buchleitner had been one of the people Meaghan had saved in Residence Square that day, more than a dozen years ago. She had thrown the old man over her shoulder and carried him to the safety of a side street and he had wandered away – half blind because he'd dropped his glasses – and collapsed right in front of this shop, which had been for lease at the time. In the years since, he had turned it into a museum for artifacts from the terrible war that had been fought in this city, a way to honour those Shadows who had fought and given their lives for its people. Many had mocked him and some had been furious, but Herr Buchleitner insisted upon educating them about the Shadows, trying to make people understand that they could be angels or devils, as they so chose. Much like ordinary human beings.

KING OF HELL

The Museum of Shadows had not won the kind old gentleman any friends.

Neither did his cigars, Octavian thought.

But as the thought occurred to him, he realized that he could smell only the faintest aroma of the stinking things.

Footsteps came from the rear of the little museum. Octavian glanced up as the tall, painfully thin man emerged from the gloomy back room, putting on a pair of round spectacles. But as the man stepped into the light, Octavian saw the unruly brown hair and the bright eyes behind the glasses. There were wrinkles on his face, but far too few. The features were familiar, particularly the beak of a nose, but thirty years too young.

'*Ja?*' the man asked.

'I'm looking for Herr Buchleitner.'

The man narrowed his eyes, studied Octavian for a moment, and then glanced over at a display case. Octavian recognized one of the items inside – an antique pistol that had once belonged to Will Cody. There were photographs there as well.

'I know you,' the man said in English. 'Peter Octavian.'

'I don't know you,' Octavian replied. "I'm looking for—'

'Herr Buchleitner,' the man interrupted. 'So you've said. And I'm sorry to report that I am the only Herr Buchleitner you will find within these walls. I am Lukas Buchleitner. Julian – the man you knew – was my uncle.'

'Was,' Octavian echoed.

'Heart attack,' Lukas replied. 'In April of this year. On his birthday, believe it or not. Nobody should die on his birthday.'

Octavian exhaled heavily and glanced away. He swore under his breath and ran a hand over his stubbled chin,

25

studying the objects in the cases around the room, the daggers and ledgers and crucifixes. In a small frame on the wall was a black eyepatch that he realized must have belonged to Sister Mary Magdalene, one of the members of Liam Mulkerrin's sect of Vatican sorcerers. Suddenly, the whole place seemed ghoulish. Somehow, Julian Buchleitner's genuine academic curiosity had made it all more palatable.

'You were friends,' Lukas prompted.

'Perhaps,' Octavian allowed, turning toward the man, who so looked the part of museum curator. 'Though that might be overstating it. He was a man of courtesy and intellectual honesty, and I admired that. He also brewed excellent tea.'

Lukas smiled. 'That, at least, I believe I've inherited. I could make you a cup.'

'Thank you, but no. I don't want to give you the impression that my reaction to the news of his death is simple grief. I *am* quite sorry to hear it, but it's also one in a series of recent losses. It feels very much like the world is moving on—'

'You're talking about the vanishing,' Lukas interrupted. 'What the new church is calling "the Excommunication".'

Octavian frowned. Now that Buchleitner had said it, he thought perhaps he had heard that the restored Roman church had begun to trumpet the expulsion of vampires and demons from the world as an excommunication, taking credit for something Gaea had done.

'Yeah,' Octavian admitted. He smiled, surprised at his willingness to share. 'I guess I feel left behind.'

'I can only imagine,' Lukas said. 'Are you sure I can't interest you in tea? Or coffee? I do an excellent mocha. I get the chocolate from Gerstner's and melt it down myself.'

Over the long weeks since Nikki's murder by the vampire Cortez and the demon incursions that led to Gaea's radical solution, Octavian had retreated to a dark place within himself. He had neither sought human kindness nor shown it to others, and so the gentle sympathy Lukas offered took him by surprise. Something released in his chest, a coiled intensity that he had been relying on to get him through each day.

'I'm grateful,' he said. 'But I lost a lot of friends during the so-called Excommunication and I mean to get them back. To sit and have tea and talk of Salzburg . . . the guilt would be too much for me, Lukas.' The darkness began to seize him again. 'My friends are in Hell, you see.'

Herr Buchleitner crossed his arms, hugged himself as if he felt a chill. 'I'm sorry. Obviously, there's much I don't know about the fate of the vampires.'

'Shadows,' Octavian corrected.

'Of course,' Lukas said, nodding. 'How can I help you?'

Octavian pointed to a shadowy corner behind the antique desk where the old man had always sat and watched visitors over the tops of his glasses, hoping to be asked a question so that he could share his knowledge and passion.

'There used to be a case over there in the corner with two large pieces of silver, broad and flat like hardened puddles.'

Lukas nodded quickly, expression troubled. 'Yes, of course. I should have known right away. I was just startled by your visit. You see, I had thought you must also have been taken from the world that day and to have you walk through the door . . . well, you can imagine.'

Octavian stared at him. 'You said you "should have known".' Should have known what?'

The younger Buchleitner, now and forevermore the curator to *le Musée des Ombres*, rushed over toward the desk.

'The case is gone, my friend,' he said. 'Destroyed on the same day that your friends were taken away. I came into the shop the next morning and found it dismantled, simply shattered. Not merely the case, either, but the floor beneath it. You can see where it's been repaired.'

Indeed, Octavian could see where the damaged floorboards had been cut away and newer, younger wood had been fitted into place. In his mind's eye, he saw the portals that had opened up beneath Allison and the others during their battle against Cortez and the huge, living roots that had dragged them down into the Earth – feeding them through those portals into another dimension . . . into Hell.

'And the silver?' he asked, hope dimming.

'Gone, I'm sorry to say. Vanished.'

'Not vanished,' Octavian replied. 'Taken.'

The silver had been his last real hope. For all intents and purposes, it was real silver, but it had once been the flesh of vampires and contained the blood of demons. He had thought that he might be able to use sorcery to force it back to its original form, to make it flesh and blood again, and that Gaea would have to create a portal to expunge it from the world. If it had worked and he had been standing there waiting, he had hoped to slip through.

Lukas put a hand on his shoulder. Octavian blinked in surprise but did not pull away.

'Tea has remarkable healing properties,' the curator said, smiling. 'It's good for the memory, and for the soul. Surely, your friends wouldn't begrudge you a single cup . . . not when it's so good.'

Octavian couldn't help himself; he chuckled. 'Do you make it with the same honey your uncle used to have?'

'From the old nun who keeps the bees at Nonnberg Abbey,' Lukas confirmed. 'Of course. When she dies at last, there'll be no point in ever drinking tea again.'

Octavian glanced at the space where the silver had once lain in its case and then at the door, but the street outside did not beckon because he had not yet figured out his next step.

'Well, then,' he said, 'it would be foolish to refuse.'

Lukas smiled. 'Excellent.'

A short time later, they sat in the little office in the back of the museum, where a nineteenth-century Biedermeier sofa with an oak sleigh-back sat amidst stacks of books and musty boxes. A hand-knitted blanket had been wadded up on one end to make a bed for an ageing brown Pinscher. The dog had given Octavian a single, damp-eyed glance and then proceeded to ignore him.

While they waited for the tea to brew, the two men spoke of Lukas's late uncle and Octavian noticed that the young curator had changed very little in the small office. The clutter had become more orderly and one bookshelf had been given over to digests devoted to international affairs, but Herr Buchleitner's antique turntable and racks of vinyl albums were still there. The old man had enjoyed classical music as well as ragtime from the early days of the twentieth century and Octavian was pleased to see a dust-free record still on the turntable, as if Lukas had recently played it.

'That was his favourite Scott Joplin,' Lukas said, noticing what had caught Octavian's attention.

'"Maple Leaf Rag"?'

Lukas smiled as he carried a tea tray over to the desk and placed it between them. 'That's the one.'

Octavian smiled. 'With all the music I've heard in my life, somehow I still manage to remember that one. Probably thanks to your uncle.'

Lukas added honey to the tea and slid a cup toward Octavian, who took it, stirring the honey in with his spoon. He sipped it, not waiting for it to cool, and found it just as wonderful as he remembered. Amidst all of the grief and horror of the past weeks, he had almost forgotten that one could find a moment's peace in such a simple pleasure.

'Would it be prying,' Lukas asked, 'if I asked how it happened?'

Octavian cocked his head, teacup in hand. '"It" being . . .?'

'The so-called Excommunication. The world was in danger, Mr Octavian, perhaps facing human extinction if the invading demons couldn't be pushed back—'

'Worse than that,' Octavian interrupted. 'They weren't just invading. Understand, Lukas . . . there are infinite dimensions. The barriers between them are invisible but tangible. You could call them walls but they're softer than that and more malleable, a kind of metaphysical fabric. I've heard mystics call the barrier a veil, and maybe that's not so far off. The walls that separate our reality from, well, let's call it Hell—'

'It's not Hell?'

'It's *one* Hell. A dimension full of what we'd call demons, including the ones we're most familiar with from our religious history. Since humanity first learned to reason, we've had contact with them. Either they've managed to slip through, to influence and corrupt, or we've found these places where the barriers were weak or torn. Belief has an effect on it as well, because the idea that some souls are dragged into this Hell after physical death, are punished for some period of time . . . that's true.'

Lukas stared at him. Octavian thought the man had stopped breathing. His narrow features pinched even further and he had turned pale.

'That's not funny.'

'I'm sorry to say I'm not trying to be funny,' Octavian told him, and sipped at his tea. 'You were curious. Maybe you'd rather I say no more?'

The slender, bespectacled man frowned, but then picked up his own tea and gestured with the cup.

'Go on.'

'There are no hard-and-fast rules,' Octavian said. 'If you expect Hell, then it's easy for them to draw your spirit there. The one thing I can tell you is that most souls manage to escape that suffering fairly quickly. It doesn't take long before they believe that they've been punished enough.'

Lukas studied the ripples in his teacup, the result of a trembling hand.

'And this is where your friends have been sent?' he asked.

Octavian sat back in his chair and glanced out the window. 'It's a long story. You know of the Gospel of Shadows?'

'Of course,' Lukas replied.

Octavian nodded. The man had inherited the Museum of Shadows. He would have to know the story of the Gospel of Shadows. For two thousand years, the Roman Catholic Church had battled demons and other supernatural forces and mostly kept them at bay. Vatican sorcerers had used the magic passed down over the ages, compiled in the Gospel of

31

Shadows, to keep the world safe. Only the Shadows – the vampires, whom they called the Defiant Ones – had been able to resist them. But the sorcerers had become sadists and madmen and attempted to exterminate all of the world's Shadows at once, no matter the cost. Octavian had led his people's resistance, been victorious, but ended up in Hell. When Lazarus and Alexandra Nueva and Meaghan Gallagher had gone in search of him, they had brought the Gospel of Shadows with them and promptly lost possession of it. By then, he had acquired enough magic that he *sensed* it and drew it to him and studied it over the course of months. When they at last managed to set him free, Lazarus had been left behind . . . and so had the Gospel.

'Without the Vatican sorcerers and the spells from that book, the barriers between our world and various Hells kept getting thinner. A vampire called Cortez tried to blow them all wide open. It wasn't just a flood of demons into our world; left unchecked it would have meant almost a merging of the two dimensions. Literally, Hell on Earth. We fought back, tried to keep the planet from being overrun, and we were doing all right, but we would have lost in the end if not for Gaea.'

Lukas paused with his teacup halfway to his lips and arched an eyebrow. 'And by Gaea, you mean . . .?'

'The goddess of the Earth. The spirit of the world,' Octavian explained. 'Yes, she does exist. It's fascinating that you can believe in demons like Beelzebub, that you can have seen the things you've seen, and you find it so hard to believe that your planet has a soul.'

'It's difficult to wrap my mind around,' Lukas admitted.

'Nevertheless, she sealed us off from other dimensions. Her vitality's been restored, thanks in part to a connection with my friend Keomany Shaw. It turned out that Cortez was just taking orders from someone he called the King of Hell, and the go-between was ... well, that's another story. It's enough to say that the go-between is dead; but I believe Cortez survived, dragged through into Hell along with Kuromaku, Allison, and too many others.'

Lukas nodded. 'And you're trying to find a way through to them? A way to bring them back?'

Octavian frowned as he studied his tea. After a moment, he looked up.

'I haven't talked much about this since it happened,' he confessed, gauging the curator's inquisitive eyes. 'Most of the people I could confide in are gone.'

Lukas took a small sip of tea, then set his cup down with a clink as he leaned forward in his chair.

'I'm not writing a book, Mr Octavian.'

'Peter.'

'Peter, then. I'm not a journalist and have no interest in research, nor do I have my uncle's fascination with Shadows and sorcerers and you in particular. I loved his passion because it was *his* passion, but I have no interest in learning magic. I appreciate that you were always kind and courteous to a little old man who thought the world should understand that not all Shadows were sinister creatures.'

Octavian glanced over at the late Herr Buchleitner's record collection again.

'He was a gentle soul. This world has too few like him,' he said, letting his gaze linger on the unmoving turntable before he turned back to Lukas. 'I am trying to find a way to reach them, yes. It was never a simple matter to go into Hell. Its geography shifts like the coastline after a storm, so going in to find them . . . Still, I have to try. I'd thought the silver from the death of Beelzebub might provide a key to breaking through Gaea's barriers. Now I'll have to think of something else.'

'It's just so extraordinary,' Lucas said. 'Knowing what you're capable of, the extent of magic, is one thing, but to know that you've been to other dimensions . . . it's just extraordinary.'

'I agree,' Octavian said. 'Sometimes I lose sight of that.'

They fell silent for several moments, neither reaching for his tea. Octavian felt as if they had reached the natural conclusion of the conversation and knew he ought to make his departure. The silence lingered a bit too long, growing awkward as each of them contemplated the conversation.

'Well,' Octavian said as he slid back his chair and started to rise.

'Isn't there a back door?' Lukas asked.

Octavian sat back down, resting on the edge of the chair. 'What do you mean?'

'Gaea blocked entry to these Hell dimensions, but isn't there some less direct way to enter them? Something unorthodox? You've said there are infinite dimensions. Could you get into one of those and then circle back from there?'

Octavian stared at him, turning the idea over in his head.

'It's risky,' he said. 'Trying to navigate something like that . . . I'd probably end up lost between worlds. I'm not like . . .'

He faltered.

'Like who?' Lukas asked.

Octavian glanced over at the turntable again – at the racks of old vinyl records – and a grin spread across his face.

'Son of a bitch,' he whispered.

Lukas cocked his head worriedly. 'What's wrong?'

Octavian stood and extended a hand for him to shake. Lukas took it, rising along with him.

'You've sparked a crazy idea, Herr Buchleitner,' Octavian said. 'I thank you for it.'

'Well, I hope you'll come back and tell me about it,' Lukas said, walking with him out of the office and back through the shop toward the front door.

The bells rang overhead as Octavian opened the door and stepped out of the shop. Somewhere not far away, music drifted out of an upper story window – Mozart's Piano Fantasie in D Minor. The smell of something baking floated on the air. Nearly vibrating with possibility, he managed to tamp down his excitement enough to pause and focus on the young curator.

'If it works,' he said, 'I'm not sure I'll be *able* to come back.'

He hurried away, leaving Lukas speechless behind him.

Octavian never saw Salzburg again.

3

Westminster, London, UK

Several blocks from the famed recording studios in Maida
Vale, the Black Hart stood as it always had. Little about the
pub had changed over the past hundred years and those who
frequented it presumed the coming century would alter it
even less. Why tamper with perfection, the barman often
asked. The dark oak of the bar and the booths was buffed to
a midnight gleam and the aroma of spilled ale had soaked so
deeply into the wood that it could never have been banished,
no matter how many times the floor and counter might be
washed down. Famed musicians made their way into the
Black Hart from the studio, sat on the stools or in intimate
corners and drank fruity Belgian beers or red wines or trendy
vodka. The locals took their whisky straight and their ales
from the tap and they laughed and bragged and flirted with
each other's partners.

Above the pub there were rooms for let, three small flats on the second floor and two on the third. The flats at the front of the building were of course more appealing, as they faced the street and that particular corner of Maida Vale included pleasant façades and shops whose owners decorated them prettily at Christmas time. Much like the Black Hart, the intersection had changed little in the past century, and many took comfort in its quaintness. The front-facing third-floor flat was larger and caught much more of the sunshine, on those days when the sun deigned to emerge from the grey English sky for more than an hour's time.

But Peter Octavian hadn't come for the quaintness or the warmth or the working musicians who gathered for darts at the back of the pub while the stars made themselves visible at the front. He had rented the flat at the rear of the building's topmost floor, where loud laughter rose up inside the water pipes from the pub below. There had been a tenant, an old woman resistant to the idea of vacating the premises, but Octavian had insisted. He would have used magic if necessary, but instead kept upping the amount of money he was willing to pay both landlord and tenant for just a few nights' use of the place, and at last they had relented. In his experience, cash had a magic all its own.

The sitting room had two high-backed chairs whose musty smell permeated the air, but he had chosen a Victorian oak spindle arm chair and pulled it over by the window that overlooked the alley behind the pub. The window stood open a few inches, letting in the chill of the October night. A pair of antique smoked-glass lamps, their globes decorated with hand-painted roses, provided only the barest illumination, but he had brought a modern floor lamp in from the bedroom and plugged it in using an extension cord purchased at a shop down the road.

He set the floor lamp beside one of the high-backed chairs and cocked the lampshade so as to throw a spotlight on the chair that was bright enough to delineate every stain and unraveling thread. But it wasn't the brilliance of the light that concerned Octavian. Rather, he required the light in order to create an effective shadow. The brighter the light, after all, the darker the shadow.

He had purchased the vintage turntable in a secondhand shop just off of Holborn Street. Nothing like the beauty Julian Buchleitner had owned, it consisted mostly of plastic and dated back to the late seventies or early eighties. Octavian had waited patiently while the shopkeeper had selected a vinyl album and demonstrated that the turntable's needle still worked and then paid for it without dickering over the price. On the way back to Maida Vale, he had stopped and bought a litre of thirty year old Talisker Single Malt. Now the turntable sat in the deep shadow behind the chair, with a tumbler of scotch beside it.

'All right,' Octavian said to the murky room, 'let's have a little music.'

The album itself had been hard to track down, especially in London. The jacket had yellowed and had a musty odor, but the heavy vinyl seemed in good condition, without any deep scratches. There wouldn't be any skipping. Octavian went to the turntable and put on the record, cueing it up to the track he wanted. Static crackled from the speakers, a hiss that the advent of compact discs and then digital music had eliminated from the experience, and he found that he had missed it. Then the horns kicked in, and he smiled as the memories came back to him.

The last time he'd played this record it had been in this very room, in the spring of 1979. Even then the music had been ancient, a tune from the 1930s called 'Long About Midnight', by Louis Prima and His New Orleans Gang. Now Prima's raspy voice filled the room again after so many years, and it felt right.

'Don't keep me waiting, old friend,' Octavian said as he walked back to his chair, where he picked up his own tumbler and poured himself a drink. 'You take too long and I'm liable to drink all the scotch.'

On the small table beside the chair was a Styrofoam take-away container from which wafted the spicy aroma of his dinner, a five-alarm jalfrezi he had picked up at the curry place across the street. The gentleman who'd taken his order had promised that the dish was so hot it would melt his plastic fork. Octavian liked a challenge when it came to curry and the jalfrezi did not disappoint. He sipped his Scotch and ate his dinner and listened to Louis Prima, rising every few minutes to start the track over again.

He had just played it for the twelfth time, the Styrofoam container set aside and a fresh glass of Scotch awaiting him, when something shifted in the deep shadow behind the high-backed chair. Halfway back to his own seat, he froze and listened. A floorboard creaked and something bumped the turntable. The needle skipped, scraping across the vinyl to the middle of another song entirely.

Octavian scowled.

'Damn it, Squire, you just scratched the hell out of it,' he said as he turned.

But the figure that loomed in the shadows was not the one he had expected. It stood, rising into the light, and he saw the ragged pits where its eyes must once have been. Some kind of wraith or revenant, tall and skeletally thin, it had jaundice-yellow skin and wisps of white hair. A long black tongue that slithered from its mouth, probing and searching, as if it hunted by tasting the air.

He'd meant the music as a summoning, but he'd summoned something unintended. It twisted its head toward him, tongue stretching obscenely as it took a single, stalking step in his direction.

'Son of a bitch,' Octavian whispered, as green fire ignited around his hands. The magic that flowed through him surged and ebbed, skipping like the scratched record. Whatever the hell this thing was, its presence seemed to make his magic unpredictable. It would still do the job, but he worried that it might have other consequences as well, like burning the building down or blowing out a wall.

Fine, he thought, glancing about the room for a weapon. *There are other ways to kill.*

The thing threw its head back and loosed an ululating scream that ended in a keening cry and, finally, a hiss. It lunged for him and Octavian leapt aside as it crashed into his chair. A mental catalogue of potential weapons passed through his mind – lamp, chair leg, liquor bottle – and he knew he'd have to make it to the kitchen and get a knife if he wanted to rely on something other than himself.

It flailed and twisted, scrambling to its feet, and he knew he didn't have that kind of time.

'Enough,' he said, and extended a hand, fingers curved.

Green light erupted around his hand, crackling as he sent a bolt of pure, destructive force at the creature. Its probing tongue lashed out to catch the sizzling light as if drinking it down. Twisting and elongating, its tongue wrapped around Octavian's wrist and slithered up his forearm, yanked him closer as it consumed and absorbed the hex-bolt he'd cast, and he let out a shout of surprise.

There were a hundred ways to kill it but quick and deadly would be best. He muttered a phrase in German and clawed the air with the fingers of his free hand, meaning to turn the beast to stone.

Its tongue raced the rest of the way up his arm and its pointed tip speared him in the shoulder, tearing through flesh and bone and muscle. Octavian roared in pain as the creature grabbed hold of him and slammed him to the ground. Left hand tightly curled, he punched it again and again even as its tongue stabbed deeper. The whole right side of his body felt cold, and that chill began to spread.

Right arm twined tightly, he used his left hand, grabbed hold of its slick, leathery tentacle of a tongue and began to rake it against the creature's own teeth, sawing back and forth. Spells filled his head, ways to turn it to ice or make it age so fast it would rot right in front of him, but he understood now. The flicker he'd felt in the magic he wielded at his core, the way it had just absorbed his attack . . . the thing was a magic eater.

Its tongue wriggled inside his wound, draining him.

Octavian grimaced. A chair leg wouldn't help him, and neither would a liquor bottle, broken or otherwise. Not against this thing.

'I wouldn't waste the scotch,' he muttered. He released its tongue and grabbed its throat instead. 'I guess the question is, "How hungry are you?"'

Anger boiled up inside him and he let the magic rise with it. At the deepest part of him there existed a well of power, a core unlike his human heart. The magic he drew on came from both within and without. Spells allowed him to pull the threads of the universe, to unravel them and weave them anew, and any real sorcerer could do that. But he had not merely studied magic in Hell, he had accumulated it, transforming a spark within him into a blazing sun. Across infinite worlds there must be other mages with power like his, but not here . . . not in this world.

'Have it, then,' he whispered as he reached down into his core and tapped into that magic. His entire body shook and he felt it rush through his veins, searing his bones. It ebbed and flowed, grew and diminished as the creature consumed every bit of magic he could provide, nursing as if at its mother's breast. But then it, too, began to shake and Octavian could not contain the power that erupted inside him.

'Feast!' he cried.

Its head exploded, spattering grey, stinking ichor on the floor and the table and the rose-hued, hand-painted lamp.

Trembling on his knees, Octavian ripped the thing's tongue from the wound in his shoulder. Weak, his head pounding, he uncoiled it from his arm and slumped onto the floor, wishing the thing had not broken his chair. He blinked as he remembered the scotch and cast a hopeful glance about the room, only to discover the bottle of Talisker on its side, most of the golden liquid pooled on the floor around it.

'What a waste,' he said.

Something shifted behind the chair. Octavian cursed at the sound, knowing instantly what it must mean. He turned and saw it – a second one, hollowed out eye sockets, probing tongue, thinner and more ancient-looking than the first.

It made him feel tired.

'Okay,' he breathed, shaking off the weariness as he started to rise. 'Just give me a second.'

A soft, chuffing laugh came from the deeper shadow just behind the thing – the shadow of a shadow.

'Take your time, old man,' said a familiar voice. 'I got this.'

A sword cleaved the creature in two from behind, even as it turned to defend itself. Its halves slapped wetly to the floorboards as a short, stout figure stepped into the light, an ugly, gnarled little hobgoblin with a smile that revealed rows of jagged shark's teeth and an oversized orange sweater even uglier than he was.

'Squire,' Octavian said, smiling in spite of himself. 'It took you long enough.'

'You . . .' Squire said, pointing the oversized sword at Octavian as he advanced across the room. 'You spilled the fuckin' Scotch.'

Another World
Ardsley-on-Hudson, New York, USA

Riverside Medical Center had been named more for its grand aspirations than for its achievements. The little hospital sat on a tree-lined hill overlooking the Hudson River, its parking lot only half full. It looked more like a generic industrial park than a place where anyone would go looking for help if they were sick.

To die, though? Phoenix Cormier thought. *It's as good a place as any.*

She sat on a bench forty yards from the front entrance and took a long drag on a Marlboro Light pinched between her fingers. She held on to the cigarette with a tight resentment, hating every puff, despising the comfort she drew from the nicotine and the smoke and the simple act of tapping the ash into the metal and concrete receptacle the hospital had provided here in the designated smoking area. Phoenix had smoked all through her years at Boston College – usually Dunhills, thinking they were somehow classier than other cancer-sticks – but she'd quit within a month of graduation and managed to stay off them for nearly three years . . . right up until the day she'd gotten the call telling her that her father was dying.

Not yet sixty years old, Professor Joe Cormier had stage-four pancreatic cancer, and tumours in his liver and along his spine. Two rounds of chemotherapy and radiation at the finest Manhattan hospitals had restored his ability to walk by taking the pressure off of his spine and put him into remission, but pancreatic cancer was a bitch – a fucking monster – and it was going to get him one way or the other.

So here they were, Phoenix sneaking out for a smoke on a bench and her dad snug in a room in Riverside Medical Center because there was no longer any point in him going into Manhattan to someplace better. They could let him die just as comfortably here as at Mount Sinai, and the professor liked the people here. He had lived just down the road in Dobbs Ferry for seven years – ever since the Uprising – and had done his best to live like a local. Now he wanted to die like one.

Phoenix puffed on the cigarette again. She felt the urge to flick it into the parking lot, to just get it *away* from her, but her body wouldn't let her. It was something to hold on to.

In her pocket, her cellphone buzzed. Switching the cigarette to her left hand, she dug the phone out with her right and saw that it was her mother calling. Joe and Marie Cormier had been divorced for a very long time. His work had made him an absentee husband and an absentee father until Marie had told him not to bother coming home. Phoenix's father had taken the instruction to heart, buried himself even further in his work, and barely seen his daughter except when he came up for air long enough to feel guilty.

That had changed when Phoenix turned eighteen, the summer before college. They'd made a last ditch attempt to repair their broken relationship, interrupted by the Uprising. The horror of that event might have driven them further apart, but instead it had given them a new start. The professor had been catatonic for most of the day, his psyche locked away in a place that no one living could have reached, but they had still endured the crisis together . . . and both of them carried guilt for some of the deaths that had occurred that day.

'Shit,' she whispered. The cigarette shook in her hand as she lowered her head and bit her lip, trying not to cry. The guilt had been easier to bear when she could share it. Now she would have nobody to lean on – nobody who could really understand.

The call went to voicemail and she slipped the phone back into her pocket without waiting to listen to the message. Phoenix couldn't talk to her mother right now.

A silver pickup truck made its way into the parking lot, disgorging a sad-eyed man who carried a small vase of flowers. Phoenix tried to imagine who he might be visiting – wife or girlfriend, mother or daughter, just a friend – but judging from the dullness of his eyes, she figured whoever the flowers were meant for didn't have a lot of time left in this world. *Someone else who came to Riverside to die*.

The wind off the river kicked up and she shivered. It couldn't have been much past five o'clock but already the shadows were growing long. Normally, she loved October, but not this year. This year, all she could think of was the old druidic calendar, in which October heralded the beginning of the season of the dead. She shivered again and reached up with her free hand to turn up the faux-fur collar of her coat. Tight designer blue jeans, slim boots, a snug green turtleneck that cost triple what the jeans had, a dyed-blonde slashed bob of a haircut that she thought matched her green eyes better than her natural brown – the look hadn't come cheap, and she'd topped it with a battered brown jacket that she'd had since high school. Like the cigarettes, it gave her comfort.

Her father had weeks to live. Days, if he couldn't kick the infection that had settled into his lungs. Once upon a time, she had saved his life by killing someone else.

She flinched, closing her eyes as she remembered the gun, remembered the feel of her finger on the trigger. Could the gunshot really have been as loud as it was in her memory? Maybe not, but Phoenix thought it should have been. Ending a human life – taking a life – should make enough noise that the whole world would take notice.

In her case, the whole world *had*.

'Phoenix?' a voice said.

Brow knitted, she turned to see a nurse approaching her from the direction of the front entrance. The young black woman wore a thick blue zippered hoodie with Fordham lettered across her chest.

Phoenix's heart clenched and she started to rise. 'Is he . . .?'

The nurse shook her head. 'No, no. I'm sorry. I just . . . I wanted to talk to you for a minute.'

Sinking back onto the bench, Phoenix took a drag on her cigarette, the familiar bile of resentment rising in the back of her throat.

'Please just go away,' she said.

'But you *are* her, right? You're Phoenix Cormier?'

Phoenix glared at her, lips already forming the words *fuck off*. But the pain in the nurse's coffee-brown eyes made her hold her tongue. Instead she flicked the ashes off of the tip of her cigarette and glanced at the river in the distance.

The nurse sat down beside her. 'I'm Ronni Snow. Look, I'm sorry to disturb you but I came out for a smoke and I recognized you and then I couldn't walk away.'

'You couldn't?' Phoenix asked.

Ronni averted her gaze. 'I guess I . . .' she began, and then shook her head. 'Actually, no. I was going to say I could have, but that would be a lie.'

Phoenix studied the pain in her eyes. 'That your real name? Ronni Snow?'

'Short for Veronica, yeah.'

'So what can I do for you, Veronica? Or, wait, let me guess: you want to talk about the Uprising? You want to give me your opinion on whether or not I was justified in killing Eric Honen, even though the cops and the FBI and the goddamn President of the United States confirmed that shooting him ended it faster and saved who-knows-how-many lives? Some people thank me and others tell me I'm going to Hell because I'm a murderer. Usually, I can tell right away, but I'm not sure with you, Ronni, so let me ask you, if the dead were rising from their graves right now, today, hunting and killing and eating the people they loved the most when they were alive and you knew you could stop it with a single bullet, what would you—'

Ronni's eyes were cold. 'I'd shoot him.'

Phoenix blinked. 'What?'

'Right here, right now? Same circumstances, some guy I knew but not that well sitting in front of me, a gun in my hand, and one bullet would solve it all? I'd put the mother-fucker in his grave.'

All the breath went out of Phoenix. Grief strangled her and she glanced away.

'Jesus,' she whispered. 'If only I could see it as clearly as you do.'

Seven years had passed and she still had nightmares about that moment. Not the day, really. Zombies were the stuff of nightmares, but it wasn't them that she dreamt about. Her father had been one of the preeminent psychic mediums in the world. To promote his latest book on the subject, he'd arranged a séance to be held on *Sunrise*, the number-one rated morning show. Professor Joe Cormier and two other mediums, working in concert, would conduct a séance that would allow everyone within a certain distance of the studio to communicate with their dearly departed, all at once. They had intended to make television history, but what actually happened was so much more than they had ever imagined.

A circuit formed. The cruellest and most vengeful of lost souls caught the professor and the other two mediums – Annelise Hirsch and Eric Honen, who was a little younger than Phoenix – in a kind of psychic feedback loop. They had held hands around the table with the two hosts of the morning show and all five of them had been frozen, paralyzed with a catatonia so severe that their hands could not be separated. When those in the studio realized that it was this connection that was allowing the dead to continue to rise, it became clear that one of the mediums would have to die to close the circuit. An argument ensued, and Phoenix settled the argument with a bullet and the death of Eric Honen.

'Listen, I'm sorry I bothered you,' Ronni said, getting up.

'You wanted a cigarette,' Phoenix reminded her.

Ronni hesitated, then turned to her. 'You don't mind?'

'That we're probably both going to get cancer? Not if you don't.'

'Gallows humour,' Ronni said. She reached into the pocket of her sweatshirt and pulled out lighter and a crumpled pack of Parliaments. 'The smoker's best defence.'

Ronni tapped out a cigarette, put it to her lips and fired it up.

'So, what did you want to ask me?' Phoenix said.

'You sure?' Ronni arched an eyebrow.

'Yeah,' Phoenix said. 'I was a bitch. It's a reflex.'

Ronni drew in a lungful of smoke and plumed it out through her nostrils. She had a confident air about her when she smoked, but it vanished the second she started to speak again, and the pain returned to her eyes.

'My grandmother's dying. Fluid in her lungs and around her heart – everything's just shutting down. She's in a nice hospice in Chappaqua.'

'You're worried she's going to come back from the dead?' Phoenix asked.

Ronni gave a soft, humourless laugh. 'No. I mean, not any more than we're always worried that it's gonna happen again.' She paused, smoked, and hesitated further before going on. 'I was living with my dad in California when it happened. I saw it on TV, like everyone else who wasn't in the northeast at the time. But you – man, you saw it up close, and with your dad being who he is, I figure you understand it better than anybody.'

Phoenix took a final drag and then stubbed out her cigarette in the ashtray. From somewhere far off there came the sound of an ambulance siren, rising as it drew nearer.

'I guess,' she said. It was the best she could do.

Okay, so I'm asking,' Ronni said, sitting beside her again. 'Those things weren't just corpses, right? I mean, it wasn't some kind of meteor going by or some voodoo bullshit. Their souls came back?'

Phoenix took a breath, tempted to tell the nurse to buy her father's book and read about the difference between the soul and the spirit. Instead she shrugged.

'More or less.'

'We're talking ghosts,' Ronni went on. 'Our souls . . .'

'Hey,' Phoenix said, leaning toward her. 'If you're asking me if there's an afterlife, just ask.'

'You were there, eye to eye, right up close, so yeah . . . I'm asking.'

Phoenix managed a smile. 'I don't know what it is or where we go, but this,' she said, gesturing at the industrial-looking hospital and the parking lot around them. 'This isn't all there is. I can't tell you anything more than that.'

Ronni nodded. 'That's okay,' she said, tapping ash from her Parliament. 'It's something to hold on to. A comfort.'

'I'm glad,' Phoenix said. She gave Ronni's leg a pat as she stood, and shoved her hands into her jacket pockets. 'I've got to go back upstairs. I don't want my dad to think I've gone home.'

'Of course,' Ronni replied. 'Thanks so much.'

'You're welcome.'

Phoenix left her there on the bench. *I'm glad*, she'd said, but she had been biting back the reply that had first occurred to her. *Is it a comfort, knowing your soul lives on without knowing where it goes? Because that scares the shit out of me.*

She went inside the hospital and it felt like stepping into a prison, leaving freedom and the cool October air outside. The door swished shut behind her, cutting off the world, and she crossed the sunlit atrium lobby toward the elevator banks, giving a wide berth to the damp area around the yellow caution standee in the middle of the floor. Someone had thrown up or something, she figured.

There's a job I'd never want. Bless people who clean hospital floors.

It reminded her of a silly joke her father had made when he had taken her to the circus. She might have been ten or eleven years old and the professor had pointed out the man following the elephants around with a shovel and a wheelbarrow.

'What do you do for a living?' he had whispered to her. 'I shovel shit at the circus. The pay isn't great, but the tips are *enormous*!'

He'd cracked himself up that day and Phoenix had laughed along. The joke hadn't struck her as very funny, really, but it had been so rare for him to spend time with her and she didn't want to discourage him. Professor Joe Cormier didn't know how to deal with children – not even his own. It had gotten easier for him once she had reached adulthood, and easier for her as well. She would never really forgive him, but at least she understood him and knew that it had been his failing, not her own. Despite the horror that had brought them together, Phoenix felt grateful for the closeness they'd achieved in the past seven years. It didn't make up for the time they had lost before that, but it was something.

It's all the time you're going to get. The thought struck her as she tapped the elevator's call button and she felt a sick twist in her belly. Her eyes began to well with tears.

The elevator dinged and the doors slid open. Only when she stepped inside did she notice the heavyset middle-aged woman who had come up to wait behind her. Short and grey-haired with wiry eyebrows and the sort of overcoat she associated with the old Italian ladies at the farmer's market, she followed Phoenix onto the elevator. When Phoenix pressed the button for the fourth floor, the old woman chose five.

'It's okay, dear,' she said with a slight accent. 'No need to feel embarrassed. If there's a place for tears, this is it.'

Phoenix couldn't look at her. Only when the elevator stopped on the fourth floor and she had stepped off did she glance back.

'Thank you,' she said.

The woman nodded as the doors slid closed. Phoenix took a deep breath, there on the linoleum near the nurses' station. Machines beeped softly up and down the corridor. She had always hated the smell of a hospital ward, that unique combination of dirty mop water, antiseptics and the powdery rot-stink of dying people. But she wouldn't leave her father alone. She could not.

The nurses didn't take any notice of her, as if she were a ghost wandering the halls. If she glanced into any of the patients' rooms and someone – patient or visitor – happened to catch sight of her, she would get that familiar nod. That we're-all-here-for-the-same-reason-and-boy-does-it-suck nod. Phoenix had given that nod herself more times than she could count.

At the door to room 427, she turned and went in, putting on a smile the way she would her makeup. Her father lay in his hospital bed, a little pitcher of water and a cup on the overtable that she had slid into place before she went out for a smoke. Frail and grey, he looked seventy instead of fifty.

Seventy. Hell, he looks a hundred.

The professor lay with his head lolled to the left, staring out the window.

'I'm back,' she announced.

He replied so quietly that it took her a moment to make out the words. She frowned as she sorted them out.

'Something's coming,' he rasped. 'Something *other*.'

'Dad?'

He turned his head to gaze at her. 'Something terrible.'

Joe Cormier looked at his daughter with someone else's eyes. Phoenix stared at those wide, dull, frightened eyes and she knew that her father had gone away. She had seen this phenomenon many times. As a medium, he often allowed the dead to speak through him. But she had the awful feeling that this ghost had not asked for permission. Those were the eyes of a frightened animal, as if this lost soul had fled into her father's body in search of somewhere to hide.

53

This spirit had no flesh and blood, and yet it was terrified.

The thought sent ice through her veins.

'Get out,' she said, moving toward him. 'Leave him alone!'

The lost soul's eyes went even wider, as if seeing her for the first time and registering her fury. Her father bucked twice against the hospital bed, knocked over the pitcher and the water cup and sent the overtable rolling away on its little black wheels. That unfamiliar light vanished from his eyes and then he went still. He lay sprawled there, one hand dangling over the edge of the bed, and the remote control slipped off of the sheets and struck the floor with a clack.

'Daddy?' Phoenix said, her voice very small.

The intruding spirit had departed, but not alone. The medium could no longer channel spirits into the land of the living, for he was no longer among them. She thought of shouting for help, but he had given instructions that he not be resuscitated and as riddled as he was with cancer, she would not betray his wishes. He'd had enough pain for one lifetime. All that remained on that hospital bed was a husk, so thin and hollow and grey that it barely resembled the distant, absent-minded man she had worked so hard to love.

Phoenix sat on the edge of the bed and held his hand as it grew cold.

4

Westminster, London, UK

'Am I wrong,' Squire asked, 'or are you slightly less dead than the last time we met?'

Octavian smiled. He could always count on Squire to boil complex issues down to something simple. The hobgoblin had waited patiently while Octavian had gone downstairs and persuaded the bartender at the Black Hart to sell him the best bottle of Scotch in the place, though the man had extracted a generous tariff in exchange for looking the other way while Octavian walked out of the pub with the bottle. Shortly, he and Squire were safely ensconced in the two chairs in the flat's living room. The creatures who had come through the shadows – the magic-eaters he and Squire had killed – were gone by the time he returned. Octavian assumed that Squire had disposed of them, dumped them into the shadows somehow, but didn't bother to ask. If he had his way, they weren't going to be here long, so a couple of dead monsters more or less mattered very little to him.

'I'm surprised it took you this long to mention it,' Octavian said.

Squire shrugged, wrinkling his leathery nose. 'I was waiting for you to bring it up. Seemed rude to enquire.'

'You just did.'

'Come on, Pete,' Squire replied, draining the last swallow of scotch from his glass. 'You know me and polite ain't the best of friends. We start off okay, and then we just go off the fuckin' rails.'

Octavian smiled and poured him another, mouth of the bottle clinking against Squire's glass. 'You don't give yourself enough credit. Sure, you lack a filter—'

'I say what's on my mind.'

'Exactly. But you mean well. You're never rude out of malice.'

'That's me. I'm a frickin' prince.' Squire smiled and sat up a bit straighter in his chair, his feet dangling like he was a little boy instead of an ugly, shrivelled little hobgoblin. He leaned forward to clink his glass against Octavian's. 'A toast to me.'

'I'll drink to that,' Octavian agreed.

After they'd both drained their glasses, Squire met his gaze. The hobgoblin's eyes were lit with a dark intelligence that belied his outward persona and appearance.

'All right, Pete. Enough buttering me up. What do you want?'

'A favour.'

Squire sat back in his chair, cradling the empty scotch glass in his hands. 'Well, I didn't figure you called me here just to ply with me scotch and take advantage of me. You want to spell it out?'

Octavian poured himself another Scotch. 'We haven't seen each other in a long time.'

Squire nodded. 'Not since that thing with the naked Irish witch—'

'She wasn't a witch. She was a—'

The important thing is that she was naked.

Octavian laughed, surrendering. 'Of course. It's only just occurring to me, but I missed you.'

'Of course you did. More Scotch?'

'I'm set for now,' Octavian replied, raising his glass to show that it remained half full.

'Not you, Pete,' Squire said, rolling his eyes dramatically. He thrust out his empty glass. 'I meant, "Pour me another Scotch."'

Octavian complied, but as he did so his smile faded. It would have been a real pleasure to be able to sit there and reminisce and watch Squire get drunk enough to tell his favourite bawdy jokes, but there would be no scotch for Kuromaku or Allison. As he drank, Charlotte might be suffering the torments of Hell.

'Listen, Squire . . .'

The hobgoblin swirled amber liquid around in his tumbler, then lifted his gaze to stare at Octavian.

'Back with the naked witch?' Squire said. 'You saved my ass that night. As far as I'm concerned, I'm in your debt forever. Well, as long as you don't become a total asshole. Whatever this favour is, you know I'm on board.'

Octavian studied him a moment, then slid back in his seat, Scotch glass resting on the arm of the chair.

'I need you to get me into Hell.'

The hobgoblin's golden eyes narrowed. His usual profane humour seemed to have abandoned him and in that moment his ugliness seemed almost frightening. He took a long breath, seemed to scowl, and then sat up straighter in his chair.

'Can you say that again? I want to take a mouthful of scotch so I can get a good spit-take—'

'I'm not kidding.'

'I know you're not kidding. You went to a lot of trouble to call me here, and I can tell from the look on your face that it's no joke. I just don't know how to react to that without makin' wisecracks about it. What the hell . . . I mean, what do you expect me to say?'

The sound of glass shattering reached them; someone down on the street had broken a beer bottle or something. The floor thumped with music playing down in the Black Hart. The mage and the hobgoblin stared at each other for several long beats and then Octavian nodded.

'You haven't asked me how it is that I'm not a Shadow anymore,' Octavian said.

'Shadow? You mean "vampire".'

'We prefer the word "Shadow". The vampires here are very different from those in your dimension.'

'Semantics,' Squire said. 'But go on.'

'Have another drink,' Octavian said. 'It's a long story.'

Squire listened patiently as the story unfolded. Octavian started at the very beginning, being approached by Karl von Reinman during the siege of Constantinople and being made a vampire, but skirted only briefly over the centuries he had spent as a part of von Reinman's coven, engaging in warfare so that he could kill and drink the blood of his enemies. The coven had been less discriminating in their victims and for a time Octavian had gone along with their predatory habits, until at last his conscience would no longer allow it. He had spent most of the twentieth century living amongst humans, acquiring blood through cooperation instead of murder, moving from city to city so that his eternal youth did not give his secrets away. Then an ageing Cardinal had stolen the Gospel of Shadows at a time when the Vatican's sorcerers were launching a final pogrom against the vampires and Octavian had helped to defeat them and ended up trapped in Hell himself, along with that dreadful grimoire.

'Five years passed in this world,' Octavian said. 'In Hell, a thousand years went by—'

Squire choked on a mouthful of Scotch. 'You were in Hell for a thousand years? That's not an exaggeration?'

'It's not an exact count. Plus or minus a few years, but near enough,' Octavian explained. 'I lost my mind for a while, but I was there so long that I healed. I apprenticed myself to the dead souls of mages and to power-hungry demons, accumulated all the magic I could, thinking all along that I would be able to use that knowledge and power to escape. When the Lords of Hell caught wind of what I had been up to, they captured me and imprisoned me in a sort of crystal megalith in a field of such things that must have measured miles in every direction. At some point, the Gospel of Shadows became lost in Hell as well, and they put the book inside with me, taunting me with its nearness, because I was trapped like a fly in amber. Not a damn thing I could do about it until some friends came to—'

'Your friends went to Hell for you?' Squire interrupted.

Octavian paused, troubled. This topic had always troubled him.

'Two of them were my friends,' he said. 'One of them, Meaghan . . . we'd been more than friends. The other two were a woman named Alexandra Nueva, who'd become Meaghan's girlfriend—'

'Wait, girlfriends as in lesbians? Because this story just got a lot more interesting.'

Octavian sighed, thinking he wanted another glass of Scotch. 'Squire . . .'

The hobgoblin frowned. 'It's just the way I'm made, amigo. Sorry. Go on. Who was the third one?'

'That's where this story has been headed all along. See, there was a Vatican sorcerer named Liam Mulkerrin who'd been trapped in Hell, and he'd come back infused with dark magic. They came to Hell to find me, hoping I'd know something about Mulkerrin's time there that would be useful in the fight against him. Alexandra died shortly after they entered Hell. The third member of their party was a vampire called Lazarus.'

'Lazarus as in Lazarus?' Squire asked. 'Biblical Lazarus?'

'You have that story in your world?' Octavian said.

Squire nodded. 'It's not very different from this one. Or at least it wasn't until recently.'

'What happened to change that?' Octavian asked.

A heavy sorrow seemed to descend upon the hobgoblin. He waved it away but Octavian saw the pain in his eyes.

'That's a conversation for another day. Point is, it's a parallel Earth. Hell – the various Hells – and some of the others I've come across . . . they're parallel dimensions but not this same world. Not this planet. But my dimension's Earth is a lot like this one. So, yeah . . . Lazarus.'

Octavian hesitated, rotating his glass in circles on the arm of the chair, only vaguely aware that he was doing it.

'The short version is that we left him there.'

Squire went still for a moment. His brows knitted and then he nodded slowly, leaned forward and refilled his Scotch glass, and then took a sip. They had nearly reached the bottom of the bottle.

'This guy came to Hell to help rescue you and you left him there,' Squire said, his voice hollow, lacking in nuance. But his distaste was evident in his eyes.

'We had no choice. Lazarus became trapped in the same crystal megalith where I'd been imprisoned and it looked like it was consuming him. The portal we'd managed to open back to our world was closing. Someone had to get back to stop Mulkerrin.'

'You never went back to check on him?'

'The Gospel of Shadows was trapped there with him. I knew most of the magic in it by then, but not the secret to traveling to Hell.'

'You said you'd learned it all by heart.'

'Almost all.'

Squire sniffed, the accusatory look remaining in his eyes. 'Almost only counts in horseshoes and hand grenades, Pete.'

'The point is that we left him there. Left the Gospel of Shadows. We went back to Salzburg, Austria, where a bunch of Demon Lords were coming through dimensional tears into our world, and we stopped them. Killed them or drove them back.'

'Go on.'

Octavian studied his eyes. He didn't like the idea that Squire judged him, didn't like the way it made him feel. The

61

hobgoblin hadn't been there. The choices he and Meaghan had made – and Lazarus had made – were the only choices available to them at the time when they'd occurred. Lazarus had known the risks involved as well as the potential rewards. He had helped to save his people and in the process had sacrificed himself.

'I remember you telling me about the origin of vampires in your world,' Octavian said. 'Their origins are darker than those in my world, and older. Vampires here – Shadows – are trinity-based creatures: part human, part divine, and part demonic. Shapeshifters unlike anything you've seen—'

'You might be surprised,' Squire said. 'I know a guy.'

'The point is this,' Octavian went on. 'When I came back from Hell I was already about fifteen hundred years old thanks to the time elapsed while I was there. No vampire in this dimension had ever lived that long. At a certain point I entered a sort of . . . let's call it a cocoon state. I evolved. Those three parts of me *separated*, Squire. I was reborn, in a way, the day I emerged from that cocoon. The divine part of me went on to wherever divinity resides when it is no longer of this Earth. The demonic part became a kind of wraith creature, a shadow-Octavian. It tried to kill me, but I destroyed it. What remained was what you see now. Still a mage, yes, but human. Mortal, or at least not eternal.'

Octavian could practically see the thoughts ticking over in Squire's brain, the puzzle pieces fitting together. Most people assumed the ugly little man must be stupid because of his appearance or his crude manner, but Octavian knew better.

'How many years has Lazarus been in Hell, now?' Squire asked.

'More than a decade in our time.'

'And you never went back for him? You could have found a way.'

'We had crisis after crisis. We figured him for dead. I could give you a thousand excuses, but none of them would be good enough. You're right – I could have found a way. I have to live with that . . . and the consequences.'

Squire swirled the scotch around in his glass again, staring at the amber liquid as if its motion were hypnotizing him. The music down in the Black Hart seemed to grow louder. The muffled sound of police sirens could be heard somewhere nearby, moving through nighttime London, just one of many emergencies that would take place in a single evening in the city, and here they were talking about other worlds, other dimensions. Sometimes it seemed so impossible, but Octavian had accepted the impossible so long ago that the moment was lost in the fog of his memory.

'So, a decade. That's what?' Squire asked. 'Two thousand years in Hell-time?'

Octavian shook his head. 'It's not that simple. There's no consistent differential. It might be nine hundred or three thousand. But in any case, it's long enough that he's evolved by now.'

'If he's still alive.'

'Oh, he's alive,' Octavian said. 'Or at least a part of him is.'

Squire set his glass down without finishing it. Apparently, he had lost his taste for scotch, at least for tonight.

'Now we're getting to it, aren't we?' Squire asked. 'The reason you needed me.'

Octavian nodded and forged ahead with the story, explaining how the Vatican sorcerers had managed to create barriers that kept most supernatural creatures away from the human world and how, in their absence, those barriers had deteriorated. He did not speak of Nikki or of Cortez, aware of the time passing by, time he felt he was wasting. Instead he went on to talk of Gaea and her avatar, Keomany, and that in that last moments before all of the vampires and demons had been dragged from the world and banished, he had seen a wraith with the face of Lazarus . . . the ancient vampire's darksoul.

'What became of it?' Squire asked.

'Eaten by a ravenous ghost.'

The hobgoblin arched an eyebrow. 'You have an interesting world.'

'My dearest friends are in Hell. And though I told myself he must be dead, it's obvious now that Lazarus must still be alive there – the human part of him, anyway. I don't know how his darksoul came to be a part of Hell's effort to invade my world, but now that I know for certain that Lazarus is human and in Hell, I can't leave him there any more than I can my friends who've been taken.'

'You left him there before.'

'I told myself that I might be throwing my life away in Hell and there were people here who needed me . . .'

'But?' Squire said.

'There's nobody left in this world who needs me,' Octavian said, lifting his gaze. He shook his head. 'God, that sounds pitiful. The point is that the worst of the supernatural troubles facing this world are over and done with. The people who need me are in Hell, so I've got to find a way to get there. At this point, you're pretty much my only hope.'

'You're not gonna call me Obi-Wan Kenobi, are you?'

Octavian set his own scotch glass down. 'I'm fairly sure that's never going to happen.'

'What if I said I wouldn't help you unless you did? Unless you said, "Help me, Obi-Wan Kenobi, you're my only hope"?'

'I suspect I'd beat the shit out of you.'

Squire grinned. 'I did miss you. Partly because I enjoy your company and partly because your life is even more fucked up than mine. I mean, listen to that story you just told me. Is there a story more fucked up than that?'

'Listen—' Octavian began.

'You know there aren't a lot of direct entries to Hell. Not even from the Shadowpaths.'

'I know. But I also know you can figure out a way.'

Squire sighed. He closed his eyes, thinking hard, and then shook his head.

'Fuck. Maybe it's the scotch.'

Octavian gazed at him. 'You'll do it?'

'I don't like it. I've visited a lot of worlds in crisis, parallels where massive supernatural catastrophes are either imminent or have already happened. Worlds where unimaginable fuckin' horrors have taken over. There's just a lot of nasty shit out there these days. Hell's dangerous enough, but the Shadowpaths . . . they used to be fairly safe, but in the last few years there have been more and more things prowling around in there that don't belong.'

Octavian held up a hand, igniting a sphere of green flame on his palm that engulfed his hand and raced up his arm.

'I can take care of myself,' he said.

'I know that, Pete.'

'You said yourself that you owe me, Squire.'

Squire scowled and stood up. 'Fine. Pack up whatever you need and bring what's left of the Scotch. We're going to need weapons, and there's another stop we need to make.'

Octavian started to argue, but Squire held up a hand to silence him.

'I said there aren't a lot of direct entrances. If we want to get in without being captured or slaughtered in the first two minutes, we need to go through one of those, not some back door. We need permission to enter.'

'How are we supposed to get permission?' Octavian demanded.

Squire grinned.

'Trust me,' he said. 'I know a guy.'

Phoenix's World
Ardsley-on-Hudson, New York, USA

Phoenix stood in the corridor outside her father's hospital room trying to take some comfort in the kindness of his doctor. Many of the medical personnel she'd met had been pleasant enough but maintained the professional distance that she knew must be necessary to do this sort of job day after day. When patients were always being so uncooperative as to die in your care, she figured defence mechanisms must be important, so she never felt hurt or insulted by that distance. Then there were the ones who had adopted a cold, callous approach, without any attempt at cultivating good bedside manner.

Her father's doctor, James Song, was a rare breed. Kind and considerate, with eyes full of gentle empathy, he seemed

emotionally invested in his patients. Phoenix figured Dr
Song wouldn't last in the medical profession – at least not in
oncology, an environment in which he was sure to have
patients die with some regularity. All of that death would
break him, eventually, and he'd end up in research.

'He had such strength,' Dr Song said, his brown eyes full
of emotion, as if he'd been Joe Cormier's friend instead of
his doctor. 'I admired him.'

'Thank you,' Phoenix said, but the words came out a
mumble, spoken by rote.

Dr Song said something further. She missed it, somehow,
and couldn't put her thoughts together enough to ask him to
repeat himself. Sorrow sat heavily upon her chest, squeezing
all of the air out of her so that she could barely breathe.
Knowing her father had been given a terminal diagnosis and
watching him die turned out to be two very separate things.
She had thought that she had begun to process what it would
mean, that she'd already started to grieve, but now Phoenix
realized that was not true at all. Grief still had not seized her,
but she could feel it looming over her and it cast a terrible
shadow.

'Miss Cormier?' Dr Song said.

Phoenix blinked. 'I'm sorry. I kind of feel like I'm not all
here. My mind is floating off somewhere. I knew it would
hurt, but I didn't expect to feel so . . . *empty*.'

'Take your time,' Dr Song replied. 'Just breathe. If you
need someone to talk to, I can recommend a wonderful coun-
sellor. It's normal to feel lost when something like this . . .'

He hesitated and then just nodded, unable to go on. His
eyes were damp and Phoenix thought, *Don't do it, Doc.
Don't you cry on me. You're the doctor. You're not supposed*

to cry because if you cry then I'm going to totally lose my shit right here. For the first time, she wished he was more like other doctors.

'Thank you,' she said again. The words sounded as hollow as her heart felt.

Dr Song glanced toward her father's room, where a nurse had begun to disconnect the professor from his IV drip and the machines that had monitored his vital signs. A pair of orderlies rolled a gurney down the corridor toward them and Phoenix had a sudden vision of what would happen next. They would go into the room, move her father from bed to gurney, and cover him with a white sheet. He'd be wheeled to some staff elevator that would descend to the morgue in the hospital's basement, where he'd be held until she made arrangements for a funeral home to come and get him.

'No,' she said softly, shaking her head.

'Miss Cormier,' Dr Song said, laying a comforting hand on her shoulder. 'Phoenix, let them do their work. You need to rest now, but you'll see him later.'

'See him? I'm never going to see him again.'

'I only meant—'

Phoenix shook his hand off. 'I know what you meant.'

She moved to block the orderlies. 'Not yet. Just give me a minute, all right.'

Dr Song gestured for the orderlies to wait. Phoenix nodded gratefully, took a deep breath, and then walked back into her father's hospital room. She wondered how many other patients had died in that same bed in the years since the hospital first opened. How many, for that matter, had died in the entirety of the building in that time. People had been healed here. Cured. Many more, no doubt, than had died.

And yet she couldn't help now thinking of the whole place as some kind of death house.

Professor Joe Cormier's corpse lay uncovered. His body had become so thin and frail and his cheeks sunken and grey that he barely looked himself. Completely still, not even a breath remaining in him, he looked false in the way that the mummies of Pompeii had looked to her when she had travelled there – withered and unreal, some kind of hoax. But this was no hoax.

'Can you give me a minute, please?' she asked.

The nurse had been coiling a cable onto a hook on the heart monitor. She flinched and turned, surprised to find that she wasn't alone.

'Yes, of course,' the sturdy, fortyish bleach-blonde said. 'I'll wait outside. Do you want me to cover him up again?'

Phoenix frowned. *Such a strange question.* 'I don't think he's cold, do you?'

The nurse might have taken offence at her tone, but instead only gave her a noncommittal smile and started for the door.

'Oh, this is perfect,' a voice said.

The nurse froze and began to turn. Phoenix thought the voice – high and girlish, almost giddy – must have come from another nurse somewhere in the room. Only when she turned did her eyes confirm what her head had told her; there was nobody else in the room. She stared at her father's face, remembering the warning that had issued from his lips in the voice of a ghost.

This voice was different. Gleeful and full of malice. And when it came again, though there could be no doubt it came from her father's mouth, his lips did not move. Joe Cormier was dead. He wasn't speaking . . . he was being spoken through.

'Yes,' said the voice. 'This will do very nicely.'

'What the hell is that?' the nurse said, her voice barely a whisper. She looked at Phoenix, lower lip trembling and fear in her eyes. 'Please tell me that's a trick.'

Phoenix had no reply. *This shouldn't be*, she thought. *Can't be*. Her father had spent most of his life channelling the voices of the dead, giving them the opportunity to speak to the people they'd left behind, so if one of them had slipped in as he lay weak and dying and possessed him long enough to speak through him . . . it had upset her, unnerved her, but it hadn't necessarily shocked her.

But this . . . he was dead. How could they speak through him now?

'Get out,' Phoenix said, taking a step nearer the bed. The fading daylight beyond the window cast strange shadows on his face. 'Get out of him, now!'

Laughter bubbled up from somewhere inside her father's corpse, growing in volume, rising through the megaphone of his open mouth. Other voices joined with the first and Phoenix felt icy dread run up her spine. Memories of the Uprising rushed into her mind and she wondered if there might be some connection, if the malevolent ghosts who had manipulated her father and the other mediums that day had come back.

'Stop it,' the nurse said, frantic and loud. 'How do you stop it?'

Dr Song stepped into the room. 'Phoenix? Is everything—'

'Leave him alone!' Phoenix screamed, enraged by this violation of her father and disgusted by her own helplessness. Behind her, the laughter had stopped. She turned to stare at the pale scarecrow on the hospital bed, the husk that had once been her father. A low susurrus of whispers came from inside his mouth, a cluster of hushed voices that reminded her of an audience waiting for the show to begin.

She took another step toward the bed, and one more, straining to make out the words.

And then one last voice joined them, this one far from a whisper. Low, rumbling so deeply that she could feel it in her chest. Not the voice of a man or even a ghost. A malignant tumour of a voice.

'Don't be stupid, girl,' it said. 'I'd run if I were you.'

Her father's body twitched, then his chest and belly lurched upward as if an electrical current had been shot through it. The nurse began to pray as Dr Song fled from the room and began shouting about a code, and then simply for help. It occurred to Phoenix, in some tiny place inside her mind where terror and grief had not reached her, that Dr Song thought her father had somehow come back to life – maybe as himself and maybe as a zombie. But she had seen the dead rise before and it had never looked like this. That voice did not belong to her father.

'Please,' Phoenix said quietly. 'He's my dad.'

The corpse lurched again and the hospital Johnny rode up her father's thighs and stomach, baring his lower belly. Something pressed against that sickly pale flesh from the inside, and Phoenix screamed at the sight of it. A terrible new sound filled the room, like paper tearing, and then something punched through the sallow dead skin of her father's stomach from the inside.

Claws. Long black, spindly fingers like a spider's legs. A second hand pushed up beside the first and they tore her father's corpse open wide from within. The nurse fainted with a soft whisper of nylon and her head hit the floor with a clack. Phoenix could only stare and scream as her father's remains were torn open further and something began to emerge from inside of him, a hideous birth. It leveraged itself up from ribs and organs amongst which it could not possibly have fit, but she knew from one glimpse of it that this thing had not been hiding inside her father – it was merely using him as so many spirits had, as a medium. A passageway. Professor Joe Cormier had become a doorway into another place, and from the look of the thing ripping out of him, that place could only be Hell.

A crown of bone shards jutted from the scaly, crimson-black flesh of its face, dozens of them in an array of lengths. Broken and jagged, they seemed more as if they'd been stabbed into its skin than like horns. Its eyes were multi-faceted arachnoid things and its thin mouth curved up at the ends nearly all the way to the edges of its eye sockets, so that when it opened its mouth to speak, the lower half of its head seemed almost to come unhinged. Behind its lips were jagged, uneven teeth that matched its crown, jagged shards of bone planted in its gums, its fat black tongue darting around in back of those teeth like a serpent.

Phoenix stood frozen in horror and denial. Her father had just died, but what had happened to him now was so much worse than death. Enormous body halfway out of her father's corpse, smeared with his blood and grey viscera, the demon turned those yellow spider's eyes upon her. *Demon*, she thought. Yes, of course that was what it was. When she'd thought of Hell, she had not been thinking literally, but she saw now that had been a mistake.

'Why, hello there,' it said in that same dreadful rumble, the words filling the room. 'What's your name?'

Her mouth opened but no sound came out. There were no more screams inside her; fear had crowded them out. Had she never encountered impossible things she might have simply stood there while it completed its entrance into her world or fainted like the nurse. Instead, she turned and fled, full of hatred toward the thing that had made her leave her father's remains behind.

Phoenix careened into the hallway even as Dr Song came racing back down the corridor with a couple of nurses, an orderly and a single security guard. An old man with a rolling IV drip had paused in the hall to watch them go by and a nurse snapped at him to get back to his room.

'It's not just him,' Dr Song said as he ran up to her. He looked sweaty and frantic and more than a little lost.

What?' Phoenix managed, her body screaming at her to run even as she forced herself to stop and listen. 'What do you—'

'I just heard that there are others in the morgue,' Song explained. 'Others with the voices coming out of them.'

The nurses stopped outside the room, let the orderly and the security guard go ahead of them. The orderly paused just inside the door and looked back.

'Dr Song . . .' the orderly said.

Song looked reluctant for a moment before he started after them.

Phoenix knew she had to run. More in the morgue? So there would be other demons coming through. But Dr Song had been kind.

'Wait,' she said. 'It's not just voices—'

Someone – the orderly or the guard – cried out from inside the room, followed by the sickening sound of bones breaking and flesh tearing. Phoenix had moved down the hall a-ways but even at that angle she could see something moving inside the room, and then Dr Song erupted from within as if he'd been shot from a cannon. He flew across the corridor and crashed into the opposing wall with a wet crunch before he flopped to the ground, dead on impact, eyes wide and staring as blood leaked from his nose.

'Screw this,' one of the nurses said as she bolted down the hall in the opposite direction.

The other nurse had a different instinct; she ran to Dr Song and touched his neck, checking for a pulse though his lifeless eyes declared him unquestionably dead. His body bucked as if in the midst of some glorious necrotic orgasm and Phoenix saw what was about to happen even before the doctor's body opened like a set of jaws and a thick, taloned hand shot up from the mess of his viscera and grabbed the nurse around the throat. It snapped her neck, claiming its first kill in this world even before the demon, its flesh bruise-purple and its many eyes a bright violet, began to emerge.

The monster that had crawled from her father's corpse stepped into the corridor from his hospital room, black hooves clacking on the tiles.

'Oh,' it said. 'This world is ripe.'

Part of a torso hung from the dozens of bone shards on its head. It had gored the orderly, or maybe the guard, like a bull, and torn the man apart.

Phoenix found herself running without realizing she had begun. Really, she didn't know why she had stopped, except that Dr Song had been so kind to her and she had not wanted him to die. *Shock*, she thought now. *I'm in shock.* Her thoughts seemed muzzy and her heart fluttered inside her, a caged bird, frantic and terrified.

Others ran past her, responding to the shouts and violence before they knew precisely what it was they were running toward. Their screams of discovery and then of death followed Phoenix down the corridor as patients and visitors came out into the hall. She had a glimpse into one of the patients' rooms and saw the wan late-day sunlight streaming in and it seemed incongruous to her. Evil had come into this place and it seemed to her that it ought to have come at night, not on a gentle October afternoon.

She reached the stairwell door, hit the emergency bar and flung the door open. It clanged against the wall as she grabbed the railing and sped down the steps two at a time, the echoes of horror and death still resonating throughout the fourth floor behind her. Halfway between the third and second floors, she heard others on the stairs above her, a panicked evacuation, and she wondered how many wouldn't make it out.

The first demon, with his bone crown, had come from her father's corpse and the one with the many violet eyes had emerged from Dr Song. But what about the security guard and the orderly? What about the other orderlies and doctors and nurses and patients who were not going to be smart enough or swift enough to get out of there before something terrible befell them? Would demons rip doorways into the world through their corpses? Phoenix thought they would.

The morgue, she thought. *It's happening down there, too.*

As if summoned by her thoughts, she heard the screams and shouts coming from below and the sound of many feet coming up the stairs from the basement. She arrived at the first floor landing only a few steps ahead of the first of those who were coming up from below. Four people in a cluster, and among them was Ronni, the nurse she'd chatted with in the smoking area outside not long ago. Ronni spotted her as well.

'Why are you . . .' Ronni started, and then realization struck her. 'It's happening up there, too?'

Phoenix grabbed the latch and flung the door open and then they were all barreling into the lobby. Ronni caught up with her, grabbed her by the wrist as they ran for the front doors. The receptionist shouted something at them and two security guards were milling by the door.

'What the hell are they?' Ronni asked.

Phoenix tore her hand away, refused to look into her frightened eyes.

'Hold on right there, folks,' a fat-bellied young guard said as he blocked their way. 'We're in lockdown until the police get here.'

'Screw that,' a morgue attendant growled. 'We'll be dead by then.'

The guard scowled and reached for his baton, confident and slow, sure he could calm them all down. The morgue attendant slammed into him, knocked him on his ass, and they all kept going. The other guard had his keys out, on the verge of locking the doors, and now he looked up in alarm.

'If you're smart,' Phoenix said to the skinny old Asian in his ill-fitting guard's uniform, 'you'll run.'

Then they were moving past him, the doors swooshing open.

'Phoenix,' Ronni called, as they ran into the parking lot.

The autumn wind whipped across the parking lot. Leaves skittered on the pavement and sidewalk as the sun sank beyond the trees and cast an unearthly glow on the choppy surface of the Hudson River in the distance.

Ronni shouted her name but Phoenix ran on. She knew only fear now, the thundering of her heart and the rush of blood to her face and the shame of having left her father's corpse behind and *Oh, daddy, I'm so sorry* and—

'Phoenix!' Ronni snapped, and grabbed her hand again. Spun her around, pretty brown eyes wide and desperate and haunted with the new knowledge they had both acquired today. 'I took the bus to work. Do you have a car? Can I come with you?'

Shaking, Phoenix stared at her, taking a moment to play back the words, unable to understand them the first time. The wind kicked up again and her cheeks were cold and only then did she realize that tears streamed down her face.

As Ronni released her wrist, Phoenix took her by the hand. 'Come on!'

Then they were running side by side as Phoenix pulled out the keys to her beat up Mazda Miata. She let go of Ronni's hand as they reached the car and she ran around to the driver's side, clicking the key fob to unlock the doors. They piled in and Phoenix jammed the key into the ignition and turned, the engine roaring to life.

'What is this?' Ronni asked. 'God, is this another Uprising?'

'No,' Phoenix said as she slammed the car into reverse, backed out of her space and then popped it into drive. She hit the gas and the little car leaped forward, gunning for the exit.

'Whatever this is, it's so much worse.'

5

Westminster, London, UK

Octavian listened to the muffled music coming up through the floor from the Black Hart pub, looked at the now empty scotch bottle and the remnants of his takeaway curry dinner, and wondered if he would ever return to the world of his birth. It surprised him how little the thought troubled him. He had been born here, lived and loved and died and lived and loved again. He had been a hero and a monster and an ordinary man. The sun had risen and set and storms had raged and there had been a great deal of laughter between the grim and bloody battles. He would miss the laughter, he supposed, or he would have if there were anyone around with whom he could still have shared a laugh.

There was nothing left here for him. No anchor. The compass of his life spun and spun, with no true north except for the salvation of the friends who had stood by him whenever they were called.

'You ready, Pete?' Squire asked.

Octavian nodded, but it took a moment before he could tear his gaze away from his surroundings. He had left a mess for the owner of the flat – broken furniture and scratches on the floor that hadn't been there before – but he had paid enough for the privilege.

He turned to Squire. The ugly little hobgoblin stared up at him with narrow yellow eyes. The bright lights Octavian had brought in had been turned to focus on the kitchen door, a heavy oak piece that swung in either direction. Squire had propped it halfway open and positioned the lights so that they shone on the outside of the door, which turned the space between door and wall into the darkest of shadows.

'I'm good,' Octavian said. 'Time to go.'

'Y'know,' Squire replied, 'I'm surprised you never tried this yourself . . . getting onto the Shadowpaths, I mean.'

'I considered it,' he admitted. 'I even found a couple of spells that might have worked, but you and I both know that if I'd gotten in, I'd have been lost in about thirty seconds. Without a guide, I'd be trapped in there forever.'

Squire smiled, his shark-like teeth turning the look into a gruesome grimace. 'Well, then, I guess you better stick close, huh? Don't want you wandering off somewhere.'

The hobgoblin went first. Guiding Octavian behind him, he stepped into the deep shadows between the door and the wall. Octavian studied the texture of the wooden door and the paint on the wall, stared into the shadows, looked down at the back of Squire's head, and wondered how the hell it worked. He and the hobgoblin had allied themselves in the past and he had seen Squire quite literally diving into shadows as if they were pools of water. Squire could step through into the Shadowpaths without working any magic – no words or gestures or rituals. Octavian had never seen magic more subtle, more simple and innate, than this.

Maybe it's not magic at all, he thought, and frowned at the idea. The dimensions were all there. Perhaps hobgoblins were born with the ability to see the curtains drawn between worlds and find the gaps between. The thought intrigued him.

Squire's next step was into darkness. It enveloped him completely and Octavian found himself reaching into the shadows, his right arm missing halfway to the elbow. Invisible to him, already gone, Squire gripped his hand and tugged and Octavian knew he could not let go. The shadows seemed to blur at the edges of his vision and then Squire came into focus again, just a shape in the dark, yellow eyes gleaming.

The Shadowpaths.

The first thing that struck Octavian – aside from the utter darkness – was the silence. The flat in Maida Vale had been full of noise that his conscious mind had barely registered, from the music in the pub and the growl of passing traffic to the hum of the refrigerator and the ticking of a clock. On the Shadowpaths, the loudest thing he could hear was the beating of his own heart.

'Dark, right?' Squire said.

Octavian laughed. 'Yes. It's dark.'

The hobgoblin whacked him on the arm. 'Then why don't you shed some light? All that magic you were braggin' about, I'm sure you've got a simple illumination spell in your arsenal.'

Octavian let go of Squire's hand and turned his palm upward, a ball of golden fire igniting. It rose into the air and became a sphere, the flame-like ripples smoothing until the orb glowed brightly, floating just a few feet away. The light did not reach very far. It turned the shadows at their feet to a grey smoke and the nearest dozen feet of darkness to a rich indigo. But the dark went on forever in here, and the paths were the only safety. There were monsters in the dark, waiting there for travellers who lost their way. *Not so different from other worlds*, Octavian thought grimly.

'As you wish,' he said.

'As I wish,' Squire repeated. 'I don't need the light, pally. I can see just fine without it. You, though . . .' He turned and began to stride along through the darkness ahead, along a path that Octavian could barely make out. 'Fuck's sake, use your noodle, Pete. I can't think of every damn thing.'

It amazed Octavian that Squire continued to be able to get a smile out of him in spite of the gravity of the journey he had just begun and the uncertainty that lay before them. As they walked the Shadowpaths, they shared some of the events of the long years since they had last been together, both the pleasant memories and the painful ones. But when it came to the most recent years, which Squire had mostly spent on a parallel Earth quite like Octavian's, the hobgoblin became reticent and they soon fell silent, letting the haunting quiet of the darkness envelop them. Even their footfalls made very little noise, the sound absorbed by the strange, shifting ground.

Even breathing had an odd quality about it, Octavian thought. There must be air in the dark or he would have suffocated, but it seemed to him as if he were breathing the darkness itself, taking it into himself and becoming a part of it in some way. Somehow this was not as unnerving a thought as he would have imagined. The darkness must have hidden all sorts of dangers, but he felt as if it cloaked him and cradled him and he took peculiar comfort in that.

The orb floated along with them as Squire led him along a labyrinthine route, turning left and right, climbing and descending slopes. At one point, they heard a deep, rhythmic groan off to the left, as if some huge beast lay in wait, rasping its hungry breath, or some great factory loomed in the distance, its machines moaning, stacks belching smoke into the shadows.

'What is that?' Octavian asked.

'A Black Well.'

'Which is?'

'Black hole,' Squire replied.

'Meaning?'

Squire halted and turned to look at him. The light from the orb cast odd shadows on his face, deepening the wrinkles there. It should have made him uglier but instead those dark crenellations added a profound solemnity to the hobgoblin's face. With all of his profanity and sarcasm, Squire made it easy to forget how intelligent he really was. Studying his bright eyes, Octavian hoped never to make that mistake again.

'You think this place goes on forever,' Squire said. 'And I guess it does, in a way, but even forever has its limits. Even eternity isn't really eternal, is it? There's a before and after to everything. You travel far enough on the Shadowpaths and you're going to come across a Black Well. Like black holes in space, their gravity is dragging at the shadows all the time, pulling matter in. Half the reason it's so impossible for most anyone to find their way here is that the paths are constantly warped by the drag from the wells. You go one way now and an hour from now the path is completely different and you end up wandering off into the dark and that's it for you.'

Squire set off again, turning down a curving slope.

'These wells—' Octavian began.

'You fall into one and you're going to be falling a long time,' Squire interrupted. 'Until you're not. Then you're in the Hollow, which is basically a big nothing, the bottom of the wells. And nobody and nothing is getting out of there.'

Octavian nodded, grateful for the knowledge. The Shadowpaths were unknown territory to him and he wondered how many other worlds he had still to discover.

Infinite, he thought. *Infinite worlds.*

'So, stay on the path, then?' Octavian said.

'Don't get cute, smartass. That's my job.'

As Squire spoke, Octavian felt a prickling on his skin and the hair at the back of his neck bristled. A subtle shift in the pressure of the darkness sent a sharp pain through his skull; he winced and reached up to massage his left temple.

'You all right?' Squire asked.

'Something weird just happened.'

'Transition. We moved between worlds.'

Octavian shook his head. The pressure in his skull had subsided but his amazement did not.

'And how did we do that?'

'You just gotta feel your way.'

'And someone who isn't a hobgoblin?'

'Nah, you'd be screwed. Just stick with me and you're fine. Otherwise, you'd either be trapped in here or end up

CHRISTOPHER GOLDEN

coming out in some shithole world where the sun's exploded or some interstellar leviathan has swallowed it whole.'

'That happens?'

Squire didn't reply. Octavian thought this another attempt at humour – the hobgoblin's fallback position – but, as they continued round the bend in the path, he caught a glimpse of Squire's profile in the light from the orb and saw the sorrow and the grief etched in his features and he knew the truth.

After that, he didn't trouble his friend with the need for conversation.

They walked on for what might have been twenty minutes or an hour – Octavian found it difficult to gauge time here – and then Squire halted. He glanced around and seemed to be listening carefully, as if he worried that some hidden observer might lurk in the shadows.

'Kill the light,' the hobgoblin said.

With a wave of his hand, Octavian complied. The darkness seemed even more complete than before, utter blackness that swallowed even the yellow, internal gleam of Squire's eyes. In that darkness, Octavian felt Squire take his wrist and they stepped away from the path. The ground became soft and yielding underfoot, as if they might sink right in if they weren't careful.

A muffled clank came from straight ahead. Squire paused a second, there came a creak, and then the orange glow of fire-light appeared before them, outlining a low doorway. Octavian had only a second to marvel at the presence of a door here in this vast, barren nothing, and then Squire pulled him inside and shut the door behind them, throwing a heavy bolt.

Octavian glanced around, feeling cooped up now that they were actually inside. A further door led into a room from which that firelight glowed brightly, and the heat that poured out of it had him sweating instantly. The low, steady crackle of the flames – a sound that had been inaudible out in the shadows – made a soft bed of noise below the solid presence of the place.

'Home sweet home,' Squire said.

But Octavian had known it already. The walls of this entry room were lined with hundreds of weapons, swords and daggers and battleaxes made to be held by gigantic hands and tiny ones. There were ornate guns with fat barrels and lengths of hooked metal, morningstars and maces, masterfully crafted bows and arrows fixed with feathers that must have come from creatures Octavian could not imagine.

'You wanna go to Hell, you're gonna have to kill some demons,' Squire said. 'I know you're all frickin' Houdini and such, but I think I can help.'

Looking at the armoury the master weaponsmith had created, Octavian wasn't about to argue.

Yet Another World
Boston, Massachusetts

Danny Ferrick sat on the steeply sloping tiled roof of Mr Doyle's townhouse, nearly hidden between a pair of dormer windows, one of which led into his bedroom. He often sat out here after dark, perched like a gargoyle in the moonlight, and listened to the city. Tonight a light rain fell, so the only people on the streets were walking their dogs under wide umbrellas or rushing through puddles to fight over a taxi they hoped would take them home from work.

Louisburg Square was a tiny, private enclave on Boston's Beacon Hill, a garden park surrounded by a black wrought-iron fence around which a ring of brick townhouses sat, austerely watching over the gardens. Observing Louisburg Square, it would have been easy to see the city as unchanged – to imagine a world that had not suffered the unknowable horrors of a cosmic evil and barely survived. Boston had not grown any quieter, though so many had died. But the sounds of the city had changed. There were more tears, now, and more screams. And as Danny sought the inner calm that nearly always eluded him, meditated and tried to extend his senses outward, there were areas of the city which sent back nothing – parts of Boston so charred and blighted that not even scavengers would set foot in the ruins there.

Once upon a time, he had been careful, those nights on the roof, not to be seen by passersby in order to avoid scandal and terror. In those days, no one had ever seen a demon before. Danny had been born in Hell and switched at birth with a human child, the way so many fairies seemed to have been. A glamour had been cast upon him so that he had the appearance of a human child, but when he had reached puberty that had slowly begun to change, so that by now – at the age of twenty-two – he had the black-red horns and leathered skin and scarlet eyes of a devil. His horns weren't long, perhaps six inches with a slight curve at the tips, but no hat would hide them now.

Yet it wasn't his diabolical appearance that kept him indoors most of the time. People might be terrified of him, but most Bostonians recognized him as part of Mr Doyle's Menagerie – and the Menagerie had sacrificed everything to combat that cosmic darkness. *Everything*. They were heroes.

No, Danny mostly stayed indoors because he hated people. Hated humans. He had no desire to live in Hell, though the minions of that infernal realm were always deferential toward him, but that said more about his hatred for Hell than his love of Earth. Nothing remained for him here. Other twenty-two-year-olds in Boston were freshly graduated from college, just starting their first jobs or their first semester of grad school. Danny Ferrick spent his days playing video games and watching movies or Internet porn, eating pizza and Chinese food whose delivery men would barely look at him, men who stood on the front stoop and handed the food in to him, then could barely wait for payment before they fled. One pimple-faced kid had pissed on the steps.

The memory made Danny snicker. The edges of his lips turned upward in something approximating a smile, but he knew from experience that his smile these days would terrify any ordinary person. Once, he'd looked like a typical kid, decent-enough looking and in need of a haircut. Now he looked like a monster, and he spent every day wrestling with the question of how he could keep himself from letting his monstrous outside from seeping under his skin, corrupting him down to his heart.

So far, he hadn't come up with an answer.

Laughter rose into the air, an eruption of girlish giggles that came from several blocks west. Danny scowled, shifted his weight on the rain-slicked roof tiles, and shot an emphatic middle finger in that direction.

'Die,' he growled.

He hated them all, but the pretty girls the most.

No. That's a lie. He hated his parents the most – not his human mother, the woman who had never lost her faith in

CHRISTOPHER GOLDEN

her boy, no matter how monstrous he became, but the demons who had snatched her human infant and left him, their own offspring, in its place. He wished he had never seen the human world, never had his first taste of human food or listened to the hauntingly beautiful music of ordinary people. He wished he had never made a friend in this world, never known the smile of a girl. It would have been better to have spent his life in Hell than to have known a taste of humanity. Now he lived in a limbo inside Mr Doyle's house and he felt more like one of the damned than if he'd spent his life in a pit of fire.

But the rain felt nice.

Danny exhaled, letting the trickles of October rain that ran down his face and neck make him shiver. Despite all the horror that had befallen this world, the night air smelled fresh, and the flowers that remained in the park down in the square still gave off their lovely scents. If he just stayed out there on the roof in the dark, in the rain, he thought he might be able to keep himself from going mad.

He froze, one pointed ear cocked toward his open bedroom window. His lips curled back again, baring sharp teeth, but not in a smile. Something had made a noise inside the house and he strained to hear more or to catch a scent.

Footfalls.

A roof tile cracked as he darted toward his open bedroom window and lunged through it to land on the sodden, ruined, moldy carpet. Wings fluttered. He'd spooked one of the birds that nested in his open closet. Crouched in the centre of the room, he heard voices coming from elsewhere in the house and rushed to the bedroom door, where he paused and tilted his head, inhaling deeply. Leftover Chinese food rotted in containers on the bureau, but over its stink he could make out most of the smells in the house, all of them familiar. All but one.

Squire, Danny thought. The hobgoblin had returned after a long time away.

His eyes narrowed. Squire hadn't come alone.

The claws on his feet tore the carpet as he darted into the corridor. As he raced down the hall to the stairs that led to the second floor, he sniffed the air and caught another scent, the faint trace of something he had not smelled in this house in a very long time.

Mr Doyle? Danny thought, and a spark of hope ignited within him. Mr Doyle and the others had always made him feel as if he had a place in this world, as if he wasn't alone.

On the second-floor landing he raced to the dusty balustrade that overlooked the grand foyer. Squire stood in the centre of the foyer, near the ruin of the great chandelier that had once hung overhead. Beside him, Danny saw a tall, thin man with greying hair. His back to Danny, the man gazed around the foyer and up toward the second story. An axe hung at his side and he had a sword slung across his back, tied in a leather and burlap scabbard. There would be daggers, Danny felt sure, and other hobgoblin-made weapons. At his other hip, a bulge showed through his black wool coat – a morningstar or something.

Danny flinched back from the balustrade. They'd come ready for battle, or just for killing. The beast in him, the demon in his heart, felt a savage paranoia. Had they finally realized he had no place in this world and come to destroy him?

CHRISTOPHER GOLDEN

No, he told himself. *Not Mr Doyle. The old mage would never—*

The man turned. Glanced upward. Met Danny's gaze.

Squire had not brought Mr Doyle home after all. Danny had never seen this man before in his life. The hobgoblin noticed the trajectory of his companion's glance and looked up to see Danny against the balustrade, in the shadows of that second floor corridor that ran above the foyer.

'Hey, kid,' Squire said, smiling. A little worried. 'Love what you've done with the place. Maid's day off?'

Danny frowned, a growl building in his chest. He blinked, searching inside his memory for what the grand foyer of Mr Doyle's townhouse had originally looked like. Elegant. Gleaming wood. Beautiful artwork. Now the art had been torn or shattered and the wood dulled and scratched. A layer of dust covered it all. Squirrels and pigeons had made the place their own and their droppings were all over the floor. Several windows in the house were broken and Danny had never bothered to fix them. The elements did not trouble him, so it had never seemed important.

Stop, he thought. *You don't have to explain yourself. This is your house*.

He launched himself over the railing, dropped through the air and landed half a dozen feet from the intruders. Rising to his full height – half a foot taller than Squire's companion – he loomed above the hobgoblin.

'Who is he?'

'A friend,' Squire said.

'Not my friend.'

The hobgoblin held up his hands. 'Kid, give it a rest, will ya? A friend of a friend is a friend. We ain't here for trouble.

Besides, I still have a place here, don't I? I mean, I've got a room. I still live here, too.'

Danny felt brittle, vulnerable, though he could have torn both their hearts out. *Maybe. Squire, yeah, but the other . . .*

'You haven't been here in months!' Danny roared, stalking toward Squire. 'I've been alone!'

'I know,' Squire said. 'And I'm sorry. I've been wandering a little and what I'm finding ain't pretty. There's a lot of nasty shit going—'

Danny turned toward the other. The visitor. The *friend*.

'Who are you?'

'Peter Octavian. I'm . . . not from here.'

Danny narrowed his gaze, studying the man, then slid toward him. He sniffed the man's hair, caught the scent of his breath, and his frown deepened. The flesh at the base of his horns itched, as it nearly always did, and he reached up to scratch himself. Most were terrified of him, especially this close. Nobody endured his attention without flinching, but this man seemed entirely untroubled. Whatever he was, he had not lied. Underlying the other scents on him was the peculiar odour that Squire always brought with him when he'd been travelling the Shadowpaths to parallel worlds.

'I guess you're not,' Danny agreed. He scratched at his horns again.

'Danny—' Squire began.

'I smell magic,' Danny said.

'He's a mage, like—'

'Mr Doyle,' Danny finished for him, and his loneliness blossomed anew. He stared at this newcomer, this Octavian, another moment before turning sadly toward Squire. 'I thought it was Mr Doyle coming back.'

The hobgoblin's yellow eyes softened. 'Oh, shit, kid, you know Doyle's gone. They're all gone, and they ain't comin' back.'

Danny lashed downward and struck Squire with the back of his hand, knocked the little man to the filthy floorboards. A bright green light crackled to life in the gloom and Danny turned to see spheres of emerald fire burning around Octavian's fists. Magic.

The devil laughed.

'Pete, no,' Squire grunted, climbing to his feet. Danny rounded on him again but Squire showed no fear. 'Kid, you need a friend. *I'm* your friend, remember. Still and always. And Pete here . . . he's my friend. I've told you a million times that any time you want to get out of here, I'll take you wherever you want to go. Any place, any world.'

'I've got nowhere to go,' Danny said, turning away. 'Besides, Mr Doyle left me to watch over the house.'

'He gave you the damn house, kid. It's not the same thing.'

Danny strode away from him, not liking the thoughts in his head. He used the heel of his right hand to pound on his temple. Took a deep breath. Then another. His stomach grumbled and he realized that he hadn't eaten or drunk anything since the frozen waffles he'd had at breakfast.

'Maybe we shouldn't have come,' Octavian said quietly to Squire.

All the breath went out of Danny. He spun around and held up his hands in as friendly a gesture as he knew how to make.

'No, no. It's okay,' he said quickly. 'I'm sorry. I'm just . . .' He pounded his temple again. 'I'm not used to company.'

Stupid, he thought. If he drove them off, he'd be alone again.

'You guys want something to eat?' He smiled and then forced the smile away, not wanting to look more frightening than he already did.

Squire looked dubious. 'You have food that hasn't been shit on by squirrels?'

'I have—'

'Wait,' the hobgoblin interrupted. 'This food wouldn't happen to *be* the squirrels?'

'Fuck you, Squire,' Danny said. 'I don't eat squirrels.'

Squire laughed and some of the tension went out of the house. Danny exhaled in relief. In truth, he had eaten the occasional squirrel, but he had always cooked them first.

'The kitchen is in okay shape,' Danny said. 'I don't have much besides waffles or mac and cheese, but we could order pizza. I might have beer.'

'How about mac and cheese *on* waffles?' Squire asked.

Octavian groaned. 'You'll eat anything.' He looked at Danny. 'Why don't you tell me what you want, Danny, and I'll order something in for us. Anything.'

Danny opened his mouth to reply, thinking of the Tex-Mex place that had survived the great cataclysm but didn't deliver. If Octavian would go out and pick it up, bring it back . . .

'Why are you here?' Danny asked, before he could stop the words from coming out. 'What do you want?'

Don't, he chided himself. *Tex-Mex*.

'Kid,' Squire started.

'No,' Danny said, shaking his head. 'You haven't been here in months and then you show up with this guy, armed to the teeth for a fight with someone. I know you, Squire. Maybe you would've stopped to look in on me and maybe you wouldn't, but you didn't bring this guy here for a social call. You want me to fight.' Danny's stomach gave a sickening twist. 'I'm done fighting,' he rasped. 'I don't want to kill anyone else.'

He felt Squire's warm, leathery hand clasp his and almost pulled away before he realized that this was the first contact he'd had with anyone in . . . he couldn't remember how long.

'Danny, I didn't come to ask you to fight. I wouldn't do that to you. I promised, and I mean to keep that promise,' the hobgoblin said. 'But I did come to ask a favour. Pete, here . . . I owe him. He's a good man, Danny, and he's asked for my help. I intend to give it to him, but that's going to be hard to do without you.'

'No fighting?' Danny asked, staring at the floor.

'I promise,' Squire said.

Danny glanced up at Octavian. 'So, what's the favour?'

Octavian ran a hand over the stubble on his jaw, his eyes full of sorrow and determination.

'Let's get something to eat, and then I'll tell you.'

Danny held his breath for several seconds, and then nodded. What could it hurt just to listen? And, after all, there would be Tex-Mex.

6

Phoenix's World
Dobbs Ferry, New York, USA

Phoenix drove with both hands on the wheel, knuckles white from the strength of her grip. Her heart pounded in her chest and thumped in her ears and her thoughts whirled in a maelstrom of fear and grief and confusion. The tyres skidded in road sand as she took a hard turn onto Route 9, headed south into Dobbs Ferry. In the dimming of the day, the sky looked more like a painting than reality and it played into the strange, dreamlike feeling that had gripped her since the ghosts had possessed her father, just before he died.

'Talk to me,' Ronni said, her voice small and afraid. 'Please, you've gotta talk to me. You've been through something like this—'

'No.' Phoenix snapped her head around to stare at her. 'I told you I've never seen anything like this. The Uprising . . .

that was dead people coming back to life. Part of them was still inside them. Yeah, it was the ugly part, but this is not the same. The ghosts who manipulated my father . . . they were spirits. Lost souls. Human souls. Those things weren't human at all.'

The light ahead went from green to amber and Phoenix hit the accelerator. Cars were headed the opposite direction and she glanced at them, stunned to see that the drivers looked calm. Bored. Half-asleep, like the rest of the world. A thirty-ish Latina talked on her cell phone.

The light turned red and Phoenix sped right through it. She frowned, turned and glanced at Ronni. 'Wait, you did see one, right?'

'Three,' Ronni said, her voice cracking. 'I saw three. One of them came out of a dead girl's abdomen, split her open from inside and started to . . . to climb . . .'

She tried to put the window down but the electrics didn't go fast enough. Ronni hit the lock and opened the door – the car doing sixty – and hung out over the pavement, straining her seatbelt, to loose a stream of vomit into the air. Some of it splattered the rear door as the wind and their speed whipped it away.

'Stop it!' Phoenix shouted. 'Damn it, stop!'

She grabbed the nurse's sweatshirt and tried to pull her back in. Ronni hung out there for a few more seconds, fighting the pull, and then yanked the door shut. She threw herself back against the seat and began to sob and pray and hyperventilate.

'Shut it!' Phoenix snapped.

Ronni had gone beyond listening. Something inside her had broken. Phoenix couldn't think with the woman braying like that. The night drew around them as dusk turned to darkness and up ahead a red beer truck had pulled to the side of the road, hazard lights on, back open wide and ramp down. The driver came out of the yawning truck back with a keg on a dolly.

'God damn it, Ronni!' Phoenix yelled.

'Butbutbut . . . oh, Jesus, girl, they were demons.' She grabbed at Phoenix's arm. 'This is the end, isn't it? I never believed in the Rapture, but this has to be it. It's here, but God didn't take any of us. He's left us all behind and now the demons are—'

'Shut up!' Phoenix screamed, fresh tears springing to her cheeks.

She tore her arm free, twisted the steering wheel, and the car swerved toward the back of the beer truck. The delivery guy spotted her and leaped off the ramp onto the sidewalk as the dolly fell over and the keg thumped and rolled onto the pavement. At the last second, Phoenix jerked the wheel to the left and the car caromed off the side of the truck, tearing off her mirror and sending up sparks. *Objects in mirror*, she thought, *are closer than they fucking appear.*

Her heart thundered and her chest clenched and her breath came in hitching gasps. Ronni had never stopped sobbing. Phoenix turned and punched her in the shoulder as hard as she could.

'You bitch!' Ronni screamed. 'What the hell—'

Phoenix stood on the brake. The car skidded to a halt and she popped the gearshift into park.

'Get out,' she said, her face flushed, a little bit of madness creeping in around the edges of her mind.

Terror lit Ronni's eyes. 'No, please. I didn't mean it. I'm sorry. I'll be—'

'I don't know you,' Phoenix said quietly. 'I don't need you. Whatever this is, I intend to live through it. I'm not going to get very far with some chick who can't stop being hysterical for two seconds.'

'It's—'

'The Rapture? Maybe so, but I don't believe in that shit. If I learned anything in the Uprising, it's that we're on our own. This is crisis time, *Veronica*, and I promised myself that I'd never be taken by surprise in a crisis again. I didn't plan for . . . demons, or whatever the hell those things are . . . but I do have a plan, and it doesn't involve holding your hand.'

The night had quickly overtaken them. In the dashboard light, Phoenix watched Ronni struggle to compose herself.

'I'm . . .' Ronni said, sniffling. 'I'll do whatever you need. Just don't leave me here. I have friends. You could drop me . . .'

Phoenix had stopped listening. A siren wailed and she stared through the windshield at the police car that sped toward them, light bar flashing. She popped the door open and climbed out, and once out of the car she could hear the beer-delivery man shouting at her. She turned to see the man standing beside his truck, hands thrown in the air.

'Are you drunk or are you blind?' he called to her. The heavyset, broad-shouldered guy had torn his work shirt and the knee of his pants when he'd jumped from the ramp. Now he gestured to the long scrape on the side of the truck where some of the metal had buckled and torn. 'What the hell is wrong with you?'

Phoenix couldn't breathe. The man looked furious, but he had every reason to be. Being angry with her – that was the normal response. The ordinary reaction.

The police car raced by them, ghostly blue lights flashing across the beer man's face and his scarred truck and the plate glass windows of the liquor store and the sub shop in the little strip mall beside which she had stopped her car.

'Hey,' a quiet voice said behind her. 'There's another one coming.'

A strange stillness came over Phoenix as she turned and saw that Ronni had gotten out of the car. The two of them watched as not one but two more police cars roared past them. The truck driver stepped into the street and tried to flag them down but the cops kept going as if they hadn't seen him.

'Damn it!' the driver snapped. 'What's going on around here?'

Phoenix pointed past him, above his head. 'That.'

The grizzled driver had come within fifteen feet of her, but now he turned. Ronni came up behind her and the three of them stared at the plume of black smoke that rose into the sky to the northeast, near the river. Ronni said nothing but Phoenix knew they were both thinking the same thing – *the hospital*.

'What's going on?' the driver asked. Phoenix noted the name sewn into the shoulder of his shirt: *Wayne*. 'That a fire or an explosion?'

'Maybe both,' Phoenix said slowly.

The chaos in her mind had begun to settle and she turned to look south along Route 9, which was also called Broadway and which would have taken them all the way into the heart of Manhattan if they kept going. Here, though, they were twenty yards from the turn in the road just before the downtown part of Dobbs Ferry, a charming little Westchester County town.

'Ronni, stay with the car,' she said, and started toward the bend in the road. Her pace quickened to a run and the driver shouted after her.

'What about my truck?'

You've got bigger problems, Phoenix thought.

At the corner, she looked left. The street lamps along the little downtown of Dobbs Ferry had come on. People were parked all along the road. The shops were open and she could smell pizza and hear teenagers shouting at each other and laughing. A fiftyish man jogged toward her, listening to an iPod as he ran. Beyond him, a group of twentysome-thing women came out of a tavern. A pickup truck came toward her and she could see several cars stopped at the light at the intersection two blocks down. The whole of Dobbs Ferry seemed to be functioning as if nothing at all had happened.

Then a siren blatted and began to shriek and she saw a long fire truck turn a corner onto the main road and growl as it picked up speed, headed her way. Another came behind it, joining the chorus of wailing emergency vehicles.

Phoenix started back toward her car, where Ronni and Wayne the Budweiser man watched the fire trucks go by in numb fascination. Wayne seemed stunned that the police had passed him by, was mumbling about it to Ronni as Phoenix walked up.

'What'd you see?' Ronni asked.

'Nothing. It's just an average night in Dobbs Ferry,' Phoenix said. 'The chaos up there . . . it hasn't spread this far yet.'

'What chaos?' Wayne demanded. 'You know something, don't you?'

Despite her smooth, dark skin, Ronni looked pale. 'You wouldn't believe us if we told you,' she said, then looked at Phoenix. 'What now? Do you think they'll be able to get it under control?

Phoenix thought of Dr Song, and the fact that each person the first demon had killed had become the doorway for another.

'Not a chance.'

'Then what do we do?'

Phoenix stared at the plume of smoke in the distance, grey against the indigo sky. Her heart kept fluttering in her chest but her thoughts continued to click into place like pieces of a puzzle she never imagined being able to solve. During the Uprising, they had come to realize that the connection the three mediums had made – the circuit – had allowed the spirits of the dead to come through, and that only breaking that circuit could end it. Phoenix had shot Eric Honen to make that happen.

'It started at the hospital,' she said now. *With my father*, she thought but did not add. *Again, with my father.* 'If we can figure out why and how, maybe we can stop it.'

'Us?' Ronni said, staring at Phoenix. 'Are you out of your mind?'

'If not us, then who?' Phoenix demanded, thoughts racing, growing surer by the second that they were leading her in the right direction. An image filled her mind, the sight of those hideous claws bursting from her father's belly, but she pushed it away. 'You think the cops are going to fix this? What we just saw is evil, Ronni. Bullets aren't going to stop demons. They're going up there just to die.'

Wayne put a heavy, calloused hand on her shoulder. He had fear in his eyes, but intelligence, too, and a quiet, iron strength.

'Evil and demons? Maybe you better tell me what this is all about.'

Phoenix shook her head. 'Sorry. I wish you luck, man. But I don't have time to stand here and convince you. Stick around long enough and you'll figure out what's real and not real.'

She shrugged off his hand and turned back toward her car. Ronni kept staring at the smoke in the distance for a second and then hurried to follow.

'Where do you think you're going?' Wayne said, but doubtfully now. 'Look at this damage to my truck. You've gotta give me your insurance information.'

'Don't worry about your truck, Wayne,' Phoenix replied as she pulled open her car door and slipped inside. 'Worry about your life insurance.'

As Ronni climbed in, Phoenix slammed the door, fired up the car and drove off. She glanced at Wayne in the rear-view mirror but he hadn't even bothered to watch them pull away. He had turned to the northwest to watch the smoke, even as another police car screamed by, blue lights flashing.

'You have any idea where you're going?' Ronni asked.

'To see a friend who might have some answers. You want me to drop you somewhere?'

'Hell, no,' the nurse said, glancing nervously over her shoulder. 'Seems to me that right now the safest place for me is with you. Though if that changes, I'd appreciate you letting me know.'

Phoenix kept both hands tight on the wheel, hoping she didn't get Ronni killed.

On and Off the Shadowpaths

Octavian followed Squire and Danny through the shifting darkness of the Shadowpaths. He had conjured another light sphere and it floated ahead of them, its warm golden illumination dimmed by the constant drain placed upon it by the hungry blackness of this limbo world. *Nature abhors a vacuum*, or so Octavian had read. But the darkness of the Shadowpaths abhorred the presence of light.

'Why couldn't we have just crossed over from your world?' he asked.

Squire glanced back at him. 'It hasn't been sealed off the way your world has, but after the last time it was nearly destroyed, Doyle and some of the others weaved a spell to keep it hidden from other dimensions. It was the last thing the old man did before he left us and I'm not going to screw it up by letting Danny find and open a doorway and let Hell know we're here.'

'Mr Doyle sounds like a formidable mage. I would've like to have met him.'

'Nah,' Squire scoffed. 'You're not uptight enough. He would've hated you.'

'That's not funny,' Danny said.

'Doesn't mean it ain't true.'

They marched onward. Despite the vastness of this in-between place, the air felt close and Octavian had the occasional shiver of claustrophobia. It seemed hard to breathe here, as if they were climbing Everest instead of wandering the least travelled corners of a seemingly endless dark labyrinth normally trodden only by hobgoblins and other dimension-hoppers.

'Do you ever run into other people walking the paths?' Octavian asked.

Squire and Danny had been talking as they walked, quietly catching up on the time that had passed they had last seen one another. From what Octavian had overheard, this mostly consisted of Squire apologizing for not visiting in so long and the demonic young man reaffirming their brotherhood.

Now Squire paused and glanced back at him. 'Why? What did you see?'

'Just wondering,' Octavian said. Though in truth he did feel . . . something. Some presence, the focus of some aware-ness, as though their passing had been observed from the deepest darkness.

'I've run across monsters in here,' the hobgoblin admit-ted, his yellow eyes narrowing. His voice lowered to a rasp. 'And once in a while some ordinary citizen stumbles in by accident – through a rift or portal or whatever – and those poor souls are fucked up, let me tell you. In darkness like this, their minds break down pretty quick.'

'They go crazy?' Danny asked.

'Batshit crazy,' Squire confirmed. 'But it's not often. The Shadowpaths ain't exactly a high traffic area.'

Danny uttered a soft, chuffing laugh, amused by the wit of his old pal, Squire, whom he had seemed ready to tear limb from limb only an hour or so before. From the moment they had entered the Shadowpaths, Octavian had made sure not to turn his back on Danny. The devil seemed pleasant enough now, but he was unlike anyone else Octavian had met – not fully a demon but not at all human, except in his heart. From what Squire had said, he had never quite fit in anywhere until he had gone to live with the mage, Mr Doyle. He'd had friends and allies there, but after the cataclysm on their world, he had been left alone, and now loneliness and self-loathing had taken their toll. Danny talked about crazy as if he could differentiate between sane and insane, but Octavian had doubts about the devil's objectivity.

'So, Danny, how does this work?' Octavian asked. 'Do you have a secret password or something?'

Danny glanced back at him, brow knitted in consternation. All-too-human irritation. And yet with his size and those red eyes and the horns, Octavian could not help but see malice in that glance. Even malevolence.

'It's Hell,' the devil said. 'The only currency is fear.'

'You're that much of a badass?' Octavian replied. 'Hell's sentries are going to just bow down before you?'

Danny showed his teeth in a snarl. 'Fuck off, man. I don't know you. I'm not here for you, and I can head on home if you—'

Squire halted so abruptly that Octavian nearly collided with him. He turned, black mist shadows drifting across his face.

'What are you trying to do, Pete?'

Octavian stared at him. 'I don't know what you mean.'

'You asked for my help and I'm helping you. Danny's willing to help *me*. You want to get into Hell, you won't find a better way than this, if you find another way at all. But here you are antagonizing the kid—'

'I'm not—'

Squire reached up and jabbed one stubby finger into Octavian's chest. 'Don't poke the bear, Pete.'

'Sorry,' Octavian said, throwing up his hands. He looked at Danny and tried his best to look sincere. 'I've got a lot riding on this, that's all. People depending on me. Friends.

You're meant to be our ambassador, supposed to get us through the door, but you don't exactly seem stable and that worries me.'

'Damn it—' Squire started.

Danny put a hand on the ugly little man's shoulder. 'No. I get it.' His red eyes burned brighter. 'You're not wrong. It's just that you don't have much choice.'

He turned and soldiered on, following the glowing orb that had paused with them but now floated ahead along the path as he strode away from them. Squire shot Octavian a withering glance.

'How is this supposed to work?' Octavian said. 'This guy is more likely to get us killed than help us invade Hell.'

Squire took a deep breath, glanced over to make sure Danny had passed out of earshot, and then stepped nearer to Octavian. The darkness had begun to close around them now that the orb had floated off, and the hobgoblin's eyes seemed somehow both brighter and darker than ever, burning amber coals instead of bright yellow.

'He's of the bloodline, okay?'

Octavian held out a hand and blue light ignited around it, casting pale light onto Squire's face.

'The bloodline. Of Hell,' Octavian said.

'That's why the sentries will fear him. He may have been abandoned on Earth as a baby, but his father – who figured him for the runt of the litter – is a Demon Lord.'

Octavian nodded. Their confidence made sense to him now, but only to a point.

'We don't even know if that hierarchy still exists.'

Squire rolled his eyes. 'It's Hell. You spent long enough there to know its politics. Old loyalties linger, and if the

Demon Lords have been killed or deposed, loyalty to them will only have grown. The kid knows it, see? But he grew up with a human mom who loved him and now he lives in a house alone and he's blacked out the mirrors so he doesn't have to see what he really is. That house is like his prison. He's not really welcome in the human world and he won't let himself belong to Hell. That's why he's just making the introductions and then going home, and the only reason he's helping us at all is because he wants a little company. He's broken, Pete, and he's never going to be right again. So don't poke the bear.'

Octavian opened his hands in surrender. 'I'll do my best. It just worries me how on edge he is. Sometimes broken people keep breaking.'

'That's a chance you'll have to take,' the hobgoblin said. 'Like the kid said, it's not like you have much of a choice.'

Without awaiting a reply, Squire turned and hurried along the path after Danny, shadows swirling in his wake, filling in the space where he had just been. Octavian followed, weapons clanking against him as he picked up his pace.

He had barely had time to take an inventory of the weapons he'd acquired from Squire's armoury. The last time they had gone into battle together, the hobgoblin had been able to jump in and out of the Shadowpaths, bringing Octavian and his comrades whatever weapons they desired. It had been a massive boon, giving them the upper hand in that battle, but Squire claimed that sort of aid would be impossible on this journey, that he had no direct access to the Hell dimensions from the Shadowpaths. Octavian suspected that this was a half-truth. It seemed illogical to think that the hobgoblin could not move from the paths to Hell – as if there were no shadows in the inferno from which he might emerge. No,

Octavian thought perhaps it was only that Squire feared what might happen if he slipped into Hell from the Shadowpaths, feared that in doing so he might inadvertently show something in Hell the way *out* . . . and onto the paths.

For now, he chose not to push the issue. Instead, they were seeking another way in, taking the long way around. Squire intended for them to emerge in some other parallel dimension and then go from there into Hell. To do that, they needed a world with direct access to the demon dimensions, a doorway or portal that would allow them to enter directly, without using the Shadowpaths as a bridge between two worlds.

'Pete?' The hobgoblin had rushed ahead to catch up with Danny and now his voice drifted back to Octavian through the shadows. 'You coming?'

Octavian glanced around. It had seemed to come from everywhere and nowhere at once. He raised his hand and the cold blue magic that emanated from his fingers brightened, dispelling the deepest part of the darkness. Without Squire, he would never find his way home, but he could at least keep himself from stepping off of the path. He thought of the Black Well they had passed and the way it had breathed and groaned. The noise it made would keep him from stumbling into one now that he knew what it was, but there were other things out there in the dark.

Something shifted off to his right and he turned to peer into the shadows. *Other things*, he thought again. It was as if he had summoned something just by thinking of it. But as he stood there, listening without breathing, he recognized the same feeling he'd had before – the sensation of being observed – and knew whatever was out there had been following them, just as he'd feared.

With a gesture, he ignited the shadows. The part of the darkness where he'd sensed that presence lit up with blue flames and Octavian gazed into the abyss. Nothing moved or breathed or fled, and the sensation of being observed vanished, yet he felt sure he had not imagined it.

'Show yourself!' he called.

He neither expected nor received a reply.

'Pete, come on!' Squire shouted back to him. 'What are you doing?'

Octavian stared for another long moment into the dark as the shadows moved in, obliterating the illumination he had created. Then he tore himself away. Whatever was out there, it either feared them too much to attack or it would come for them eventually.

He nearly ran into Squire and Danny, who had back-tracked to check on him.

'Don't be stupid,' Squire said. 'You wander off and I can't find you, that might be the last you see of any world.'

'Sorry,' Octavian replied. 'Just thought I saw something.'

Squire frowned.

'Like what?' Danny asked, Octavian's earlier antagonism apparently forgiven.

'Maybe nothing,' Octavian replied.

'Let's hope so,' Squire said. 'But it won't matter in a second anyway. There's a place up ahead that's perfect for our needs. Exactly what I'm looking for. The shadows have a shitload of branches.'

'What does that even mean?'

Squire sighed. He nudged Danny and the two of them started onward again, the sphere glowing as it drifted beside them. Octavian took one more glance off the path and then caught up to them, weapons weighing on him. The shadows were so quiet that he felt almost foolish carrying so many implements of war, but he knew the quiet would end soon enough.

The path forked once and then a second time, and Squire kept to the left at each of them. Time felt fluid on the paths but Octavian thought only a minute or two had passed before they came to a place where the sphere illuminated what seemed at first like a dead end. With a wave of his hand, Octavian made the sphere glow more brightly and he saw that instead of ending, the path had splintered into many narrow paths that stretched out into the swirling mists of darkness.

'Branches,' Octavian said.

'Obviously,' Squire replied.

Danny cleared his throat, a sound like a growl. 'Now what?'

'Just follow me and stay close,' Squire said. 'When I tell you, make sure we're all in physical contact.'

'You want us to hold hands?' Danny asked.

'My boot up your ass would do it, too, if you want to go with that option,' Squire replied.

The devil surprised Octavian by laughing. Danny rolled his eyes and reached out with both hands, linking Squire to Octavian with a powerful grip. The strength in those hands could have crushed bones to powder but Danny took hold of them carefully, almost gingerly.

'Go on, then,' he said.

Squire nodded and started off. Octavian stared downward, tried to keep the path beneath his feet in view, but the mist moved in and obscured it despite the light from the sphere.

Then that light winked out and they were plunged into near total darkness. He summoned the magic that he'd used before, the blue light around his fingers, just in time to see his right hand – the one holding on to Danny – vanish into the shadows ahead. Squire and Danny were gone, as were the many branches underfoot. The darkness swirled around him and he paused, only to feel himself tugged forward.

Three more steps, and Octavian cursed aloud and threw his free hand up to shield his eyes from the abrupt daylight. Coming out of the dark, he had been unprepared and now he squinted against the bright sunshine and glanced around. They were in the cold shadows at the edge of a late autumn forest.

'Damn it, Squire, you could have warned me,' he snapped.

'This ain't an exact science, pally,' Squire muttered. 'Time of day, weather, that kind of thing ain't part of the deal.'

'It is beautiful, though,' Danny said.

Octavian blinked, his eyes beginning to adjust, and glanced around. The kid – the devil – hadn't been exaggerating. They were in a field of knee-high yellow grass that stretched a hundred yards until it reached what appeared to be a sheer cliff that dropped away to an ocean of roiling whitecaps. Out to sea, dozens of rock formations rose from the water like stone towers. Some of them were crested with ice or snow. On one of the most distant towers, Octavian could make out the shape of an enormous house – a castle with smoke rising from its chimneys.

'What is this place?' he said, moving through the grass toward the cliff's edge. 'I've never seen rock formations like this and I've wandered my world quite a bit.'

'Somewhere else,' Squire said.

111

Octavian shot him a dark look. 'Yes, but where else? Don't you know anything about this dimension?'

While they paused to talk, Danny kept walking through the high grass toward the cliff's edge. He seemed mesmerized by the ocean and the stone towers and the plume of smoke that rose from that distant castle.

'I told you,' Squire said. 'It doesn't work like that. I've never been here before and we don't have time to play tourist.'

'Check this out,' Danny called to them.

Octavian and Squire exchanged a glance. For the first time since they had encountered him, Danny sounded almost like an ordinary young man. Squire had said he was in his early twenties, but Octavian had been focused on how unstable the devil had seemed, how depressed and unstable – distant and borderline psychotic.

Danny turned toward them, grinning an actual grin. 'Guys, seriously. Check this out.'

Grass rustling around them, they strode across the field toward him, then picked up the pace to catch up with him as he kept walking. Twenty yards from the edge of the cliff, he stopped and pointed as they came abreast of him.

'Look down there.'

At the base of one of the stone towers, a plateau of stone jutted out perhaps a half dozen feet above the water. In spite of the cold, six or seven naked figures lay basking in the sun. There were both males and females as far as Octavian could see, and they were human. Or at least he thought so until he saw an enormous seal swim up to the edge of the rock, launch itself from the water and slide to a landing on its belly just feet away from them. Then it stood up and stripped off its seal skin, not as if it had been in disguise but as if it had been a seal one moment and now was a lovely naked black-haired girl who held the seal skin in her hands.

She put the seal skin with a pile of others and then lay down a few feet from her companions, small perfect breasts gleaming wetly in the sunlight.

'I think she might be a little young for you, kid,' Squire said, patting Danny on the back.

'No,' the devil sputtered. 'That's not what I . . . I just . . . I mean, this place is beautiful, right? Just smell the air—'

'Focus, Danny,' Squire said, reaching up to tap him on the chest. If he could have reached the devil's chin, Octavian was sure he would have grabbed hold and forced Danny to lock eyes. 'Can we get into Hell from this world?'

With one regretful glance back at the selkies – or whatever they were – Danny closed his eyes and frowned. With his wicked-looking horns, the innocent look of concentration seemed slightly absurd.

'He can sense the presence of Hell?' Octavian asked.

Squire gave a nod. 'Sort of.'

'It pulls at me,' Danny said in a quiet growl. 'Like it wants me. It gets stronger all the time.'

Octavian said nothing. He had an idea by now of just how much Danny's struggle with his true nature had wreaked havoc on his heart and mind, and didn't want to make it any worse.

'No,' Danny said. 'Nothing here.'

'Right,' Squire replied. 'Let's get going.'

Wistful, Danny glanced back toward the stone towers and then down at the naked figures sunning themselves on the stone plateau above the whitecaps. With his horns and his red eyes and rough skin, he might well terrify them if he tried to speak to them. Octavian figured the very same thoughts must be in the kid's mind and he wanted to offer some reassurance. They had no way of knowing if this world even had a devil myth, if they would know what demons looked like or just think of Danny as different. These shapechangers were pretty different themselves.

'Do we have to?' Danny asked.

Squire patted his back. 'For now, kid. But maybe you can come back. Find some sexy little sea lion to be your sweetie.'

Octavian thought they were seals but didn't want to interrupt.

After a second, Danny sighed and gave them a wry glance, and then the three of them trudged back across the field to the shadows of the trees.

7

On and Off the Shadowpaths

Octavian stepped out from the deep shadow beneath a massive water tank on a rooftop in New York City. Squire and Danny followed him as he strode out to the edge of the roof, but once there, all he could do was stare.

'Holy shit,' Squire muttered.

'It's New York, isn't it?' Danny asked.

'Lower Manhattan,' Octavian said. 'Or it used to be.'

'Looks to me like the whole frickin' place is "used to be",' Squire replied.

They stood for a long minute in silence, just staring out at the other buildings and at the streets below – or where the streets had once been. Now they were canals. At some point in the history of this dimension, a cataclysm had taken place – earthquakes or melting polar ice caps or something – and Lower Manhattan had either sunken into the water or been flooded or both. Waves rolled through the canals that had once been broad avenues and narrow streets. Small boats with loud, buzzy motors that spewed black smoke churned the water, navigating by rusted street signs. Higher up, a network of bridges and ropes and planks connected building to building, some of them makeshift and others real works of architecture or engineering.

'Whatever happened here,' Danny said, 'it happened a long time ago.'

Octavian gave a slow, sad nod. 'Yet people still live here.'

'What about it, kid?' Squire asked. 'Anything?'

Danny closed his eyes and began to turn in a circle. After two revolutions, he lay his head back and turned his face upward as if toward the sun, but there were only clouds overhead.

'I don't feel that pull,' he said, opening his eyes. 'But I feel something. Not the Hell we want but something else – something cold and so far away that it almost doesn't feel real. And old.'

Danny shivered, and it felt odd to Octavian, seeing the fear in the devil's eyes. Even with his horns and the savage sharpness of his teeth, he looked vulnerable.

'Can we go?' he asked. 'I feel like if we stay it might . . .'

'Might what?' Octavian asked.

'Might *notice* me.'

Danny didn't have to say any more than that. They turned and retraced their steps to the shadows beneath the water tank, joining hands without hesitation. It had become second nature to them now. They had visited half a dozen parallel dimensions already and none had provided Danny with the tug he sought.

As they entered the shadow beneath the tank, all of the light bled out of the world around them. Octavian's field of vision went grey and then they plunged into darkness once more. The three of them had developed a pattern by now and Squire paused to let their eyes adjust, even as Octavian summoned the same bright, floating sphere to illuminate their journey through the Shadowpaths.

They remained in that same small corner of the limbo of darkness, the juncture where the path splintered into dozens of narrow branches. One after another, they had tried them without good fortune, but all they could do was continue.

'You ready?' Squire asked in the darkness.

Octavian grasped his hand and then reached out for Danny's. 'Go.'

Once again, they were off, soldiering into the deeper darkness. The sphere winked out and the black mist swirled in front of Octavian's eyes and they strode a dozen steps until they emerged in a bright, moonlit forest, standing in the nighttime shadows of enormous evergreens.

'Wow,' Danny said. 'It's quiet, here.'

Octavian knew what he meant – compared to several of the parallels they had visited, it was indeed quiet – but he could hear night birds calling and the breeze through the trees and the rush of a nearby river. The distant sound of a ringing bell reached him, a rich tinkling noise, but slow and leisurely. The air smelled faintly of oranges and for a moment Octavian allowed himself to wish things were different and that he could stay in this place. It felt peaceful to him.

The urge made him ashamed. His friends were in Hell and he wanted peace.

'Let's go,' Octavian said.

But Danny had already set off through the trees, headed for the sound of the river.

'Wait up, kid,' Squire called as they pursued him, pushing branches aside.

'Do you feel something?' Octavian asked. 'Is there a doorway here?'

They found him at the edge of the trees, just a few feet from the riverbank. Danny stared along the water's path at an enormous waterfall.

'Danny—' Octavian began, faltering when he took a second look at the waterfall.

The river flowed upward, rising up to a rocky ledge at least a hundred feet high.

'Now there's something you don't see every day,' Squire said.

'It's . . .' Danny began. Then he smiled and glanced at the hobgoblin. 'I feel like I read this in a book. Or my mom read it to me when I was little. The Up-River.'

The sound of the ringing bell grew louder and Octavian turned to scan the opposite bank of the river. Something moved in the shadows between trees and the ringing quickened. He caught a glimpse of the figure that darted from one tree to the next, hurrying on his way but aware of their presence and trying not to be seen. The little creature was low to the ground and swift, despite its waddling gait.

The thing did not carry a bell. It had arms and legs and a head but its body *was* a bell, and as it waddled the clapper inside swung side to side. Ringing. A living bell.

'Danny?' Squire said. 'Do you—'

'No,' the devil said. 'Not here.'

'Then we should go,' Octavian said.

'Shit, yeah. Y'think?' Squire replied. From the look in his eyes, it was clear that he had also seen the bizarre denizen of this strange wood.

Squire led the way. Danny was still mesmerized by the Up-River and when Octavian pulled him by the wrist, he came only reluctantly. The childlike wonder in Danny's expression changed him and for the first time Octavian saw the little boy he must once have been, before his true nature revealed itself. Before he had been left alone with his regret and self-loathing. Before he had begun to lose his mind.

'It's okay, kid,' Octavian said, adopting Squire's use of the word. Danny might have been twenty-two but for the first time it seemed to fit him. 'You can come back someday.'

'I don't think so.'

Octavian glanced at him as they pushed branches out of the way, plunging back into the forest.

'Why not?'

Danny would not meet his eyes. 'I'm just not meant for a place like this.'

They caught up with Squire, joined hands, and were back in the darkness before Octavian could think of a reply, and when he did he knew it was not something that would have offered any comfort. The only thing he could possibly have said that would have been true, the only honest response, would have been *neither am I*.

With a flourish of his hand, Octavian brought the sphere of light blazing back to life, casting its yellow light into the Shadowpaths. Squire stood staring at the ground, studying the many thin branches at their feet as he tried to determine their next move. Octavian took a breath and moved up beside him. They could not keep searching at random; he thought there must be some way to narrow their options.

A shudder ran up Octavian's back, skin prickling with the strange heat particular to being observed. Whatever had been stalking them through the darkness on their previous journeys through the Shadowpaths had returned.

'Squire?' Danny said, his voice floating in the shadows. His tone carried a warning.

Magic rushed up through Octavian as he spun around to see a stranger amongst them. Rippling occult energy flared from his hands and an amber aura emanated from him, so that he seemed to be armoured in that seething magic. Danny snarled at the newcomer and hooked his fingers into wicked claws.

'Who the hell are you?' Octavian demanded.

'Merely a passerby with a friendly word of advice.'

On the surface, the new arrival did not appear to be a threat. Tall and slight, the pale man had a hawk nose and a long grey beard tied halfway down its length round an iron ring. His blue eyes were like ice, conveying a chill despite the smile he wore. In his brown wool greatcoat, thick cotton shirt and heavy trousers over scuffed boots, he reminded Octavian more of some ageing hippy college professor than any deadly enemy, but Octavian had not lived so long without realizing things were often not what they seemed.

Sparks flew from Octavian's fingers and amber mist spilled from his eyes. They were on the Shadowpaths – there were only monsters and travellers here, and few of the travellers would be innocents.

'I'll ask you again—' he began.

'Smith,' Squire said, sniffing in disapproval. 'What the fuck do *you* want?'

Octavian glanced at Squire. The ugly, misshapen hobgoblin had come up beside Danny and now stared up at the newcomer with obvious distaste. The bearded man inclined his head in the very slightest of bows.

'Squire,' he said.

'You know this guy?' Danny demanded.

Squire nodded. 'I know him. Him and all his kin. Meet Wayland Smith, boys. There's one of 'em in every dimension, weaponsmiths and dimension-walkers. Sorta like hobgoblins, only not so pretty.'

'You never quite understood,' Wayland Smith said. He tugged on the iron ring in his beard, then combed his fingers through the grey hair. 'My brothers and sisters and I . . . we are all Wayland Smith.'

'Ain't that what I just said?'

'Not quite,' Smith replied. 'There is no—'

Squire sighed. 'Yeah, yeah. Fascinating stuff. What the hell do you want?' The hobgoblin gestured toward Octavian. 'Speak fast, or my boy here is going to melt your face.'

'As I said, I've come with a word of advice.' Wayland Smith turned his icy blue gaze upon Octavian, ignoring the others. 'All of this tramping around between dimensions is going to lead to no good.'

Octavian glanced at Squire. 'What's he talking about?'

'Nothing. The Smiths just like to stick their noses in.'

Danny rose up to his full height, at least half a foot taller than Wayland Smith, and stared down at the intruder, red eyes gleaming in the dark.

'What is it you really want?' the devil asked. 'Why do you care what we do?'

Wayland Smith sighed, more irritated than frightened. 'I should have known better. People on a crusade never listen. But I had to try, didn't I?'

'Try what?' Octavian said, the amber magic churning around him slightly diminished. The power in him wanted to be used; over the years he had found that once summoned, magic had an urgency to it – spells wanted weaving, hexes desired to be cast.

'To send you home, Nicephorus Dragases,' Wayland Smith replied.

Octavian shivered. 'How do you know that name?'

'It is your name, is it not?'

'My birth name, yes. But I've died and lived again since then, and lived countless days. That name no longer has meaning.'

'Whatever name you choose, you're a son of your world,' Smith said. 'You're not meant to be in the lands between, whether the paths of shadow or the Grey Corridors walked by Travellers such as myself. It's dangerous for you and young Orias to be here. Every time you cross between worlds, you risk drawing others back in after you – perhaps powerful others. There are too many dark-intentioned creatures wandering these paths already. I won't have you polluting them further."

Squire laughed softly. 'Fuckin' Travellers, always trying to act like you're in charge. Look, this isn't my first goddamn rodeo. If memory serves, the last time we had something really nasty slip into the in-between it was because one of your people fell in love and tried to save a whole tribe of—'

The dagger appeared in Smith's hand faster than Octavian's eye could see. 'Hold your tongue, 'goblin, or I'll cut it out!'

Octavian let the magic surge from his left hand, a spell intended to knock the blade from Smith's grasp. He stared in astonishment as the magic split on the blade, the edge so sharp that it cleaved the spell in two. Wayland Smith had forged a weapon impervious to magic.

'Put away the knife,' Danny snarled, his horns casting strange shadows in the light of Octavian's sphere. He took a step forward and Smith moved back, wary, ready for a fight.

'Danny, back off,' Octavian said. He scratched at the air, fingers contorted, and this time the magic that surged from him struck Wayland Smith full in the chest, knocked the Traveller backward so that he reeled into the dark mists around them. 'This is a waste of time.'

The devil leaped into the darkness after Smith and Octavian called out, thinking Danny meant to kill him and would be killed himself. But a moment later the towering young demon hauled Smith back into the light, dragging him by the iron ring in his beard.

'You called me something,' Danny growled. 'Something that isn't my name. What was it?'

Smith grabbed his wrist and twisted, forced Danny backward with a show of startling strength.

'But it is your name, Orias,' the Traveller said, dagger held warily before him. 'Just as his is Dragases. You are Orias, son of Oriax.'

Danny scowled. 'My demon-father was Baalphegor-Moabites, and he's dead.'

Smith shook his head. 'Moabites claimed you, stole you away for his own purposes, but you are the son of Oriax, and you would be a fool to go home.'

'What are you . . .' Danny began, but faltered. His eyes narrowed with sudden realization. 'Home. You don't mean Mr Doyle's place.'

Magic still pouring from his hands, amber sparks falling from the power that misted all around his silhouette, Octavian stepped between them.

'I don't understand you or the things you seem to know,' he said, glaring at Smith's cold blue eyes. 'But unless you want to try yourself against us, I suggest you move on. Find another path.'

'I only want to dissuade you—'

Squire barked a laugh. 'With a blade. You think I don't have a dozen blades close at hand that could snap yours in two? Your kind can work metals, I'll grant you, but any hobgoblin with half a brain could—'

'Enough!' Octavian commanded.

Squire began to argue but Octavian stilled him with a glance. Danny seemed ready to attack, but all Octavian could think about was the time they were wasting. He turned to Smith.

'Are you willing to fight us to stop us from going on?' Amber magic rippled through him, suffused his body so that he was charged with it.

Wayland Smith arched an eyebrow and then scoffed at him. 'I'm old, Dragases, not stupid. I do my best to dissuade the haphazard efforts of amateurs who manage to slip between worlds, in order to protect myself and my kin. But if reason won't sway you from your course, then I certainly don't have the power to force you to abandon it.'

Danny grunted in approval.

'Then why are you still here?' Squire asked.

Octavian glanced over at the hobgoblin and when he looked back, the Traveller had gone. Whether he had stepped back into the shadows or simply vanished altogether, Octavian couldn't say.

'You never told me there were other races who could navigate the Shadowpaths,' Danny said, turning to Squire.

The hobgoblin shrugged. 'You never asked. Anyway, the Smiths are pricks. They think just because nobody else can find their way in the Grey Corridors, somehow that makes them better than my kind, like they're the transdimensional police or something.'

Octavian frowned. 'Are you sure they're not?'

Squire scowled. 'You want to get your friends back?'

'You know I do.'

'Then let's keep moving. Before Smith arrived, I had started reaching into this one dimension and I caught a whiff of a horrible stink – like burning kittens or something.'

Squire turned and started along one of the branches that splintered away from the main path. He went more carefully than before, afraid of what kind of world he might fall into.

'You think it's Hell?' Octavian asked.

Danny gave a soft laugh. 'Not the hell you mean. I'd feel it.'

'No, not Hell,' Squire added. 'But whatever it is, it ain't Happytown. If we want to find an open doorway to Hell, that's the kind of place we need to be looking for.'

'Then lead on.'

Squire nodded, took a breath and reached back to take Octavian's hand, who took Danny's hand in turn. The sphere of light that had floated alongside them winked out once again and they plunged into the darkest shadows, a place devoid of all light.

The smell hit Octavian even before light and colour returned. He flinched away from the acrid stink of burning flesh even as he felt Danny's grip tighten.

'My God,' the devil rasped, and Octavian thought better than to correct him on the casual prayer.

They stood in the shadow of a tall building, its architecture nothing like that of Octavian's world. It towered two hundred feet above their heads, bent like a reed in the deep current. Its exterior had a pale rose hue but otherwise seemed to be made of something akin to blown glass, elegantly curving without need of seams or frames or beams. Around them spread a city of such buildings, or it had been a city before catastrophe had claimed it. Corpses had been heaped into piles in the smooth streets and set aflame, funeral pyres that had burned down so that all that remained were flickers of flames amidst the charred dead and huge plumes of lilac smoke that drifted skyward.

'I don't want to be here,' Danny whispered.

'We have to be,' Squire said. This is the kind of place we . . .'

The hobgoblin turned away, knelt, and vomited in the street. Octavian and Danny averted their eyes while Squired heaved again and then he crouched, taking sips of the air, steadying himself.

'Kid, tell me you feel that tug you were talking about?'

Danny hesitated, unsure. Octavian watched him a moment but then curiosity drew him away. He wandered along the street a few yards, taking in the atrocities around them. Other bodies lay strewn in the streets, humanoid figures that had been flayed open or torn in half. Along a side street, several of the blown glass buildings had come down, but instead of debris, they seemed to have melted like candles left to burn. A massive hole in the middle of the street bore investigation.

From somewhere far off there came a high-pitched scream that sent a shiver along his spine. These people weren't human – not the way he understood humanity – but he sensed that this was no scream of terror. Whatever horror had been visited upon this world seemed to have passed. Instead, the scream rose and fell, a keening wail that could only have been a cry of grief. Of loss.

He started moving in the direction of that sorrow.

'Pete,' Squire called. 'Don't.'

Octavian turned to face his companions as they strode toward him.

'Can't you hear—?'

'Whatever ugliness was going to happen here, it's happened already,' Squire replied. 'It's too late for you to try to play the hero. You want to stay here and help the survivors rebuild, or do you want to try to save your friends?'

For several long seconds – an eternity – he could not reply. Allison and Kuromaku were like his sister and brother, but they were seasoned warriors. If anyone could survive in Hell, it would be the two of them. Santiago and Taweret and Kazimir as well, though he had never been as close to them as to the others. But Charlotte . . .

She'd been nineteen years old when Cortez had made her a vampire. The girl had no family, no place in the world, and little experience as a warrior. In the face of true evil, her spirit might shatter. She might have a noble, courageous heart, but even that would not keep her alive for long. Octavian had taken her under his wing, in a sense, intending

127

to redeem her. He had promised her that she would be a part of his family, just as Kuromaku and Allison were. No way could he leave her to an eternity of torment.

With one more glance in the direction of that mournful scream, he turned to his companions.

'Danny,' he said. 'Is there a way through from here? Did you find a door?'

The young devil nodded his heavy, horned head, crimson eyes gleaming.

'I think so,' Danny replied. 'If you're sure it's what you want.'

Octavian did not hesitate. 'Show us the way.'

'Oh, joy,' Squire muttered as Danny started off along the street. 'Next stop, Hell.'

Phoenix's World
Manhattan, New York, USA

The whole frantic drive into Manhattan, Ronni had felt sure that Phoenix would be pulled over, or that the whole city would erupt into chaos around them the way it had done during the Uprising. At first, as night fell, they had seen State Police cars headed north and once they got off the Henry Hudson Parkway, there did seem to be an inordinate number of cops out on the streets, on alert in the event the chaos did spread. But otherwise the world beyond Ardsley seemed unaffected by the events unfolding there. That would change, Ronni knew. Even if the cops up in Westchester were able to get control of the situation and those – *demons*, she thought, *call them what they are* – could be killed, word of what was happening would spread like wildfire soon enough. It had been barely more than an hour since she and Phoenix had fled the hospital. The whispers were due to start any minute now, and then the TV news would be all over the story, if they weren't already.

Unless it gets covered up, Ronni thought. She supposed that was possible, if they could keep it from spreading. The very idea made her wonder how many other hideous, impossible things might have happened in the world that most people would never know about.

Phoenix turned on 82nd Street and by some miracle found a parking space under a streetlight halfway between Columbus and Amsterdam. Ronni studied her as she parallel parked, doing a crappy job of it the first time and starting all over. They had ridden much of the way in tense silence, only their heartbeats for company. At one point, Phoenix had turned on the radio, searched for news of the chaos in Ardsley, and then shut it off again. Ronni had a hundred questions but most of them were stupid, things that Phoenix wasn't in any better position to answer than she was herself.

'Now's your chance,' Phoenix said as she put the car in park.

'For what?'

Phoenix switched off the engine and turned to look at her. 'To take off. You're in Manhattan. You can get anywhere from here. Hop a cab to Penn Station and get a train out of town. It's what I'd do—'

'But it's not what you *are* doing.'

'My father died today. We had a lot of bad blood between us, once upon a time, but we made up for that. *He* made up for it. I know he loved me. The first of those things that came through . . . it came through him. And there are more, and likely to be more and more and more, and I can't walk away from that.'

Phoenix opened her door and stepped out of the car, so Ronni followed suit. The sounds of New York City reached them, but seemed distant there on the quiet, tree-lined residential block. Autumn had brought many colours to the leaves and the sidewalks and gutters were littered with those already fallen, but it was beautiful there. Serene. Ronni wondered if Phoenix was thinking the same thing that she was – that it was an illusion.

'I'm not the type to run,' Ronni said, smoothing her sweatshirt, feeling stupid in her hospital scrubs.

'Bullshit.' Phoenix locked the car and slammed her door. 'Outside the hospital earlier, you knew who I was on sight. You recognized me from all the attention I got after the Uprising, but that happened seven years ago.'

'You're famous,' Ronni said.

'My father's famous. *Was* famous. I had a lot of attention for a while and yeah, I guess some people might still recognize me from that, but you were . . . you were fascinated. I know you're not some kind of stalker, that you actually work at the hospital, but if you've got some weird fucking fetish for the Uprising and you're obsessed with me or whatever, then—'

'Do I seem like just some fan girl to you?' Ronni demanded, bristling.

'Then why the hell aren't you running? You don't need to stay with me!'

Ronni clenched her jaw, pressed her eyes shut, and then sighed as she opened them. She closed the passenger door gently and stared across the hood at Phoenix, who had come around the front of the car.

'Firstly, I've already told you part of this. Yes, I admired you. If you really don't know how famous you became, then you're delusional.'

'Famous for killing someone,' Phoenix said bitterly.

'Famous for doing whatever you had to do. I saw this one interview you gave and you were in so much pain, but you kept your head up. Tough girl. The look in your eyes was like, I'm in Hell, but I'd do it all again if I had to—'

'I don't know if I would.'

Ronni spread her arms. 'Look around, Phoenix. You may have to. Point is, one of the reasons I'm not running is because of you. Someone's gotta stand by you in this, help you do whatever it is you're going to do. I don't see people lining up for the job.'

Phoenix hesitated, then took a deep breath, and nodded. 'All right. What's the other reason?'

Ronni gave her a humourless smile. 'I've got nowhere else to go.'

A taxi rolled by and they had to step out of the way. Phoenix gave Ronni another glance and then started across the street. Three doors down from where they'd parked was a three-storey building so narrow it seemed to have been erected merely to fill the space between two others. A low black wrought-iron gate ran along all of the buildings on the block and there were unruly bushes and still some flowers in bloom behind the fence.

Phoenix opened the gate in front of the narrow building and walked toward the small set of steps that led to the entrance.

'Admit it,' she said, glancing back at Ronni. 'You just want to meet Annelise.'

Ronni smiled. 'Well, yeah . . . but not *just*.'

With a clank, the front door opened before they reached it and a grey-haired, crinkly-eyed woman in her mid-sixties appeared on the threshold. The older woman pressed a hand to her chest, a baleful sorrow in her eyes. Ronni recognized her immediately. Annelise Hirsch had been one of the mediums whose televised mass séance had caused the Uprising. With Eric Honen and Professor Joe Cormier dead, she was the only one of them left alive.

'Oh, my, they were right,' Annelise said in a light, Germanic accent. 'You really *are* here.'

8

Phoenix's World
Manhattan, New York, USA

Phoenix hesitated.

'You're talking about the spirits,' Ronni said. 'They knew we were coming?'

Distinguished and elegant, Annelise frowned as she looked at Ronni. 'Strange that they didn't mention you would have company.'

A chill went through Ronni, then, a ripple of unease that caused a twist of dread in her gut.

'What do you . . .? I mean, why wouldn't they—'

Phoenix slipped her arms around Annelise and began to cry, shaking with grief. 'He's dead,' she said. 'My dad's gone.'

Wrapped in that comforting embrace, Phoenix could not have seen it, but Ronni noticed a dark shadow passing across the older woman's eyes. As a nurse, she had seen a similar shadow in the eyes of a hundred doctors; it came whenever they had difficult news to share.

'You'd better come in,' Annelise said, stepping back to allow them entry into the foyer of her apartment.

The medium occupied the entire narrow building. Ronni expected old fashioned tastes – antiques and delicate furnishings – but despite her dignified airs, Annelise seemed a thoroughly modern woman. Her front parlour seemed to be still recovering from a shabby chic stage, with comfortable chairs and lots of earth tones and framed art pages from *The Adventures of Tintin* books, which Ronni assumed had been a childhood pleasure for the Austrian woman, though they had originated in Belgium.

'I would offer you tea . . .' Annelise began.

'But if you've been consulting the spirit world, you know there's a crisis going on,' Phoenix said.

'Just so,' Annelise agreed, then she glanced at Ronni.

'Oh, I'm sorry,' Phoenix said. 'This is Veronica Snow. She's a nurse at the hospital where . . . where it's all happening.'

'Nice to meet you, Veronica,' Annelise said. 'Despite the circumstances.'

'Ronni. People call me Ronni,' she replied, and immediately felt stupid. They didn't have time for tea or for small talk and pleasantries. 'What have the spirits been saying?'

'What aren't you telling me?' Phoenix asked.

Brows knitted, Annelise reached out to touch Phoenix on the arm. 'Please, both of you, sit down. Perhaps it's best if you hear it directly from them.'

Ronni perched on the edge of a loveseat, while Phoenix took a plush chair whose wine-dark upholstery was the only splash of real colour in the room. It made Ronni shudder, thinking of blood, but she said nothing as Annelise turned on a small, frosted-glass-and-nickel-plate lamp in the corner and then went to switch off the fixture overhead. Diffuse yellow light, soft and warm, bathed the parlour and Annelise sat in a plush beige chair.

She lit no candles, played no music, burned no incense. Ronni found herself slightly disappointed to discover that Annelise was a thoroughly modern medium.

'All right, my friends,' Annelise said quietly, glancing about the room. 'She's here.'

'What about Taki?' Phoenix asked. 'I thought he was your spirit guide now?'

Annelise closed her eyes and lowered her head, her voice becoming little more than a wisp. 'Oh, he's here. But others have been waiting to speak . . .'

The grey-haired woman fell silent. Head down, her wrinkles seemed to deepen and she looked much older. Ronni watched her as the seconds ticked by and then glanced at Phoenix, confused. If the spirits had been waiting—

'*Please,*' Annelise said in a tremulous voice that was not her own.

Ice ran through Ronni's veins. All the breath went out of her lungs as fear engulfed her. She had romanticized the work of a medium, but that single word had brought the truth home to her – the voice belonged to someone dead, speaking to them from after death, wherever that might be.

'Oh, God,' she whispered, and she saw her own breath fogging the air in front of her. The temperature in the room had dropped forty or fifty degrees in a matter of seconds.

135

She shivered, alone there on the loveseat, and wanted to run. The thought made her sit up and rub her arms to keep warm. Ronni Snow wasn't going to run.

'Please what?' Phoenix asked, staring at the drooping head of the ageing medium. 'I'm here. Talk to me. If you know what's going on up north, you've got to tell me what to do. How can we—'

'*We're frightened*,' another voice said, a rasping male voice. '*They're coming through our world to get to you, in here with us, and they don't belong. They can hurt us. Destroy us.*'

'*Eat us*,' another voice said, and tears ran down Annelise's face as the ghost spoke through her. '*Some of them eat us.*'

Ronni raised a shaking hand to her mouth to make sure she would not speak out of turn. She had never heard such despair before. All her life she had pretended that death did not scare her, but she would never be able to persuade anyone of that lie again.

'What are they?' Phoenix asked. 'Demons?'

'*Evil*,' the first voice said, quavering. '*Devils. Cruel beasts. The first one through . . . he is letting the others pass into the world of the flesh.*'

'*Your father . . .*' rasped the male voice.

Phoenix jerked upright, staring, her chest rising and falling with shuddering breaths. 'What about my father? Is he there with you? Can I speak to him?'

'*He is the door*,' the ghost rasped. '*Dark magic has made him their doorway, and all of the other dead who have been taken and used . . . they are only windows. If you destroy his flesh, it's possible they will all be closed. No more devils will pass through.*'

'No,' Phoenix said, cringing. 'I can't—'

'What about the others?' Ronni asked. 'If all of the . . . the doors and windows are closed, what happens to the demons that are already here?'

'*We suspect they would remain,*' the trembling girl's voice said. '*But at least there would be no more.*'

'No way,' Phoenix said, shaking her head. She shot Ronni a hard look, perhaps angry that Ronni had so readily agreed. 'Hasn't my father been used enough?'

Annelise's head whipped up. Her eyes had rolled back to white and she darted a hand out to grip Phoenix's wrist.

'*Don't be stupid, Fee,*' yet another voice said, the voice of a young man.

Phoenix's jaw dropped. 'Eric?'

'*He's being used right now . . . his body's been torn up, contorted, and tainted by demons. If you can burn up what's left of him, don't you think he'd prefer that?*'

'Eric, I . . .'

Annelise jerked in her chair, blinked several times, and then moaned as she slumped back. Her eyes were aware of them – she had control of herself again, no longer possessed.

'Are you all right?' Ronni asked. 'Do you want some water or something?'

Annelise ignored her. Her hand still gripped Phoenix's wrist. 'They're right, you know. It's what he would want.'

Phoenix ran her hands over her face and through her hair, sighing deeply. Then she nodded and stood up. 'Okay. You're right. *They're* right. Shit, I can't believe I'm going to go back there.'

'Now?' Ronni blurted. 'I mean, right now, you're getting in the car and driving back up there?'

Phoenix gave her a blank look. 'You saw demons today. You just listened to the wandering spirits of the dead speak through Annelise. These things . . . they made my father a part of this, and that makes me a part of it. They're right, he's tainted. There's only one way to fix that.'

Annelise rose and put a maternal hand on Phoenix's shoulder. 'I wish I could tell you not to go. I think of you caught up in such evil—'

'Tell me about it,' Phoenix interrupted. 'I wish I could tell *myself* not to go.'

Ronni leaned forward, elbows on her knees, and stared at the hardwood floor. She felt like she might puke. This girl had been her inspiration, but what she planned to do now . . . this was totally batshit crazy. The screams of the people in the hospital were so fresh in her memory that she could still hear them echo off the tile walls. And the image of the body she had seen being wheeled toward the morgue on a gurney – the hands that had burst up through its abdomen – she couldn't get that out of her mind.

'You be careful, too,' she heard Phoenix say. 'If they used my dad that way, you're not safe. Don't try to channel the dead, at least until this is over.'

'I can't help it,' Annelise said quietly. 'They're here with me now. Always with me.'

'Hey,' Phoenix said. 'Ronni Snow. You take care of yourself.'

'We're the only ones,' Ronni whispered.

'What's that, dear?' Annelise asked.

She looked up at them, trying to keep her breathing steady. A dreadful chill had settled into her flesh, sinking to the bone.

'If this thing can really be stopped, we're the only ones who know how.'

Ronni stood, shook her head with a little laugh of disbelief, wondering if good sense would kick in and stop her, but then she heard the words coming out of her mouth.

'Let's go,' she said, as she started toward the front door. 'Before I change my mind.'

A World of Ruin

Danny led the way through what he had quickly come to think of as the melted city, and every block seemed haunted. Octavian and Squire had started out by asking him a billion questions about what he felt, trying to get him to describe the tug inside his chest that drew him toward what he felt sure must be some passage to Hell, but he had done a poor job of it. A fish hook, he'd said, but attached to some part of him so deep it wasn't bone or muscle or organ – it was *in* him, and though he fought, it felt like Hell kept trying to reel him in.

But that had been only half true, a metaphor they could understand. What he didn't say, what he could never admit to anyone, least of all himself, was that the lure of Hell was a kind of pied piper's song that made him want to follow. Temptation filled him with self-loathing and the closer they drew to a place where he would be able to cross over, the more repulsed he became with himself. He wanted to find a small, warm corner and curl himself into a foetal ball and wait until his mother came home. The trouble, of course, sprang from the fact that his mother was dead.

Danny breathed in the humid air of the melted city and reminded himself that even if his mother had still been among the living, she would never have found him here. He could scream all he wanted, weep and pray, but nobody would come looking for him. He had no proper home, but as long as he stayed in Mr Doyle's house he could persuade himself otherwise. There, at least, he could look at the rooms and corridors and see the echoes of friends who had accepted him for himself. Who had loved him and cared for him as best and for as long as they could . . . until they could no longer care even for themselves.

'Kid, you sleepwalking or something?' Squire asked.

'Daydreaming,' Danny said.

The hobgoblin sighed. 'Well, pay attention, would you? Are we getting any closer?'

'Not far to go, now.'

Danny gestured vaguely ahead, but he didn't like to look too closely at their surroundings. The city had been beautiful once, with the shimmering colours in the elegant, translucent material used to construct nearly all of the buildings and the peculiar, ropy growths that functioned like trees, placed along the sides of the streets to provide shade. He had stopped to run his fingers along the surface of one of the intact structures and found them to be contoured and textured, not as smooth as they appeared. This world's glass reminded him of amber, and he'd had the momentary thought that the buildings seemed almost to have been grown instead of constructed, that they might be organic.

Whatever beauty remained in this city – in this world – it had been wounded and scarred by the evil that had come here. Piles of the scorched dead were everywhere. Remains had been hung from the trees and on the blocks where the buildings had melted and run like wax, the wind seemed to shriek, although it blew no harder than elsewhere. A glance inside one building had revealed a honeycomb structure inside and he thought the shrieking might be the wind blowing through it, but another part of him felt sure it was the screaming of the dead.

Hell seemed as if it might be a relief.

'How far?' Squire asked.

Danny shot him a withering glance and bared his teeth. 'You think I want to be here?' He reached up and scratched the dry skin at the base of his horns. 'We're almost there. It feels . . . down, somehow.'

'Down?' Squire repeated. 'That's helpful, thanks.'

'Maybe it is helpful,' Danny growled. He turned on Squire and felt his fingers hook into claws. 'I think it's underground.'

Squire raised a stubby finger and pointed at him. 'Listen, kid, don't get—'

'Cut him some slack,' Octavian said. 'He's doing his best. And if his thoughts are drifting, well, who wouldn't rather daydream than take in what's happened here?'

Danny frowned. He had made up his mind not to like or trust Octavian, but the mage made it difficult when he spoke kindly. Danny had begun to feel that Octavian might be on his side, that he might be a friend, and it confused him. He had decided months ago that he would never have the opportunity to make another friend. He was a ghost in his own house, a gargoyle on the roof, a monster in the attic.

A demon. You're a goddamn demon.

But inside, he was still the same Danny Ferrick, who'd always loved football and skateboarding and hipster indie rock and girls with ginger hair. The same little kid who'd gone from Thomas the Tank Engine to Godzilla with hardly a stop in between. At the core of him, his emotions were simple – they were, he imagined, just like everyone else's. But when he allowed himself to feel the strength in his limbs and the heat in his gut or when he ran his tongue over his mouthful of wicked sharp teeth – things became complicated again. There were no mirrors left in Mr Doyle's house; Danny had covered or destroyed them all. He did not want to look at himself. Did not, if he was being completely honest, even want to live.

But Squire had asked for help, and Danny did not have enough friends that he could afford to refuse, even if the hobgoblin had begun to fray his nerves.

So he walked through the melted city, crunched charred bones underfoot and breathed in the burning embers that floated on the air, and he led them toward a doorway that his gut told him he ought to enter. Some primal voice inside his head told him that beyond that door was the place he belonged – his true home – but he refused to acknowledge it.

Someday, somehow, Mr Doyle and Eve and Clay would come back, and only then would he be home. With his friends.

They passed through a block of buildings that seemed untouched by the savagery that had swept the streets, but a closer look showed many places where dark blood and viscera were smeared on the inside of the glass. Smoke rose from the roof of a spire across the street, and Danny wondered how many demons had been a part of the massacre and how long it had taken them to slaughter an entire city.

'This is nuts,' Squire said.

Octavian glanced at him. 'It's not crazy. It's evil.'

'Yeah, no shit,' Squire replied. 'I meant it's just . . . it's frickin' amazing to me that we haven't seen even one survivor.'

They walked the rest of the block in silence, glancing around, and Danny knew that each of them sought some evidence of life. The question seemed to have gotten under Octavian's skin, because he did not reply.

At the corner, Danny turned to the right and they found themselves facing a structure unlike any they'd seen thus far. A massive, sprawling thing, its spire fell short of the height of many others on the cityscape, but it seemed to go on for an entire block. The translucent exterior, that blown glass substance, hung on some kind of internal skeleton so that the whole thing reminded him of nothing so much as a circus Big Top. Its surface had a rainbow of faint hues, like oil on a pool of water.

'What do you think?' Octavian asked. 'Some kind of cathedral?'

Squire grunted. 'Church or concert hall or something.'

'Whatever it was, this is where they first came through,' Danny said.

Octavian started toward the building, moving around a hole in the smoothness of the street that appeared blackly bottomless. Squire followed but Danny hung back.

'Why do you say that?' Octavian asked, not noticing his reluctance.

Squire studied him. 'Danny? What is it, kid? Trouble ahead?'

Danny stared at him, a sick feeling roiling in his gut. God, how he wanted to go on. The lure of Hell had grown more

powerful with every step and now it felt as if he were in a
swift, deep river current. He wanted to cry.

Instead, he laughed. 'Trouble? You're going to *Hell*.'

He gave in and let the current carry him along, though at
this point Octavian and Squire would not have needed a
guide. The glass cathedral had an enormous hole in one side
and as they drew closer the details became unnerving. Long
strings and spikes of smooth glass jutted from the edges of
the hole, as if it had melted and then been pushed and twisted
and teased outward only to harden again. Whatever had
destroyed this city had come from inside the cathedral and
forced its way out like some infernal birth. That blown glass
wall was a melted caul.

Octavian could find no door and the hole was too high for
Squire to climb up to it. The mage lifted a hand and a wave
of golden light burst forth. An opening appeared in the cathedral wall like a curtain being drawn back and Octavian
entered. Squire followed, both of them silent. The tide of
Hell swept Danny after them. His horns banged off the upper
edge of the opening and he bared his fangs in disgust. How
often would he forget his size, forget his horns, forget what
he had become?

Reaching into the pocket of the jeans he had forced himself
into, he clutched at the object within – a small emerald ring
that had belonged to his mother. After her husband had left
her, the ring was the only gift he had ever given her that she
had kept; it was her birthstone, and she had loved that ring, its
style and setting. Before they'd left Mr Doyle's house,
Octavian had cast a spell upon it that would act as a sort of
homing beacon – once Danny made it back to the Shadowpaths
it would lead him home, with or without Squire to guide the

way. Squire had shown him how to get back into the paths, how to feel for them, and Octavian had assured him that if he went in at precisely the point where they had emerged, he should be able to pass through, but Danny wasn't sure.

He caressed the ring for a moment and then removed his hand from his pocket, leaving the ring there. His good luck charm.

Inside the glass cathedral, they found themselves in a chamber forty feet wide and twenty high. The walls and ceiling were scorched black. The dim light from outside carried through the massive, twisted hole overhead and in that illumination they could see a broad stairway vanishing downward beneath an arched ceiling. Dead things lay at the top of the steps, statues of misshapen ash, and as they approached the top of the broad stairs, Danny felt a coldness spreading through him. Not a chill on his skin or in his bones, but an icing of his heart.

Hell loomed so near. There, desires were encouraged. Destruction permitted. As he took the first step downward, he felt as if the skate kid he'd been – the kid with the torn Red Sox cap and the old comics – was being left behind.

'That's just disgusting,' Squire said.

Danny blinked. He had fallen into a kind of trance and only now, three steps down, right behind Squire and Octavian, did he see what they must have noticed the moment they had reached the top of the stairs. At first glance, it appeared to be a circular mirror, perhaps twelve feet in diameter, its silver surface smooth and reflecting the charred carnage around them.

The frame of the mirror had been sculpted from the flesh and bone of one creature, a citizen of this city. Its hands dangled loosely at either edge of the mirror, flesh grey and bloated, and at the top sat its head, stretched so badly that it had split up to the forehead, exposing bone and the dripping yellow matter of something that must have been its brain.

'You sure this is a good idea?' Squire asked.

Octavian laughed and glanced at him. 'It's a terrible idea,' he said. 'But if it was you in there, you'd want your friends to come after you.'

Squire continued to descend the steps. He shot a look back at Danny. 'How are you doing, kid?'

Danny only stared straight ahead and continued downward. He could see Octavian and Squire in the mirror, and he could see himself, small but growing larger as they approached. For a second, he averted his gaze. It had been a long time since he had allowed himself to look in a mirror, to come face to face with his own monstrosity. But now a little spark of excitement ignited in his chest. He raised his head and studied himself. In that reflection, he towered over the mage and the hobgoblin. His long fingers hung like talons and his eyes burned with a deep crimson. The demon inside Danny couldn't help itself – it smiled.

'Something funny?' Squire asked. He'd seen the reflection of that smile. ''Cause now seems a weird time to be—'

Whatever he might have said next was lost as the silver mirror surface rippled and a huge, taloned hand emerged, palm up, motioning them to halt. The demon stepped out of that mirror as if sliding from a pool and the silvery liquid mirror wavered behind him and went still.

Not a mirror, Danny thought. *A portal.*

But he'd known that from the moment he'd seen it. From before he had seen it, really. This was the door they had come looking for.

The sentry – for surely this was the guardian of the door – stood at least a couple of feet taller than Danny. Its sickly, jaundice-yellow flesh revealed many eyes, which seemed to look in several directions at once. Its tongue slipped out of a narrow slit mouth, long and forked and darting like a snake's. A massive prick swung between its legs and Danny registered the spot as a vulnerability.

In its right hand, the sentry held a long sword whose blade seemed to be made of bone on one edge and a strange ebony, perhaps volcanic stone, on the other.

The demon's roving eyes locked on Octavian and Squire, who still led the way. It barked a command in its own guttural tongue. Danny had lived his whole life speaking English and even his thoughts were in that language, but he realized that he understood.

'Not another step,' it had said.

'Move aside, asshat,' Squire replied.

The demon's eyes twitched and blinked and its darting tongue paused a second, and then it reached back through the mirrored portal with its free hand, made a gesture, and another – the twin of the first – emerged.

'I could just kill them,' Octavian muttered.

'If you want all of Hell down on your damn head,' Squire muttered. 'They're sentries. You don't think killing them would raise some kind of alarm?'

When the magic began to flow through Octavian, Danny felt it. The skin on his arms prickled and the air seemed to contract around them. A rich blue light began to glow around the mage's fists and to spill like mist from his eyes. The two demons raised their swords, hissed and thrust out their tongues, and started forward.

147

'Isn't this what we brought you for?' Squire snapped at Danny.

The boy he'd been raised to be wanted to whine and complain that he didn't know what to do, but the devil he'd been born felt the power within him. Danny took a step down, pushed between Octavian and Squire, and then took two more steps to meet the demons' approach.

They were hideous to look at and they didn't smell much better.

'Turn back or die,' the first sentry said in that same demonic language.

His twin grunted in laughter. 'No, no, brother. Too late for them to turn back.' He cocked his arm, prepared to bring his sword down.

'You don't want to do that,' Danny said.

The blade whistled as it came round in an arc meant to take off his head. Danny ducked enough that the ebony edge of the sword struck one of his horns, sparks flying, and then he stepped up and punched the sentry in the forehead as hard as he could. The sentry staggered backward but Danny held on to his wrist and twisted the sword out of his grip. He kicked the sentry to the ground even as his brother roared and jumped forward, halting as Danny brought the sword up and pressed it to his chest, right between two furious eyes.

'If I was you—' he started to say.

The one he'd knocked down cried out in pain and began to puff up, growing in stature and girth. Its head split into an impossibly wide mouth full of rows of jagged teeth and green, frothy drool spilled from its lips.

'Danny—' Octavian began, but Danny shot him a wary look.

'Don't screw this up for yourself,' he warned, and Octavian hesitated, the magic swirling around his fists diminishing.

As one sentry grew into an even more hideous monster, Danny focused on the demon who had yet to change, who had paused at the end of the stolen sword Danny pointed at him.

'You better chill for a second and listen,' Danny said, wondering if they could understand him. 'Whatever lower demon you report to, whatever thing that crawls in the pit, it's not going to be happy if you kill the son of a Demon Lord.'

The one at his swordpoint scoffed. 'You? What Lord would ever claim you as his son?'

Apparently, it had understood him just fine.

Danny hesitated. He'd heard several names for his father in the time he'd known Mr Doyle, but when they had encountered Wayland Smith and the Traveller had given a name, it had felt more right and true than any he'd heard before.

'I am Orias, son of Oriax,' he said, feeling foolish, like he was in the middle of the weirdest Shakespeare performance ever. 'And I command you to stand aside and let my companions enter.'

If his skin had not already been a leathery red, he felt sure he would have blushed. The words had felt absurd coming out of his mouth. But the sentry actually looked alarmed and backed up a step, and the other – its twin – began to shrink and regain its original appearance.

Danny blinked in surprise. Behind him, Squire gave a small grunt of something that might have been appreciation. Whoever Oriax might have been, he carried some weight.

149

Danny wondered if his father was still alive, and then he hated himself for wondering – the only parent he cared about was the only one who had shown him unconditional love, and she was dead. He had no interest in the monsters who had conceived him.

'Prove yourself,' the first sentry said, raising his sword and gently parrying Danny's, turning it aside so that they both lowered their blades. 'We take no commands from impostors.'

'How do you propose I—'

'Blood,' Octavian said, stepping up on Danny's left, eyes still leaking an intimidating aura of magic. 'They'll need to taste your blood.'

Danny frowned. 'What, you mean like a vampire?'

The sentries made noises of revulsion.

'There is a reason our breed are made sentries,' the first said. 'We don't need to drink your blood, but we must taste it. You can draw your own blood.'

Danny stared at them.

Squire stepped up behind him and gave him a nudge. 'Kid.'

'Fine, whatever,' Danny said. He reached up and drew a sharp talon along his cheek, sliced the flesh with a leathery tearing sound, and felt the warm blood spill down his face and run along his jaw, beginning to drip.

The second sentry – its mouth even wider and more grotesque than when it appeared – stepped up and reached out a hand, running its three fingers across Danny's jaw. He managed not to flinch from its stench as it drew its fingers toward its mouth. That revolting tongue snaked out and slithered across its fingertips and instantly the demon stiffened.

With so many eyes, the sentry could not hide the shock of its reaction, followed by obvious confusion. It reached out and smeared Danny's blood on its brother's searching tongue.

'This is just nasty,' Squire muttered.

'Hush,' Octavian said.

The first sentry – the second to taste Danny's blood – hung its head in indecision but only for a moment before it knelt on the stairs before him, placing its sword on the step above. Its brother followed suit an instant later.

'Well, well,' Squire said happily.

Danny punched him in the shoulder and the hobgoblin grunted. *Don't blow it*, he wanted to say, because there was no way these idiots ought to be kneeling to him. Yeah, okay, maybe his father was a Demon Lord, but Octavian knew a lot about the workings of Hell and hadn't told him to expect this kind of reception. It made him uneasy, but part of his discomfort stemmed from the fact that he liked it. A lot.

'Get up,' he said.

'You are Orias, son of . . . of Oriax,' the first sentry said, all of his eyes downcast.

Octavian tapped Danny on the arm. 'What is this? All the time I spent in Hell, I never heard of a Lord named Oriax. How does he warrant this?'

'That'd be my question, too,' Squire said. 'But it works for me.'

'Get up,' Danny said again. He thought maybe he should say *rise* or something more formal like that, but he felt stupid enough as it was. 'Seriously.'

The sentries did as instructed. The second, whom Danny had embarrassed by disarming him, still seemed unsure, as if the temptation to say or do something gnawed at him.

'Stand aside,' Danny told them.

After a moment's hesitation, they did so. Suddenly the allure of Hell swept over him, more powerful than ever before. He stared at that mirrored portal and the primal, diabolical part of him wanted to laugh and hurl itself through. What wonders awaited him?

No, he thought. *Not wonders – horrors.*

It took all of the will he could muster for Danny to turn his back on Hell. He reached into his pocket and fiddled with his mother's emerald ring, hoping it would really lead him back to Mr Doyle's house, because that was home. That world, that building, the memories there, and the people – if they ever returned.

'Danny,' Octavian said, 'are you sure you won't come with us? I've got people I love in there and it would go much easier if I didn't have to fight to get them out.'

Squire sniffed. 'You've got magic practically falling out of your ass and a sword I made, just in case we run into anything your magic can't kill—'

'Which we will,' Octavian said. 'You better believe we will.'

'You'll be fine,' Squire told him. 'Let the kid alone.'

Danny studied them, the ugly little hobgoblin and the tall, handsome mage who looked more like a grizzled gunfighter than a sorcerer. They were noble company and in any other circumstance he would have wanted to go with them, but if he went along now, he knew it would not be to help.

'If I go through that door, I'm afraid I won't be myself anymore,' he said.

The sentries grew agitated. The conversation troubled them, but whatever fealty they owed Danny because of his heritage kept them from speaking up.

'I understand,' Octavian said.

'What about you?' Danny asked. 'You'll find your way?'

'I lived here for a thousand years. I'll manage.'

Danny nodded. They said their farewells and he watched as they slipped through the mirrored portal, which rippled for a few seconds after their passing and then went still. Somehow he felt better when they'd gone, as if by not choosing to go with them he had already begun his journey back to the human world.

Clutching the ring in his pocket, he turned to the sentries.

'You won't speak of this,' he said. 'I forbid it.'

Forbid. More Shakespeare-sounding crap. But they nodded their heads in acceptance and he felt pretty certain they would obey, otherwise they would have cut his head off already.

Hell tugged at his heart, but he turned his back on the doorway, walked up the steps and out into the melted ruins of a city he had never known, a civilization no one had been left alive to remember. The thought made him realize that his life as a gargoyle perched on Mr Doyle's roof had a purpose he had never realized. Extraordinary people had lived there and had gone from that place. They had been heroes, and no one had erected a marker in their honour. So Danny would remember. Until the day they returned, he would be the keeper of their memory.

Compared to that, Hell had no allure at all.

9

Hell

The difficulty in navigating Hell sprang from its malleability.
There were regions and districts that were defined, the strong-
holds of Demon Lords and the fields of the damned and the
dungeon, the absolute sub-basement of Hell where those
lords and high-ranking soldiers who had betrayed their brothers and sisters were imprisoned for eternity. These were not
traitors who had stabbed other demons in the back – that was
the bloodsport of Hell, and to be expected – they were the
hellions who had turned to the light, who had sought kindness and love as if such things could be within their grasp.

Like Danny, Octavian thought, though the young devil
had achieved that very thing. Believing in the light was one
thing – he would not be punished for that – but attempting to
spread that belief, to bring light into the dark fires of the
inferno, for that he would be twice-damned.

'Hey,' Squire said. 'You got a single clue where we are?'

'More or less.'

'How much less?'

Octavian glanced around. They were in a massive chamber with no discernible ceiling and a pit so deep there seemed no bottom. Stairs had been carved into the walls and there were doorways from time to time that would take them into other caverns, other tunnels. Flames erupted at odd intervals from cracks in the walls and stairs and black, four-winged, mindless predator demons flew on the thermal drafts that belched up inside the throat of that cavern. They stank like shit and sickness, but in Hell, that was as good as it was going to get.

'A hundred feet or so down, there'll be a door, and we'll be out of the throat. If the geography's even close to the same – and it's probably shifted, I just don't know how much – then we'll be in the stronghold of Belial—'

'That doesn't sound very smart.'

'Belial's dead. Even while I was here there were a hundred lower demons fighting for his seat. With luck it's still in disarray and we can pass through without much trouble.'

'You're in Hell relying on luck?' Squire said. His yellow eyes gleamed as he narrowed them. The hobgoblin had looked nervous from the moment they had crossed over, and Octavian had wondered from hour to hour if he ought to have come alone.

'Listen—'

'Shut up, dickhead,' the hobgoblin said. 'I'm here to help. I'm helping.'

'Don't tell me you didn't have anything better to do,' Octavian said, as they moved carefully down a broken segment of stone steps. Fire erupted ahead of them and Squire grabbed his wrist, held him back.

'I pay my debts,' the little man said. 'And I've lost too many friends these last few years. I don't have enough of them that I can afford to lose any more.'

'Aww, that's sweet,' Octavian teased.

'Screw.'

Octavian heard a leathery rustle off to his left and turned just in time to avoid the talons of one of the four-winged fliers. It let out a shriek like an infant's cry of pain as it flapped its wings and banked, gliding higher on the hot air rising from the furnace of the pit below. The one that had attacked circled around the throat of the cavern, turning glittering silver eyes downward, tracking them.

'That ain't good,' Squire said.

'Hurry.' Octavian quickened his descent. Two circuits on the stairs would bring them to the next exit from the cavern. He had hoped that they could descend much further than that without difficulty, but if the predators were going to come after them, they had to be smart about it.

Squire grunted and huffed as he came down after the mage. 'Easy for you to say. Have you not seen how stumpy my legs are?'

The infantile shrieking began again and Octavian glanced up to see two other predators joining the first in its flight pattern. There were dozens of others above and below – sometimes darting at the stone walls of the cavern to cling for a moment and dart their sharp beaks into holes where massive worms and insects might be found – but these three flew in formation and there could be no doubt that they had a purpose in mind. They were hunting.

Running down the steps, Octavian's heart pounded in his chest. It would have been so much easier if he could just use magic – he had a hundred ways to destroy these winged demons – but he knew that every time he cast even the tiniest spell or summoned the magic within him, he ran the risk of alerting the Demon Lords to his presence. Like the scent of smoke on the wind, the frisson of sorcery in the air would carry. Some types of demons would react like sharks to blood in the water, and the Demon Lords would learn of their presence.

Swords and daggers and other weapons jostled in their scabbards and banged his legs as Octavian raced down the stairs, careful to jump over cracks in the stone and to keep as near to the wall as he could manage and keep his speed. He had made it once around Hell's throat when he heard Squire shouting behind him again.

'Here they come, Pete! Don't you fuckin' leave me up here!'

Octavian glanced back the way he'd come. Squire had kept up better than he'd thought, now only a dozen or so steps behind him, but the winged things – Hell's blackbirds, he thought – had banked and now dove toward the hobgoblin.

Damn it, Octavian thought, and he drew the sword Squire had given him and started back up the steps.

Squire could have escaped by diving into the shadows, but had he done so, there was always the chance that demons would find a way to follow him onto the Shadowpaths, and Octavian knew he would not run the risk.

Instead, the hobgoblin cursed loudly, reached behind his back and produced a small, double-sided battle axe. As the first of the demon birds came at him, Squire cleaved its skull in half and the thing careened into the cavern wall beneath the hobgoblin's feet, wings slapping wetly before it tumbled all the way down into the flames far below. The second bird slashed Squire's forehead and the hobgoblin roared his displeasure even more loudly and swung the axe in time to slash the two wings on its right side as it flew away. Unable to stay aloft, the thing plummeted, its screeching baby wail even louder than before.

The third demon bird passed by Squire and the hobgoblin started running.

'Go!' Squire snapped. 'What the hell are you coming this way for?'

'To help,' Octavian said as he halted and reversed direction yet again.

'Yeah, good job with that. A lotta fuckin' help you—'

Shrieking, the third bird came at Octavian's back. He ducked, grateful for the warning, and it flew over his head, one talon slashing his scalp. As it went by, he thrust out his sword and cut its belly open; stinking viscera spilled out and hung in loops as it hit the stairs and began to roll and bounce with a crack and snap of bones. When he reached the dying, twitching thing on the steps, he kicked it off into the flames.

'Getting there!' Squire called.

Another three-quarters of a circuit around and they would be able to leave the throat. But the death screams and the blood of the three hell-birds had drawn the attention of the others. Octavian heard Squire shout and turned – nearly losing his footing on the carved steps – and saw six of the things converging on the hobgoblin. Several others rose up on the thermal drafts and darted toward Octavian. He could feel the magic thrumming inside of him, power begging to be unleashed. It pulsed as his core, a flood pent up behind a dam, and from the way his fingers prickled he knew that its energy had begun to spark and emanate from there.

No, he thought, tamping it down. With a hack and a slash of the sword, he killed the two that dove at him. The diamond-like side of the blade did the job, but the ebony side cut demon flesh with zero resistance. Of course it did; Squire had made it.

'Oh, you motherfuckingsonofabitch!' the hobgoblin roared.

Two of the demon birds that had attacked Squire were dead but the other four were slashing at him and more were circling like vultures, ready to dart down for a strike. Octavian saw several headed toward him and knew he had to go back up again to help Squire. But the moment he had taken his first step in that direction, the hobgoblin shouted at him.

'Go! Just go! I'll get there!'

'How—'

Birds slashed at Octavian's face and he hacked them in two, spattered with their blood.

'Go!' Squire shouted as he slammed himself against the cavern wall, crushing one or two of the birds, each of which had to be more than half his size. Talons hooked through his coat and in his hair and he thrashed against them as they tried to pick him up. Octavian had an image in his mind of gulls carrying their prey high and dropping it to stones far below in order to break it open and feast on the insides.

But Squire insisted he had it under control. Hesitating a moment longer, Octavian turned and hurried down the steps.

If he had to use magic, he would do it, but it might just save Squire's life for a moment as it brought hundreds of the birds down on them at once.

Sword in hand, he ran along cracked steps made slippery with the stinking dung of the demon birds. A blast of fire shot up through a crack ahead of him, so close it singed his face as he pulled back. It subsided only slightly and he leaped over it, continuing, only a half-circuit around the throat to go, and he glanced over at Squire just in time to see the hobgoblin hurl his axe out over the bottomless inferno, the weapon turning end over end until it struck the cavern wall just beside the door below, where it cut the stone and stuck fast.

Octavian stared. Squire had killed a couple more of the birds but now he had no weapon in his hands – they were all sheathed or holstered – how would he . . .

The hobgoblin jumped from the stairs. Octavian shouted his name, but then he saw that Squire had not jumped alone. He had his left hand around the talons of a demon bird and his right clenched around the throat of another. The one he strangled could only wheeze but the first let out a scream of fury and perhaps embarrassment as Squire jerked at them, diverting and directing them. Others picked at them and he shot out a kick or three to keep them back. The one he strangled began losing altitude but the other fought to stay aloft, rising higher, and with a shock Octavian realized that Squire would beat him to the door.

'You cunning little—' he began, and then a blast of fire shot from a crack behind him and knocked him headlong down the stairs.

Octavian rolled, the back of his coat on fire as he slammed into the wall and stairs and nearly went right off the side and into the pit. His fingers scrabbled for purchase and found it and his left arm wrenched in the socket hard enough that he let out a yell and a bit of magic flashed from his eyes, but not a spell or a real summoning of power, and he hoped it would not be enough to send up an alarm.

Grunting, bleeding, he got to his feet just as a demon bird dove at his face. He brought his sword up just in time for the thing to impale itself. More blood splashed him and he would not have minded – the blood of demons would help them pass unnoticed in the bowels of hell – but the stink made him want to vomit.

He staggered down half a dozen steps as he got his bearings again and then realized he was only ten feet from the crude doorway hewn in the cavern wall. Squire stood waiting for him.

'You're out of your mind,' Octavian said.

The hobgoblin worked his axe out of the cut it had made in the stone wall and then turned to smile at him.

'Maybe, but you can't say I don't know how to show a fella a good time.'

Days passed, though in Octavian's world that might have been merely minutes. They took several wrong turns and killed dozens of demons, large and small, and never with magic. Squire's weapons were more than adequate to dispatch the low-level devils that they encountered along their path and those that might have proven a challenge had been thus far easy to circumvent.

There were nexus points in the infernal lands, spots where the borders of one Demon Lord's territory led to that of another that might not be geographically adjacent. Science might have called these nexus points wormholes, but Octavian felt sure it would be foolish to attempt to apply the physics of the human world in Hell. The infernal lands were inconsistent, constantly in flux, so one realm might be firmly beside another for years and then shift elsewhere in the blink of an eye. There were constants, of course, roots so firmly planted in this dimension that they could not be moved. The nexus points were reliable because they led to their original destinations no matter where those destinations might have moved, but there were other fixed bits of geography as well. Octavian knew most of them, but it had been a long time since he had been in the caverns and plains of Hell and his memory proved imperfect.

'Where are all the people?' Squire asked.

'People?'

'The dead. The damned.'

Octavian exhaled. He had been very careful thus far to avoid the fields of the dead as much as possible, and the halls of torment even more so. Squire had accompanied him here but there was no point in putting the hobgoblin through that if it wasn't completely necessary.

'They're here,' was all he said.

'I can hear them.'

Listening, Octavian discovered that he, too, could hear distant cries of suffering and despair. His heart clenched with sorrow but he forced himself not to slow down.

'Try not to listen,' he said. 'There's nothing you can do for them.'

'I could get them out,' Squire said. 'Some of them, at least.'

Octavian turned to stare at him. 'I thought you couldn't travel directly from Hell to the Shadowpaths.'

'You know that's not true. I just . . . don't want to be the one to compromise the paths. But all these people, suffering like that . . . if I could get even some of them out—'

'Do you even know what you're saying? Trillions of souls, maybe more, into the Shadowpaths, with all the demons of Hell on their trail.'

Squire lowered his gaze. Octavian had never seen him so completely at a loss, so ordinary. So human, though he was not that.

'Maybe I could—'

'Squire,' Octavian snapped, and the hobgoblin glanced up at him. 'This place will destroy you if you let it. Despair will weigh you down until you feel like you can't move another inch, and then they'll get you.'

'They'll . . .'

'Yes. You'll let them. You'll reach a point where you think you deserve to be here. So listen to me carefully – all of these souls here, they can't leave. They're here because they believe they deserve it, or because they committed such atrocities that they are truly evil, now, and no other dimension would have them. All you'd be doing is flooding the Shadowpaths with demons, just like you feared, and who knows how many other worlds they'd invade because of it?'

Squire stared at the smooth rock floor underfoot. For several long seconds he seemed to be listening to the distant cries of the damned.

'I can't not hear them,' he said. 'I can't not care.'

'Then you have to weigh their suffering against all of the other suffering you would create if you tried to free them.'

The hobgoblin breathed in and out, in and out, then he shuddered a bit, shook his arms and head, and forged ahead.

Octavian followed, but he would watch Squire carefully from now on, not only because his plan depended on the ugly little man but because he considered Squire a friend – a friend who had only come to Hell because Octavian had asked him.

They walked down a long slope inside a canyon whose walls rose up so smoothly that they seemed to be made of metal instead of rock, steel that had been melted down and then painted on. It stretched hundreds of feet on either side of them, but all around this floor of this strange Hellish canyon were crumbled ruins of what must have been structures. They reminded Octavian most of the worst of Pompeii's ruins, eroded to the rudimentary representations of structures until they looked like mere impressionistic suggestions of structures than actual buildings. Once, this had been a legendary city of Hell called Malizia. It had been built in a time when the Demon Lords were united and their relations more civilized, but entropy had taken hold and the natural savagery of demons overcame any attempts at order. This was a place of chaos and disharmony, after all. Malizia had never had a chance at enduring.

As they continued down the long slope of Malizia's ruins, they passed through the shadows of gigantic bones that jutted from the ground and curved thirty or forty feet into the air. These were the remains of Demon Lords who had gone to war in the time of the city's destruction. The bones were dry and pitted as dead coral, but Octavian still felt an ancient power resonating within them, as if these antediluvian demons were not dead but only inert, and the dust might blow and gather around their bones and return to cruel, raging, primal and infernal life. The dead were not often so full of potential, but evil tended to linger long after the flesh had begun to rot.

High above them, holes in the ceiling let in a strange, pale light whose source he had never been able to discover. It fell in shafts like sunlight through breaks in the clouds, but this illumination did not come from any star or sun, nor did it have the familiar orange glow of hellfire. Regardless, it lit their path and caused the ruins and the bones of giants to cast great shadows across the canyon floor.

As they crossed the ruin of Malizia, Squire surprised Octavian by remaining almost completely silent. Whether happy or angry or terrified, the hobgoblin always seemed to have a great deal to say. Words were just as much his stock in trade as weapons. But somehow those enormous bones and the hushed aura of evil around them caused Squire to hold his tongue, and perhaps even his breath. Only when they had reached the far end of the canyon, where the walls came together to form a single, narrow ravine, did Squire exhale.

'You're awfully quiet,' Octavian said as they entered the ravine, which became a low-ceilinged, claustrophobic tunnel within a dozen paces.

Squire glanced back the way they'd come. Instead of being troubled by the fact that they were now closed in – the walls and ceiling narrowing further with each step – he seemed relieved.

'Damn right, I'm quiet,' Squire said. 'Good thing you were, too.'

'I don't understand.'

Squire shot him a dark look. 'Don't bullshit me. It's the giants, Pete.'

Octavian wondered if this was some ancient enmity between hobgoblins and giants, some ancestral memory haunting the Squire.

'Honestly, I don't—'

'I was afraid to wake them, all right? And so were you, the way you tiptoed around the joint.'

Wake them? Octavian frowned as they kept moving through the narrow space. He wondered if Squire had seen something he had not, if his human eyes – regardless of his sorcery – had been blind to some truth that the hobgoblin had no difficulty seeing. He nearly asked, but Squire still seemed spooked and so he thought better of it. A conversation for another day.

If there is another day.

They came to a place where the tunnel had narrowed so much that they could barely slip through. Most of the larger demons would be unable to pass this way, and certainly that had been intentional. Whatever dark power had built this nexus had wished to control how and when it could be utilized, but they had never counted on a human mage and a hobgoblin surviving in Hell long enough to pass this way.

'No screaming in here,' Squire said. 'Nice.'

Octavian led the way and they passed through the gap and found themselves inside a circular room, standing on the rim of the bowl-like floor. The air inside the round room shifted, strange lights undulating and floating. Octavian thought of the aurora borealis, but these were not the icy hues that drifted in the sky in the far north of his homeworld, they were the colours of hell – of stone and fire and blood.

'So this is going to take us to the dungeon you were talking about? To the City of Dis?'

'The City of Dis is a myth. Or a euphemism, really. Think of Hell as a tree with its branches moving in the wind. The trunk is stationary but even that can bend. The only things that never change are the roots. But at the deepest part of Hell there's only one root, and that's the dungeon. Dis.'

'Sounds like fuckin' paradise. You think that's where your friends are being kept?'

'Maybe,' Octavian said, staring at the shifting colours of the nexus. 'In my time here, intruders would often be taken there. It's where they first took me when I found myself on the wrong side of a portal. So it makes sense that we make that our first stop . . .'

Squire studied him. 'But it isn't, is it?'

'No, it's not. Do you remember I told you about seeing that wraith with Cortez down in South America, when Gaea was expelling all of the vampires from my dimension?'

'Yeah. Not a wraith, though. You said it was the, whadd-ayacallit, the shade of Lazarus. The one who came to Hell to rescue you and you fucked him over and left him behind.'

Octavian felt anger and humiliation burning in him. He turned to glare at Squire. 'It wasn't like that.'

'Well,' Squire said, cocking his head, 'it was a little like that.'

'The point is this: Cortez killed the woman I loved, but there was more to it than that, someone or something pulling his strings. If it really was Lazarus's shade I saw, then the human Lazarus might still be here in Hell. I left him behind once; I'm not going to do it again.'

'And the fact that seeing his shade makes you think he might know who was behind what Cortez did has nothing to do with your sudden urgent need to find him?'

167

Octavian did not reply. Instead, he drew the sword that Squire had given him – best to be prepared – and slid down the side of the bowl into the centre of the room. The swirling lights of the nexus made his skin prickle and the hair stand up on the back of his neck, quite like the magic he was so used to commanding. He heard a grunt and looked up to see Squire sliding down to join him.

'Grab my coat,' Octavian told him, and he felt the tug of the hobgoblin's grip.

He stepped out of the swirling light, bent into the climb, and opened his eyes as he scaled the bowl back to the rim. Squire followed on his heels but Octavian heard the hobgoblin muttering under his breath as they entered the narrow gap again.

'What's that?' Octavian asked.

'I don't get it. What was the whole point of—'

They had stepped through the passage to find the tunnel gone. There was no canyon, no Malizia, no bones of the ancients. Instead, they found themselves on a broad, dusty plain with a nighttime sky stretching out in every direction overhead, its darkness broken by the light from bright fires that shot from the earth like geysers all around them. Burning embers drifted on the searing wind that buffeted them. Rock formations rose all around them, some natural and others very clearly constructed.

'Where the fuck is this?' Squire asked, an edge of panic in his voice.

Octavian breathed deeply of the blast-furnace air, so familiar to him. This whole scene had been branded into his mind. He had spent lifetimes with this vista the only thing his eyes could see.

'The surface,' he replied.

Squire punched him in the arm and Octavian flinched and turned to glare at him.

'Did you just say the surface?' Squire demanded. 'The goddamn *surface*?'

'We passed through the nexus. There are several fixed locations it could have taken us, but this was our destination, so yes, we're on the surface.'

'Of Hell. The surface of Hell.' Squire glanced around and then up at the tiny, white pinpricks of stars. 'Hell is a fucking planet?'

'What did you think?' Octavian asked.

'It's the underworld, dumbass. I thought it was *under*!'

'And it is. Under this,' Octavian said, spreading his arms wide. 'Did you think it was under Cleveland?'

Squire shrugged. 'Kind of.'

'Look, you've got to get your shit together. I need—'

'Blahblahblah your needs. Yeah, all right. Hell is a planet. Got it. Keep walking, because at some point I'm gonna have to take a piss and I'd rather do it somewhere I won't get my dick burnt off.'

'You might want to take care of that now,' Octavian said. 'It's a long walk.'

Squire grumbled but made no effort to find some privacy. Octavian took that as a sign that they should move on and started walking, and after a moment Squire fell in beside him. They struck out for a mountain ridge far in the distance, where flames shot high into the air from crevices throughout the mountains – so much fire that it looked as if the sun were rising beyond the mountains. But no sun ever rose on the fire plains of Hell. Octavian had spent centuries imprisoned amidst that burning twilight.

169

Pa-Bil-Sag, one of the most putrid of the Lords of Hell, had bartered his location with Meaghan and Lazarus all those years ago, but the demon was not his friend. Octavian knew if he encountered Lord Pa-Bil-Sag here, he would have to strike first and swiftly, kill the disgusting bloated monstrosity before Pa-Bil-Sag had the chance to kill him. When he had contemplated which among the Lords of Hell might have sent Cortez – which might have ascended to such power that he or she would dare launch a full-scale invasion of Earth – he had not considered Pa-Bil-Sag. The bloat was too self-indulgent, too focused on his own immediate pleasure to bother with ambition. But as he considered it again, Octavian realized he could not judge so quickly. Much time had passed in Hell since he had last walked these plains. Anything was possible.

Hours passed. They drank what little water Squire had brought along, but their bodies did not seem to require the same sustenance that they would in another dimension. Whatever field of magic kept them from burning up in the atmosphere and allowed the damned underground to be tormented over and over, to die again and again, sustained them. They passed over vast areas where the sandy surface had been scorched with such heat that it had turned to glass.

Only when they had already passed by did Octavian realize they had gone beyond the gate to the glass city. The gate, it appeared, had been destroyed. Only a broken tower that had once been part of the frame remained, and even that had been scoured away by the wind and sand. Whatever power had once claimed this place for itself had long since abandoned it and any responsibility for its upkeep.

On the outskirts of the glass city, the spires and buildings were little better off than its gate. Shattered spires lay in pieces, half-buried in the sand. Structures that might once have been lived in – though not in Octavian's time – had collapsed and begun to return to the desert plain of Hell's surface.

As they walked, however, they discovered that much of the vast city remained, abandoned but still intact. Some of the glass buildings seemed modelled after those in the human world, with turrets and balconies and dormers, but others were completely alien to the sort of design that might be found on Earth. Octavian believed these had been inspired by the civilizations on other worlds – other realms where societies existed in fear of demons and damnation. But they were perversions of actual homes, because these housed only the Suffering.

The spires were the one constant in the city, rising up like towering glass knives. Some of the spires were part of the design of other buildings, but most seemed to have no other purpose but to stab at the sky.

'It's a ghost town on the planet Hell,' Squire muttered as they walked. 'Yeah, I'm not gonna have nightmares about this.'

Octavian wished he could have smiled, but he simply couldn't bring himself to do it. They walked on for another hour and soon drew close to the burning mountains. The structures became rarer while the spires became more plentiful, until it was like striding through a forest of glass.

'Here,' he said. 'It was near here.'

Squire sighed. 'Better be. I've had burning cinders in my boot for the past half hour. I need to sit.'

'Soon,' Octavian promised.

'I don't see a prison,' Squire observed.

Octavian laughed without humour. 'It wasn't that kind of prison. The spires . . . in the heart of the glass city they're mostly decorative. Out here on the fringe, near the mountains, they serve a different purpose. Some of the spires you see . . . they were the prisons, glass cages where the damned and other captives might be encased for eons, unable to do anything but think.'

'I'd go out of my mind,' Squire said.

'Madness the only rational result,' Octavian said. He expected Squire to ask how he had remained sane, but the hobgoblin said nothing more as he glanced around, contemplating the spires. The truth was, Octavian had gone mad in the end. Meaghan had brought him back from that.

Meaghan, who was dead now. Far too many of the people he'd loved were dead. He did not intend to lose any more.

'Are there . . .' Squire began. 'Christ's sake, there are people in there.'

The hobgoblin had stopped to stare through the glass wall of one of the larger spires. Closer up it was easy to see that the reddish tint of the glass did not come solely from the reflection of the fires. Octavian knew what caused the red tint, but nothing would be gained by explaining it to Squire.

'Don't stare,' Octavian said. 'It's torment to them, knowing we're out here and can do nothing to help them. Better to just walk on.'

Inside the glass, frozen in place, were two women and a man. They seemed to have been caught unaware, paralyzed in the midst of a moment out of their lives – but a terrible moment, for each of them seemed to be screaming. They had bright red skin and wide eyes and they were trapped in the glass like flies in amber.

'You mean they're alive?' Squire asked.

'Not quite. Like the rest of the Suffering, their physical bodies are dead. As best I could ever work it out, these are manifestations of some sort.'

'But they can feel pain? And they know we're here?'

'Yes. So let's move on. There's nothing you can do to help them.'

'Screw that,' Squire said, pulling out his axe. He began to hack away at the glass, but the best he could do was to carve off splinters and fragments. After a moment, he began to beat at the glass with his free hand and then swore, yanking his hand back and staring at the terrible burn that had been seared into his skin.

Octavian put a hand on his shoulder. 'There are billions of Suffering here. Trillions. More than that, I'm sure, from a hundred civilizations.'

'But they're . . .' Squire said, staring at his hand as the meaning of the burn on his wrinkled flesh became clear. 'Son of a bitch, Pete, they're burning in there. The glass must be searing their skin constantly.'

A ripple of anger went through Octavian. He dropped to one knee and spun Squire around to face him, stared into the little man's yellow eyes.

'Listen to me. You, my friend, are in *Hell*. There is nothing here but suffering. I'm sorry that I needed you to bring me here and I appreciate your help, but if you expect either of us to get out of here, you've got to get it together.'

Squire scowled at him, baring his little shark teeth, but then he faltered and his leathery, misshapen face crumpled with emotion. For a second, Octavian thought he might actually cry – not for himself but for the Suffering – and then Squire took a deep breath and nodded.

'Go on,' he said.

And so they walked. The fire that engulfed the mountains grew louder as they approached, and the ash fell softly from the sky like a fine snowfall. Ash had accumulated so that soon they were walking through low drifts of it. Octavian recognized their surroundings all too well, now. Years had passed, but he could have found his former prison with his eyes closed. Nearer to the mountain than any of the others, the spire that had once been his cage climbed so high into the darkness that they could not see its tip.

As they walked toward it, Octavian picked up his pace, for within the reddish glass of the spire he could see the silhouette of a person. One of the Suffering. A prisoner of Hell.

'Who is it?' Squire asked, hurrying to keep up. 'Is it Lazarus?'

Octavian stood inches from the hot glass and stared inside, trying to make sense of what he saw.

'Not really how I imagined Lazarus would look,' Squire muttered.

'That's because it's not Lazarus.'

'No shit? Really?' Squire said, unable to rein in his sarcasm, even here. 'You know her, though. I can tell by the way you're gawking at her.'

Octavian did know her. They had been friends and allies once, blood-children of the same vampiric sire, Karl von Reinman. And, later, they had loved the same woman . . . the woman who had dragged her into Hell along with Lazarus to try to bring Peter Octavian back to Earth. She had died in the attempt, or at least that was what Octavian had always believed. But then, this was Hell, where one could die again and again and again, in order to suffer.

'Her name is Alexandra Nueva,' Octavian said. 'In all the ways that matter to me now . . . she's my sister.'

10

Hell

Octavian and Squire took turns carving away at Alexandra's glass prison. It had taken Meaghan and Lazarus weeks to chip through the crystal spire in order to release him, but they hadn't had weapons forged by a hobgoblin weaponsmith. Both edges of the sword Squire had given Octavian were sharp enough to shear off whole sections of the spire, but the black edge did it smoothly, with only the lightest resistance.

As they worked – Octavian with his sword and Squire with the axe that seemed to have become his preferred weapon – Octavian kept stealing glances at Alex's frozen features. He had not seen her in the flesh since before his own time in Hell, and yet he had recognized her immediately. When Karl von Reinman had made new vampires to bring into his coven he had required them to abandon their human names and had rechristened them with names that included numbers, thus Nicephorus Dragases had become Peter Octavian. Whatever Alexandra Nueva's birth name had been, Octavian had never learned it. They had been allies and sometimes even friends, but often they had feuded the way siblings so frequently did. Her rich, deep brown skin might be the furthest thing from his own complexion, but they were family in a way that went far beyond such simplistic definitions, siblings not from birth but rebirth. An entirely different sort of blood relation.

'She's a beauty,' Squire said as they carved away. A huge chunk of crystal calved off and crashed into the thick blanket of ashes to the hobgoblin's right. 'I'm gonna go out on a limb and assume she's single.'

Octavian took his turn, brought the sword down and whittled off a six inch section near her abdomen.

'Not funny,' he said.

'It's a little funny.'

'You keep saying that, which suggests to me that you actually believe it. You're like the girl with the horrible voice who sings the loudest at parties because her mommy always told her she sang like an angel.'

'Now who thinks he's funny?'

Squire hacked off another chunk of glass. They had come within a foot of Alex's chest. Her arms hung at her sides as if she were unconscious when she had been pushed into the malleable, still-cooling crystal spire. Octavian studied her perfect features, her chocolate skin, and the serenity of her expression and he faltered.

'No, no,' he said, and he brought the sword down hard, cleaving another shard away, this time close to her face. 'Don't fucking do this.'

'Who are you—' Squire began.

'Look at her,' Octavian said. He let the sword rest at his side, point against the ground, and gestured at Alex. 'She burns inside, you understand? Alexandra Nueva's one of the most intense creatures I've ever met. She can be a cruel bitch or a savage ally, but she's fierce. She'd have fought this, but look at her face. Even demons could not imprison her here without her fighting back, but she looks so damn peaceful.'

'Last I checked, vampires from your world were molecular shapeshifters,' Squire said. 'The only way to kill them is to destroy them completely, or convince them they're dead.'

Exhaling, Octavian nodded. 'Normally, that's true. But this is Hell. Even I'm not sure what's possible here.'

'Look, it's much more likely that she was just unconscious when they put her in there,' Squire said. 'They do torture people, if you'd forgotten.'

Octavian sneered angrily at him and Squire held up a hand in surrender.

'I know, I know. I'm not funny,' the hobgoblin said. 'All I'm saying is, if she's dead, she's no worse off than you thought she was when we got here. We trekked over here looking for Lazarus and we found your sister instead. Let's just get her cute little ass out of there and we'll see what's what.'

Ignoring him, Octavian stared at Alex through the jagged crystal. *Can you hear me?* But of course she could not. Shadows who shared the same sire could communicate with their minds, read each other's thoughts, but he hadn't been a vampire in a very long time.

Squire hefted his axe.

Octavian held up a hand to stop him. 'We've done enough. We're almost through to her flesh, but there's a faster way to finish this. The way I got out of here.'

Sheathing his sword, Octavian drew a dagger Squire had given him and began chipping away at the glass around Alex's face as if it were a block of ice. It took several minutes – during which, Squire winced several times and admonished him to be careful and work more slowly – but at last he cracked a bit of the crystal away from her left cheek. Emotion well up within him, the pain of a sentiment he had not allowed himself to feel since before he'd discovered Nikki had been murdered. Yes, he believed Allison and Kuromaku and the others were still alive somewhere in Hell, but no living creature had known him as long as Alex had. No one could understand the road he had travelled the way she could.

Sister, he thought again. The word had never had so much meaning.

He poked the pad of his left index finger with the point of the dagger, just enough to draw several beads of blood.

'Alex,' he said. 'Time to wake up. If you're alive in there, I need you to open your eyes.' He pushed his finger through the hole in the glass and smeared his own blood on her cheek. 'Come on, now. You're not alone anymore.'

Nothing happened. He prodded her flesh and found it soft and yielding, scalded by the superheated glass but otherwise unharmed.

Octavian slammed his hand against her crystal prison. 'Alex, come on! Wake up! I need you!'

He struck the spire again and again, until Squire put a hand on his arm.

'Pete, step back a second. Let me take a few more whacks at it and we can pull her right out. It might help if—'

Alex opened her eyes. They were bright red, wide with fury or madness or both, and Octavian felt sure that if she could have opened her mouth she would have screamed.

'Mist,' he told her. 'You can get yourself out. Just shift and you can . . .'

Alexandra Nueva did not need his instructions. She disincorporated, transforming herself from flesh to white mist, and poured herself out as if that crystal spire had simple exhaled her. The mist fled the hollow inside the spire and began to coalesce, but the incorporation seemed sluggish, as if her consciousness had trouble remembering what she was supposed to look like, how to sculpt herself anew.

'Alex, focus!' Octavian snapped. 'You're Alexandra Nueva, blood-daughter to Karl von Reinman, one of the Defiant Ones. You *know* who you are!'

It took several seconds longer, but the mist took on solidity and at last Alexandra Nueva stood naked before them, head hung as she stared at the thick layer of ashes underfoot.

'Oh, my,' Squire said, entranced by her nudity.

Octavian took a step toward her. 'Alex, it's me, Peter. Do you know me? Do you remember yourself?'

She snapped her head up, red eyes locked on him, and she began to tremble as her jaws opened wide and her fangs grew long. With a ravenous snarl, she lunged at him. Octavian shouted at her to stop as he brought the dagger up to defend himself. Her claws raked through his jacket and slashed his shoulder even as he buried the blade between her breasts. Alex roared with pain and staggered backward, almost feral in her rage and hunger.

'Goddamn it, Alex, listen to me!' Octavian shouted. 'It's Peter!'

Her blood-red eyes locked on him again, but this time the madness had receded and a fierce intelligence glittered therein. She glanced down at the dagger jutting from her chest and then she turned to mist again. The blade fell into the ashes with a whisper and then she reformed in front of him, lashed out and grabbed him by the throat . . . lifted him off the ground so that he began to choke.

Fangs bared, she shoved her face toward his so that they were eye to eye.

'I know exactly who you are,' she said. 'You're the motherfucker who got my girlfriend killed.'

Which was when Squire buried his axe in the back of her head.

She screamed and reeled away, crashing into the shattered face of her crystal prison. With a roar, she ripped the axe from her skull and turned on Squire, ready to cleave him in two with his own weapon even as the wound he'd made knitted itself closed.

'Alex, stop!' Octavian shouted at her. 'I don't know how you know Meaghan's dead, but it wasn't me who killed her. Mulkerrin returned and brought Lord Beelzebub with him. Meaghan sacrificed herself—'

She spun on him, unsure, fingers flexing on the axe. 'Not what I heard.'

'From who? Lazarus? How could he know what happened? He's been here the entire time that you have. When he and Meaghan came to rescue me, we used the *Gospel of Shadows* to open a portal back to our world but one of the spires impaled him, trapped him even as he finished casting the spell. We were already passing through the portal and it was closing! My thoughts and memories were a mess, just like yours are now. It took a long time for me to put it all back together, to remember all the magic I'd learned. When I did, I should've come back for him—'

'For us!' Alex cried, but some of the red had left her eyes.

'I thought you were dead. We all did. Think about it, Alex. If Meaghan had known that you were still alive she never would've left you here. She'd have let the portal close with her on this side if it meant she could have stayed with you.'

The vampire hesitated. 'I . . .'

Then she whipped her head back and forth as if trying to shake loose thoughts and voices that troubled her. The axe remained in her hand but she had forgotten it had been Squire who had tried to kill her with it. She had eyes only for Octavian.

'I know your story. He told me,' she said. 'He told me you were human now, and I can *smell* that it's true. Smell your blood.'

'Pete . . .' Squire said, his tone full of warning. The hobgoblin reached into his coat and drew a small dagger, but if the axe had done nothing, he could not possibly think this blade would be any more effective.

'It's been so very long since I've tasted human blood,' Alex said. Her body bent forward and her arms began to elongate, fingers turning to talons. 'And it's only right. It's what Meaghan would want . . . what she deserves. We came to save you and you got her killed.'

Octavian swore under his breath. Deep inside, his magic waited. He had sublimated it as much as he could, buried it in his heart and his gut and held the reins tightly. But he had come to Hell to rescue his friends and he was not going to let anything stand in his way. If that meant using magic – even if it sent up a flare that would bring every demon in Hell down on their heads – he would fight.

'What else did he tell you?' Octavian asked. 'Did he tell you I'm a magician? A sorcerer? Did he tell you I know a dozen ways to kill a vampire, even a Shadow in full control of her abilities?'

Alex crept toward him, eyeing his hands warily. Octavian felt the tingle in his fingertips and understood why – a silver aura had begun to crackle from his hands and he could feel the power misting from his eyes. *No*, he thought, tamping it down, tightening his hold on the reins of his own magic.

Squire shifted, moving directly behind her. The ugly little man glared at Alex's back, yellow eyes narrowed to slits. He held the dagger loosely, and then he reached his left hand into his jacket and withdrew a heavy revolver. Octavian had not seen him pick it up at the armoury and it seemed much too large for him to have hidden in his coat, which made him wonder if the voluminous inner pockets of that coat might be somehow supernatural.

The click of the hammer made Alex freeze.

'Silver bullets, honey,' Squire said. 'It doesn't have to be like this.'

'The thing is,' Octavian went on. 'You're not in full control. I don't want to hurt you, Alex, and I really don't want to kill you. But if you could shapeshift with a thought the way Shadows are meant to, Squire and I would already be dead.'

'*What are you doing here?*' Alex screamed. 'I know you didn't come for me. You thought I was dead. So why the fuck are you here? You finally came back for Lazarus?'

183

Octavian considered lying. Instead, he shook his head. 'I have other friends I believe are here. You know some of them. Kuromaku. Taweret. Santiago. There are no Shadows left in our world, no vampires at all. They were all shunted here. At least I—'

'No. You're lying.'

'He's not,' Squire said quietly.

'Meaghan—' Alex began.

'She loved you,' Octavian interrupted.

'I know she loved me!' Alex screamed, and tears of blood began to run down her face. 'You son of a bitch, I *know*!'

'She loved me, too,' Octavian said quietly, the hot wind and flying ash nearly stealing his words away. 'Doesn't that mean anything to you?'

Alex stared at him with wide eyes, her eyes fading from vivid red to her own warm and beautiful brown. The axe fell from her hand and she began to crumble, folding her arms across her chest as grief overcame her. Bloody tears dripped from her chin and vanished in the ashes at her feet.

She turned to mist again, but this time she did not reform. The searing wind blew burning cinders across the surface of Hell and took Alex and her grief along with it.

Phoenix's World
Ardsley-on-Hudson, New York, USA

As she drove north, with Ronni in the passenger seat, Phoenix felt remarkably calm. Her grip on the steering wheel stayed light and her pulse and breathing both remained steady. It couldn't have been a lack of fear; only a fool or a madwoman could have chosen the path they were taking without being terrified of it. Yet her heart swelled with purpose and she kept her eyes on the road, and when they came to a road-block in Dobbs Ferry she rolled down the window and waved to the police officer standing in the street, then turned and weaved her way along back roads that would still get them where they were going. She hadn't grown up here, but knew the area well enough by now.

As they drove, making their way along old roads and through neighbourhoods of ageing Victorians and 1960s Colonials, they could see smoke rising off to the northwest. Not from the hospital, as least as far as Phoenix could gauge their location; the smoke had to be coming from the surrounded woods or homes. Hell hadn't just come to Earth . . . it was spreading.

'This is . . .' Ronni began, followed by a hollow laugh. Phoenix turned along a narrow, curving road lined with dense forest, grateful they couldn't see the smoke anymore. 'Holy shit, this is . . .'

Phoenix glanced at her, cold autumn breeze blowing through the window she had forgotten to put back up. Ronni had high cheekbones and full lips and a wide nose that amounted to a kind of perfection, but she also had a long scar on the left side of her throat and several smaller ones at the temple and hairline on the same side. Phoenix had noticed these scars before but paid little attention to them. They had spoken very little during their journey together, mostly about their parents and the houses they had grown up in, and a little bit about the Uprising, the topic that seemed foremost on Ronni's mind tonight.

'Are you okay?' Phoenix asked.

Ronni twisted in her seat, staring. 'Fuck no! How the hell are *you* okay?'

'I'm not okay.'

'Bullshit, look at you. No wonder you survived the Uprising. I always figured you had to be pretty damn chill to be able to do what you did, but we're going back to the hospital after . . . I mean, they're demons! I just don't know how you can—'

'I said, "*I'm not okay!*"' Phoenix snapped.

Her hands gripped the wheel and she looked at Ronni.

'I'm as terrified as you are. But my father is at the centre of this. He died this morning but he's . . . they're *using* him, Ronni. I don't know what that means for his soul, if it's already at peace or whatever, but I know either way that what they've done to his body is an abomination. I'm going to put an end to that, whatever it takes, and yeah, that's given me a kind of weird serenity. But it doesn't mean I'm not afraid or that I don't know how crazy this is or what we're up against, okay?'

Phoenix exhaled, tried to focus on the road, and realized she'd missed her intended turn. She swore under her breath as she slowed and made a U-turn.

'Sorry,' Ronni said, her brown eyes wide and searching. 'I'm freaking out.'

'You're not alone,' Phoenix said, as she drove a short distance to the dead end circle at the end of Tomko Road, put the car in park, rolled up her window and then killed the engine.

The engine ticked loudly, cooling.

Ronni reached over and covered Phoenix's hand on the wheel with her own.

186

'Neither are you.'

Phoenix nodded slowly, then plucked the keys from the ignition. 'You don't have to come, y'know? This isn't your fight.'

When Ronni didn't immediately reply, she popped open her door and climbed out. It took a second, but then the passenger door swung open and Ronni emerged, looking at Phoenix over the top of the car.

'It's everybody's fight.'

'You know what I mean.'

Ronni slammed her door. 'Yeah, I do.'

'People are going to be running away, not toward this. They're going to leave it to the cops and the National Guard and get as far away as possible as fast as they can. It's what I would have done during the Uprising if I could have, if I didn't have to look out for my dad and if I wouldn't have been ripped apart and eaten alive the second I reached the street. It's what I would do tonight, right now, if this didn't involve my father.'

'I don't believe that,' Ronni scoffed.

Phoenix slammed her door and clicked the button on the key fob that engaged the locks. The chirping sound made her frown. *Locking the doors?* Apparently, she thought she might actually be coming back. The odds were ridiculous, but the thought gave her hope. She went to the rear of the car and opened the trunk, hefting out one of the plastic gas cans they had bought and filled up at a Shell station on the way.

'What about you, Ronni?' she asked. 'Why are you here?'

'I already—'

Phoenix smiled. 'Nah, come on. Maybe you've told me part of it – the surface part – but there's got to be more. You

CHRISTOPHER GOLDEN

live in Westchester County but, other than some casual friends, you don't have anyone here. No way did you have to come all the way across the country to get a nursing job, so that's not it. Maybe you feel like you've got nothing to lose or nothing to live for, but I don't think that's it, either.'

Ronni knitted her brow and wetted her lips with her tongue, as if she had something to say but couldn't find the words.

'Is it redemption? Something you feel like you have to do penance for or something? Because I know all about penance.'

Ronni rubbed at her arms, but Phoenix didn't think it was the October evening that had put a chill into her.

'I told you when I met you today how much you inspired me,' Ronni said.

'And that's sweet, and maybe it's even true,' Phoenix replied. 'But?'

Ronni took one of the gas cans from her and started walking, heading for the path that led from the circle into the woods.

'Hey!' Phoenix called to her, not moving. Ronni turned to face her. 'If I'm about to do the stupidest, most terrifying thing imaginable, if I'm basically walking into Hell, I deserve to know who I've got beside me.'

She could see the conflict in Ronni's eyes, but after a few seconds the woman shook her head with a laugh.

'I don't talk about this.'

'I get that,' Phoenix replied.

'But I figure we're probably going to die, so . . .' Ronni said, and shrugged.

Phoenix walked over to her and they stood together at the entrance to the woods. The hospital was maybe three hundred

188

yards away, along the path and up a steep hill. If they had any chance of sneaking in without being torn apart by demons, this was it.

'Okay,' Ronni said, and she took a shuddering breath. Her eyes brimmed with tears but she fought to keep them from falling. She swallowed hard. 'My senior year of high school, I was out of control. A party girl. The guy I was seeing – Spence – he had a party one night when his parents were away and he thought it would be funny if we got his little brother drunk. Matt was fourteen, a freshman, and kind of a dweeb. You could see he was going to be handsome once he grew out of his nerdiness, that he was gonna be something one day, but all he wanted was to impress his older brother and I know he thought I was hot.'

Ronni gave a soft laugh. 'Shit, I *was* hot.' Any other time, Phoenix would have told her that she still was, but the pain in her eyes and her voice went too deep to be interrupted. Ronni gazed off into the trees but it was clear that she was really looking into the past.

'We got him *so* drunk. Outrageously shitfaced. All the girls loved him and they took care of him and babied him even after he'd puked. But even as drunk as he was, he knew enough to be embarrassed and when me and Spence had found something else to amuse ourselves – screwing in his bedroom upstairs – Matt left the house.'

Ronni lowered her gaze, staring at the pavement beneath her feet. Phoenix had never seen anyone look so hollow, or so alone.

'I got shitfaced that night, too, even though I was driving. I always told myself as long as I could walk then I could drive, and somehow I always managed to get the car back into the driveway back at my house without wrapping it around a tree. But the thing is, Mattie . . . he was so drunk that he just fell over. Just passed out right where he landed, which happened to be at the end of his driveway.'

Phoenix's heart lurched.

Ronni began to cry. 'Backing out . . . headed home . . . I ran him over.'

'Oh, my God,' Phoenix said, reaching for her arm.

Ronni pulled away, refusing to be comforted, the heavy plastic gas can swinging in her hand. 'He was dead by the time the ambulance came. Really, he was dead pretty much the second I ran him over. I knew that, but we all waited for the ambulance like somehow they'd be able to perform a miracle.'

She lifted her teary gaze and stared at Phoenix. 'Nothing was ever the same after that. Nothing was ever right or good, and every time I looked into the eyes of the people who somehow, after that, still managed to love me, all I could feel was their pity and my own shame. My own guilt. I couldn't stand seeing that in people's eyes anymore, and so when I decided to be a nurse – that being a nurse was the only way I could live with myself – I came out here for school. I've never gone back.'

Ronni wiped at her eyes and then threw up her hands. 'So now you know who you've got beside you. Another killer. But you killed someone to try to save the damn world, and I did it because I was a drunken little bitch who thought it would be okay to make a fool out of a fourteen-year-old boy.'

Phoenix wiped at her own eyes and found that she was crying, too. There'd been far too much of that today. She reached for Ronni again, but this time when Ronni tried to push her away she would not be pushed. She held her by the shoulders until Ronni had no choice but to look into her eyes.

'Don't tell me I don't have to do this,' Ronni said, her jaw clenched.

'Whatever you think of yourself, whatever mistakes you've made,' Phoenix said, 'you're here now. Almost anyone else would have run screaming.'

Ronni shuddered but only nodded, all out of words.

Phoenix nodded in return. 'All right. Let's go.'

And they turned together and started into the woods. From the top of the hill ahead of them, through the trees, they heard someone begin to scream, a long, horrible keening – the most completely hopeless sound that either of them had ever heard.

But they kept walking.

Nothing would turn them back now.

II

Hell.

Drenched in the blood of demons, hacking his way through minor imps, damned madmen, and enormous armoured worms that he thought might not be demons at all, Peter Octavian lost track of the days. His swinging sword was the pendulum that marked the passage of minutes. He could taste the filthy ichor on his lips and every inhalation brought its stink inside him, but he had been here before – been coated in the blood of hellions and had the rotting stench of hell seeping into his clothes and hair and skin – and he had survived. Octavian set his jaw and narrowed his eyes and fought on.

They were on the Stairs of Remembrance, fighting their way down the spiral passage carved down through solid rock, and images kept firing in his brain. As he and Squire descended those one hundred and sixty-nine steps, Octavian had to fight more than just the demons in their path. His thoughts whirled with ugliness, from the girls' hearts he had broken as a boy to the lives he had taken as a vampire; every moment of blood and sorrow played across his mind, including the deaths of all those whom he had loved. But these horrors – meant to haunt the damned as they rotted in the dungeon of Dis – only hardened him and honed his purpose. Once, perhaps halfway down the steps, he glanced at Squire and saw that his eyes were red and damp, but the hobgoblin did not hesitate.

They had moved from battle to battle, sometimes walking for eons without encountering any resistance, but as they had approached Dis they had found it all but abandoned, another ancient ruin where one of Hell's greatest cities had been. In the crumbled ruins, they had relaxed their guard as they sought the entrance to the Stairs, and only then had then stumbled upon an orgy of heaving, grunting demon flesh, as Chermosh and other sons of Moab raped the damned, both male and female. There had seemed neither joy nor malice in this torment, only a listless cruelty, as if the sons of Moab had forgotten the point of their evil entirely and performed out of rote obligation.

The sight had made Octavian feel sick. He had urged Squire onward, but it was too late – they had been spotted, and that suited Squire perfectly well, for the ugly little man had turned on Chermosh then and loosed a volley of profanity and disapproval, after which he and Octavian had been forced to run. There were too many demons and too many places in the ruins to hide. They had made it to the Stairs of Remembrance, and now – as they descended – they whittled down their attackers one by one.

193

Octavian found himself a dozen steps from the bottom, Squire safely below him, and turned to face Chermosh himself, the last of the demons who had pursued them into the cramped little spiral Hell of memory. Black spines covered his body and they rippled with even the slightest motion. A constant hiss escaped the demon's lips, as though the spines stabbed his flesh as he moved, and perhaps they did. Upon his chest was a soft slit with labial folds the colour of midnight, and it was from there the hiss originated, a voice of pain that seemed to rise from the very heart of him.

And when he spoke, the words emerged from that same slit, the spines on his chest clicking against one another with the undulation of his flesh.

'Go, then, man-flesh,' the hellion said, his voice thick with mucous. 'But you'll have to come out of the dungeons eventually, and there are so many more of us in the ruins above.'

'There are other ways out of the offal pits of Dis,' Octavian replied warily, watching as the demon shifted on the stairs, spines clacking.

'Don't fuckin' talk to it,' Squire muttered from behind him. 'Cut it in half.'

Chermosh narrowed his eyes, staring at Octavian. 'How would you know that?'

Octavian brought the sword around in an arc that shattered hundreds of the demon's spines. Chermosh let out a roar of pain and twisted away, leaving his side vulnerable for Octavian's blade. The spines prevented a deep wound, so Octavian held the sword with both hands and slashed downward, opening the demon down to his crimson bones. Black blood and purple viscera spilled out, crawling with worms and other parasites. The stench that wafted up off of Chermosh's innards was worse than any they had thus far smelled, and both Octavian and Squire held their breath and hurried down the last dozen spiral steps to the dungeon's giant door, which stood open and rotted and canted to one side as if something had burst its way in instead of breaking out.

They crossed the threshold, weapons held out before them.

Octavian had been prepared for the despairing screams of the Suffering, but they were met with silence. A faint red dust floated in the air as they walked began to explore, first the anteroom and then the vast central cavern, whose ceiling echoed back their footfalls. Chains and hooks were strung for miles along the walls, which were lined with empty cells. The bright light of Dis, generated by anguish, had gone dark.

'I take it this ain't what you expected to find,' Squire said.

'Nope.' Octavian sheathed his sword.

The hobgoblin's yellow eyes gleamed in the dusky grey light that filtered into the dungeon from Hell's burning places.

'So where are all the souls that are supposed to be here?' Squire asked, putting away his axe.

Octavian frowned. 'Nobody's supposed to be here. This is Hell's Hell. Or it was, once upon a time. As for where they are, there are fields of punishment all through Hell. Infinite caverns of sorrow and pain—'

'You should write the vacation brochure,' Squire muttered.

Octavian wished he could have laughed at that.

'There are a couple of other places I can think of,' he said. 'One in particular . . . the Pit. Outsiders are often taken there.'

195

'It's Hell, Pete. It's full of pits. Fire pits and blood pits and pits of screaming babies.'

'This one is special,' Octavian said, forging ahead with purpose now, remembering the last time he had been in this place and the madness that had seized him. There were cold places in the dungeon of Dis, frozen corners where the walls were made of ice – and ice could be broken. That would be their exit.

'What's so special about it?' Squire asked, hurrying to keep up.

Octavian glanced around, listening to the echoes of the past. 'The war between Heaven and Hell ended eons ago, but even now, from time to time, an angel will fall. When angels fall, they go to the Pit. I saw giants there in my time, as well as boggarts and kelpies and, once, the god of bats. If Kuromaku and Allison and the others are here and they're alive, and they're not in the dungeon, my best guess is the Pit.'

'And if they're not there?'

'Is it possible for you to be optimistic, just for maybe half a second?' Octavian asked.

Squire scowled. 'Excuse the fuck out of me, but we *are* in Hell. Down here, optimism's for assholes.'

Octavian felt a draught and glanced at an alcove up ahead and to the left. A cool mist swirled out of it and he knew he would find a wall of ice there, blocking an ancient passage. When the dungeon had been inhabited there would have been guards there, though the crevices inside were treacherous and most who tried to escape that way would have died in the attempt.

'That's where you're wrong,' he said. 'When you're in Hell, a little shred of optimism may be all that keeps you alive.'

Squire nodded as if impressed. 'Wow. Somebody call Hallmark. You could make a million bucks with crap like that.'

Octavian paused and stared at him. 'I could just leave you here.'

A smile spread across the hobgoblin's ugly, leathery features. 'Good thing I'm so cute, huh?'

Octavian lifted a hand and ran it over his face, first covering his eyes and then scraping his palm across his stubbled chin. He tried to stifle the soft chuckle that rose in his throat, but couldn't do it, and quiet laughter whispered its echoes off of the walls of the dungeon of Dis. He suspected it must have been for the first time.

Drawing his sword, he lifted it over his head and brought it down with enough force to shatter the ice wall. Searing heat rushed all around them, sucked into the frigid chimney beyond the wall. Red dust stung their eyes and they shielded themselves as the burning air buffeted them for long moments, until at last it slowed.

'You want to explain this?' Squire snapped.

'I'd be guessing,' Octavian said, stepping through the gap he had created by shattering the ice. The walls were frosted but there were wide ledges all around that would make for simple enough climbing, if they were careful.

'How is it so cold?' Squire asked as he followed. The hobgoblin bent to peer down into the deep crevice that fell away below them. 'And what is this place? You said the dungeon was the basement of Hell or whatever. But this looks like it goes down forever.'

'Maybe to the centre of the planet,' Octavian replied. 'I don't know.'

'But it's fucking freezing cold in here. It's like we're in a vent, but the breeze is coming up at us. How can that be? I mean, Hell's all fire and brimstone.'

'Not all the way through. At its core, Hell is ice cold.'

Octavian began to climb. His boots gripped the icy ledges well enough, but his fingers slipped several times. From below him came Squire's grunts and the rustling of the hobgoblin's rough clothing. With every new step – every handhold – Octavian expected to hear a cry for help and he prepared himself for the possibility that he would need to use magic to save his companion. Only his prowess as a warrior, honed through the centuries, had kept him from having to use magic thus far, but his skill with a sword or in hand to hand combat would not save Squire if he fell.

Yet they climbed higher and higher and the frigid air became slightly less frigid and still Squire scrambled upward without requiring help. An hour passed and another and the muscles in Octavian's shoulders and arms weakened, a burning sensation passing through him, and Squire held on.

When they emerged, Octavian crawled out onto scorchingly hot stone and lay there for a moment to catch his breath. Squire sighed and stretched and let out an enormous belch and then stood over him, yawning.

'I can't lie down or I'll fall asleep. You ready to move along?'

Octavian stared a moment and then nodded. 'Ready. Just let me get my bearings.'

For once, the hobgoblin did not have a snappy retort. Octavian furrowed his brow and glanced over to see that Squire had wandered away. Rising quickly, Octavian pursued him up a small rise. They had emerged from the ice vent into a crater in the stone floor of a cavern and when they had climbed to the crater's rim, Octavian felt his heart sink. A quiet chorus of whimpered prayers and whispered promises filled the air, along with the soft weeping of the truly hopeless. They were surrounded in all directions by hundreds of the damned – perhaps thousands – all of them on their knees with their heads hung.

'Don't stop,' Octavian said quietly. He grabbed Squire by the arm and propelled him forward, finding a path amidst the kneeling damned. 'And whatever you do, don't listen. The sorrow can be crippling.'

'Wait,' Squire said, yanking his arm away.

On their knees, the Sorrowful – for that's how Octavian had always thought of them – were about the same height as Squire, so when he looked at them he could not help but see the contours of their regret.

The hobgoblin glanced up at him and Octavian saw the uncertainty in his eyes.

'Where are we?'

'One of the fields of punishment,' Octavian replied. 'I'd hoped to avoid you seeing one of these.'

'But there are no demons here. Nobody's getting their skin ripped off or their guts torn out or . . . I mean, what kind of Hell is this?' he asked, voice pinched by the depth of his horror.

'During my time here, I saw fields where the damned are eaten by putrescent demons and then shit out again, over and over for eternity,' Octavian said. 'Places where they're flayed over and over as their skin grows back each time, or where they're forced to fuck forever until their joy and passion *becomes* their Hell. But this . . . this is the worst. All these

CHRISTOPHER GOLDEN

people jammed together, but they can't see or hear or feel the presence of the others. They're in a crowd of thousands who could give them some meagre comfort, but they think they're alone, forever.'

'Forever?' Squire echoed. 'They feel that for eternity?'

Octavian nodded.

'So much for whoever said, "Hell is other people."'

'Only the people who believe in Hell and that they deserve to be there end up coming here,' Octavian said, looking out over the sea of the Sorrowful. The lonely. 'Them, and the truly evil ones. Hell is ourselves, my friend.

'Hell is personal.'

Phoenix's World
Manhattan, New York City, New York

Sometimes, Annelise thought she could see the ghosts. Tonight she sat in her usual chair in her little kitchen – the one with the rip in the seat, a little stuffing coming out – and she sipped tea from a cup that belonged to a set her grand-mother had bought in Austria in 1923. The tea had a healthy spoonful of honey and a twist of lemon in it, just the way she liked it. The lemon and honey helped with the rasp that had begun to sneak into her voice over the past decade, the result of her being a secret smoker. Oh, some of her friends knew that she still smoked, but for the most part she hid it well, kept her smoking to the little balcony at the back of her place and aired out her clothes any time the acrid scent of cigarette smoke seeped into them.

She wanted a cigarette tonight.

Her hands shook as she picked up her teacup and a drop of it sloshed over the rim to stain her faded flannel nightgown. The spot soaked in and spread a bit but she paid it no mind. It would wash out.

'*Please, Annelise,*' Manolo said. '*You must listen.*'

His imploring voice did not make her look up from her teacup, for there would be nothing to see. Manolo normally had a gentle way about him, a sweetness that sometimes became playful flirtation, which she allowed to go on because there were so few men willing to be playful or flirtatious with her. Of course, Manolo was not like other men. She did not look up when he spoke because she would not be able to see him. Manolo had been killed in an accident six years earlier, when he'd fallen onto the subway tracks at 125th Street. A young mother had taken her eyes off of her baby stroller, texting or something, just long enough for the stroller to roll across the platform and onto the tracks.

Manolo had retrieved the infant, but there hadn't been time for him to climb back up before the train had barrelled through, brakes and driver and waiting commuters all screaming. His death had been gruesome, but at least it had been instantaneous.

Some weeks later, Annelise had been riding the subway across town, nowhere near the site of the accident, when she had heard his kind voice whispering in her ear. *A little birdy told me you could hear me,* he had said in his pleasant, thickly accented voice. *Is this true?* When she had replied – a low mutter under her breath to avoid drawing attention from other riders – she had heard the sound of quiet weeping as he was overcome with joy at the thought that his connection with the world of the living had not been completely severed. Years had passed since then, and in all that time she had never heard Manolo sound afraid, until now.

Annelise sipped her tea, relishing its earthy flavour and the sweetness of the honey. It might need a bit more lemon, she realized.

The salt shaker on her little kitchen table fell over, spilling a few grains across the autumn-themed table cloth. Annelise frowned.

'That's not very nice, my friends,' she said. 'Manolo, was that you?'

A chorus of voices replied, all speaking up at once, and a spike of pain went through her head. Her hand shook and more tea spilled. Her hand began to jitter so badly that he forced herself to put the cup down.

'Quiet!' she snapped.

But the spirits did not comply. A dozen of them spoke to her at once, worried for her or frustrated with her, or both. Loudest among them were sixteen-year-old student Thandie Carver, seventy-eight-year-old painter Priya Lahiri, and a butcher named Stroud, who had been dead two hundred years and somehow managed to linger on. Once, she had used a spirit guide to help mediate her interactions with the dead, but after the Uprising that had become virtually impossible. The dead knew her, now, and how to find her, and they haunted the corners of her mind just as constantly as they did the shadowed corners of her kitchen.

'Please,' she said, and buried her face in her hands with a deep sigh. 'I know you all mean well, but what do you expect me to do?'

The refrigerator hummed and the faucet released an occasional drip. A truck rumbled by on the street outside and she could hear the thump of club music coming from the building that backed up to hers. *Inconsiderate little shits*, she thought. More than once she had wished that she could send some of her accumulated ghosts over to spook them.

Annelise blinked. The spirits had gone silent.

She glanced around the kitchen, though she refused to look at the water marks on the floral wallpaper where the rain had seeped in during last year's worst storm. Soon, she would get it fixed, inside and out, but that would mean new wallpaper, and she had always so loved this pattern and its colours.

'*You've got to run,*' said Stroud the Butcher.

Breathing deeply, focused and calm, Annelise raised her cup and took another sip of tea. This time she did not spill a drop. Stroud's first name was Herman – a family name – but he despised it because it had been his father's name, and his father had beaten him so often and so badly that in life he had been deaf in one ear.

'I'm not going anywhere,' she said.

'*Annelise,*' Manolo begged. '*You must stop listening to the dead and seek only the voices of the living. Evil is coming, don't you understand? We can all feel it, in here with us. It feels us, knows us, overhears us even when we whisper.*'

A shudder went through Annelise. Despite the sagging of her skin and the iron grey of her hair, she rarely felt truly old, but now an icy chill passed through her that she could feel in her bones. It made her want to cry, not in fear but in sorrow. What her friends were asking was impossible.

'Where could I run?' she asked the empty kitchen, its corners full of ghosts. 'Where could I hide from my own soul?'

'Run!' other voices cried out. Priya, quavering with age. Stroud, almost angry with her.

Annelise stiffened. Her body began to quake and the teacup fell from her grasp, struck the edge of the kitchen table and shattered, fragments raining to the floor. With a sharp inhalation of breath, she felt the cold weight of a spirit slipping inside of her, the fullness of its presence. The sensation was familiar, going all the way back to her ninth birthday, when the ghost of her grandfather had used her as a vessel to speak to his wife.

Manolo, she thought, anger rippling through her. Tears slid down her cheeks. With the exception of her grandfather, she had only ever served as a medium to those spirits she invited, those she welcomed. During the Uprising, she had been betrayed by the dead, but for the most part it had been a tremendously satisfying existence, offering herself as a conduit in that way. But this . . . this was a violation.

Her slippered feet pushed against the floor and her chair slid back from the table. Without her help, her body rose from the chair.

You bastard, she thought.

'I am sorry,' the dead man said, using her mouth. Her lips. Her voice, though the accent belonged to him.

Annelise fought him, but the other spirits cheered Manolo on as he walked her across the kitchen, manipulating her as if she were some kind of puppet.

'Oh,' her mouth said, and she felt a sudden fear, deeper than any she had ever known. In that moment, the tears on her face were not her own. 'Oh, no.'

Manolo left her. Where the spirit had been, a void appeared within her, a hollow place that made her feel bereft. Annelise frowned, listening to the shadows and to the spaces between spaces, the whispers of the spirit world. They were truly silent, now, as if there had come a sudden exodus of ghosts. The last time Annelise had felt so alone, she had been a child.

The whole building seemed to hold its breath. The only sound that reached her in that moment was the tick-tock of the moon-and-stars clock on the wall.

Something struck her, some invisible presence that knocked her reeling across the kitchen. She crashed into the refrigerator but she did not feel the impact. Annelise felt herself pushed, felt her own spirit forced deeper into herself, and she was not alone inside her flesh. What had joined her there, what had barged its way into her body, was not one of the ghosts with whom she was so familiar. This was no lost soul.

The malevolence of its thoughts crushed down upon her and she would have screamed if only she had control of her own lips.

Its mind touched hers and she knew her soul was forever tainted. It was a putrid thing, a foul sentience, but for just a moment she could see into it just the same way that it could see into her, and she knew that it had been searching for her. Not her, precisely, but someone like her. A medium. It wanted doorways, and it had found some already. Joe Cormier had been the first and the place he had died had become the locus of an incursion of evil so pure that her soul screamed at its touch.

Yet she sensed some other purpose beneath that. This malevolence served another, and they sought mediums only for their ability to act as conduits. They were coming to this world with vengeance in mind, hunting one specific individual, one man. Annelise could almost read his name in the demon's thoughts.

'Well, well,' it said, speaking with her lips, every word a cancer on her tongue. 'What have we here?'

Leave me, filth, she thought. *Get out*.

'I don't think so,' the demon replied.

Inside, where voices and mouths were unnecessary, it whispered to her heart.

Instead, I think I'll tear you apart.

Hell

Squire knelt in the shadows on a rocky outcropping overlooking the Pit and wanted to run as far and as fast as he could. If he'd had a tail, he figured it'd have been tucked between his legs. Hobgoblins didn't scare easy, but he didn't fancy the idea of dying, either, and after being down in Hell this long he had come to regret offering Octavian his help.

'I might puke,' he whispered, and glanced up at his friend – this mage who used to be a vampire.

'Do it quietly,' Octavian replied. He lay flat on his stomach on the rocks, observing the activity down in the Pit like a general planning his strategy.

Octavian had always had the kind of rugged quality that most women found attractive, but now that he was human again, he'd begun to go a little grey and had a sadness in his eyes that made him even more handsome. Squire considered him a friend – it would've been hard to find a nobler companion – but he would've liked him better if he hadn't been so good looking and if he hadn't decided going to Hell would be a good way for an ageing hobgoblin to pay off his debts.

'Wish I'd brought my golf bag,' Squire said.

Octavian shifted, turning to stare at him. 'What about this situation makes you feel like playing a round of golf?'

Squire laughed softly. 'Never mind.'

No point in explaining that he often carried around many of the weapons he'd made in a golf bag. The image it summoned even in his own mind seemed silly, but it worked like a charm when Mr Doyle and his Menagerie were in the midst of a battle and he had to get weapons to them quickly.

Had worked, he reminded himself. The Menagerie had scattered far and wide – at least those who were still alive.

'You recognize anyone down there?' he asked.

Octavian slid forward a bit, trying to get a better look into the Pit. Ironic, considering that Squire wanted to look anywhere else. He had imagined that it would be another of Hell's canyons, but the Pit was a broad crater, maybe two hundred yards in diameter. Compared to the scale of some of the other spots they'd visited on their scenic tour of the netherworld, it didn't seem that vast, but the sight of it turned his stomach.

The base of the Pit seemed to be composed of a damp, living tissue, a greyish pink layer of slick flesh that gave off a stench that made Squire's stomach roil in protest. Fissures split the spongy surface of the Pit, belching black smoke and fire that burned a deeper red than any he had ever seen. Figures writhed in the fleshy floor, stuck as if in some grasping quagmire, and if they managed to pull themselves out far enough that they might have a hope of freedom, grey tendrils formed on the ground, stretching out to wrap around the

CHRISTOPHER GOLDEN

Suffering and drag them down again to suffocate in the malleable flesh of the Pit. Squire saw no angels – no wings, at least, and he expected wings on angels – but there were several figures trapped there which did not look human, and one huge, roaring thing that could only have been some kind of troll or bogeyman.

Demons roamed amongst them, nine-foot sentries who acted as jailers. Of all the evil things Squire had seen in Hell, these looked most like the kinds of devils he associated with this place. No gasping mouths in their chests or worm-like slithering or flesh split with a hundred vaginas. They had horns and hooves and thin, powerful bodies, the perfect image of a demon of legend except that their entire bodies seemed composed of yellowed bone and their faces were nothing more than skulls with a bit of muscle to move the jaws and hold the eyes in place.

The sentries carried pikes made of sharpened bone no different from that which seemed to comprise their bodies, and bone phalluses hung between their legs, equally as sharp as the pikes. As Squire and Octavian watched, they worked their way through the Pit, smashing their hooves down on the heads and arms and backs of the damned, sometimes stabbing them with their pikes until their blood pooled into the flesh of the pit. When the damned would scream, the sentries' phalluses would grow with arousal.

'Pete?' Squire asked.

'I'm looking.'

Even as they spoke – careful to whisper – two sentries reached into the pink muck and dragged a bloody figure up and out, tearing her away from the grasping tendrils. Their hollow laughter could be heard echoing around the walls of

208

the Pit as they carried her, kicking and screaming, toward one of the fire-belching fissures. One sentry slammed her to the ground and then trapped her there with one hoof while he thrust his pike through her back, pinning her. A torrent of hellfire roared from the ground and ignited her face and hair.

Amidst the screams and laughter that followed, the other sentry handed off his pike and approached the young woman, whose clothes were ragged tatters. Squire could make out very little detail, except that she had red hair.

'I can't watch this,' he said. 'I know these are the Suffering, but I can't just sit here while—'

'You're going to do just that.'

Squire bristled. 'Are you serious? I know this is Hell and shit like this happens all the time, but you're going to let them rape—'

Octavian snapped his head around to stare at him. 'How many of those sentries do you count? Fifty? Sixty?'

'Still—'

The mage shook his head, and Squire saw a fury in his eyes that cancelled out his rugged looks. In that moment Octavian was not handsome at all – he was terrifying.

'The girl's name is Charlotte,' he said. 'She trusted me, and she ended up here. My friend Kazimir is down there, too. You've proven a fiercer warrior than I'd expected, Squire, but you're staying right here so I don't have to worry about you, too.'

Down in the Pit, the sentry with the raging hard-on dropped to his knees above Charlotte, grabbed a fistful of her hair, and forced her legs apart. The fire engulfing her head diminished for a moment and she planted her feet and pistoned herself forward, taking with her the pike buried in her back and knocking over the sentry who'd been about to violate her.

Snarling, charred skin hanging in flaps from her face, she leaped to her feet and turned on them.

'Why doesn't she shapeshift?' Squire demanded.

'Confusion. Something about the Pit keeps them disoriented; that's why they're here.'

The two sentries attacked Charlotte and began to beat her, drove her to the ground and kicked her with their hooves.

Octavian rose, but Squire grabbed his arm. 'It's like fifty to one, Pete. What are you going to—'

The mage grimaced and held out both hands. Blue light erupted around them, crackling like fire, and mist began to seep from his eyes. The sheer power emanating from him made Squire flinch and the hair stand up on the back of his neck.

'Well, yeah,' said the hobgoblin. 'There's that.'

So much for keeping a low profile, Squire thought. Octavian thought that using magic like this in Hell would be like sending up a flare announcing their presence. Squire hoped he was wrong.

'Don't go anywhere,' Octavian said, and he launched himself over the edge of the Pit, suddenly engulfed in a sphere of that blue light, which rocketed him toward the sentries brutalizing his friend.

'Where the—' Squire said, before he realized that Octavian, in the midst of it all, had made a joke.

12

Phoenix's World
Ardsley-on-Hudson, New York, USA

Getting into the hospital turned out to be simple enough. The wooded hill behind the facility led up to within thirty feet of the loading dock, where the exodus of employees trying to survive had left the doors wide open. In the dark, Phoenix and Ronni slipped across the pavement and climbed onto the dock and then they were inside, simple as that. The hospital's fire alarms were ringing, the noise like a dentist's drill to the brain, but Phoenix welcomed the cover the sound would give their sneaking and shuffling.

On the way up the hill, the weight of the gas can had gone from a burden to a struggle. Her shoulder ached with the pull of it. Ronni seemed to be in better shape, but still it couldn't be easy on her, and by now they were both lugging their respective cans rather than just carrying them. Halfway up

211

the hill, they had debated leaving one behind and taking turns with the remaining gas, but Phoenix liked the idea of a second can. A backup. They weren't going to get a second chance at this.

Phoenix glanced around the loading area, where the most recent deliveries for the hospital were still stacked, waiting to be added to the inventory. She had no idea what might be in those boxes – maybe bedpans and surgical gowns – but it wouldn't be pharmaceuticals or syringes or anything else the government regulated.

She rushed across the open space with a glance out the wide open door, making sure that none of the demons had spotted them from outside. Ronni padded across the concrete floor to an open door whose small inset window had been smeared with blood. Phoenix forced herself not to linger on that crimson streak and instead pushed herself against the wall beside Ronni.

'Tell me you know your way around down here,' she said, right up close to Ronni's ear so that she could be heard over the alarms.

Why the fire alarms? she wondered. They hadn't seen any smoke and couldn't smell it now that they were inside. *Maybe the whole place is just going batshit crazy.*

Ronni nodded, then gestured for her to follow as she ducked through the open door and down a long concrete corridor. There were signs on the walls, but most of them were just numbers and letters, codes that must have meant something to those who worked down in this sub-basement but which she could not decipher. They came to a pair of double doors and took up position on either side, wary of the rectangular inset windows.

Phoenix edged forward and glanced through the glass. Beyond the criss-cross wire mesh embedded in the window, she could see a pair of bodies on the ground. At least she thought there were only two of them, though it was hard to tell with all of the blood spattered on the walls and the way the hospital employees had been torn apart. She stared for a second, unable to breathe, and the gas can seemed to become too heavy to hold.

Ronni shuffled forward to glance through the other little window and that shook Phoenix from her momentary paralysis. They scanned the corridor on the other side of the door for half a minute, waiting to see if whatever had killed these people would show itself. Was it even still down there? The demons might have left the hospital, spreading out to continue their slaughter, but they couldn't be sure.

Taking a deep breath, Phoenix tried the door and found it locked. 'Shit.'

Ronni reached into her top and tugged out an ID card that hung from a lanyard around her neck. Immediately, Phoenix understood that this was not just her ID, but a key card. For just a second, she wanted to turn and run. The possibility that they would not be able to get any further into the hospital, that they might be thwarted, had sparked a selfish hope inside her. But then she thought of her father and how the demon had defiled him, and the hundreds they had likely already murdered in the hospital – and the untold numbers that might die if those demons weren't cut off from Hell – and felt ashamed.

A simple pass of the card in front of a pad by the door, and the lock disengaged long enough for Ronni to open it. Phoenix pushed through first but she paused just inside the door. The copper stink of blood filled her nostrils and her thoughts were flooded with memories of the Uprising. The bodies on the floor weren't going to get up and attack her, especially not with how badly they had been savaged, but the dull, staring eyes of the dead had haunted her sleep for over a decade and just a glimpse of these corpses took her breath away.

A wave of hatred rocked her.

Phoenix had smelled blood before, seen slaughter before, confronted horror before. But the malevolence behind the Uprising had been unknown until it was nearly over; they hadn't even known there was an enemy other than the cruel, risen dead. This was different. She had seen the demon that had torn its way out of her father's cadaver, had heard its voice. The spirits that had spoken through Annelise claimed that her father had been used as a kind of gateway, and Phoenix figured this demon must be the gatekeeper – the one who had made her father's flesh into an abomination. She pictured the demon with its crown of bone shards and those spider-eyes, saw its crimson-black flesh and the grin that split its face all the way up to its ears, and that was enough.

Phoenix walked through the blood, careful not to slip, and paid no attention to the scarlet footprints she left behind. Ronni seemed less sure, but after a moment she followed suit. There was no path forward that would have allowed them to avoid the blood.

Soon, they came to another junction and she let Ronni take the lead again. There were more signs, but these were more direct, indicating which corridor would take them to the morgue or the laundry or the cafeteria. Suddenly, Phoenix realized just how completely lost she would have been if she had managed to convince Ronni not to come, and the thought made her stomach lurch.

Ronni hesitated for a single, indecisive moment before choosing the corridor that led to the cafeteria. The plastic can thumped against Phoenix's thigh as she followed, sure that this approach must have been for employees only. Patients and visitors would not have been allowed to wander these faded, industrial halls. The entrance she remembered from her own visits to the cafeteria had potted plants in front and little signs up advertising the specials of the day. Nothing greeted them except the stink of whatever had been left to burn when the demons had rushed through the hospital. Down here, they would have emerged from the morgue, and not for the first time Phoenix wondered why they had seen so few corpses thus far.

Over the aural assault of the alarm, they almost didn't hear the other noises at first. But as they paused outside a single door and Ronni shifted her gas can from one hand to another, ready to use her key card again, Phoenix frowned. Had she heard a clanging of metal, there in the valleys amidst the clamour of the alarms?

She grabbed Ronni's wrist, stopped her from opening the door. Ronni glanced at her and Phoenix shook her head. Her heart thundered in her ears but she ignored it, listening carefully, trying to hear whatever noise might be beneath the klaxon.

The clatter came again, the crash and clang of something in the kitchen. Something heavy that thrashed against the counters and ovens and knocked over cookware and plates. Phoenix realized they had not come to the back of the cafeteria, but the rear entrance into the kitchen. Food deliveries would have arrived this way, and perhaps employees entered here for their shifts.

Phoenix shook her head again. They couldn't go in that way unless they had no other options. Ronni read the hesitation in her eyes and they stood there together, riveted, listening for demons. The reality of it struck Phoenix afresh and she held her breath. Discovery would mean more than mere failure. If they met demons now her father would never be purified and the portal that crowned demon had opened would never be closed, but more imminently, she and Ronni would die.

Torn apart, like the orderlies whose blood she had tracked along the sub-basement halls.

Something slammed into the door from the other side and they both jerked backward. Ronni clapped a hand to her mouth to keep from screaming, eyes wide with terror. Phoenix nearly dropped her gas can but managed to hang on to it, even as she raised a hand to stop Ronni from running. Ronni stared at her, terror plain on her face. *It knows we're here*, the nurse's eyes seemed to say. *It's coming for us*.

Phoenix wasn't so sure. Trying to steady her hitching breath, she stared at the door. The demon had been crashing around the kitchen and she thought it might have struck the door at random.

She hoped.

They stood and they breathed and tried not to make a sound, and then they heard another crash beyond the door, this one further away, and Phoenix exhaled. She glanced at Ronni, whose brow was knitted in thought for a second before she gestured to Phoenix and fled back the way they'd come, careful to go quietly.

Don't think, Phoenix told herself. *If you think, you'll scream. If you think, you'll go out of your mind.*

She tried her best. As she followed Ronni, she marvelled at the other woman. Ronni had been so inspired by her courage, so impressed by Phoenix's actions during the Uprising, but she had begun to think the nurse far braver than she would ever be.

When they reached the laundry room, Phoenix wanted to cry. Stacks of clean towels and sheets and pillow cases had been overturned and blood painted everything, spatters and pools and long stripes of it. There were three bodies she thought were mostly complete, two women and a man, but even with only a glance she could see there were too many arms in the main room. A cart full of dirty laundry had strings of gore dangling from it, and she thought a flap of skin draped over the edge of the cart might be a human face.

But there were no demons there to stop them. No demons to kill them and spray their blood across immaculate white sheets or leave pieces of them hanging from the light fixtures overhead.

Numb, they went on.

Beyond the laundry room there was a service elevator, and just past that a fire door marked EMERGENCY EXIT – EMPLOYEES ONLY. They took the stairs, tracking more blood, and kept their hands off of the railings in order to avoid touching the bits and pieces and smears that had been left behind. As they passed the first floor landing, they could hear distant screams amidst the constant, maddening alarms, human voices filled with the kind of anguish that came from the soul. Hopeless voices. The screams of the dying. Ronni stopped to breathe and Phoenix thought she might vomit, but it seemed to pass and they started up the stairs, happy to have the screams behind them. Soon – startlingly soon, given the nightmare they'd just been through – they found themselves on the second floor.

Phoenix set down her gas can and massaged her shoulder a moment before opening the door just a crack. The carnage in the corridors was worse than anything they had encountered. In the midst of it, a white-coated doctor had been hung upside down from the ceiling, suspended with bloody sheets and his own entrails. Despite the terror and agony that had made a gruesome mask of his face, Phoenix recognized Dr Song.

The hatred came back. Images barged into her mind, her father lying dead while that dreadful voice spoke through his open mouth. The talons that thrust up through his abdomen and chest. The crown of bones pushing up through him, an obscene, Hellish birth.

She picked up the gas can and slipped open the door. Ronni said her name – Phoenix heard that over the alarms – but she had given up on her own fear. By some miracle, they had made it this far and she wasn't about to stop now. There were no demons in the corridor, nothing in sight but ravaged corpses and upended gurneys, and she navigated the bloody mess with her shoes squelching and smearing the blood. Ronni hurried to follow, glancing quickly through the open doors they passed. Phoenix did not bother. Hatred fuelled her, and it seemed to her to have created a strange bubble around her, as if she weren't even really there in the hospital at all – as if she floated through some nightmare world, untouchable and unseen.

Only the weight of the gas can seemed real.

Behind her, Ronni muttered prayers, but Phoenix kept walking. She reached the open door to her father's hospital room and went in, stepping over the nurse who lay on the floor, legs spread so wide she had torn up the middle, pelvic bone broken and jutting sharply through the skin. Her face had been torn away and something had gnawed at the muscle beneath.

When she let herself look at her father – at the pale, slack features and dead eyes of Professor Joe Cormier – the illusion shattered. Her breath hitched and she began to shake and something broke anew in her. Hot tears coursed down her face but she forced herself not to hesitate. She twisted the cap off of the plastic can and upended it, gasoline gurgling out. Phoenix poured it on his face first, as if to reassure herself that he was dead. If he were alive he would fight, now. He would wake up. She recognized the ridiculous fantasy of this notion – his chest and belly were torn and distended, stretched so wide that the lower half of his body no longer looked remotely human. Just meat, now. Just meat.

She soaked the meat with gasoline and then dropped the plastic can, which clattered on the linoleum as she fished the lighter she'd bought at the same Shell station out of her pocket. The drilling noise of the fire alarm dug into her skull, made her brain hurt and fed into her desire to set it all on fire – not just her father's remains, but the whole goddamned place.

She flicked the lighter, which sparked but did not ignite.

Behind her, Ronni loosed an ear-splitting shriek so loud that it cut right through the alarm.

Phoenix did not turn. She *knew*.

She flicked the lighter again and the flame appeared, flickering as it danced into life. I love you, Daddy, she thought as

219

she thrust her hand forward, the stink of gasoline filling the room.

Something tangled in her hair and jerked her head backward. A dark shape darted past her, thick tendrils wrapped around her hand and wrist and smothered the flame. The lighter broke in her hand, plastic shards cutting into her palm, and she felt herself yanked backward off her feet. She hit the ground hard, thumped her head against the floor as the impact knocked the wind out of her.

She tried to catch her breath as it dragged her through the bloody wreckage of the dead nurse and out into the hallway. Blinking, head ringing, she managed to clear her vision enough to see Ronni's legs dangling in the air, kicking hard. Alive, then. At least she was alive.

Hunched and bloated, its green flesh made of scales and blisters, it stared at her with rheumy, piss-yellow eyes. Its four arms were long, fleshy tubes and its fingers the thin tentacles of a young octopus. In one hand – one set of those dripping tendrils – it held Ronni off the ground, fingers wrapped around her face as she gasped for air and tried to claw at its grip.

With another hand, it hoisted Phoenix off the ground by the hair while a third released her right hand, which opened reflexively to release the shattered remnants of her lighter.

It opened its mouth – a gaping maw at the centre of its chest, full of hundreds of wavering cilia, like long reeds beneath the sea – and bent to push her head inside.

Somehow, even over her own screams and the clamour of the fire alarm, Phoenix heard a single, spoken word.

'*No.*'

Ronni still kicked and fought. The demon flopped Phoenix to the floor, jarring her bones, but did not release its hold on her hair. She could sense its irritation as they both turned to see the figure that now approached them along the corridor, its hooves clacking and splashing in the drying, sticky blood.

'*Naberus,*' the tentacled demon said, its voice thick with phlegm.

Fucker, Phoenix thought. *So that's your name.*

Crimson-black flesh. Spider eyes. That crown of bone shards, now stained with blood and strung with viscera. This was the demon that had defiled her father, the one that had chosen him to use as its doorway. Fear and rage waged a battle in her heart, and her rage won. She wanted so badly to see the crowned demon dead.

'*Bring them,*' Naberus said. '*His arrival is imminent and he may want tribute. Let* him *decide what to do with them.*'

The tentacled demon snuffled and spit onto the floor in frustration, but he dropped Ronni to the ground, tendril-fingers wrapping around her body, and then began to drag both women toward the stairs.

Him? Phoenix thought. Naberus had created the doorway that brought them here, but apparently he answered to some-one else.

Ronni kept screaming, kept fighting, but Phoenix let herself be dragged, biding her time.

Hoping for a chance, not to live, but to kill.

Hell

Octavian swept down across the Pit with rage in his heart. Perhaps, he would later think, a little bit of Hell had crept inside of him since he and Squire had descended, or perhaps it had never left him after his imprisonment here. The skeletal sentries sensed him at once and turned to face him, red eyes gleaming in those strange, jagged skulls. The damned screamed all the louder and the flesh of the Pit dragged at them covetously, as if sensing that he wanted to take away its playthings.

The sentries roared and shook their heads like beasts. Nine feet tall, they began to leap at him, talons raking the air. Their hooves split the flesh underfoot when they landed, forcing fresh gouts of flame from the fissures that split the soft quagmire. Octavian reached a hand out to the nearest of them as he lowered himself nearly to their level, and he felt all his fury boil out of him in that single gesture. The demon blew apart, bony limbs shattered, torso exploding. Its skull split in two and one half of it, horn intact, speared through the eye of another sentry nearby.

Pink-grey tendrils reached up for him and jerked back in burning pain at the touch of the magic that surrounded him. Some of the damned had seen him and were crying out in hope – and he would help them if he could, but not until he had secured the freedom of his friends. The sentries who had savaged Charlotte had turned from her, focused on Octavian, and he knew he had given her a few moments' reprieve. Kazimir was nearer – only twenty yards away – and Octavian saw his huge fists reaching up from beneath the suffocating flesh of the Pit.

How many times had he turned enemies to stone or ice?

This required a different transformation. As Octavian swept toward Kazimir in a crackling sphere, the hue of that magic turned bright white and he searched his memory. He had no spell for this, but the magic in him went to the roots of his consciousness and when he consulted all that he had learned, he was able to make adjustments, to create intuitive magic. The Pit was a place of punishment, and these evil creatures deserved nothing less.

His fingers contorted even as he spoke the words – not in Latin or old German or any other language of Earth, but in the guttural tongue of the Demon Lords – and he felt the spell tear from him with such force that he roared in pain. It struck half a dozen of the sentries at once, all those who stood near Kazimir, and then began to tremble and cry out as a change came over them. Yellow bone turned to soft pink skin. Their horns withered and slid from their foreheads and the demons stared at one another, horrified by what they saw. What they felt.

They were flesh and blood, now, and the tendrils of the Pit reached up and grabbed hold of them and dragged them down, screaming and burning.

But Octavian fell as well. The spell had hurt him. Weakened him.

'Son of a bitch,' he muttered as he landed on his hands and knees in the slick flesh of the Pit and it began to suck him down, swallowing him like quicksand.

'No!' he snapped, and green flame burst from his hands, igniting the flesh around him and causing it to recede, retreating from his touch.

As he rose and ran toward Kazimir, it flowed away from him. Tendrils wavered but did not attack for fear of his magic, and as he approached, it pulled away from his friend as well. Kazimir lay naked on a stony surface – whatever the true floor of the Pit was, beneath that demonic flesh – and he dragged himself to his hands and knees as Octavian reached him.

'Peter,' the bearded giant said in his Slavic accent. 'We meet in the strangest places.'

The mountain of a man rose to his feet, nearly seven feet of muscle and flab, and glanced around at the sentries who had begun to surround them. Despite his flippancy, Octavian saw a hatred in his eyes that seemed to verge upon madness.

'Let us kill them, shall we?' Kazimir asked.

'By all means,' Octavian replied. Drawing his sword, he handed it to the Shadow warrior, and Kazimir smiled, and his smile was death for the sentries.

'Charlotte—' Kazimir began.

'I know,' Octavian said. 'Stay with me.'

They turned together, Octavian thinking of the others who had been dragged into this damned dimension. Kuromaku and Allison, Santiago and Taweret. There had been more, but these were his friends, the ones he had come to save.

With Octavian's magic keeping the flesh of the Pit at bay, they started toward Charlotte. Kazimir held the sword with both hands and cleaved a sentry in two, hacking at it a second time to split its skull. Octavian felt weakened by the spell he had created and tasted blood in the back of his throat, and thought better of trying it again. But still he had sorcery at his command that they had no hope of defeating. He turned two to stone and drove one mad with a muttered hex that caused it to pluck out its own eyes. His magic was rarely so brutal, but the image of what they had done to Charlotte would haunt him always, and he needed them to feel at least some of that.

Something screamed in the air above them and Octavian looked up. In the darkness of the caverns overhead, something winged through the shadows. Its talons were enormous and its wingspan breathtaking, but he could make out little else before Kazimir let loose a battle cry and ran at the sentries that separated them from Charlotte. There were fewer than thirty left. Octavian saw several of them turn and flee, realizing that they had better chance of surviving the wrath of their masters than the magic he wielded and the madness behind Kazimir's sword.

Across the Pit, forty yards or more, Charlotte struggled to rise. Her body was contorted, face caved in, one arm broken. The tendrils wrapped around her legs and waist but she lunged at one of the sentries who had assaulted her and used him as an anchor. She could not shapeshift – not until Octavian reached her and forced the flesh of the Pit to retreat – but still she was a vampire with all the strength and ferocity that entailed. Charlotte sank her fangs into the sentry's throat with a crack of bone, and Octavian realized that while they might not be beings of flesh and blood, they at least had marrow at their core.

He unleashed a bolt of concussive force that blew another sentry apart—

And then he let out another cry of pain and clamped his hands over his ears. Kazimir did the same, nearly dropping the sword. Octavian looked up and saw the giant beast swooping down upon them, some demonic bird of prey that looked more pterodactyl than falcon. He snarled, fought the pain in his ears, and brought up one hand to burn it from the air, but the bird snatched a pair of sentries from the Pit and dashed them against the walls with enough force to shatter them, cave in their chests and crush their skulls.

The bird turned and descended again, changing as it fell, diminishing in size until it took a familiar shape and alighted on the ground, its wings the last to vanish.

Alexandra Nueva shattered the chest of a sentry with a single punch and then stood beside Charlotte as the tendrils of the Pit attacked them both. Octavian and Kazimir hurried toward them, killing more sentries as they did, and the rest of them fled in terror, recognizing their defeat.

Kazimir threw his arms around Alex. 'Oh, my friend, I am so happy to see you alive. We have thought you dead for many years.'

Alex pushed him back and gestured at his nakedness. 'Happy to see you, too, Kaz. But not that happy. Find some pants.'

Kazimir laughed and clapped Octavian amiably on the back.

'I didn't expect—' Octavian began.

Alex put up a hand. 'Don't. I was a bitch. Doesn't mean you don't have things to answer for, but we've all lost too much to fight about it now. We've got to save whatever's left of our blood before we spill any more of each other's.'

Charlotte had her arms crossed across her chest, covering up the tatters of her clothes. But now that her ability to shapeshift had returned, both her body and her garments repaired themselves. Her red hair and green eyes were vivid colours in the grimness of Hell. Nineteen when Cortez had made her a vampire, she seemed young and fresh and beautiful, all of the things that Hell abhorred, but her eyes revealed that her innocence had been stripped from her long ago.

But perhaps not all of it. She hurled herself at Octavian and he thought she might hit him. Instead, she embraced him, held him so tightly that it hurt, and then she rose on her toes and kissed him once on the cheek.

'Kazimir said you'd come, that you'd find a way,' she said, and her eyes were rimmed with bloody tears. 'I'm sorry I didn't believe him.'

'I could never have made it myself,' Octavian replied. 'A friend brought me. You'll meet him soon.'

Kazimir tapped his shoulder and Octavian turned to see the massive Shadow gesturing toward the damned who were still trapped in the Pit. Those nearby had stood, since Octavian's presence made the flesh and its tendrils shy away from him, but the others were still held fast.

'What about them?' Kazimir asked. 'Any way to get them out of here?'

Octavian frowned. If there were any way—

'Not a fucking chance,' Charlotte said. 'We're alive, Kaz. We were dragged here, bodily, and these people are all dead. I pity them, but there's no way we're going to be able to get them all out of Hell. Where would we bring them even if we could? They're dead souls. Let's focus on finding our friends who are still alive and getting our asses out of here.'

Alex ruffled Charlotte's hair and glanced at Octavian.

'Y'know,' she said, 'I think I'm going to like the new kid.'

13

Phoenix's World
Ardsley-on-Hudson, New York City, New York

Naberus – whom Phoenix found herself thinking of as the doorway demon – led the way down the stairs. The sticky, tentacled demon followed, and dragged Phoenix and Ronni along. Had the thing wrapped its tendril fingers around their ankles or legs instead of their heads and chests, they would likely have broken their skulls open on the steps. Instead, Phoenix tried to keep her feet in the air, pedalling and pushing off to avoid having her spine and tailbone smash on each step. Her chest burned and her head ached from oxygen deprivation – she could breathe, but not well.

Ronni kept screaming the whole way down to the first floor.

When they left the stairwell and entered the corridor that led to the lobby, Naberus paused and lifted a finger to his lips, that slashed grimace turning into a mocking jack o' lantern grin.

'Sssshhhhh,' the crowned demon said. His jagged, broken teeth were stained with blood.

Phoenix hocked up a gob of spittle, but before she could loose it at him, the tentacled demon slammed her against the wall hard enough to make her teeth clack together. She tasted her own blood and the image of Naberus's broken, crimson-tinted fangs swam into her head again. The comparison made her retch. Tendrils wrapped more tightly around her chest and thumped her against the wall again and it was all she could do to try to breathe.

Ronni would not be silenced, even when it slammed her against the opposite wall. The impact caused a little hitch in her breath, but that was all.

Naberus grunted in apparent disdain, though his spider-eyes were impossible to read. With a sound like a clogged drain, the tentacled demon gave a mucous-filled laugh, and commenced to dragging them again. Phoenix's head rang and dark spots flashed in her mind as she tried to get a full breath of air, but still a single clear thought kept repeating in her head. Naberus had prevented the tentacled demon from killing them so their fate could be decided by *him*. If she only knew who *him* might be, she reasoned, she might be able to guess the odds of them living to see the morning.

They approached the lobby, an enormous atrium with a glass-paneled ceiling and tall potted plants all around. When the tentacled demon dragged them around the corner, it twisted them about and dangled them like marionettes, facing into the atrium.

Only then did Ronni stop her screaming.

'Oh, my God,' Phoenix whispered.

Hundreds of demons congregated in the vast atrium lobby. Huge things hunched in the corners, thirty foot horrors more like gigantic insects than any image of the devil, although there were plenty of those as well. She saw hooves and horns, tails and whipping tongues, damp scales and dry leather, crimson-black and putrid green and urine yellow. The stink of them struck her all at once, a wave of nauseating rot and offal that made her stomach lurch again. They were twisted nightmares with too many eyes, some with bodies so contorted and stretched or so geometrically wrong that Phoenix could barely make sense of what her eyes beheld.

The reception area had been broken into pieces and crushed to the ground. The glass exit doors had all been shattered and glass shards scattered the floor like crystal knives, though most of them would have fallen outside as people crashed through – attempting to escape – and demons raged after them. Splashes of blood were everywhere, but other than torn clothing and strips of flesh that hung from the shards that were still stuck in the window frames, there were no corpses or even body parts on the floor.

No, not on the floor.

'Phoenix,' Ronni rasped, her voice ragged from screaming. 'What is it?'

How could she not know? Phoenix had taken one look at the grotesque sculpture that filled the centre of the atrium and knew immediately what it represented. The demons had collected many of the corpses of the patients and staff and forced them together like children building rudimentary sandcastles. Limbs had been snapped, bones bared and then stabbed into other flesh, legs twined together ... but something else had been used as well, some hellish paste or mortar that held them together, and the demons had sculpted the dead into an arch twenty-five feet high. Even the base of the arch – the threshold – had been forged of broken bodies.

The opening in the arch should have allowed them to see right through to the other side, to see all of the demons gathered there and all the way to the far end of the lobby. Instead, a scarlet mirror seemed to hang there, rippling and undulating, a vertical pool of bright red blood beneath which something seemed to swim.

Don't you get it? she wanted to ask Ronni. *Don't you see? It's a door.*

As if summoned by the thought, a hand emerged from the archway, pushing out through the blood as if piercing some grotesque membrane. The figure that emerged with it shocked her, but not with its ugliness. Phoenix caught her breath in surprise at the utter normalcy of the man who came through that portal. He looked to be no more than fifty years old, with olive skin and greying hair. Average height, average build. A beard slightly more silver than his hair.

The new arrival took a deep breath and a grin spread across his features. He laughed as the demon throngs bent their heads lower, chanting something short and guttural that might have been the man's name or some greeting.

'But he's just . . .' Ronni began. 'He's *human*.'

Naberus struck her so hard that her lip split and one of her teeth flew out to skitter across the floor.

'*Hush, woman,*' the crowned demon spat. '*You will kneel to the King of Hell.*'

The tentacled thing dropped them to the ground and used its extra arms to turn them into puppets again, making them

231

kneel. Phoenix did not fight it; her focus remained on the newcomer. He might look human, but she had not needed Naberus's reassurance to know that was not the case at all. A dreadful energy had begun to pulse around his hands, a bruise purple light that grew and spread. His eyes glowed with the same dark light and a crackling mist began to spill from them.

The demons chanted again and the man turned and gestured back at the portal. A single tendril of purple light unfurled from the energy thrumming around his right hand and shot through the bloody membrane of that doorway and a moment later he stepped away from the portal to make room for two figures who shuffled through into Phoenix's world with a sleepwalker's gait. An Asian man with long black hair tied in a knot at the back of his head, and a pale woman with long brown hair framed her face in an unruly tangle. Their eyes glowed the same bruise purple but they seemed nearly dead.

Not dead, Phoenix realized. *Mesmerized.*

The man clapped his hands together with a smile that seemed almost jubilant.

'This is it,' he said. 'This is just . . . perfect.'

Even his voice sounded ordinary.

'Home sweet—' he began.

With a furious roar, Ronni tore herself from the tentacled demon's grasp. She flattened her hand and drove her fingers into its eyes and it shrieked, and then she ran. Its grip on Phoenix loosened and she realized that its grasp upon them both had been slipping ever since the sorcerer – for that was what he had to be – had stepped through the portal. The demon had been distracted by his master.

'Run, Phoenix!' Ronni screamed.

Phoenix tried to pull free, but she had lost precious seconds and now the tentacled demon tightened its grip so ferociously that she felt bones popping inside her. Not broken, not yet, but compressed. She tried to breathe and could not, and knew that the demon would kill her.

Naberus caught Ronni in three long strides, picked her up with those huge, sharp hands, turned and flung her toward the congregation of hellions. Ronni struck the floor and rolled, limbs flailing. Demons made way, staring at this human who'd been tossed into their midst. Some of them laughed, but Phoenix could barely hear them. Tentacles tightened around her and she thought her skull might just burst.

A skittering demon, a kind of cyclopean praying mantis, clambered on top of Ronni as if laying claim to her.

'That's enough!' barked the sorcerer. The ordinary man. The King of Hell.

The demons, his minions – even Naberus – obeyed without question. They turned toward him, the mantis-thing sliding off Ronni. The tentacles around Phoenix loosened again and she drew a massive gasp of air, heart thundering as the blood rushed back through deprived parts of her body.

'Bring them!' the sorcerer commanded.

Phoenix fell again, slapped against the floor as the tentacled demon dragged her toward the portal. She struggled and swore, because something in the eyes she could see beyond that bruise-purple mist told her that whatever happened, she did not want to go through that portal. Not ever.

And yet . . . he looked so human. Her mind had been screaming at her about demons, thoughts full of panic and horror, and here was a human being, something ordinary instead of grotesque. Unless his grotesquerie was simply not visible from the outside.

'Please . . .' she managed, as she was whipped around and forced to her knees again, only a few feet from the sorcerer and the two mesmerized slaves he had brought through the portal after him. They looked human as well, but how could Phoenix know?

The tentacled demon slammed Ronni down beside her.

'Now, now. Gently, please,' the sorcerer said. He smiled at them, came forward and reached out rough hands – human hands, crackling with that purple light – to touch Ronni's hair and stroke her cheek.

'Who are you?' Ronni asked in a quavering voice.

The power that burned around his hands seemed to diminish, as did the veil of mist in front of his eyes. He turned to Phoenix and one corner of his mouth lifted in an amused, lopsided smile.

'Oh, my darlings, you'd never believe me if I told you.'

The sorcerer raised his hands and the demons chanted those same, choking, guttural syllables once more and then raised their heads. They remained on their knees – all except for Naberus and the tentacled demon – but they were watching their master now. Their king.

'Let's make a little bargain, you and I,' the sorcerer said, glancing from Ronni to Phoenix. 'You tell me what I want to know, and I'll let you live as long as your species survives. You'll be the last two human beings I let the hordes of Hell devour. How does that sound, good?'

'Oh, sweet Jesus,' Ronni said, a plaintive, broken prayer.

The sorcerer snapped his head around and glared at her. 'Oh, he's not coming. Trust me. That son of a bitch is the ultimate fair weather friend.'

Phoenix shuddered and hung her head, but the sorcerer bent, stroked her chin, and lifted her face so that he could gaze upon her.

'Tell me all you know about the current status of Peter Octavian and his fellow *Shadows*.'

He said the last word as if merely speaking it soiled his tongue. His nose curled in distaste as he pronounced it. Phoenix frowned, shaking her head.

'Never heard of them.'

Anger furrowed the sorcerer's brow. 'Look around you, girl. Hell has come to Earth. For all the time Octavian has spent repelling such incursions . . .' He took a deep bow. 'Here we are. I don't know why you would want to protect them unless . . .'

The man cocked his head, studying Phoenix and Ronni. Then he turned to the mesmerized pair he had brought through the portal with him.

'Kuromaku. Allison. Are these two your kind?'

The female – Phoenix figured this must be Allison – glanced at the sorcerer with that bruise-purple glow in her eyes. Without a word she strode toward Ronni, dragging her feet a bit as though somewhere inside she fought the control the sorcerer held over her. Her companion, Kuromaku, struggled a moment before marching stiffly toward Phoenix.

The tentacled demon released them as the sorcerer's minions approached. Allison grabbed a fistful of Ronni's hair and dragged her to her feet, studying her eyes. As Kuromaku strode toward Phoenix, she flinched and took a step backward, bumping into a thin, wraith-like demon who seemed little more than wispy skin and thin bones – a black-red kite of a creature.

'What are you?' Allison asked, brown hair veiling one eye.

'I . . . I don't understand the . . . the question . . .' Ronni stammered.

Allison snarled, nostrils flaring and eyes going wide as her teeth lengthened into glinting needle fangs. Ronni screamed and Phoenix spun to face Kuromaku. He sneered at her and she saw his own fangs, saw his fingers lengthen into hooked talons, and she knew.

'Holy shit,' Phoenix whispered. 'They're vampires.'

Absurdly, surrounded as they were by demons, Ronni closed her eyes tightly as if she could make them go away merely by pretending, and said, 'But there's no such thing as vampires.'

Allison cut her cheek with a talon and blood welled up in the gash. Ronni cried out and tried to flinch away, but the vampire had her by the hair and leaned in to lick the blood that dripped down her cheek.

'Don't move,' Kuromaku told Phoenix, and she did not argue.

I'm going to die, she thought. *Shit, I'm practically dead already*. A terrible sadness crushed down upon her heart. Naberus had to pay for defiling her father. And this sorcerer – if what Annelise's spirits had told her was correct and demons were flooding out of Hell – he was responsible. She wanted to kill them both. Destroy them all. She had the will and the determination and the fire of hate burned inside her, but her only weapons were her two fragile human hands. Any one of the demons in that room could have killed her with barely a thought.

'She's human, Lazarus,' Allison said, turning toward the sorcerer.

The purple light around the sorcerer's hands – Lazarus's hands, if that was his name – pulsed and turned darker, even as it grew and spread along his arms. The static mist spilling from his eyes increased but behind the mist they glowed brightly. The lights in the atrium flickered and Phoenix felt a ripple pass through the air like the brunt of distant fireworks thumping her chest. Two panels of the ceiling glass shattered, raining sharp fragments down upon the portal, and the October wind howled.

'Human,' Lazarus said, the word like a curse. 'Listen to me, human women. I am going to ask again, and this time I will be very clear. You will not get another chance at an honest answer because you will be dead.'

'No, please,' Ronni said, averting her gaze, unwilling to look into the vampire's purple, mesmerized eyes. 'Anything you want.'

Kuromaku loomed over Phoenix, who nodded. 'Me, too. We're not hiding anything.'

'What do you know of Peter Octavian—'

'I swear to you,' Phoenix said, 'we've never heard of the guy.'

The sorcerer shook with rage. The aura of magic burning around him darkened further, nearly black now.

'Do you expect me to believe—'

Kuromaku grabbed Phoenix by the throat and hauled her toward him. He showed his fangs and she thought he would tear out her throat.

'You've never seen a Shadow . . . never seen a vampire before,' he said.

'Of course not!' Phoenix cried, shaking.

Kuromaku turned to stare at Allison. 'She said vampires don't exist.'

Eyes wide and desperate, Ronni tore her gaze from Allison and stared at Kuromaku. 'They don't! Until right this second, we thought vampires were just legends, monsters from movies and books. The same thing with demons.'

A wave of reaction went through the gathered hellions. They shifted and grumbled and some of them laughed. The motion raised a cloud of stink, the stench of gore and shit and charred flesh. Phoenix caught a glimpse of Naberus, who stared at Ronni with those spider-eyes. The crowned demon seemed to take a step back, glancing anxiously at the demons around him.

Lazarus stood frozen, outlined against the vertical pool of blood that made up the portal behind him. His features had gone slack, but abruptly he began a low chuckle, the laugh of a madman.

'Oh, no,' the sorcerer said, as if to himself. 'That just won't do.'

'It's true,' Phoenix said quickly. 'I don't know why you expect us to know—'

'The whole world knows!' Lazarus roared. 'Vampires and demons and Peter Octavian . . . the whole damned world knows!'

Phoenix shook her head. 'Not this world.'

Lazarus stared at her and then buried his face in his hands. At first, she wasn't sure if he was laughing or crying, and she thought maybe he wasn't sure either. But then he sighed deeply and glanced out over the congregation of demons and the damage and slaughter they had committed in his name.

'I believe you,' Lazarus said with a too-wide smile. 'That's the problem. I believe you completely. This world . . .

it's so like the world of my birth, but more innocent. Or it was, until today.'

The sorcerer's smile faltered. He spun and gestured toward the crowd of demons. Purple-black light arced from his fingers and struck like lightning, lancing into Naberus. The crowned demon let out a cry of pain and protest as that lightning tangled itself around him and dragged him toward the portal – and toward his master.

'Lord Lazarus, wait!' Naberus shouted. 'I told you we couldn't be sure—'

'You said you would open a doorway to my world!'

'And I will!' Naberus snapped, struggling to stand as that purple-black light arced around him, holding and searing him. 'If this isn't your world, it's very close. A twin. Don't do anything—'

'You presume to tell me what to do?' Lazarus shouted, and that dark lightning dragged Naberus up off the floor, his hooves scratching the linoleum as he dangled aloft.

Lazarus strode toward him, fury on his features. Phoenix held her breath as she watched, thinking the sorcerer would kill the crowned demon – wishing for it, praying for it. Ronni had ceased her whimpering, givng up on crying and fear, and now Phoenix could hear what sounded almost like a growl coming from her.

'Go on,' Ronni snarled at Allison. 'Kill me.'

Allison's eyes narrowed, features pinched as if in pain. The vampire squeezed her eyes shut and when they opened, some of the violet hue had faded from them.

'I don't want to,' the vampire said.

Phoenix blinked in surprise. Allison was struggling. She and Kuromaku might be monsters, but they were in the thrall

239

of Lazarus. *Fighting him,* Phoenix thought. *They're fighting him.*

For a second, she let herself hope that she and Ronni might not be on their own, that the vampires might be their allies, but then she glanced up at Kuromaku and saw the hunger in his eyes and the glint of light off of his fangs.

'Kuromaku! Allison!' Lazarus snapped. 'Get them out of my sight. Take their blood if you want, but kill them. And don't let me hear them scream. We can't afford any more distractions.'

Phoenix's mind rejected the words. She tried to tell herself the sorcerer wasn't talking about her, that he'd just ordered someone else's murder, but then Kuromaku grabbed her by the wrist in an iron grip and she could not help it – she screamed. The sound burned up out of her throat as if it came from somewhere else entirely, someone else.

Kuromaku struck her in the face so hard that when she blinked back the dark spots at the corners of her vision, she thought she might have gone unconscious for a few seconds.

'Didn't you hear him?' Kuromaku said. 'No screaming.'

The demons began to shuffle toward Lazarus, closing the circle around their king. Phoenix caught a glimpse of Naberus being drawn nearer to the sorcerer, who barked commands at him – orders and warnings about what would happen if he failed a second time – but she could not focus on those words. Kuromaku dragged her from the atrium and Allison followed, one hand fisted in Ronni's hair. The demons flowed aside to let them pass, much more focused on their master's disappointment and wondering what came next than they were on the two women whose fates had already been decreed.

'Ronni!' Phoenix shouted. 'I'm sorry. I never meant—'

Kuromaku hurled her from the lobby and into the corridor that led to the elevator banks. Phoenix hit the floor and rolled, smashed her elbow and cried out in pain. Her thoughts were muzzy and she thought she must have a concussion, but still she rose on her hands and knees and glared at the vampire, with his severe eyes and black hair in a tight ponytail. In his black pants and a tailored white shirt – now torn and stained – he looked as if he'd spent the night at a party somewhere trendy. Only his fangs and those glowing purple eyes gave him away.

The vampire reached down to his side and drew a long sword out of thin air. One second there was nothing there and the next he held a Japanese katana, which gleamed along its arc as he raised it and strode after her. Somehow, after a day of horror and impossible things, she still managed to be astonished, to reject the reality of what she had just seen.

Then Allison came around the corner and into the corridor, dragging Ronni by the hair. Ronni fought her, screaming, and though they were away from the atrium now – out of sight of the demons and their king – the screams must have echoed all through the lobby.

'You don't have to—' Phoenix began.

With a single, primal shout, Ronni reached up to grab hold of the hand that was gripping her hair. She got her feet under her and crabbed backward, twisted, and swung her legs at Allison's. The vampire tripped and the two of them fell in a bone-jarring tangle of limbs.

'Go, Phoenix! Run for it!' Ronni screamed. 'Finish it!'

On her feet now, Phoenix stared at Kuromaku. The violet glow of his eyes seemed to dim a moment and then he turned to glance back at Allison. Phoenix bolted, racing along the corridor toward the elevator banks. Her breath came in small gasps and her heart thudded in her ears and the slap of her shoes on the linoleum was so loud. So fucking loud. And she knew she would never escape, that she was going to die. In a building full of demons, with a window into hell in the goddamn lobby, with vampires ordered to kill her, how could she hope to survive? Why was she even bothering to run?

Running, she thought. *Oh, my God*. She had left Ronni behind. Ronni, this brave woman who had become her friend in just a few short hours of terror, who had just attacked a vampire in order to buy her precious seconds to try to get away. Who had wanted nothing more than to redeem herself for the terrible accident that had coloured her whole life.

Guilt threatened to swamp her, and then Ronni's words caught up to her racing thoughts. *Finish it.*

Jaw set, fists clenched, she raced past the elevators toward the stairwell door. She could feel the vampire bearing down on her, imagine its jaws opening wide – too wide – and those fangs tearing her flesh, splashing her blood onto its face, the monster drinking it down, face smeared crimson. But her father's corpse still lay in his hospital room one floor above them, soaked in gasoline, and one small flame would do the trick. Maybe end this, but at least cleanse him.

Behind her, she heard Ronni cry out again, but the sound had changed.

As she reached the stairwell door, she glanced back to see Kuromaku staring at Allison and Ronni. He hadn't moved. Instead, he put his sword away, sliding it into an invisible scabbard, where it vanished. Allison held Ronni's hair and yanked her head back, opened her jaws wide and sank her fangs into the creamy coffee skin at Ronni's throat. Ronni screamed louder, the sound filled with regret and profound sorrow, and then Allison silenced her forever with a single, swift jerk that snapped her neck. The crack of bone echoed along the corridor.

Shaking, numb and hollow with grief, Phoenix slammed the door open. Just before she raced into the stairwell, she saw Kuromaku whip his head around, his gaze locked with hers, and then he gave chase.

Phoenix didn't have a chance. Bruised and exhausted, she was only human, and Kuromaku was not. She managed to make it to the seventh step before he caught her, and she twisted to fight him, beat at his face, tore furrows in his cheeks with her nails. He struck her again and she went limp, waves of pain flowing through her skull.

In his arms, she felt herself being carried and wondered why she wasn't dead.

Down, she thought. *Why are we going down?*

Blinking, she drew a ragged breath and her vision swam back into focus. Her ears rang from the blow but she worked out that the pain meant he had not killed her. Instead of tearing her throat out, he carried her down past the first floor landing and kept going until he reached the door that led into the basement level. There were two corpses blocking the door and he slid Phoenix gently to the ground before picking up the bloodied corpse of a woman in scrubs and tore her arm off as if she were a Christmas turkey. Blood and gristle spattered the ground and then he tossed the corpse aside and turned to glare at her, the dead woman's arm in his hand.

The purple hue of his eyes had dimmed even further.

243

'It's all I can do to keep from . . . killing you . . .' he managed. He shook the bloody arm at her. 'This is to prove that I *did*. If you can escape from down here, do it. If not, just hide, and I'll find a way to get you out as soon as I can.'

He turned and left her there, taking the steps two at a time with inhuman speed. In a blink, he was gone. For several long seconds, Phoenix could only sit and breathe, astonished to be alive.

Just hide, he'd said.

But she had other ideas.

14

Hell

In a small alcove of gleaming black volcanic rock, Octavian conversed with Kazimir and Charlotte while Squire stood watch at the entrance to that shadowed grotto. Moans and screams drifted to them from distant corners of this circle of Hell, but they had found respite here after fleeing the Pit. As shapeshifters, their abilities were not confined merely to flesh and blood. They changed themselves on a molecular level, could alter their appearance to look like anyone or become anything, so manifesting clothing had not been a problem. They were all grateful for that, except for Squire, who had been disappointed when Charlotte was no longer nude.

'How long had you been here before they captured you?' Octavian asked.

'Weeks,' Kazimir said, his accent thick with emotion. 'Months, I don't know. Time is fluid here; you know that.

Important thing is that when they finally catch us, they took us to Lazarus—'

Octavian frowned. 'Not to Abraxas or Balberith? There are dozens of Demon Lords they could have taken you to. Unless he knew you were here somehow, had people out looking for you, it's a pretty damn big coincidence that the demons who finally captured you—'

'We kill many of them.'

'—would be working for Lazarus.'

'Peter,' Charlotte said. 'You're not thinking.'

She put a hand on his chest and he glanced down at her, met her gaze, and felt the connection between them instantly. Not a sexual thing, but a bond and a rapport that made her important to him. With her fox-red hair and narrow features, she was beautiful, but so young that his greatest urge was to protect her and to teach her how to protect herself, not to take her to bed. They were friends, but as with a small handful of those he had called friends over the years, he felt as if they were growing toward becoming something like siblings.

'All right, little sister,' he said. 'What should I be thinking?'

Charlotte narrowed her gaze. 'He's got the run of the place. We were separated, but the demons captured us and dragged us all to the same Pit. Us specifically – your friends. Allison and Kuromaku, Santiago and Taweret, and me and Kazimir. Allison and Kuromaku were taken away. We don't know to where, but it was at Lazarus's command. You think he could get away with this without the Lords of Hell knowing about it and coming down on his head?'

'Not unless he had some power over them,' Octavian replied.

'He does,' Kazimir said. 'That's what we're trying to tell you. Lazarus . . . he's like you, Peter. He's a powerful mage. Peter . . . he killed Taweret and Santiago, and maybe others as well.'

In the baking heat of Hell, Octavian felt his blood run cold. 'You're sure. Shadows are hard to kill.'

'I have seen you do it,' Kazimir replied. 'He is magic, like you.'

Charlotte took her hand off Octavian's chest, but kept her eyes locked on his.

'Lazarus isn't just a mage,' she said. 'We heard the demons talking, heard him giving commands. Balberith and all the others – I don't know the names, this is all new to me – but all of those Demon Lords don't try to stop him because they can't. They already tried and he defeated them.'

Octavian stared, ice forming in his gut. 'What?'

'Yes,' Kazimir said with a nod. 'Lazarus . . . he is King of Hell.'

Squire had been listening from his position keeping watch. Now he let out a humourless bark of a laugh.

'You gotta be fuckin' kidding me,' the hobgoblin said.

'No,' Kazimir replied. 'No kidding.'

'From what we overheard,' Charlotte went on, 'Lazarus killed a couple of Demon Lords – one of 'em was Moloch or something like that. The rest saw they didn't stand a chance and some even rallied behind him. Demon politics are just like politics in our world, I guess. Once they saw he was a winner, everybody wanted to kiss his ass.'

'The demons say that Lazarus promises to break down all walls between Hell and other dimensions,' Kazimir said. 'They can spread everywhere, make little demon babies.

Lazarus is going to lead them, but he has told them there's one thing he must do before he guides them to conquest. One task they have to help him accomplish first.'

Octavian stared at the huge Shadow, with his dark eyes and grim features, and he saw the message there. He glanced at Charlotte.

'Cortez murdered the woman I love,' Octavian said. 'I know he did it at Lazarus's command. So it's not hard to guess what this one task is.'

Charlotte nodded slowly. 'The King of Hell has told all the demons under him that he will basically give them the universe, but only when he has killed *you*, Peter. Only when you're dead.'

'Fuckin' marvelous,' Squire said from his post.

'He's not even in Hell right now, I don't think,' Charlotte said. 'Lazarus is out hunting for you, trying to track you down. He must be trying to get into our world to find you the same way you were trying to get into Hell to find us.'

Octavian tried to still his heart. Hate and rage could be fuel, but he had to make it burn cold and calm. If he could not keep his head, they would all pay the price.

'I wish it hadn't come to this,' he said.

For the first time, he regretted having brought Squire with him. There were only two ways for them to find Lazarus now, either let themselves be captured or work their way up the hierarchy of Hell until they found a demon well-connected enough to know where the dark realm's new monarch had gone. Either way, the level of peril they faced would increase. As if Hell itself weren't dangerous enough, now they were going to have to spit in its face. Squire had proven himself more capable in combat than Octavian had imagined but when it came time for them to do battle with the Lords of Hell, how much could one hobgoblin do?

Damn it. He had to send Squire back, and despite the risk, the hobgoblin would have to use the Shadowpaths to get home or else Octavian would have to travel with him in order to protect him on the journey. He owed the little man that.

'Peter?' Charlotte said.

Octavian glanced over at Squire – and froze. He blinked a couple of times to clear his vision but it was not the heat haze rising off of the stone floor. Squire had vanished from his sentry post.

'Son of a bitch!' Octavian snapped, rushing from the alcove.

'What is—' Kazimir began.

'Squire!' Octavian shouted, scanning the entrance to the alcove and the glassy-black rock that sloped away from where they had gathered. Gleaming teeth of that volcanic stone jutted up from the slope and he could have been hiding behind any one of them.

He stopped to listen, holding up a hand to silence Kazimir and Charlotte as they joined him. The tunnel they were in was forty feet wide and almost as high, and stretched a hundred yards or so before it opened out into the vast cavern where the Pit was located. They had killed all of the demons on guard there, but by now more would have arrived. Hundreds of tunnels branched out of that cavern, so a search would take time, but he had to wonder if somehow the searchers had gotten lucky.

No. If they had been found – if Squire had been attacked – there would have been noise. Hellions from the Pit would not have snatched a hobgoblin and spirited him away, they would have attempted to wreak vengeance. In the distance, out in the cavern, huge jets of flame shot toward the ceiling. The cries of the Suffering continued, no different now than the sound of the surf against the shore – omnipresent, ordinary. The idea troubled Octavian, but he had already argued with Squire about the nature of the damned and he couldn't be distracted by them now.

Octavian glanced at Charlotte and Kazimir, who seemed equally mystified.

'Where did he—'

A birdlike screech tore through the air and echoed off the alcove walls behind him. Octavian glanced up at the ledges overhead, jagged stone plateaus that hid shadows within shadows. A cry of pain burst forth and the sounds of a scuffle ensued.

'Damn it,' Octavian said, magic flowing from his hands, bathing the alcove in bright blue light.

'I've got it,' Charlotte said. She leaped upward, flesh rippling and diminishing instantly as she transformed into a bat. Octavian had a moment to cringe at the choice, but he knew it was second nature to her. She had been made a Shadow by Cortez, and he had embraced the darkest parts of vampire lore.

Before Charlotte could reach even the bottommost ledge, two small figures came tumbling over the side. In the light of his own magic, Octavian saw Squire grapple with a squirming crimson demon as they plummeted to the ground. It had its spiny tail wrapped around the hobgoblin's throat but Squire managed to twist himself around just in time to be on top as they hit the black stone floor. The demon cried out at the impact and its tail loosened enough for Squire to breathe.

'You spying little motherfucker!' the hobgoblin yelled. He raised his axe and hacked off the vicious little imp's tail.

It let out another bird-screech and tried to claw at Squire's face.

With a gesture, Octavian struck the imp with a hex that made it jerk and shudder and then go still, moaning quietly. Squire took the opportunity to launch a kick at its side, his heavy boot cracking something inside the demon.

'I hate these little things,' Charlotte said, moving to stand above the imp. 'They're filthy, always groping. Fingers everywhere.'

Squire glanced up at her, yellow eyes gleaming. 'I'll cut the little bastard's fingers off if you want. Have 'em as a keepsake or something.'

Charlotte arched an eyebrow. 'Gross.'

The hobgoblin shrugged. 'Fine. Just don't ever say chivalry's dead.'

Kazimir crossed his arms. 'You say this thing was spying?'

Squire nodded, still clutching his axe. 'Perched on the ledge up there, just sitting in the shadows listening. At first, I thought there were more of them, but when I snuck up there I only saw the one. Little prick was just listening, trying not to be seen, but if there's anyone who's going to notice something skulking in the shadows, it's me.'

'I don't get it,' Charlotte said. 'It didn't attack and it didn't raise an alarm. What's the point of spying on us?'

Octavian crouched above the imp. Standing, it would've been under four feet in height, and its arms and legs were thin and wiry, little more than bones with thick, cabled muscles wrapped around them. Its sunken eyes and tipped-back ears would have made it look like some kind of exotic

251

monkey if not for the deep crimson hue of its leathery skin and the small nubs of horns on its forehead. Its primary weapon would have been the tail, which looked just as long as the imp was tall. The spines on the tail were painted with Squire's blood, an observation that made Octavian glance worriedly at the hobgoblin. Squire's coat and trousers were spotted with bloodstains but other than looking pissed off he seemed little worse for wear.

'You okay?' he asked.

'Right as fuckin' rain,' Squire said. 'Even better when you let me chop the asshole's head off. Those spines hurt, I don't mind tellin' ya.'

Octavian frowned. 'You're gonna have to wait a while.'

On one knee, he waved a hand and the sizzling blue light engulfing the imp disappeared. The demon leaped at him, claws out and hissing, but Kazimir snatched it up from behind, held its arms back so far that Octavian thought the huge Shadow might snap the little imp like a wishbone.

'Who are you spying for?' Octavian asked.

The imp spat in his face. Its spittle burned, but the magic in Octavian healed his skin instantly, without him sparing a thought to do it. Larger injuries required focus, but this was nothing.

'Do you know who I am?' he asked the imp.

Its tiny pink eyes burned deep in those sunken sockets, full of hate and fear.

'I think you do,' Octavian said.

'I'll say,' Squire added. 'I think he just pissed himself.'

Octavian ignored him. The imp tried to struggle and Kazimir gave it a bone-jarring shake so that it fell limp in his huge hands.

'What's going on?' Charlotte asked.

'Let's find out,' Octavian replied. He opened his hand and a bright, coppery light flickered to life upon his palm.

'Hurt me, cut me, snap my bones,' the little imp dared them. It uttered a high, grating little laugh. 'What can you do to me that hasn't been done? This is Hell, stupid magic-man.'

Octavian let the copper fire play across his hand and over his fingers. The others all seemed mesmerized, but the imp resolutely refused to look at the flame.

'You know who and what I am,' he said darkly, moving his face nearer the imp's so that they were nearly nose to nose. 'I will forge a little bottle and lock you inside, not like some djinni – that would almost be kind. I will bring you back to my world and put you on a shelf in a room where human children would come and gape and you and shrink from you and laugh at you all day, every day, for as long as humanity exists. And when the last light of humanity is extinguished, I will travel the Shadowpaths with my friends and find another world where there are children to mock and to shudder in revulsion at your ugliness and your pitiful flesh. You will never feel pain again. Never feel anything again, except within you.'

Kazimir leaned forward and whispered into the demon's ear. 'There is more than one kind of torture.'

The imp averted its eyes but Octavian saw the way its mouth quivered, as if it might cry. In all the time he had spent in Hell, he had never seen a demon cry. The desire to witness such a phenomenon did not make him feel ashamed. Evil could feel pain, but never sympathy, and so he would lend it none of his own.

'Talk, you little—' Squire began.

The imp spat acid at him and the hobgoblin jumped back, swearing.

'Little?' the demon wheezed. 'What is little to half a man? Stay here in Hell, 'goblin. Here, at least, you swim in an ocean of ugliness and no one will notice your face.'

Squire raised the axe, but Octavian gestured for him to stay back.

'Do you honestly think I'll let you be killed before you tell me what I want to know?' he asked.

The mage raised his hand and the copper fire that burned there began to take shape, becoming a small, ornate bottle. The imp let out another screech and tried to scramble back away from him, but Kazimir held it tightly.

'Charlotte,' Octavian said, 'go and stand watch. He's going to scream bloody murder when I'm putting him into the bottle.'

'All right!' the imp said, lower lip quivering like a child's. 'What do you want to know?'

'Most of it I can guess easily enough. You're spying, and you're afraid to talk. Is it a Lord of Hell you answer to, or the king?'

The imp sneered. 'I am in service to His Majesty the Twice-Resurrected.'

Squire snorted. 'Wow. I mean, Lazarus is seriously full of himself, ain't he?'

'And you weren't alone up on that ledge, were you? There was another – at least one – and it's run off to snitch,' Octavian said.

With a nervous shudder, the imp averted its eyes. Octavian whacked it in the skull with the now solid bottle and it cried out.

'Yes!' it barked. 'My brother! It was my brother.'

'And what is your brother's name?' Kazimir asked.

Its pink eyes glared hatred at Octavian, though he had not been the one to speak.

'Thresu,' the imp said. 'He is Thresu. And I am Teucer. And now you will do with me what you will, but I'll tell you no more.' It shuddered and then whispered, as if to itself, 'Oh, my lovely tail.'

Octavian nodded. 'That's all right. I don't have any other questions.'

'Wait, what?' Charlotte asked.

Octavian held the bottle up in front of the imp's mistrustful eyes. 'Take us to Lazarus. Show us the door he's used to get wherever he's gone.'

'What?' the demon asked. 'But I don't know—'

'Your brother's gone to tell him we're here. You were left to keep watch. If Thresu knew where to find your Twice-Resurrected bastard of a king, then you know as well,' Octavian said. 'He'll reward you, if you live, Teucer. You'll be a hero in the eyes of your king. What does he want? He wants Octavian. What better way to serve him than to bring me to him?'

The imp had a terrible smile.

Phoenix's World
Ardsley-on-Hudson, New York, USA

Kuromaku felt submerged inside his own body, floating weightless in the capsule that his flesh had become. And yet his will had not been completely subjugated. From the moment Lazarus had seized control of him, Kuromaku had found that if he focused he could extend his will out into his extremities and take temporary control of his arms or legs. The magic flowed around him like mercury and it could be shifted, just a little. He was a passenger inside his own body, but he had thought that with some effort, he might grab hold of the wheel – just for a moment.

Now something had changed.

Lazarus had set him after this girl with the green eyes and the blond bob as if he were a housecat and she a mouse in the sorcerer's kitchen. She and her friend, the lovely creature in the nurse's uniform, with such beautiful dark skin—

Allison had murdered the nurse. Drained her blood. Broken her neck. Yet Kuromaku had not killed the blond. Somehow he had wrested control of his body. The magic still lingered, the impulses that he knew came from Lazarus instead of his own brain. That dark power caressed him, moving his limbs, and he let himself go with the flow.

Let himself. That was the difference. He had a choice, now. He could feel the potential for control, that if he exerted himself he would be able to resume command not just his arms or his legs but his whole body, just as he had done on the basement stairs when he had come face to face with the young blond woman.

The ground shook underfoot and dust rained down from the ceiling as he walked back down the corridor toward the atrium lobby. Allison sat against the wall just a few feet away from the nurse she had killed. She wiped furiously at her face with a bit of fabric she'd torn from the dead woman's sweatshirt, and at first Kuromaku thought she was just trying to clean off her victim's blood, which had drenched the front of her own shirt. Then he saw the blood in her eyes and the crimson tears that slipped down her cheeks as she dabbed at them anew.

They were being used, but it was worse for Allison. Kuromaku had killed more than one innocent in the early years after his transformation. As far as he knew, she never had.

'It's all right,' he said quietly as he strode toward her.

Her gaze locked on him and she frowned, understanding that something had changed – that he had regained control. She would ask him how, he thought, and he would have to tell her that he did not know, and guilt would tear her apart. If he had been able to fight the sorcerer's power, why had she been unable to do the same? What had he done differently?

Suddenly he knew.

The sword.

Kuromaku frowned and reached down to grasp the handle of his katana, which manifested with a mere thought, an act of pure will. He had not altered his entire body, but forging that sword from the fabric of the world around him had been a form of shapeshifting. The Shadows controlled their bodies on a molecular level. Somehow, altering himself had disrupted Lazarus's control.

'Allison, listen,' he said, hurrying toward her.

She stood abruptly and turned from him, walking toward the lobby. Confused, Kuromaku wanted to call out to her, but then the flow of dark magic increased around him and he understood. They were being summoned.

He could have fought Lazarus's power, but there were hundreds of demons already and more coming through all the time. He had no plan, and if he struggled now he might give himself away and be killed. Kuromaku had lived many centuries, long enough that the idea of dying in battle did not frighten him, but he had no intention of dying for nothing.

A fresh tremor swept through the hospital. The sounds of breaking glass and quaking earth grew louder and when he entered the atrium, he saw that a new phase of destruction had gotten under way. Most of the demons had already gone outside, but there were perhaps a dozen remaining to guard the portal in the centre of the lobby, and more were emerging in ones and twos – devils and putrid slitherers and imps. They paid no attention to him or to Allison, their focus riveted on the parking lot beyond the shattered glass. October air blew through the atrium, but it had grown warmer now, and Kuromaku could see why.

A chasm had opened just outside the hospital, and a demon the size of a blue whale began to rise from the fires within. Liquid flame spilled from the plates of its armored skin and burned in its five oval eyes. Kuromaku had seen many demons in Hell but his senses had been overwhelmed there and the presence of the monstrosities had a rightness about it. Here, in this ordinary world of grass and pavement and human construction, the thing seemed more abominable. Unimaginable. It had the thorax of an insect and the spear-shaped head of a squid, with both tentacles and the spindly front legs of a mantis. His senses could barely take it all in and he tore his gaze from the Hell being born outside and stared at the floor.

Too many disparate pieces of information filled his head and, like trying to hold a complete image in his mind of the Demon Lord in the parking lot, he could not put them all together. Lazarus sought Octavian and the gatekeeper

Naberus had made an error, brought them to the wrong world. That much was plain.

But what of the women? The blond and her dead friend, whom Allison had murdered.

Kuromaku whipped his head up and sought out Allison, grateful to find that she had paused to watch the Demon Lord rise. *Lazarus is distracted*, Kuromaku thought. *His grip has loosened.*

If he intended to do something, Kuromaku knew he might not get a better opportunity. Once they were outside, Lazarus would not be so careless with how tightly he held the reins on his pet Shadows.

Puzzle pieces jumbled in his brain, but the ones that didn't fit were those two women. He and Allison had been in this world only minutes, but it seemed very clear that most if not all of the patients and staff in the hospital must be dead or have fled when the incursion had begun. Yet he had looked into the eyes of the young woman to whom he had just shown mercy, and now that he pictured those eyes again, he understood something vital. She wasn't going anywhere. Her expression had been fearful but determined.

She has a plan, Kuromaku thought.

The idea brought him up short. He frowned, staring at Allison's back, feeling the low-level current of Lazarus's magic. Naberus had brought the two women as tribute, but had he captured them when he had first opened a door into this world, or only recently? Kuromaku couldn't be sure the question was significant, but it felt as if the answer mattered.

If she's not going to run, he thought, *what's she up to?* Whatever it might be, it seemed clear that she knew something Kuromaku did not. Had she discovered some way to fight Lazarus, to stop the incursion? It seemed unlikely, but the grim purpose in her eyes made him think there must be some truth to that.

He would have to find out, but he couldn't leave Allison in Lazarus's thrall, and he could think of only one way to snap her out of it.

With a single swift thrust, Kuromaku drove the blade of his katana through her back. She let out a grunt but he clapped his hand over her mouth even as she tried to twist around to fight him. Her eyes were full of rage and he felt her fangs tear the flesh of his palm.

'That's right,' he whispered. '*Change.*'

Her left hand reached back over her shoulder and grabbed a fistful of his hair and with her right she managed to claw at his cheek, talons slashing down to the bone. His blood spilled onto the blade between them, sticky and warm on his fingers where the gripped the handle.

'Your name is Allison Vigeant,' he said quietly.

'I know my name, you bastard,' she growled. 'Can you take the fucking sword out of my back?'

Kuromaku gave a single, curt nod and slid the blade out of her flesh. Allison turned toward him and for a second or two they only stood there, wounds healing as they stared at one another.

'That hurt,' she rasped.

Beyond her, a new wave of demons crept through the shimmering crimson portal in the atrium. One of them glanced their way and its eyes narrowed, but then the ground shook again and a chant arose outside, and it turned and followed the others out through the broken windows to show fealty to its king.

'You feeling yourself again?' Kuromaku asked.

Allison reached up to press her temples. 'More or less. But he's still in my head . . . and not *just* my head.'

"If you feel like he's trying to get control again, change form. Don't give him an anchor."

She nodded. 'So what now?'

Kuromaku took one more look at the portal and then started to slip out of the atrium, back into the corridor, beckoning for Allison to follow.

'Now,' he said quietly, 'there's an attractive blond I need to track down.'

Allison frowned, opened her mouth and then closed it again.

'Screw it,' she said. 'I'm not even going to ask. Just lead the way.'

Lazarus stood on the cracked pavement in front of the hospital and watched as Haagenti rose from the fiery passage that had appeared in the middle of the parking lot. Of all of the Lords of Hell, Haagenti had been the most supportive of his plans to expand the influence of the Realm Infernal. It reproduced in massive broods every few months and desired a place where its spawn could run rampant instead of being eaten or slain for sport by other hellions.

As Haagenti crawled and slithered from the flames, front legs breaking through the pavement as its tentacles drew it forward, Lazarus watched the Demon Lord with a mixture of pride and revulsion. Once, the sorcerer had gazed upon the face of God. The Son of Man had called him friend. Later, he had become an immortal, with the soul of an angel and the heart of a devil, and he had indulged both sides of his nature before he at last understood what his kind could become. He had ventured into Hell to retrieve Octavian because it needed to be done, and he had always believed that heroes were simply people who did what needed doing, and did not require any reason other than that necessity.

For his trouble, he had been abandoned.

He wasn't a Shadow anymore – not a vampire. Both the angel and devil parts of him had left him, but he had been in Hell so long that the only thing he still knew how to do was survive. For the first few centuries, he had held on – held out hope of rescue – and when hope had died, he had gone mad.

Lazarus embraced his madness, cherished and nurtured it the way one might shield a candle flame from the wind. Like that candle, madness had been the only light sustaining him in the dark heart of Hell. It had been born of regret and resentment, and in time it had grown into a bright fire of vengeance.

'Isn't it glorious?' a voice said at his side.

The sorcerer flinched, unhappy to be shaken from his reverie. He grinned because anger and amusement were close cousins in his soul, and turned to see Naberus standing beside him. Spite roiled in him.

'You ought to be hiding from me,' Lazarus said.

Naberus twitched and took a step away, lowering his gaze. Was it possible he had not expected recrimination? Demons were self-involved and could be blinded by their own arrogance, but surely . . .

'I hoped you would be pleased with Lord Haagenti's arrival, Majesty,' the demon of thresholds said. Naberus scratched at a place on his forehead where a fresh shard of bone had broken through the skin. 'A portal of this size is not easy, and I have opened several on this world, and dozens that are smaller.'

Lazarus's grin widened. He twisted his fingers, muttered in a language older than the Lords of Hell, and tendrils of black smoke billowed from the pores of his left hand. Naberus staggered backward, eyes widening at the sight of that smoke, and it was all Lazarus could do not to kill him. When he'd uttered the spell, that had been his intention, but a cold splinter of sanity stabbed his brain and he reminded himself that if he killed Naberus, he would have to summon another gateway demon from Hell and that would take time.

Instead of killing Naberus, Lazarus took an eye. The smoke shot toward the gateway demon's face, touched his left eye, and it too became smoke.

Naberus clapped a massive hand to his face and fell to his knees, screaming.

Lazarus knelt beside him as a dozen black-hoofed demons, his personal guard, rushed to surround them both.

'It is the *wrong world*, you imbecile,' Lazarus snarled.

Naberus cursed him profusely, but quietly.

'What was that?'

'I am heartily sorry, Majesty. Once I can identify your source world, I will begin again. Though I'll have to start with one portal, an anchor point, just as I did here, I swear to you that I will bring your whole army through. It's only that we used cells from your body as a base for the search for your world, and there have been versions of you on so *many* worlds.'

'You'll have to be more precise, then, won't you?' Lazarus replied.

Haagenti let out a cry that shook the sky and shattered every window at the front of the hospital, as well as the glass in all of the cars in the lot that had not already tumbled into the flaming hole in the ground. It was a joyous cry of celebration, and Lazarus stood, brushing grit from his knees. So magnificent was Haagenti, so enormous, that Lazarus would have to use magic just to communicate with it, but he gazed upon it now with wonder and anticipation.

Most of the Lords of Hell despised him, but paid obeisance out of fear or practicality. Haagenti may have felt the same, though Lazarus was confident in their alliance. Their goals were the same, though their purposes divergent.

'If you don't find the way into my world by dawn,' Lazarus said, not even glancing at Naberus, 'I will offer you to Haagenti as host for its next brood and I will use all the magic at my disposal to make sure you don't die as his spawn begin to hatch inside you.'

Naberus stood much taller than Lazarus, but now he seemed to shrink.

Black hooves clacked against pavement as his personal guard shuffled aside and a scaly, yellow devil pushed through, leading a crimson-fleshed, spiny-tailed imp behind him.

'Majesty!' the imp said breathlessly, glancing up at the much larger demons in fear of being crushed beneath their hooves.

'Thresu,' Lazarus said, frowning in surprise. He had left the imp and his twin to stand watch over the Shadows he had left to suffer in the Pit, to warn him in case they managed to escape or others of their kind arrived. He felt sure he had not discovered all of the vampires who had been flushed into Hell by Gaea. 'Don't tell me they've actually escaped.'

The imp wrapped himself in his own tail, spines piercing his flesh and drawing beads of thick black blood. Thresu did not even flinch. Such pain was a comfort to his kind, like his own mother's caress.

'Not escape,' the imp replied, eager to share the news. 'They were rescued, Majesty.' He bowed his head, bobbed it twice, and his tail unfurled from around him before he straightened to meet Lazarus's gaze.

'Octavian is in Hell, tracking down his friends,' Thresu said. 'Teucer is keeping an eye on them.'

A wave of ecstasy went through Lazarus and this time his smile was one of joy. The imp had spoken the sweetest words imaginable.

Lazarus turned to Qennes, the captain of his personal guard.

'If you have Thresu's scent, you can find his brother. Track Teucer until you find Octavian. You won't have to capture him to lure him here. He's looking for his friends. Just tell him Allison and Kuromaku are with me.'

Qennes bowed and rushed off, taking two of the other black hoofs with him.

As the captain went, Lazarus frowned and glanced at the hospital. He reached within himself and took up the magical tethers he had used to bind the two Shadows and tried to summon them. Only then did he realized that he could barely feel their presence, and when he attempted to exert control over them, his magic could not grasp them. They were still here, somewhere inside.

But the Shadows had slipped their leash.

15

Phoenix's World
Ardsley-on-Hudson, New York, USA

The metal door felt cool to the touch. Phoenix pressed her hand flat against it and then leaned her whole body onto its smooth surface and put her cheek to the painted steel, appreciating its solidity. Its ordinariness and reliability. If not for the tremors that vibrated the whole building around her, she might have been able to pretend that nothing had changed, that she had come here to visit her father and gotten turned around enough to end up in the employee-only stairwell.

If there had ever been a time for pretending, it had passed. Anything but direct and drastic action was a luxury, now. Even this moment, appreciating the cool touch of the metal door, was an indulgence. When Kuromaku had spared her life she had hurried through the basement, but she'd had no intention of leaving. It had been the work of ninety seconds and two swift but wrong turns to find the dismembered body of a maintenance worker and to wipe the blood off his ID card, which doubled as the key that had let her into the secure stairwell that was meant only for staff. She and Ronni had used the same stairs.

Ronni, she thought, forcing her eyes shut and pressing her forehead against the door. Regret and grief washed over her. She had barely known the nurse but in the short time they'd spent together, Phoenix had come to like and respect her.

She made her own choices, Phoenix told herself. And yet she could not help but feel responsible. Whatever she did now would be as much for Ronni as it would be for herself.

There had been no demons blocking her way down in the basement, nor on the stairs. They had all made their way to the lobby to kneel and worship Lazarus, the sorcerer who was apparently their monarch. That ought to make it easy for her to do what she needed to do. The spirits who'd spoken through Annelise believed that burning her father's corpse would close the door Naberus had opened – that it might close all of the doors that had been created afterward, as if they were all somehow tied to the first one. And maybe they were; this shit was magic, and what did Phoenix Cormier know about that?

In her pocket, she had a blue Bic lighter, the crappy plastic kind available at every gas station and convenience store in America. The maintenance worker from whom she'd taken the ID badge had a pack of Winston cigarettes tucked into his shirt pocket. From what had remained of his facial features and the grey of his hair, she pegged him at about fifty. The good news was he wouldn't have to worry about lung cancer anymore.

CHRISTOPHER GOLDEN

A smile touched her lips and she let out a soft sound comprised half of laugh and half of whimper. *Not funny, Fee,* she imagined her dead father saying. And he'd have been right. He might have had a serious deficit when it came to his social skills, but Professor Joe Cormier had nearly always been right.

All she had to do was open the door, go down the hall about fifty feet and into his father's room, and flick her Bic. Her father's corpse had already been doused in gasoline. He would burn like kindling. If she could just breathe, she would be able to move. If she could just grip the door knob and give it a twist. If she could just push her fear down a little deeper. Keep her hands from shaking. Erase the faces of demons that seemed to haunt her mind. If she could just . . .

If she could just.

Phoenix knocked her forehead against the door, took a breath, and then peeked through the narrow, rectangular window at the blood-painted corridor where Dr Song still hung from the ceiling. He had dropped lower, his intestines beginning to sag. Bile rose in the back of her throat and she choked it back.

'Go,' she whispered.

She waved the stolen ID badge in front of the security pad, heard the lock disengage, and hauled the door open. Sticking the badge into her pocket beside the Bic, she hurried into the corridor. On the floor were the bloody footprints she and Ronni had left behind earlier, and she followed them as if they were a yellow brick road. Lights buzzed and machines beeped and she could hear the muffled chanting of demons from outside and the rumble of the earth, but nothing moved in the corridor. The sound of her own heartbeat and the soft, sticky pad of her boots on the linoleum seemed inordinately loud.

212.

214.

216.

The demon that stepped out of room 218, her father's room, moved like an orangutan, hunched and grunting, its long arms dragging along the floor. Its flesh sagged on a frame of jutting bones, skin oily black with the wet, shifting colours of an oil slick.

Phoenix froze. She and the demon stared at each other.

Should've found a weapon, she had time to think, and then the demon extended its impossibly long left arm and pointed at her. Its mouth opened almost comically wide.

'Oh, this is perfect,' it said. 'Malthus, come out here. Didn't I tell Naberus someone needed to guard the door?'

The thing that appeared in the doorway of room 218 behind it seemed ordinary by comparison – a devil, crimson-fleshed and black-horned. Its eyes glowed a sickly orange and it grinned as it spotted Phoenix.

'Let's eat her,' it said.

Shit, she thought. She had failed her father again. Her only choices were to run or die, and if she lived, at least she could try to warn the world. With that thought came an epiphany. She had wanted to be the one to purify her father's remains, and close the doorway if she could. But she didn't really *have* to be the one – an airstrike would do the same thing, if she could manage to get out of the hospital alive.

She backed up a step.

Down the hall the way she'd come, the security door swung open. Phoenix spun to see Kuromaku and Allison emerge, and she felt her heart clench. *Vampires*, she thought, and she sank against the blood-streaked wall.

Not for the first time that day, Phoenix knew that she was about to die.

Not for the first time that day, Phoenix was wrong.

The orangutan-demon, the bag of bones, gave the vampires a wary look. 'What are you two doing up—'

Kuromaku moved so fast that he took Phoenix's breath away, streaking past her with such speed that she did not even see him draw his sword. One moment, his hands were empty and, the next, he had bridged the distance between himself and the bag of bones and his katana sliced a whickering arc across its neck. The blade cut so deeply that its head toppled backward, dangling on a knobby cable of spine. Kuromaku reached in with his free hand, grabbed hold of that bit of spine, and snapped it, dropping the orangutan-demon's head to the floor.

The devil behind it reached for Kuromaku but something lunged at it through the air, a thing like a lion but with the wings of an eagle. It knocked the devil down, clawed open its chest, and then snapped its jaws over its head, cracking bone in its teeth.

Phoenix stared as the winged lion – *Gryphon*, she thought, *it's something like that* – stood on its hind legs and its flesh seemed to *flow*. A heartbeat later, Allison stood in its place and Phoenix understood that these things weren't anything like the vampires she'd read about in stories.

Kuromaku stared at her, dark and intense. 'You have a plan,' he said. 'You came up here for a reason.'

She pulled out the lighter, the little piece of blue plastic seeming more absurd than ever.

'My father's corpse is in that room. The demon with the crown of bones – Naberus – he made my dad the doorway that started all of this. I soaked him in gasoline before. I think if I burn him—'

'Do it,' Allison interrupted, and Phoenix saw a hint of purple light in her eyes.

'Are you—' Phoenix began.

Kuromaku stiffened, the same light coming into his eyes as well. 'Do as she says. We have a fight of our own. Finish what you started and be quick about it.'

Phoenix took a breath, nodded, and started into her father's hospital room, stepping around the two demon sentries that the vampires had just slaughtered.

The door at the end of the corridor exploded inward and vivid emerald light shone through, so bright it made Phoenix twist away, but not before she saw the silhouette of Lazarus stepping through the wreckage of the door frame. She glanced up as the light faded and saw the massive, black-hoofed devils that followed him.

'Go!' Kuromaku snapped.

Phoenix didn't need to be told. She ran into the room as the vampires turned to face the master whose influence still shone in their eyes. Her father's corpse lay ruined on the bed, his whole belly and chest open, and now she could see a black nothingness pulsing at his core. The door Naberus had dug through her father's body remained open.

She glanced at her father's face, wished she had time to give his forehead a kiss, and struck the thumbwheel on the lighter. A small jet of flame arced up from it and she brought it toward his pale, dead, outflung arm, thinking that it would be like lighting logs in the fireplace, needing to ignite one spot and then another. But it caught instantly, the gasoline soaked into the sleeve of his hospital Johnny blazing into flame that roared and spread across first fabric and then flesh and hair, engulfing the last earthly remains of Professor Joe Cormier so fast that Phoenix held her breath.

In the corridor, something cried out in pain. She heard the sounds of savagery and bloodshed and something that had to be the static hiss of magic. Kuromaku and Allison were fast and impossibly strong and could transform, it seemed, into almost anything, but Lazarus had defeated and controlled them once. They had no chance.

'Goodbye, Daddy,' Phoenix said. Something else she had done more than once today.

The black pit at his core wavered as the hungry fire consumed his flesh, and then the whole room seemed to undulate, as if reality had become liquid. The room contracted somehow, drawn toward her father's corpse, and then with a pop as loud as a gunshot, it released. The pit remained, but now she could see it shrinking, falling away into an endless abyss inside her father's chest. Diminishing as he burned.

Phoenix didn't even hear the black-hoofed demon enter. Huge hands closed on her skull and left arm and then it tugged her off of her feet and slammed her against the wall. Bright sparks of pain lit her up and she knew bones had broken, but then the demon smashed her into the wall again and she felt ribs snap, sharp edges stabbing her deep inside, puncturing and tearing.

She stared at the demon's sneering face.

Dying, Phoenix thought. *I'm dying*.

When the slender, female hands slid around the demon's head from behind, it seemed almost like a dream. Those hands grabbed it tight and twisted so hard that the demon's head reversed direction, and Phoenix found herself staring at the back of its skull as it fell to the ground.

Allison stood behind it. 'You done?'

Phoenix didn't even have time to answer as the vampire snatched her up in powerful arms and carried her across the room. Allison twisted as she hurtled them both toward the window, taking the impact herself. With a leap, she threw them both at the glass, shattering it, and then they were out in the October night, falling through the darkness, plummeting toward the ground that was all too close.

It was kind of Allison, she thought, to try to save her life.

Too late, though.

Too late.

Hell

Octavian's sword dripped. Blood and marrow decorated the blade and spattered his long coat and the front of his shirt. The toe of his left boot had been smeared with pink brain matter. It had been years since he had felt the bloodlust that was the curse of the Shadows, but in moments like this, when his heart raced in the aftermath of battle and his skin felt flushed, he remembered that hunger very well.

'Well, wasn't that a party?' Squire said. He produced a cigar from an inner coat pocket and proceeded to light it up.

'Too early to celebrate, 'gob,' Alex said curtly.

Squire made a pouty face and then shot her the middle finger, puffing on his stogie. He glanced at Octavian.

'You never mentioned your "sister" was such a bitch.'

273

Octavian ignored them, watching Kazimir and Charlotte as they moved through the ornate chamber, checking to make sure that all of the demons they had just fought were truly dead and not just faking it. They had come too far to turn their backs on any hellions who might then get the drop on them. Teucer had led them to one of the temples of Lord Abraxas – a temple that the imp claimed had been ceded to Lazarus. The doors had been open, with hundreds of demons camped outside and legions more approaching. This was the army Lazarus had been amassing.

'We can't stay here,' Alex said.

Octavian glanced at her. 'I'm aware.'

'So what are—'

'I'm thinking,' Octavian said.

Teucer had led them here along a narrow crevice, a treacherous path that only a spy would ever choose. Kazimir had only managed it by transforming himself into mist and drifting after them, and Octavian wouldn't have made it without magic.

Massive fists hammered at the doors to the temple. Octavian saw Charlotte flinch. The young Shadow stared at some of the carvings on the walls that showed the kind of torment that the worshippers of Abraxas could expect as reward for their loyalty, and the sound of the demons outside attempting to crash through the door made her rightly nervous.

Charlotte seemed to sense the weight of his attention and turned toward him with a worried, pleading look.

'We need to go,' she said.

She and Kazimir had suffered much in the Pit, but Octavian was more concerned about Alexandra. The torture and imprisonment she had endured would have driven most

– even immortals – over the brink of insanity. When he'd been similarly imprisoned, he had studied magic and nurtured the spark of it, honing his skills, learning the Gospel of Shadows, but Alex hadn't had anything like that.

'Hey,' he said, moving toward her.

Alex lifted her chin in defiance, as if she expected some kind of challenge or accusation. 'You done thinking?'

'In a second. Are you ready for this? When we go through there are likely to be hundreds of demons. I don't know how overrun this world is going to be and there are only going to be four of us.'

Kazimir stomped his massive foot down onto the skull of a demon with a wet crunch and then glanced at them. 'Five.'

'Four,' Octavian said again.

'You don't think I'm going to stay here,' Alex said.

'Not you. And not my point. It's just going to be us. I need to know you can focus once we're in the middle of—'

'I can handle myself.'

'You're one of the most merciless fighters I've ever seen, yeah. No question. But I need you there with a clear head.'

Alex stared angrily at him, but then her gaze softened and she nodded slowly. 'It's as clear as it's gonna get for a while. Maybe ever.'

The hammering at the temple door became louder and more insistent and Octavian thought he heard stone begin to crack. Teucer sat in a corner, curled into a fetal ball and whimpering. He'd been like that since Octavian and his friends had assaulted the demons inside the temple – what Teucer called pilgrims, because they were on a journey to a new world. The roar and shriek of demon voices reached Octavian and he felt satisfaction at their fury.

'Teucer,' he said, striding toward the imp and crouching beside him. 'You know that if we get through this nexus – the gateway Lazarus is using – and I find out you've been lying to me about any of it—'

The imp snapped his head around and stared at Octavian with its sunken eyes. 'The bottle, I know. Oh, why must I suffer? I tell my brother all the time that I was born to suffer.'

'You were born in Hell,' Squire said. 'That's a start.'

Charlotte and Kazimir had finished the job and stepped across the carnage they had all created to join Octavian, Squire, and Alex.

'Peter, we've got to get out of here,' Charlotte said, wiping her bloody hands on her clothes. 'What are we waiting for?'

Octavian glanced at Squire. 'I have an idea.'

'If it involves me in a tutu, you can forget it.'

'Is he *ever* serious?' Alex sneered, glaring at the hobgoblin.

'Every other Tuesday from noon to three,' Squire replied.

Deep green fire rippled along Octavian's hands and up his arms.

'Enough!' he snapped, and turned to Squire. 'I have a job for you. That's why I said four instead of five. The more I roll this all around in my head the more I realize we need a Plan B, and that's going to be you.'

Decades past, when Octavian and Squire had first become allies and friends, he had seen many people underestimate the hobgoblin. Squire's penchant for profanity and wise-cracks made it easy to overlook his intelligence, but Octavian had never made that mistake. Even now, he saw the dark gleam of suspicion in Squire's eyes.

'I'm not gonna like this, am I?' the hobgoblin said.

'Not in the least. It's not an easy thing for me to ask and it won't be an easy thing for you to accomplish. But if you're willing to try, and it works, it may make all the difference. Whatever world Lazarus has invaded, it may not be the one where I was born, but I'd wager it's still full of life. Parallel dimension or not, people are dying—'

'You don't have to fuckin' sell me, Pete. Just give me the bad news. What's the job?'

With the others looking on, Octavian walked Squire a short distance away, stepping over dead demons. Teucer's tiny pink eyes had been alert and attentive and Octavian could not risk the imp overhearing.

When Octavian had finished, Squire hung his head a moment.

'Will you do it?' Octavian asked.

The hobgoblin glanced up at him. 'You can be a son of a bitch, you know that?'

'When I need to be,' Octavian said. He turned to the others. 'Let's go. Be ready as we go through the gateway. There's no way of knowing how many demons have already passed through. And whatever happens, steer clear of Lazarus. You kill demons and you save lives, and you let me worry about the turncoat sorcerer.'

Squire pulled his axe from its sheath. Charlotte and Kazimir stood together and Octavian approved – they were becoming something of a team, watching each other's backs. Here he was in Hell, building yet another new coven. Maybe, just maybe, they would all be able to keep each other alive.

'Come on, imp,' Alex said, snatching Teucer off the ground. The little demon whimpered.

Without its tail, Teucer seemed a pitiful creature, little more than a cur with the power of speech, but Octavian knew imps could be cunning, and did not intend to turn his back on the demon, with or without its tail.

They had been in an antechamber, full of graven images of Abraxas, but now Octavian led the way into a circular room at the heart of the temple. Blue light danced and wavered in the middle of the room, a nexus not unlike the one that he and Squire had passed through before, but with one difference. In the middle of the nexus, there floated a small crimson stain, a little puddle of blood suspended in mid-air, undulating with the shimmering of that portal.

Teucer ceased its whimpering and fell limp in Alex's grip, surrendering itself to whatever was to come next. Octavian decided they all could learn by the imp's example. He tightened his grip on the handle of his sword – its blade so bloody that he could not longer tell which side of the blade was which – and entered the nexus, as the others followed.

The world shifted around Octavian as he left Hell behind. Four or five steps, and he emerged into another world, in the devastated lobby of a hospital, judging by the insignia on the wall. The portal he'd stepped through had been sculpted from the corpses of the freshly dead, and Octavian let the horror of their mutilation envelope him. A pair of yellow-fleshed demons with long arms and three scimitar-like bladed fingers on each hand had been left to guard the portal.

With a wave of his hand and a muttered breath, Octavian turned the one on his left to stone. The other began to turn just as Alex came through the portal with a squeaking Teucer clutched in her hands, and Octavian stepped forward and brought his sword around in an arc that sliced off the top four inches of the demon's skull. It flopped to the ground with a wet slap.

Octavian turned toward the outer wall of the lobby, where all of the windows had been blown out and a cool autumn wind swept in. He counted a dozen demons lined up at the windows, watching the spectacle of a towering, tentacled, mantis-like Demon Lord dragging itself into this world with a screeching wail that reverberated across the sky like the death cry of a murdered god. Only one of them turned at the sound of the sentry hitting the floor, and its eyes went wide as it watched Kazimir, Charlotte, and Squire follow Alex and Teucer through the portal.

'Son of a—' Squire muttered. 'What did I do?'

Octavian pointed his sword and summoned a bolt of pure magical force from within. Green static buzzed around the hilt of the sword and then arced from the end of the blade and blew the demon who'd spotted them through the shattered windows, its back breaking bits of window frame as it went.

The other demons in the lobby turned toward them, startled, and the Shadows waded into battle. Kazimir and Charlotte attacked, but Alex hesitated just long enough to take Teucer in both hands and twist, snapping his neck with a crack. She tossed him to the ground and glanced at Octavian.

'Imps are treacherous,' she said. 'He'd have found some way to pay us back.'

She was right, of course, but still Octavian didn't like it. Teucer had been a demon, but Octavian had given his word.

A shambling, razor-haired demon lumbered at him, gnashing its teeth. Octavian could have turned it to stone or ice if he'd had just a second to think about it, but with a sword in his hand he was a different man. He had been a warrior long before he had become a Shadow or a sorcerer, and old habits died hard. He dodged the demon's claws and cut it across the abdomen, splitting its belly.

Then he left the others to the immediate task of eliminating the other demons in the lobby and turned to Squire.

The hobgoblin hadn't moved. He stood staring at the portal they'd come through, and Octavian blinked as he realized that something had happened. The portal had died. Through the corpse archway, he could see the other end of the lobby. This wasn't a doorway anymore. The arch had begun to collapse, cadavers shifting, sliding against one another. Octavian flinched as the broken, flayed body of a teenage boy dropped from the upper part of the arch and landed with a crack of breaking bone.

'What happened?' Octavian asked.

'No idea,' Squire said. 'I felt it shut right as I came through. Almost sucked me back through. Pulled free just in time, but it was a near thing.'

'A puzzle for later.' Octavian pointed at the deep shadows behind the upended registration desk. 'You need to go.'

Squire shot him a hard look. 'Plan B.'

'We've got to stop Lazarus, whatever it costs.'

'Only if he agrees,' Squire replied, but he had already turned away.

Octavian watched as Squire raced into those dark shadows and vanished, not quite certain if the hobgoblin would return. No matter the outcome of the battle to come, he knew that Squire would never forgive him.

16

Phoenix's World
Ardsley-on-Hudson, New York, USA

Phoenix knew she was dying. She lay on her back with one leg broken and bent beneath her. Allison had twisted as they fell to take most of the impact, but Phoenix's left leg had been tangled with the vampire's and the snap of her bones had resonated in her mind even as the impact jarred her. Pain had blacked her out and now she found herself looking at the night sky, darkness at the edges of her vision as her breath came in ragged, gurgling gasps.

'I'm sorry,' a voice said. 'I wasn't fast enough.'

Allison's face moved into view above her and, lost somewhere in her own drifting thoughts, Phoenix thought it so peculiar that such a lovely woman could be a monster. The vampire looked formidable, yes, but her eyes were full of what seemed decades' worth of regret. They were so human.

CHRISTOPHER GOLDEN

Fast enough, Phoenix thought. For some reason that seemed funny. These vampires were so fast her eyes had been barely able to track them, but still Allison had not arrived in time to keep the demon from slamming Phoenix against the wall of her father's hospital room, from crushing her. From killing her.

She cocked her head slightly to the right and spikes of pain stabbed her through the chest and back. Deep pain, not muscular. She had hurt herself in the past, broken a couple of ribs and torn muscles, but this – oh, this was nothing at all like that. Once, she had owned an antique clock, an heirloom that she had inherited from her great-grandfather at the age of nine. Too young for such a beautiful, precious item but, apparently, she had often admired it when visiting the old man with her mother, and he had wanted little Fee to have it. Within days of his funeral, she had accidentally knocked it from her bureau. The glass had broken, but glass could be replaced, so she had not been overly concerned until she had picked it up and heard little bits of the clock's mechanisms rattling around inside.

The demon that had smashed her against the wall had shattered her inner workings just the way she'd broken her great-grandfather's clock, and her mechanisms were rattling inside of her.

Her fingers were cold. She could not feel her broken leg aside from the screaming pain in her left hip.

Phoenix blinked, and the world went away.

Blinked again, and saw stars.

'You still with me?' Allison asked.

The night sky filled with distant screams and sirens and the ground trembled beneath Phoenix and she knew these were the sounds and feelings of Hell beginning to spread its influence. As she lay here dying, others were dying not far away. But how many?

'Hey,' Allison said, and nudged her.

Phoenix tried to scream but could only cough, which set broken bones moving in her chest and gave her a fresh rush of pain that lit up like fireworks in her head. Through some miracle of cruelty, she managed to stay conscious as the pain stabbed into her and her light cough brought a burble of thick spittle out of her mouth to slide down her cheek. The copper stink of blood filled her nostrils and she knew it had come from inside her.

Coughing up blood, she thought. *Not long, now.*

'What's your name?' Allison asked.

'Fee. I mean . . . Phoenix.'

'Phoenix. That's a great name. Cleansing fire, rebirth and redemption. You could do a lot worse.'

'Did it work?' Phoenix managed to ask.

Allison glanced back up at the hospital, and Phoenix realized they were not where they had fallen but fifty yards away just at the edge of the woods at the back of the hospital. At some point, while Phoenix had been unconscious, Allison had moved her . . . but not far.

'They haven't come after us,' Allison said. 'If Kuromaku had killed them all, he'd have joined us by now. He's either been killed or captured. Either way, Lazarus would have come after us – or sent someone after us – unless he encountered a sudden huge distraction. I'd guess having his portals all slam shut would qualify. So, yeah, I'd say it probably worked or we'd be dead right now.'

Phoenix thought she might be smiling. She certainly intended to smile, but could no longer tell if her facial

283

muscles were obeying her brain's commands. Tiny black motes like dust floated across her visions and the shadows encroaching on the periphery of her eyesight continued to spread.

'Soon enough,' she thought she said.

Allison frowned but didn't argue. Phoenix figured she had seen death up close often enough to know it when it lay broken and bleeding in front of her. It should have felt like victory for Phoenix. Her father's remains had been purified by fire. The demons couldn't use his flesh anymore. But somehow . . .

'It's not . . . enough,' she tried to say.

'I know,' Allison said, placing a gentle hand on her forehead. 'I'm sorry.'

'Lazarus . . . Naberus . . . they have to pay,' Phoenix choked out, frothy blood bubbling from her lips. Her voice sounded like little more than a whisper, even in her own ears.

Inside of Phoenix, an ember burned, fuelled partly by hate and anger, but at its core was love. Her mother had given her a foundation of righteous love and her father, though absent for much of her life, had helped to nurture that love in recent years through his faith in her. Could she quit now? Could she leave the fight against such evil to others?

What choice do you have? she asked herself.

Allison gazed kindly down upon her. Phoenix frowned, swallowed back some of her own blood, and found an answer.

'You,' she gurgled.

'What?' Allison asked. 'What did you—'

'Can you . . . is it like the stories? Phoenix managed. 'Can you make me . . . like you?'

*   *   *

Allison stared at the dying woman. The blood she kept coughing up had streaked both of her cheeks and pooled on either side of her head, soaking into her blonde hair. She had minutes to live, but Allison felt frozen.

'Please,' Phoenix gurgled.

A wave of nausea passed through Allison. She shook her head slowly, and then more rapidly.

'I can't,' Allison managed. 'I'm sorry, I . . .'

Phoenix's eyes narrowed. Even dying, with consciousness fleeting, somehow she had interpreted the reply correctly. Allison could see in Phoenix's eyes that she understood the nuance in her inflection. It wasn't the mechanics of it – Allison could turn Phoenix into a vampire if she chose to do so.

Though dying, Phoenix still had the ability to cry. Tears filled her eyes and slid down her temples, parallel to the trails of blood.

'Why?'

Allison had too much respect for the woman – for her loss and her courageous spirit – to turn away, so she kept her gaze locked on Phoenix's, but she did not reply. Images shot through her mind, memories that seared her soul. Though she had been in love with a man who was already a Shadow, Allison had chosen to remain human—to stay mortal. Then she had been abducted by a vampire named Hannibal, who had tortured and raped her, and who had *turned* her just so he could continue to torture and rape her for as long as he desired.

'I can . . . fight,' Phoenix said, the puddling blood making a circle at the edges of her hair, now. A crimson halo. 'I'm . . . not afraid. We had—' She coughed, features etched in pain, and a fresh spasm of blood bubbled from her lips. 'Years ago, the dead came back . . . to life. The Uprising. Zombies . . . killed thousands. I helped . . . end it.'

The dying woman fixed Allison with a flinty, unyielding look and spoke one brief sentence without the moist, guttural accent of blood in her throat.

'You *need* me.'

Allison tried to force images of rape and torture from her mind, replacing them with thoughts of love. She'd had the greatest love of her life even after being turned. She'd suffered ugly betrayal but also found great loyalty and friendship, and she had saved countless lives. Done so much good.

'This happened . . .' Phoenix continued, though her eyes could no longer focus and her head had begun to loll to one side. Death had crept closer. 'I was here and I . . . got away. Could have . . . run. I came back to burn . . . my father's body. To . . . help. How many people would – would do that?'

Allison stared at her. Once, Peter Octavian had told her the story of the night that he himself had been transformed into a Shadow. They had been within the walls of Constantinople as the Turks besieged the city. Karl von Reinman had offered Octavian the opportunity to slaughter as many of the enemy as he liked, and made no secret about what he would be sacrificing, the life of darkness and blood-thirst he would be choosing. That night, von Reinman had asked how many would accept the gift and curse he was offering, and Octavian had replied.

That reply echoed in Allison's mind now.

'How many . . .' Phoenix tried to choke out again.

Allison shushed her, took her hand.

'One,' she said.

One.

And she bent to drink of the dying woman's blood, and to share of her own.

Danny's World
Boston, Massachusetts, USA

Over the years that he had spent in Mr Doyle's house, Danny Ferrick had become a fervent reader. As his appearance became more monstrous and his public forays fewer, he had spent many evenings in a wing chair in the corner of what had once been Mr Doyle's library. One entire section of shelving remained bare, the removal of the occult tomes that had lined those shelves one of Mr Doyle's final acts before he vanished from Danny's life. But Danny had no interest in arcane texts. The magic he sought from books came from their pages, from the stories that inspired him and created fanciful landscapes in his mind.

Tonight, he sat sprawled in that wing chair, one of the few in the house that did not bow beneath his weight, and enjoyed the texture of the book in his hands and the smell of the old, yellowing paper. Candles burned on plates and in sconces around him, plenty of light for his inhuman eyes to read by, and their golden glow cast an eerie pall upon the room. Apropos, he thought, for reading Ray Bradbury on a night in October.

Every year at this time, he read a couple of Bradburys, one of which would always be *The Halloween Tree,* which he had finished two days ago. The second choice varied from year to year, and tonight he sat completely immersed in that other selection. The room had been stripped of any objects of power, but there were still carved knick knacks and mementoes of Mr Doyle's life in the room, and they made peculiar shadows in the flickering glow of candle light that permeated the room. A draught that blew through the house and the scurry of an animal in the corner of the room made Danny jump. The scritch-scratch of its claws on the wood made him realize he had a rat for company, but then he heard the hiss of a cat, and he thought they both must have discovered some space behind the walls that they believed had been reserved as the personal arena for their combat. Danny had seen mangy stray cats in the house before, and if this was the torn-eared ginger he had spotted a week or so ago, he knew the rat had no chance.

He listened to them scuffle for half a minute and then the thumping and scratching died down and he returned to his reading. It comforted him to sit there amongst the books. Over the past year or so he had begun to make great stacks of them, pulling those that interested him off of the shelves and creating his own strange catalogue of preference, piles of both fiction and non-fiction that he had decided to read. The very presence of those stacks made him feel a lovely sort of pressure, a weight of expectation that was one of the few things he could focus on when he needed to clear his head.

Sometimes the books comforted him, as they had belonged to Mr Doyle, but other times they only served to make him lonelier than ever.

The scratch of nails upon wood came again, but this time it hadn't come from any crawlspace. Danny frowned and placed a finger in his book. He looked up just in time to see the torn-eared ginger dart across the library. It scraped itself against one of Danny's to-be-read piles and the tower of books collapsed, spilling across the floor.

Danny hissed at the cat and it froze, arched its back and turned to stare at him. Spitting and hissing in return, it continued its retreat warily. He looked like the sort of creature who would eat a cat, he knew, but that was only because he might actually do it. He didn't think he ever had, but his mind slipped sometimes, grey areas blotting out places where memory ought to have been, so he could not swear that he had never partaken.

'Get out of here, you little shit,' he snarled, his voice low.

The cat slithered beneath Mr Doyle's desk, hid there a moment, and then bolted across open space to the door, vanishing into the hall. Danny hoped it didn't piss in the house but knew that it probably would. The place had become an elegant sort of zoo, a well-appointed urban animal shelter, where pigeons and squirrels and rats and even stray pets came to nest or hide or, in the case of a Dobermann with blood on its matted fur, to have babies. The animals scattered when he came near, but it gave him a bit of solace that they did not seem terrified of him.

Danny settled in again, searching the page for the passage where he had left off. He found it and remembered it quite well as one of his favourites. So much a favourite, in fact, that this page had been turned down and certain bits underlined for emphasis, so he would not forget to appreciate them each time he came upon them again.

'Sometimes, the man who looks happiest in town,' he read aloud to himself, 'is the one carrying the biggest load of sin . . . On the other hand, that unhappy, pale, put-upon man walking by, who looks all guilt and sin, why, often that's your good man with a capital G, Will. For being good is a fearful occupation; men strain at it and sometimes break in two.'

A soft exhalation came from the shadows behind Mr Doyle's desk and Danny frowned, glancing over. The cat had fled, and he wondered what manner of vermin haunted the library now.

'*Something Wicked This Way Comes*,' a familiar voice grumbled. Always one of my favourites.'

Danny stared, a big grin widening on his face as he scrambled from the chair. Turning down the page to save his place, he approached the desk, where the flickering candle light crafted oddly-shaped shadows on the features of the ugly little man who sat behind it.

'Squire! How long have you been sitting there?'

'Just arrived, kid,' the hobgoblin replied, with an uncharacteristic sadness on his face that Danny noticed and then chose to ignore.

'Are you staying this time?'

Squire drummed his fingers on the desk, staring at the grain of the wood a moment before lifting his eyes again.

'You've been a hero,' the hobgoblin said. 'You've proven that evil is a choice, that you can follow another path. But you've always been a reactor. Your mother pissed you off and you reacted. Eve wanted you to fight monsters and you reacted. But the time's come, Danny.'

Danny reached up and scratched at the dry skin around the base of one of his horns.

'Time for what?'

Squire's yellow eyes gleamed in the shadows behind the desk. 'Time to grow up, kid . . . Time to stop pretending that you're not your father's son.'

Phoenix's World
Ardsley-on-Hudson, New York, USA

Charlotte stared out through the shattered hospital windows and felt the embrace of despair. Legions of demons had already come into this world and now she and Octavian and a handful of Shadows were supposed to destroy them all? Since Cortez had made her a vampire, she had done nothing but fight and kill, and the constant conflict exhausted her. In crisis after crisis, she did nothing but fight to stay alive, but from the moment Gaea had banished her kind from Earth – her Earth – Charlotte wondered what, precisely, was the point of continuing the battle. Her ordinary life had come to an end when Cortez had turned her, and she had wished many times that he had finished the job.

Instead, he had resurrected her, tried to remake her in his own image. She had rejected that, chosen to follow the path Octavian had paved. But she had not expected to spend her every moment in combat, with the fate of worlds riding on their success or failure.

She stared out at the hospital parking lot and the town beyond. She didn't know the name of the place, but by morning there wouldn't be anything left of it. More fires were burning in the distance and plumes of smoke turned grey-blue against the night. Alarms sounded in the distance and she could hear screams. The demons chanted, most of them

291

gathered as if waiting for some signal, though others moved into the trees on the far side of the lot or shambled or slithered down the drive that led away toward the town. Over the trees, she saw a river, the lights on the far side giving it some sense of breadth, but dark things flew overhead, tendrils hanging beneath them, and she knew those on the opposite bank were not safe. No one would be safe in this world.

'You'll be all right,' Octavian said, stepping up beside her.

She glanced at him, so handsome with his stubbled chin and lopsided grin and the salt and pepper in his hair. Much too old for her, of course, though that seemed to matter less now that she was immortal. More than anything, what was remarkable about Peter Octavian was just how ordinary he seemed. Good-looking and fit and usually fairly intense, but otherwise just a man.

'Will it ever stop?' she asked. 'The chaos and the evil, the damned fighting.'

'When we win,' Octavian replied. 'Or when we lose.'

Alex and Kazimir went past them, a carpet of broken glass crunching beneath their boots as they stepped out into the demon-infested night. Alex glanced back at Charlotte and Octavian in the moonlight, her lovely features gleaming.

'Chaos is an ocean,' Alexandra Nueva said. 'It ebbs and flows and sometimes it rises to destroy those who build their lives beside it. But if you're clever and determined, you just might find a way to hold back the tide.'

Charlotte watched as she transformed, her human shape giving way to something much larger, a kind of winged harpy creature, ten feet tall and with fingers like hooked blades. Perhaps she had seen something like this in Hell, or it had existed in the strange history of the world of their birth.

'What is she?' Charlotte asked, as Alex flapped her leathery wings and shot skyward.

'Deadly,' Kazimir said. He transformed as well, becoming a massive creature not quite man and not quite bear, perhaps some kind of ursine deity from the region of Kazimir's birth. He spoke again, his words a growl. 'Use the gifts you have. You can be just as much a monster as any demon. And don't be afraid to use the sky. They might come at you from above, but you could do—'

Kazimir halted mid-sentence, staring past Charlotte and Octavian, back into the hospital lobby behind them. Charlotte began to turn to see what had caused the giant bear's eyes to widen, but Octavian shouted at her and then flung himself toward her. He wrapped his arms around her as he knocked her to the ground, both of them twisting upon impact, hurrying to rise.

A wave of putrid yellow light surged past them, boiling the air as it enveloped Kazimir. The bear-creature put back its head and shrieked. The stink of burning fur filled the air and Charlotte had a moment to think that Shadows could not really be burned, that it could be nothing truly damaging, and then Kazimir's flesh began to ripple and shift and stretch in all directions as if his body were taffy being pulled by a machine . . . and then he seemed to explode in slow motion, flesh becoming a spray of sparks that burst off in every direction, hardened and hit the ground, skittering amongst the broken glass and then exploding again, this time into sparks almost too small for the eye to see.

Octavian shouted Kazimir's name.

293

Charlotte spun toward the interior of the lobby, where Kuromaku stood with five red-horned, black-hooved demons flanking an olive-skinned man whose very ordinariness put the rest of the scene out of kilter. But the company he kept and the sickly yellow light that flowed and blurred around his hands and wept from his eyes meant she could not mistake Lazarus for anyone else.

'Kuromaku!' she shouted. When he glanced her way she saw the deep purple light gleaming in his eyes and she understood that he was in no danger from the demons; Lazarus had made him an unwilling ally.

The sorcerer turned toward Charlotte and Octavian, thrust out one hand and let loose another volley of magic. Octavian threw up a hand and a shield of sizzling emerald static instantly appeared, deflecting Lazarus's spell. Charlotte glanced over to where Kazimir had been, expecting him to reincorporate, but she saw no evidence of it.

'What did you do to him?' Octavian demanded, rising to his feet, extending that shield into a sphere that surrounded himself and Charlotte.

Lazarus smiled. 'Oh, Peter, you have made me very happy tonight.'

'That spell!' Octavian snapped. 'What *was* that?'

'Think of it as negative polarity,' Lazarus said with a wave of his hand. 'The creatures can control their own molecular structure, just as we both used to be able to do. They can reorganize themselves however they want, into whatever they want, but . . . if those molecules are mutually repellent, they simply can't come together again. Into anything.'

Lazarus glanced at Charlotte. 'Surrender yourself, and I'll let this one live.'

'You already killed the woman I loved!' Octavian raged. If he feared for Kuromaku, he did not let it show. 'There'll be no surrender for either of us. And your portal is shut – there's nowhere to run!'

'Run?' Lazarus said, glancing at one of his black-hoofed demons as if they shared some joke. 'Do you honestly think I'm going to run? I'll admit, the doorway being closed made me furious, but only because it meant a delay in hunting you down. Now you've saved me the trouble. Trust me, there's nowhere I'd rather be than right here with you.'

Octavian glanced at Charlotte. She saw a manic light in his eyes, but with it there were lines she had never seen upon his face before. He carried the rage and thirst for vengeance that drove him, but also an air of fresh sorrow.

'What are you going to do?' she asked. 'Kuromaku—'

'Go kill demons,' he said quietly. 'Go and live, and don't be afraid.'

Charlotte started to argue, and she saw in his eyes that he'd known she would. Octavian gestured toward her with his left hand and a bolt of silver light struck her chest, picked her up, and hurled her backward through the parking lot. She crashed into an old Audi, shattering the windows and caving in the driver's door, and then collapsed to the pavement.

Disoriented and angry, Charlotte rose just as a massive demon slid toward her on a serpent's tail. Its opalescent skin shimmered in the moonlight as it reached for her with thin, three-fingered hands and what she'd thought of as its head opened in a sticky vertical slit, its face like a Venus flytrap. Without thinking, she tore the broken door off of the Audi with a shriek of metal, turned, and beat the demon to death.

She struck it again and again, until its stinking viscera puddled at her feet.

She dropped the door and backed away, glanced around and froze. A spindly bone-demon clambered over the top of a pickup truck parked nearby, intent upon her. A pair of winged skeletons, like the charred corpses of angels, began to circle above her. With a buckling of metal, a massive demon with twin rows of horns up its chest – and little devil faces between each set – landed on the hood of the Audi. She saw devils and several imps, and beyond them, towering so high in the sky that it would never even notice her, the squid-mantis-like Demon Lord that Lazarus had summoned into this world.

With Kazimir dead and Alex off somewhere, Charlotte found herself alone. She had done stupid things, done cruel things, but she had also done heroic things in an effort to atone. This, though ... not long ago she had been just another nineteen-year-old girl trying to figure out what to do with her life. She couldn't handle this. Not alone. But the alternative frightened her even more.

Go and live, Octavian had said, with an air of finality that unnerved her.

'Fuck, yeah,' Charlotte muttered under her breath.

The bone-demon died easy. She leaped at it, let it spear her through the chest with one of its spider legs, snapped off one of its other legs, and stabbed it in the head three times as it twitched and shat itself and bled out. Turning, she yanked the sharp limb from her chest and willed the wound to close, molecules reknitting themselves.

This, she thought, *is what it's supposed to feel like. What we're supposed to be.*

Terror had inspired an epiphany. A leather-skinned devil rushed between cars at her wielding a sword of flame, and so she turned to fire and let it pass through her, drifting past it and reforming behind it. With swiftness even Hell could not mimic, she shifted into the body of a gorilla, grabbed the demon's head and twisted it so hard that bones snapped and skin tore and dark green blood gouted from exposed arteries.

Charlotte caught the flaming sword as it fell, changing even as she reached for it, and in a blink she was herself again. The huge demon with the horns and faces like an infernal totem pole on its chest dropped down from the Audi's crushed hood and reached for her.

She transformed herself into mist, transforming the sword along with her own flesh and bone. As mist, she slid through its twenty nostrils and ten mouths, and took on flesh again, reforging herself into a gorilla. Her transformation tore the demon apart from the inside and she stood there, breathing deeply out of habit instead of necessity. The flying things still circled above her, but the devils and imps and putrid, reeking things that surrounded her now hesitated to approach.

Charlotte's fear abated. She felt alive.

Only the two sorcerers had the power to kill her, and they were still inside the hospital's atrium, trying to kill each other. There were hundreds of demons here, and more around the world, she was sure, but all she needed was time.

Provided Octavian could stop Lazarus.

A broken, eviscerated devil crashed to the pavement ten feet from where she stood. Manifesting the sword again, Charlotte spun to see two figures striding toward her in the moonlight, and she felt herself grin. The demons backed

297

away even further, some of them actually retreating, wanting to be anywhere be here.

'Well, well,' Allison Vigeant said, tucking a lock of brown hair behind her ear. 'Look at you, with the flaming sword.'

She gestured to the woman beside her, whose angled blond hair partially veiled the wide-eyed amazement of a newborn Shadow.

'Charlotte, meet Phoenix.'

'You turned her?' Charlotte asked, staring at Allison.

'*Just* turned her. She insisted.'

Charlotte nodded to Phoenix. 'Good to meet you. You want us to buy you a few minutes to get your bearings?'

Phoenix's eyes narrowed and she turned to scan the demons, searching the crowd.

'The only thing I want is to kill these assholes. One in particular.'

Charlotte glanced at Allison. 'I like her.'

Together, the three women turned to face the hordes of Hell.

17

Phoenix's World
Ardsley-on-Hudson, New York, USA

Octavian killed two of the black-hoofed demons guarding Lazarus with a muttered spell. The magic surged up from deep within him, cloaking him in a white-hot brilliance, and entropy seized them, racing their natural physical degradation forward at such speed that they withered into ancientness in seconds, collapsed and died and began to decay. Even demons did not live forever.

Lazarus began slowly to applaud. 'Well done,' he said. 'Are you trying to show off, Peter? There must be hundreds of ways you could have dispatched them without expending so much—'

Kuromaku drew his katana and started toward Octavian, then faltered. He blinked like a drunk trying to regain his senses.

Octavian thrust out his right hand and an arc of golden light leaped from his fingers and hurled Kuromaku back through the atrium lobby, where he dropped amongst the wretched, mutilated corpses of the fallen portal.

He had turned his focus away from Lazarus for a moment, and now he realized his mistake. The magic inside of him, deep in his core, felt as if it were being drawn away like a wave receding after crashing upon the shore. Octavian spun just in time to throw up another shield. Lazarus shouted in fury as his leeching spell struck harmlessly against the shield.

No, Octavian thought. *Not harmlessly*. The spell drained at his magic, disrupted the shield he'd summoned. He knew the same spells, could return the favour, but even as he began to sketch his fingers in the air to cast the hex, the three remaining black-hoofed demons rushed at him.

Octavian held his left hand out, palm up, and muttered a spell in the arcane tongue of the earliest druids. Two of the demons turned and attacked each other with claw and fang, brutal and bloodthirsty and blinded by fury, but the spell had missed the third. As it rushed at him, Octavian felt himself slow. His heart beat once and then paused; even his breathing dragged, a single inhalation lingering on and on. His thoughts raced unhindered, but he could not even turn his head toward Lazarus to confirm what he knew – the sorcerer had cast a spell that caught him in time, slowed reality around him. The final black-hoofed demon raged toward him.

Lazarus had underestimated him. Some spells required him to sketch sigils in the air with his hands or to speak arcane incantations, to manipulate the magic already in the world around them. But Octavian had many enchantments and hexes ingrained so deeply within him that they were second nature. Instinct.

The demon careened at him, grabbed hold of his face, about to tear the flesh and muscle right off of the bone. Octavian began a long exhalation, but it required only the very first moment of that breath for the spell to work. The demon blew backward and upward, rising as if on a breeze before it began to flail. Weightless, it snarled and clawed the air but of course it could find no purchase.

The air around Octavian turned a deep purple and he felt pain in his bones as the flesh on his arm began to turn to stone, but he'd been able to collect himself, now. With a whisper, he released a burst of burnished copper light that freed him from his paralysis and blew out across the atrium, shaking the entire lobby. Lazarus staggered backward and Octavian stalked toward him.

'You're bleeding,' Octavian said.

Frowning, Lazarus wiped at his nose and stared at the blood on the back of his hand.

'You're turning to stone,' the sorcerer said.

Octavian did not even glance at his arm. He could feel the skin warming as it changed back, his magic healing him.

'What happened to you?' Octavian asked.

Lazarus sneered, his hatred like a poison inside him. 'You dare ask?'

'You knew the stakes when you entered Hell to find me,' Octavian replied. 'The portal was closing and you'd been impaled. You were being torn apart, burned by the same living crystal that had caged me. Without the proper spells from the Gospel of Shadows, we were sure that by the time we could figure out a way back to you . . . you'd be dead.'

'You could have tried!'

'We intended to, Meaghan and I . . . planned to go back one day and make sure, when there wasn't a crisis to deal with.'

'Always a crisis, while I burned in Hell?'

'And then Meaghan died. And I changed . . . went through the metamorphosis,' Octavian said, drawing magic into his hands, copper light turning a bright gold. 'Eventually, we forgot you. *I* forgot you.'

Lazarus seethed, black light spilling from his eyes and sheathing his forearms and hands.

'You *forgot*? Do you expect that to mollify me?'

Octavian shook his head as the two mages began to move in a circle like wolves fighting for supremacy of the pack.

'You were the favoured of God, Lazarus. You broke bread with His *Son*. He had brought you back from the dead once, and so we thought you must be under His protection. We didn't know we were your only hope.'

'I *burned*!' Lazarus said, and unleashed a hex bolt that Octavian could not identify. That troubled him, not knowing what spell Lazarus had cast. It signified more skill than he'd shown thus far.

Once, Octavian would have felt guilt. But images of his love, Nikki Wydra, murdered in her hotel room were seared forever into his memory. Into his soul. Lazarus had ordered her murder, and thousands – perhaps tens of thousands, across many worlds – had died because of his madness and his thirst for vengeance.

'You blame me,' Octavian said. 'And you have just cause. But I think you want revenge on me because you can't seek vengeance upon the one you truly blame, in your heart. The one who really abandoned you.'

'Kuromaku!' Lazarus shouted.

The samurai rose from the slaughtered dead. He had retrieved his sword, and now he rushed at Octavian. Lazarus had made Kuromaku his puppet. Whatever spell he'd used, no verbal commands were necessary for the sorcerer to pull the Shadow's strings. Kuromaku's purple eyes glowed more brightly and Octavian knew Lazarus had tightened his hold. Kuromaku could have shapeshifted but did not; he ran directly at Octavian, sword raised and fangs bared.

'Go on, then,' Lazarus said. 'Kill your friend. Kill your brother.'

Octavian did not know if this exhortation was meant for Kuromaku or for himself – the sorcerer would have received as much pleasure with either result – but he knew his options were few. His heart thundered and his hold on his own magic slipped just a fraction. Even clumsy and not in control of his own reflexes, Kuromaku was one of the greatest fighters Octavian had ever seen. Shapeshifting, attacking swiftly, he might be able to kill Octavian, or distract him enough that Lazarus could do the job.

He could take no chances.

I'm sorry, 'Maku, he thought as he unleashed a pair of hexes simultaneously. Kuromaku froze and crumbled to the floor as his flesh turned to grey stone. A clock began ticking inside Octavian's mind – he had used two spells inspired by Lazarus, one to transform Kuromaku to stone and another to slow time around him. If he could stop Lazarus quickly enough, he could free Kuromaku.

If.

A hissing filled the air and Octavian glanced beyond Lazarus to see a vertical silver pool forming not far from where the portal of corpses had stood. The pool grew to the size of a mirror, and then continued to grow, all in the space of moments.

'Say hello, Peter,' Lazarus said.

Octavian stared as the portal rippled with some disturbance from beyond.

'What is this?' he demanded.

'I made a deal with the devil,' Lazarus replied, that black energy crackling and misting around his hands as if with a mind of its own. 'Well, not one devil, but all of them. I'm their king, you see. They all kneel before me, now, and in return for their loyalty – and their help in finding and destroying you and the world where we were both born – I'm going to lead them in tearing this one apart. And the next and the next. It thrilled me to have you come to me, to save me the trouble of hunting you any longer, but even your death is just one step. The door you came through is closed . . .'

With a flourish, Lazarus gestured to the portal.

'. . . so we needed another.'

As Octavian looked on, a crimson-black demon with a jack o'lantern mouth stepped through the portal. A gateway demon, Octavian thought, staring at the circle of bone shards that jutted up through its scalp like a crown. It carried a woman over its shoulder.

'Welcome back, Naberus,' Lazarus said. 'I see you've brought us Plan B.'

With a dead imp in her hands, Phoenix stood frozen, staring at Naberus as he emerged from the silver mirror that had appeared inside the hospital atrium. A huge section of the outer lobby wall had been destroyed, turning the scene inside into a surreal sort of stage production, lit by the flickering bulbs and the bright searing glow of the magic Octavian and Lazarus kept hurling at each other. Naberus had a woman slung over one shoulder . . . but she didn't focus on the woman until the doorway demon shrugged her onto the floor and then reached down to haul her up by her hair. The woman might have been unconscious coming through the portal, but pain woke her. Her eyes were wide and bright with shock as she opened her mouth to scream.

Phoenix knew her.

'Annelise,' she whispered. 'No.'

She had left the ageing medium back in Manhattan. Had Naberus tracked her somehow? Had she led the demons right to Annelise? The question made her shudder, but then a cold certainty stole through her. No. The spirits had warned Annelise of disturbances on the ethereal plane, dark powers that did not belong there. The demons had been moving through the spirit world on their way to this one, and Naberus had found her father to use as a doorway, had chosen Professor Joe Cormier because the sensitivity of a medium made the perfect anchor . . .

Oh, my God, she thought.

Phoenix realized what would happen an instant before Naberus punched a taloned fist through Annelise's back. His hand burst from her chest in a spray of blood. Phoenix screamed, even as she heard Octavian shout in fury. The mage hurled green fire at Naberus, only to have it deflected by Lazarus. From this distance, Phoenix could only imagine the sound of flesh tearing and bone splitting as Annelise's blood began to form a new portal in the gaping hole the demon had torn in her chest.

'. . . No no no . . .' Phoenix said, shaking her head in horror. She had sacrificed so much in order to burn her father's remains, to purify him and to close the portals from Hell into this world – Ronni had died in the attempt – and now Naberus had begun anew, with poor Annelise.

She tried not to remember the woman's kind eyes or her gentle voice, but instead they were all she could think about, and cold rage built within her. A stinking, chattering demon stalked toward her on legs that shook with gelatinous fat. Its belly hung nearly to its knees in thick folds and huge tusks jutted from the layers of fat at its neck.

'*Pretty*,' it said, turning the word into a hiss.

Phoenix felt the strength in her limbs, but more than that, she felt the *possibility* in her flesh. In the midst of this bloody battle, she had seen Allison and Charlotte become beasts and monsters and even mist, but Phoenix didn't want to stop there. Focusing on just one hand to begin with, she found that it obeyed her mental commands. The flesh began to change, just a ripple at first and then a flood, until she had become a devil in her own right, massive and powerful and savage. The gluttonous demon never stood a chance. Screaming in fury at the murder of Annelise and at the way her world had been violated, she beat the demon to the ground and stomped on its head with heavy, powerful hooves.

Turning toward the hospital, she began to run in long strides, hooves cracking pavement.

Octavian and Lazarus crashed out through the broken lattice of the atrium's window frames in a flying melee of brutal magic, multi-hued energies clashing and searing the air around them.

A fresh wave of demons marched out through the portal Naberus had made of Annelise's flesh. He pulled and stretched her until no one could have identified her remains, widening the bloody window into Hell, and more and more demons were sliding and crawling and striding from that rift in reality.

Phoenix screamed as she crashed through into the atrium. A dozen demons turned toward her but she plowed past them. Naberus looked up at her with those arachnoid eyes and she saw herself reflected a thousand times – not Phoenix Cormier at all, but a demon like any other. Repulsed, she willed herself to change again, and as she crossed the last few yards toward Naberus and his new portal, she wore her own body. Her own face. The face of Joe Cormier's daughter.

Startled, the crowned demon took a step back from the portal. 'You . . .'

Phoenix bared her fangs. By pure instinct, she hooked her fingers into claws and they lengthened into hardened talons of bone, and then she struck, slashing at Naberus and tearing him open. She drove him to the floor amongst the hospital's dead and grabbed hold of the longest of the broken horns on his head and broke it off, shattered it so deeply that she heard his skull crack.

Naberus roared in fury and bucked against her, slammed the back of a huge hand into her face and knocked her off him. Phoenix crashed to the floor, slid, and scrambled to her feet in an instant, hissing and thirsting not for blood, but for his death.

Stumbling, one hand over the largest of the wounds she had given him, dark blood streaming down his face from the hole where she'd ripped out a horn, Naberus turned toward her.

'How?' the crowned demon asked.

'You killed my father,' Phoenix replied.

'I have killed many fathers,' Naberus said, almost as if he thought he was reasoning with her. 'I'm a *demon*.'

Weeping tears of blood, Phoenix lunged for him again. Naberus raised his hands to defend himself and she turned to mist. Finding herself abruptly without flesh disoriented her for a moment, but her senses had opened up to an extraordinary degree and she became aware of everything around her – the demons, the vampires, the sorcerers, the hospital and its slaughtered dead – and then she coalesced in the air above Naberus. As she dropped toward the floor, she reached down and grabbed hold of two of his horns – one in either hand – and twisted with every ounce of her unnatural strength. The snap as she broke all of the bones in his neck was the most satisfying sound she had ever heard.

The crowned demon fell to the ground and lay still, dull eyes vacant and staring. Phoenix stood over the Naberus's corpse, numb and full of grief, as the battle raged on out in the parking lot. She had taken her revenge . . . but it would not bring her father back to life.

'Daddy,' she whispered, and she sank to her knees and wished that she could still cry human tears.

Octavian swept his sword around in an arc that cleaved the head from a leather-skinned devil and hacked through the abdomen of a ten foot insectoid hellion. Heart hammering, thoughts racing, he sketched a sigil with his left hand and a wave of deep blue magic rippled across the parking lot and turned a quartet of attacking demons to ice that glittered in the moonlight.

'Where'd you go, you bastard?' Octavian shouted.

A scaly, eight-foot worm rushed at him and a pair of wraiths covered in jutting spikes, with tongues like scorpion tails, skittered on top of overturned cars, ready to leap. Octavian needed a shield, and if it came to that he would summon one, but before he worried about defending himself he had to find Lazarus – to end this, before the sorcerer killed more people he loved.

He hit the worm with a hex that made it burn from within. The fires of Hell might not have been able to kill it, but he lit it aflame at its core, and the worm began to scream. Octavian took two quick steps toward it as the worm reared up, and he cut its belly open with a single swipe of the two-edged sword. The ebon side of the blade cut the demon with remarkable ease, as if the sword had a desire and a strength all its own.

He whipped around, seeking Lazarus. When the gateway demon had created a new portal in the hospital's atrium, the fresh influx of demons had been too much for Octavian. He'd been surrounded and couldn't afford the distraction they presented. Killing them would have been simple enough for a mage of his skills, but not while Lazarus was there trying to destroy him, so Octavian had moved the fight out into the parking lot. Charlotte and the others had killed a lot of demons and others had fled. There were still fifty or more, the towering squid-thing included, but the Shadows had thinned the enemy ranks . . . they had bought Octavian time, and room to fight.

But he couldn't fight if Lazarus wanted to hide amongst the wave of demons flowing through the portal. This new incursion had changed the odds dramatically. Octavian and his allies could kill a lot of demons, but if the collected hordes of Hell itself poured out of that portal—

The ground shook, hard enough that Octavian lost his footing and went down on one knee. Sword in hand, he began to rise and turn, but too late. A huge webbed hand closed around his head and lifted him off the ground. Through the thin skin of the webbing he could see the flaming orange light coming from the eyes of his attacker. Its grasp muffled him, though he struggled to utter a spell. The demon's other hand clamped on his, crushing the fingers that held the sword, and he cried out in sudden pain. Octavian expected it to tear the sword from his grip, but instead it twisted his arm to change the blade's direction, then guided his hand and forced him to stab himself in the abdomen. The sword punched through his belly and the tip pushed out through his back, and the demon dropped him to the broken pavement. For the first time, he saw its hideously leering face, saw that jack o'lantern orange glow in its eyes, and knew it was silently laughing at him.

Sprawled on his side, he roared in pain as he ripped the sword from his belly.

Seconds, he thought. He just needed a few seconds to use magic to heal himself, and then another second to manifest a protective sphere.

But Lazarus was there.

The sorcerer stepped between the two scorpion-tongued wraiths and shot out a hand, sickly yellow light lancing from his fingers. Octavian closed his eyes and summoned the magic from his core, manifesting a defensive shield, but when he opened his eyes he saw that Lazarus had trapped him. Bleeding profusely, clutching at his gut, Octavian lay inside his own protective sphere, with a second – putrescent yellow – surrounding it, and contracting. As he fought that pressure, he felt something tearing inside him. Weakened, disoriented, he could heal his wound or he could protect himself from Lazarus and the demons that now began to surround him. Given a few seconds to catch his breath, he might be able to focus, but Lazarus would not give him those precious seconds.

The powerful frisson of magic made his hair stand on end as he tried to concentrate. Rage fuelled him. He and his allies had left Lazarus for dead, left him behind in Hell, but the Shadows had done the same to Octavian himself. They had chosen the known over the unknown, thought him lost, and he had understood it. Lazarus had not.

Images of Nikki filled Octavian's thoughts. In his mind's eye, he could still see the way she had looked on the stage of a club in New Orleans the first time they had met, guitar in hand and full of the effortless grace of music. He could hear her laugh, remember her scent and the warmth of her in bed beside him, recall how easily she had made him believe that being human again was a blessing instead of a curse.

He still loved her.

Octavian calmed his own heart. He turned to glare at Lazarus through the hissing static veil of their combined magic and he felt the wound in his stomach healing . . . and understood. The sword had been made by Squire. For all of his eccentricities, he truly was a master weaponsmith. The two-edged blade had not only cut through his flesh . . . it had slashed through the magic at his core. If he hadn't pulled the blade out, Octavian wasn't sure what it would have done.

That was why the blade cut so smoothly through the dark magic-infused flesh of demons. But now his magic knitted its wounds together even as his flesh did the same. Octavian tightened his grip on the sword and rolled onto his knees, still surrounded by his own protective ward and by the spell with which Lazarus had hoped to kill him. Octavian lifted his head to glare hatefully at the sorcerer.

But Lazarus was no longer looking at him. Frowning worriedly, the sorcerer had turned his attention upon the hospital atrium, and Octavian glanced over to see that – though the portal remained – the flow of reinforcements had ceased. No more demons were coming through.

'Naberus,' Lazarus said quietly, and Octavian realized that the gateway demon was nowhere in sight.

A Shadow – a young blond woman Octavian didn't know – ran out of the atrium, shifted into a fox and raced into the parking lot to join in the fight against the demons.

For a moment, Octavian felt a spark of hope, the promise of triumph.

Then a pair of huge hands pushed through the blood-red portal and stretched it even wider. The demon who stepped through had to have been twenty feet tall, and when he slithered into this world as if from some putrid, malevolent birth canal, he stood up inside the atrium. Illuminated by the bright lights of the hospital lobby, the massive demon was on full display. Its sides and chest and thighs had slits that pouted for air like gills or the mouths of fish.

Another Demon Lord, Octavian thought, and he stared in growing horror as something else pushed itself into the world, coated with blood from the portal as if it were smeared with birth fluids. Its wrinkled, folded skin had a pale translucence that displayed its interior workings, and a smattering of stray hairs that made it look sickly. Its front teeth were long and flat like a mole's, and beneath its tiny eyes – where a nose might have been – it had a nest of wavering cilia better suited to a sea creature.

This one, Octavian knew. *Lord Malephar*.

Lazarus strode toward the atrium, dragging Octavian behind him as if the spell he'd cast were a kind of magical net.

'My Lords!' the sorcerer called, as Lord Malephar stood up to his full height and shattered much of the remaining framework of the atrium.

The other lord with him, whom Octavian thought might be Xezbeth, lay back his head and let loose a cry that shook both heaven and earth. In the parking lot, Lord Haagenti had begun to move away from the hospital, headed toward the river, but now the largest of the Demon Lords halted and turned. Haagenti's tentacles hung loosely and the towering squid-thing bent its head as if to watch the proceedings on the ground, mantis legs clacking on the broken pavement near the hole through which it had emerged.

'Welcome!' Lazarus called, but Octavian could hear the uncertainty in his voice. They weren't supposed to be here, these demons.

Octavian breathed. Calmed his heart. Let his wounds – both of flesh and of magic – heal.

Something smaller moved behind Xezbeth and Malephar. Gazing up at their hideousness, bathed in the malignance and malice that radiated from them, Lazarus had not noticed before now, and neither had Octavian. Compared to the

Demon Lords, this third figure was tiny, though he stood perhaps eight feet tall.

Danny Ferrick.

The Demon Lords stood aside as Danny strode between them. The young demon seemed taller than before, and somehow more demonic, as if his passage through Hell had made him even more his father's son than ever. Beyond Danny, Octavian spotted an even smaller figure, moving just behind the massive bulk of Lord Xezbeth. *In the shadows, of course,* Octavian thought, as he watched Squire hurry to keep after Danny.

'Where is this self-proclaimed King of Hell?' Danny Ferrick shouted, and his words had a timbre Octavian had not heard from him before. Imperious and cruel, his voice resonated across the lot.

In the night sky, Octavian saw a falcon he assumed must be Allison. It flew down toward a Lexus that had slipped halfway into a hole in the ground and alighted on the grill, where wings flowed into arms and it grew to become not Allison, but Charlotte. A moment later Allison stalked from between two cars, dragging a massive devil across the ground with her fingers thrust into its eye sockets.

'I am the King of Hell!' Lazarus declared, and, as Octavian watched, the sorcerer began to levitate himself in an armor of purple-black light that spilled from his eyes, but he didn't attack, confused by Danny's arrival with such powerful Demon Lords.

The spell Lazarus had used to attack Octavian had weakened with his distraction. He looked down to see that the wound in his abdomen had almost completely healed. Octavian was not yet fully whole, but he gripped the handle of his sword and stood, tearing free of the remaining wisps of Lazarus's magic as if it were nothing more than cobwebs.

Danny glanced around at the demons gathered there. They sensed the power in him, just as Octavian did. Just as Lazarus must.

'You're nothing!' Danny shouted. 'You worked the system and bought votes to get yourself the throne. You're not a king, you're a fucking politican!'

Octavian could feel Lazarus's fury. With the Lords looking on, he had to do more than attack – he had to defend himself.

'Tell me!' Lazarus shouted. 'Before I have my legions tear you apart, who are you that you think you can speak to me this way and live?'

Danny kept walking, marching across the pavement and shattered glass and dead demons to stand just below Lazarus, staring up at the sorcerer with defiance in his gleaming red eyes.

'I am Orias, son of Oriax, of the bloodline of Shaitan himself,' Danny said. He grinned, and the cruelty in that expression made Octavian shudder with the thought of what the young man had sacrificed this night. 'I'm the rightful king of Hell, motherfucker, and I command every denizen of the inferno to cease hostilities and return with me to perdition immediately.'

Lazarus seemed about to argue when Lord Malephar loosed another earthshaking cry, and its meaning seemed clear. *This is your king. Obey him.*

Danny – Orias – glanced only once at Octavian, but it was clear the demon despised him. Then Danny turned and began to walk back into the atrium, where he stood by the portal

315

and watched as Lazarus's army marched one by one through the bloody pool that hung in the air, returning from whence they had come.

Squire nodded to Danny – Octavian saw the moment pass between them, steeped in regret and farewell – and then the hobgoblin went to stand by a dented Dodge Caravan. Allison, Charlotte, and the blond vampire Octavian didn't know emerged from the throng of departing demons to stand beside him.

'No!' Lazarus screamed. 'You can't do this! The others support me! I am the king!'

Some of the demons hesitated, but only for a moment. Lord Haagenti came along behind them, and if this ancient, cosmic evil had chosen to follow Orias, son of Oriax, they would not argue.

Lazarus turned to face Octavian. He looked lost and desperate, but then his hatred returned, magnified a hundred-fold, and the purple-black magic that burned around him flared outward like wings of malevolent fire.

18

Phoenix's World
Ardsley-on-Hudson, New York, USA

Lazarus shifted his eyes only slightly – a tiny glance to the left, where Allison and the other Shadows had alighted on and around an overturned car – but it was enough for Octavian to notice, and it bought him a precious second or two. Lazarus turned and let loose the torrent of magic that had been building up within him. Huge arcs of bruise-purple light churned toward Allison, Alex, Charlotte, and the blond Octavian didn't know. Allison and Alex dove to take cover behind a car and Charlotte began to turn to mist, but the blond – too new to her abilities – was slow to react.

An icy calm had descended upon Octavian. A grim certainty. Double-edged sword clutched in his right hand, he thrust out his left and willed his own magic to manifest. He could feel it in his marrow, and in the roots of his soul, but this

CHRISTOPHER GOLDEN

time it did not erupt from his hands or eyes. Instead, he drew the magic from the air, summoning a crackling sphere that formed around Alex and the others. Lazarus's attack collided with that shield in a barrage of dark hues and cold flames.

Entropy, Octavian thought. Lazarus had used the same spell to kill Kazimir, and now he'd tried it again.

Lazarus screamed in rage and desperation, pouring on his attack, trying to blast through the protective sphere around the four Shadows. His plans had failed – Squire and Danny Ferrick had seen to that – and now he wanted to hurt Octavian in any way he could.

'Leave them be, Lazarus!' Octavian said, striding across the cracked and buckled pavement toward him. He stepped over the broken corpse of a black-hoofed devil. 'Even with your army gone, you can still have your heart's desire. You wanted revenge against me, and here I am!'

The sorcerer sneered and glanced his way, but instead of turning his attack toward Octavian, Lazarus floated across the lot toward the overturned car around which the four Shadows were arrayed. Thirty feet from them, he faltered slightly. Octavian only felt it because his own magic powered the sphere protecting the Shadows. Lazarus descended to the ground and began to walk rather than levitating himself. His face had turned ashen, the entropy hex leeching strength from him, consuming him from the inside.

'I will kill you, Peter,' Lazarus said, 'but not until you've watched your friends die. They were lost in Hell, just as I was, and you came looking for them. You abandoned me, but braved the fires of damnation for *them*.'

At that, Alex leaped from the overturned car and pushed toward Lazarus, trying to stride out to meet him.

'You self-centred prick!' Alex shouted, moving forward, forcing Octavian to extend the sphere around her and the others, even as Lazarus's magic raged and burned against it, trying to find a weakness . . . to break through and kill her. 'You need to get over yourself.'

Octavian picked up his pace. Sweat slicked the back of his neck. 'Alex, no!'

Lazarus faltered again, but this time it was recognition that caused him to hesitate.

'Alexandra Nueva,' the sorcerer said, eyes almost completely clear of that purple-black mist. 'Is it you?'

'You left *me*, you piece of shit,' Alex said. 'Peter and Meaghan and the rest, they didn't know I was alive. But you did, and when the time came when the magic you'd learned could have gotten us both out of Hell, what did you do? You made me your prisoner! Peter should have come back – should have made sure – but what you did was so much worse. Blame him for never coming for you, but you can't blame him for your sins, you son of a bitch. You've got to lay claim to those yourself.'

Lazarus stared at her a moment, but already Octavian saw the barrage of entropic magic that churned against the shield around the Shadows begin to diminish. Charlotte must have noticed as well, because the mist she'd become took human shape again.

'Is he . . .' the blond began.

Allison held up a hand to silence her, then shot a hard look at Octavian. They didn't share the telepathy that existed amongst blood-kin, but he knew her well enough that he could almost hear the thought: *Finish it.*

Lazarus lowered his hands and the magic stopped flowing from them, purple-black light making afterimages on

Octavian's eyes as it faded. The sorcerer nodded once at Alex and then turned toward Octavian.

'I *have* sinned,' he said. 'There's truth in her words. I have made choices that I ought to regret . . . but I regret none of them. If I had not committed those sins, I would not be here to make *you* regret your own decisions.'

Octavian drew to a halt perhaps ten feet from him, so close that he could see the beads of sweat on Lazarus's forehead and the dark circles under his eyes.

'I've already told you how sorry I am,' Octavian said, and he let the magical protection around the Shadows fade. Charlotte and the blond muttered in concern and dropped behind the car for cover, but he kept his focus on Lazarus. 'Unlike you, I have many regrets, and not finding out for myself whether you still lived will always be among them. But there are others. Opportunities squandered and trusts betrayed. With the long lives we've led, are any of us without such regrets?'

Lazarus shook with rage, and perhaps with weariness. 'You dare to compare—'

'No,' Octavian interrupted. 'I'm not comparing. We've both spent too much time in Hell.'

The sorcerer's face turned into a mask of bitter sarcasm. 'Oh, listen to the sympathy in your voice. Now, what? Are you going to tell me it's not too late? That you came back from Hell and found love and became a hero, and I can do it, too, if only I would turn toward the light?'

Octavian narrowed his eyes. 'After the things you've done? Not a chance.'

The magic had been simmering inside him and now he unleashed it. Bright copper light erupted from his left hand, burning Lazarus's face for an instant before the sorcerer managed to fight back, casting a hex instead of trying to defend himself. The two mages stood nearly toe to toe, copper fire raging against a fresh wave of indigo, a furnace between them.

Close enough that Octavian saw the very moment that Lazarus realized his mistake. Too late.

He drove the sword up through the sorcerer's abdomen at an angle, the point cleaving bone as it punched out through his back. Lazarus grunted, eyes going wide, and sank down onto the sword. His hex faded but did not vanish. Already weakened, and now impaled, he tried to fight on, fuelled by madness and vengeance. And yet the resignation in his eyes made Octavian wonder if perhaps he had not been quite so much a madman after all.

Octavian focused on the spell he'd cast, feeling for the particular frequency and melody in it, and he altered its purpose. It absorbed what little power remained in Lazarus's hex and then expanded into a shimmering blue sphere that immediately contracted around the sorcerer. Octavian released the handle of the sword but when Lazarus tried to reach and draw it out, he found he could not move his arms. Octavian had bound him so tightly that Lazarus was paralyzed.

'Squire made the sword. It cleaves magic. Whatever connection you do have is being severed.'

The Shadows gathered around Octavian. Allison came up beside him, and then Alex and Charlotte and the one he didn't know.

'This is Phoenix,' Charlotte said, gesturing to the blond.

'Phoenix,' Octavian said, nodding to her in greeting. 'Rising from the ashes. I like it.'

'Are you going to kill him?' Phoenix asked, glaring at Lazarus.

'I'm not sure that's possible,' Octavian replied. 'But I have something else in mind.'

Broken glass crunched underfoot and Octavian glanced up to see Squire emerging from the wreckage of the hospital atrium. His axe hung from the thong tied to his belt, one side of the blade broken and jagged. The dark blood of demons had spattered his clothes and face and his yellow eyes gleamed with anger.

'The last of them are leaving,' Squire said. 'And Danny's gone.'

Octavian felt the weight of his old friend's bitterness and resentment, and he knew that he had earned it. He could have argued that they'd had no choice, that Danny taking up the mantle of his inheritance – sitting on Hell's throne – had saved thousands, perhaps even millions of lives, but what would be the point? Squire knew those things already. The hobgoblin's deepest pain came from the fact that he'd been the one sent to persuade Danny, and the young demon had been unstable to begin with, and easily influenced. When Octavian had sent Squire, he had known that Danny would have a difficult time refusing his last remaining friend. But Squire had known it, as well. Whatever became of Danny now, they were both responsible, and every time Squire looked at Octavian, he would feel the weight of his own guilt.

'He'll be all right,' Octavian replied. 'He's the king.'

Squire scowled at him, not even glancing at the Shadows. 'Meaning we just painted a big fuckin' target on his back. Yeah, he'll be just fine.'

Octavian knew he ought to say something, but he could think of nothing that would mend the rift between himself and Squire. With luck, the two of them would live for many decades to come, so perhaps time would do what words could not.

He glanced at Allison. 'Watch Lazarus a minute,' he said, and strode past Squire.

Kazimir had died. Lazarus had destroyed Santiago and Taweret as well. Octavian had sacrificed his life as a young man in order to fight the Turks, but all of the bloodshed that resulted had not saved Byzantium. Centuries later, he had safeguarded his entire world from demonic invasions, the goddess of chaos, and other supernatural threats. He had exposed the darkest secrets of the Roman Church. Yet, for all the good he had done, so much anguish had resulted. The ruination of the Vatican sorcerers had left the world exposed. The loss of the Gospel of Shadows had left him unprepared more than once. If he'd had that ancient grimoire, he believed he would have come searching for Lazarus years ago – he had certainly thought about it often enough – and he wondered how different things might have been. How many would still be alive?

Nikki might have lived long enough for him to become her husband.

In all of his long life, Octavian had never felt the absence of departed friends more keenly than he did in this moment. He missed Nikki and Meaghan and Father Jack and Keomany – the woman she'd been – and he found that he missed Will Cody most of all. Cody's humour would have been so welcome now.

The thought of his old friend made Octavian smile, just a little.

'Peter!' Allison called. 'What happened to Kuromaku?'

'Working on it,' he replied.

With a wave of his hand, he swept all of the glass and twisted metal out of his path, crossed the last few feet of broken pavement and stepped over the window frame and into the hospital atrium. The new portal Naberus had created still shimmered in the midst of the ruined lobby, the bloody red surface smooth and undisturbed by the October breeze. The last of the demons had already passed through and the place had become unsettlingly quiet. Octavian glanced at the oval frame of the portal, a thin ribbon of human flesh and bone that had been manipulated into this shape by the gateway demon. He saw what might have been part of the dead woman's face and looked away, having seen enough of death for one night.

Octavian stepped over dead demons and the remains of patients and hospital staff until he came to the body he'd been looking for. Kuromaku lay amongst the corpses, his skin a slate grey, cloaked in a sheen of magic that had dimmed considerably and continued to fade even as Octavian knelt by him. He put a hand on Kuromaku's arm, which had the rough texture of stone but remained pliable. A small sigh of relief escaped him and he trembled with the power of all of the emotion that he'd been holding back.

The hand that touched Kuromaku's flesh began to glow with warm amber light. The most powerful spells he knew all came from deep within him, that core that had nothing to do with flesh or bone but with spirit, but this one seemed to spring from something even deeper.

A frisson of amber light spread over Kuromaku's still form and his flesh slowly returned to its original hue and texture.

Kuromaku frowned and groaned, stretched as if waking from a deep sleep, and then opened his eyes. They had no trace of the gleam that had been in them when he had been under Lazarus's control.

'Hello, brother,' Octavian said.

'I've missed the entire battle, haven't I?' the samurai asked.

'Mostly,' Octavian replied. 'But it's not quite over yet.'

He helped Kuromaku up. The Shadow could control every atom in his body, but still the spell that had almost killed him had left him stiff and slow. They turned to walk back out into the chaotic mess the parking lot had become, but Octavian paused when he saw that Phoenix had entered the atrium behind him. The others had remained outside and Octavian could see them standing guard over the rigid, paralyzed form of Lazarus, but Phoenix stood before the portal and stared up at it. Tears of blood streaked her face and she had one hand over her mouth as if to keep from sobbing.

Realization struck.

'You knew her,' Octavian said.

'Her name was Annelise,' Phoenix said. 'She was a friend of my father's. I can't leave her like this.' She turned and looked at Kuromaku and then at Octavian. 'Will you burn her? Leave nothing but ashes. I'll let the wind take her. I think she'd have liked that.'

'I can,' Octavian said. 'But you're a Shadow now. You could do it yourself, if you'd like. You can *be* the fire that burns her.'

Phoenix hesitated a moment, and then she nodded. From the way she stood, the cant of her head, Octavian realized she wanted privacy. He gestured to Kuromaku and the two of them left the atrium for the last time. Outside, Kuromaku and Allison embraced. Octavian heard the rush and crackle of fire behind him but did not turn around.

Squire stood a short distance away, gazing across the ravaged lot and through the trees, where they could see the moonlit ripple of the Hudson River below.

'I know we both did what had to be done,' Squire said without looking around. 'And I know we have to live with it. I just don't want to be lookin' at your goddamn face as a reminder.'

'One last favour,' Octavian said. 'And then you never have to see me again.'

'I'll do it,' Squire replied, not taking his eyes from the distant, darkened river. 'But not for you.'

'Fair enough.'

On the Shadowpaths

Phoenix hurried to keep up with the others as they marched through infinite darkness. She wrapped her arms around herself for warmth, although she didn't really feel cold. Squire had called these the Shadowpaths, which made it sound as if they were *somewhere*, but to Phoenix it felt very much like nowhere at all. The ground underfoot felt firm enough, but the couple of times she had begun to stray from the path the terrain had become spongy and uneven. In those moments she had looked into the depths of thick charcoal fog that obscured everything and heard the whispers of hungry things. Now she did her best to keep pace.

Squire led the way, almost totally lost in the black fog ahead. Only he knew how to navigate the Shadowpaths, or so she'd been told. Octavian and Allison followed, with the paralyzed body of Lazarus floating in the air between them, sword jutting from his chest and a sheath of magic hissing and glowing around him. Then came Charlotte, with Phoenix bringing up the rear and Alexandra Nueva covering them all from behind. 'Guarding our flank,' Octavian had called it. Several glowing orbs floated along the path beside them. They reminded Phoenix of the ball that dropped in Times Square on New Year's Eve.

'Hey,' Charlotte said, dropping back to link arms with her. 'You all right?'

Phoenix raised an eyebrow, realized Charlotte probably couldn't make out her expression, and shook her head. 'Are you kidding?'

'No. Just hopeful.'

'I feel like I'm dreaming,' Phoenix said.

'Me, too,' Charlotte said. 'I've never been on the Shadowpaths before, but it does have a very dream-like feel.'

'Or a nightmare.'

Charlotte matched her stride with Phoenix's. 'I'm not going to talk just to make noise, Phoenix, so let me say this. When you're ready, I'll tell you my story. It's pretty ugly, but the one thing it has in common with yours is that when I became a vampire—'

'I thought we were supposed to be Shadows.'

'That's what Octavian calls us. It's a philosophical difference.'

'Philosophical . . .' Phoenix said. 'So it's nothing but semantics? We really are monsters?'

Still arm in arm with her, Charlotte slowed them down and turned to her, face close enough that even in the black fog Phoenix could see her eyes.

'I've *been* a monster. Trust me, it's more than semantics. It's a choice.'

Phoenix felt a hand on her back, a none-too-gentle shove, and she and Charlotte stumbled forward.

'Move, you two,' Alex said, coming up behind them. 'You get lost in here, you could be lost forever.'

'That's a cheery thought,' Charlotte said.

Phoenix said nothing, only quickened her pace and caught up to Octavian, Allison and Squire. Alexandra Nueva scared her and she had no interest in idle chat with the woman. A thousand years in Hell had made Octavian into some kind of master sorcerer and driven Lazarus totally batshit crazy. Phoenix didn't want to be around if Alex ever snapped.

'I know what you're thinking,' Alex said, coming up behind her again.

Charlotte had dropped back a few feet, leaving Phoenix on her own with the hardcase. Alex's dark skin gleamed with the illumination from the spheres of magic Octavian had summoned to light their way; otherwise, she would have been almost impossible to see in the shifting fog. She was beautiful, but the glint in her eye was intimidating.

'I'm not thinking anything,' Phoenix said. 'I lost my father today. I lost friends and since I was too scared to stay behind and be ... whatever I am now ... without anyone who could understand, I came along with you people. That means I lost my whole damn world. I've got nowhere else to go. So, really, I'm doing my best not to think at all.'

'I just want you to know that you have nothing to fear from me,' Alex said.

Phoenix shivered. Maybe the hardcase did know what she was thinking.

Alex spoke again, but lower this time. 'I've got my own problems.'

Well, yeah, Phoenix thought. She looked back at Charlotte, who followed only a few steps behind, not wanting to get lost but also – Phoenix was sure – intimidated by Alex.

'Octavian was a Shadow. So was Lazarus,' Alex said. 'Octavian was the first to discover that if we live long enough, we go through a kind of metamorphosis. Cocoon.'

Phoenix snapped her head around to stare and almost collided with Squire, who couldn't keep pace with Octavian and Allison.

'*Cocoon?*' Phoenix said. She glanced back at Charlotte, couldn't make out her face but saw her nodding in the fog. Confirmation.

'When we emerge, the three parts of our essence are separated. Divine. Demonic. Human,' Alex said. Her voice seemed haunted and she hung her head. 'It's going to happen to me soon. I can feel it.'

'But you'll be human again!' Phoenix said, the idea giving her a spark of hope.

'I know,' Alex said. 'The thought terrifies me. I don't know how to be human anymore.'

Hell

Orias, son of Oriax, sat on the throne of Hell and wondered who would look after Mr. Doyle's house now that he had gone. Someday, Mr Doyle would return, and then he would gather the Menagerie again ... perhaps with new allies amongst them. Orias believed this with all of his heart. It was his faith.

But he would not be there.

He would be here, on the throne. His Infernal Majesty, Orias the First. Lord of Lords. Duke of Dukes. He would sit, as he sat now, looking out over the fires and the legions of imps and devils who served him, who implemented the punishments that the Suffering demanded by their mere presence. Orias understood that, now – understood Hell, or at least he had begun to.

He reached into his pocket, but somewhere along the way, he had lost his mother's emerald ring.

It would be all right, he told himself. He would be here on his throne and the Demon Lords and Archdukes and the Great Old Ones would be in their Deep Halls and Screaming Chambers. Everything would be perfectly all right.

Until the moment that enough of them decided that perhaps his bloodline wasn't a good enough reason for him to be King of Hell. At which point he would die.

But until then, everything would be just fine.

On the Shadowpaths

The noise of the Black Well made Octavian think of the laboured breathing of a sleeping giant. It drew the dark mist in, sucking at the very substance of the Shadowpaths, and every so often it seemed to exhale, a release that caused a bellow like that of an industrial furnace.

'This worries me,' Octavian said, turning toward Squire.

The hobgoblin stood a few feet away, further from the gaping, sucking maw of the Black Well. The mist around their legs no longer swirled – it flowed like water, and the Black Well was a whirlpool. Octavian had set his legs wide apart, fighting the gravitational drag of the well, and Lazarus floated above the ground beside him. Trapped inside the spell Octavian had woven around him, with the double-edged sword leeching his own magic away, Lazarus could only stare at them with eyes full of hate.

Allison, Charlotte, and Alex had kept back twenty yards or so from the rim, where Octavian had asked them to wait, just for safety. But Phoenix's curiosity had gotten the better of her. Despite her fear and the horror of the unknown that Octavian could see written on her features, the young woman could not help coming nearer to get a better look at the man she blamed for the abominable things that had been done to her father's corpse. Octavian admired her courage, but he wished she had stayed back.

'What are you worried about?' Squire asked.

Octavian stared at the hobgoblin's gleaming yellow eyes – at the anger in them. No profanity. No humour. No *Pete*. Danny Ferrick had been given a choice and had done the noble thing, the right thing, and Squire hated it. Hated Octavian. Maybe even hated himself.

'It keeps breathing like this. A black hole is constant gravity, inescapable, but if there's an inhale-exhale, that concerns me. There's always some chance he could—'

'No,' Squire said, eyes narrowed.

'No?'

Squire turned to look at Lazarus. For the first time, Octavian noticed that the magic sheathing the sorcerer rippled at the bottom, stretching in places where the drag of the Black Well pulled at it.

'I don't know how many wells there are,' Squire said grimly. 'Dozens, that I've seen, and a hell of a lot more that

I haven't. Maybe a little air drawn into one vents from another, but look at the darkness around us . . .'

Octavian glanced at his feet, where the flow of shadows into the sucking maw of the Black Well continued unabated.

'I've been on these paths for a very long time,' Squire said. 'And the oral history of hobgoblins is long. In all that time, I've never heard of anyone escaping the Black Wells. You put him down there, weakened like this, he'll have to use what little magic he has to keep himself alive. He'll die eventually, but it's going to take a very long time.'

Octavian hesitated. If he freed Lazarus, let him draw out the sword, he couldn't be certain of the outcome.

He glanced over at Phoenix, and then beyond her at the others, his friends. They were all homeless now, with no world to call their own, but if Lazarus had been allowed to succeed, world after world would have been claimed by Hell. The living would have been damned to eternal suffering. Yet, Octavian would have preferred to kill Lazarus in open combat, like a proper warrior. This felt like an execution, and that did not sit well with him.

Until he thought of Nikki's laugh, and the way she had reached out so often just to touch his hand, as if to reassure him that she was still there. Still with him. He thought of the expression on her face when she played the guitar, and the way her whole soul seemed to show itself when she sang. And then he thought of how many people had died horribly at Lazarus's command, and the parents and lovers and children who carried the same grief and pain that weighed on Octavian's heart.

With the merest turn of his wrist, he released the spell that had held Lazarus aloft. Still paralyzed by Octavian's magic, his mouth open in a silent scream within that sheath of bright energy, Lazarus fell into the swift current of darkness that flowed around them and was swept over the rim and into the Black Well. The last Octavian saw of him the sorcerer was his back, where the point of that double-edged sword traced its own path through the black fog.

And he was gone, drawn down into the Hollow.

For a full minute or more, Octavian and Squire stood there. Despite the hobgoblin's assurances, Octavian almost expected Lazarus to emerge in a black of dark magic, ready for battle. But the seconds ticked by and the darkness kept flowing over the rim without interruption.

Squire tapped his arm. 'Let's go.'

Octavian stared into the abyss a moment longer and then blinked and looked around. It felt as if he were waking from a terrible dream only to find himself in the grip of another. The illumination from the spheres he'd summoned cast strange shapes all through the darkness that swirled around them. He looked at Squire and Phoenix, and then he joined them, moving away from the Black Well.

'So what now, Peter?' Allison asked, as Octavian, Squire and Phoenix joined her, Charlotte, Kuromaku, and Alex. 'I mean . . . Squire could get you back to our world, but with the barriers Gaea has put in place, the rest of us are shut out.'

Octavian studied her face, saw the concern in Charlotte's eyes and Kuromaku's furrowed brow. 'There's nothing back there for me, now. Wherever we go, we go together.'

Phoenix stood hugging herself, set off slightly from the others. 'Yeah, but where? I can't go back – nobody would understand what I am now – but I'm not one of you, either—'

'Yes, you are,' Kuromaku said, nodding.

Octavian went to Phoenix and took her hand, gazing into her eyes. 'You *are*,' he said, guiding her closer to the others before releasing her hand.

'Thank you,' Phoenix said softly, with a sweeping glance. 'All of you. But still . . . what now? You can call us Shadows all you like, but we can't stay here in the dark forever.' Squire scratched his head and gave a small shrug. 'You don't have to stay here. There are endless worlds out there, and plenty of them have magic in them.'

'I don't want to have to hide what I am,' Allison said. 'I'm tired of being a Shadow. I want to live out in the light without being hunted, somewhere ordinary people aren't afraid of things they don't understand.'

Alex scoffed. 'You're talking about a fantasy, now. You can search a thousand worlds and you're not going to find what you're looking for. It doesn't exist.'

'Maybe it does,' said a voice from the shadows.

Octavian spun, magic surging from his heart and igniting at the tips of his fingers, ready to fight. *Lazarus*, he thought. The sorcerer must have found a way to defeat the dark gravity of the Black Well.

But the figure that emerged from the shifting darkness, though familiar, was not that of Lazarus.

Allison shifted into a bear and Alex into a towering devil. Kuromaku drew his katana while Charlotte and Phoenix stood back to back, fangs bared.

Squire took a step toward the interloper and cocked his head. 'What the fuck do *you* want?'

'You know this guy?' Charlotte asked.

Octavian nodded. 'His name is Wayland Smith.'

'The Traveller?' Kuromaku asked.

In response, the thin old man widened his ice blue eyes and made a small bow.

'The same,' Smith replied. 'And it's a pleasure to make your acquaintance. All of you.'

Allison and Alex shifted back to human form.

'I don't understand,' Phoenix said. 'Who is he?'

'A walker between worlds,' Squire said. 'Sometimes they stray onto the Shadowpaths, but the Smiths usually stick to the Grey Corridors.'

'That doesn't help me,' Phoenix said.

'What are you saying?' Octavian interrupted, staring at Smith. 'You were following us the last time we were on the Shadowpaths – Squire, Danny and I. And now here you are. What's your game, Traveller?'

Wayland Smith tugged at the iron ring in his beard, a sadness in those blue eyes. 'No game, Peter. If you've met one of my brothers or sisters before, perhaps you know enough about us to realize that we are more than just smiths or travellers. We are pathfinders. We are patrons of the lost. And it has been a very long time since I have encountered anyone as lost as you have become.'

He extended a hand to include the rest of them. 'You have all become wanderers.'

'And you have someplace in mind for us?' Allison asked.

Smith inclined his head. 'Since the last time I saw Peter, I have consulted with a council of other Wayfarers – my siblings – and we are all in agreement.'

The Traveller locked eyes with Octavian. 'There is a world where a unique set of circumstances has unfolded. All things supernatural were once walled away from the more ordinary regions and peoples of that world, but they have

335

been reunited in spectacular fashion. I will not lie and tell you that it is devoid of violence and ignorance, but the ordinary world has been merged with so much wonder that you and your friends would barely be considered unusual. Amongst so many other extraordinary individuals, I daresay it might even come to feel like home.'

It sounded almost too good to be true. Smith hadn't promised them utopia, but . . . a place where they no longer had to fight to survive or to drive back unimaginable evils that threatened the very fabric of existence . . . that was about as close to paradise as he could imagine.

He glanced at the others, his gaze lingering on Kuromaku. These people were his family now, but Kuromaku was his oldest and wisest friend.

'Can we trust him?' Allison asked.

They all looked at Squire, who wore a deep frown.

'The Wayland Smiths always have their own agenda,' the hobgoblin said. 'But they're not malevolent.'

'Yeah?' Alex said, moving toward Smith. 'What *is* your agenda, then?'

'Guiding the lost is my only interest here,' Smith replied, tugging the iron ring in his grey beard again. 'Though I will be relieved to have you all off of the Shadowpaths. The inter-dimensional fabric is delicate, and it's unsettling to have you tromping about in here. Anything could happen.'

Octavian arched an eyebrow. Whatever other purpose Wayland Smith might serve, he felt sure that, just then, the Traveller had been telling the truth.

He glanced at his friends again, this time focused on Allison.

'What do we have to lose?' he asked. 'We have nowhere else to go.'

For a moment, no one replied, and then Allison nodded. Kuromaku sheathed his sword and the magic crackling around Octavian's hands abated.

'Excellent,' Wayland Smith said. With a sage nod, he began to turn from them. 'Follow me, then, to the place beyond the Veil.'

Octavian felt as if a dreadful burden had been taken from him. One by one, they fell into step behind Wayland Smith. As they did, the fog swirling around them turned from pure darkness to grey mist, laced with an autumn chill.

In moments, only Octavian and Squire remained, and he looked at the hobgoblin in sudden understanding.

'You're not coming.'

'Of course not,' Squire replied. 'I've never belonged to just one world. Besides, someone has to look in on Conan Doyle's house from time to time. Just in case he comes back one of these days.'

Octavian tilted his head. 'I thought you said he was gone forever.'

A wry grin touched Squire's lips. 'Shit, Pete, are any of us ever really gone *forever*?'

With that, he stepped into the shadows and vanished from sight.

Octavian frowned, certain that the hobgoblin had been trying to tell him something he hadn't quite understood. Then he heard his name being called from far ahead in the mist, along the Grey Corridors, and knew he had to hurry.

The orbs he had summoned winked out as he contorted his right hand, and blue fire ignited around his fingers as he went in pursuit of the family he had chosen for himself, and the home for which they had wished.

A little magic to light the way, he thought. *Without that, we'd* all *be lost.*

A NOTE FROM THE AUTHOR

Something strange happened while I was writing this, the last Peter Octavian novel. While plotting it, I spent some time thinking about how Octavian could get into Hell without Gaea or Keomany stopping him from doing so. I thought – *well, Squire could do it,* not actually intending that Squire . . . you know, *do* it. But then I thought, *Why not?*

That started the ball rolling.

Tom Sniegoski and I created Squire – and Danny Ferrick, for that matter – some years back for our *Menagerie* novel series. There are four of those: *The Nimble Man, Tears of the Furies, Stones Unturned,* and *Crashing Paradise.* We had always intended to do one more but have never had the opportunity. *King of Hell* takes place, strangely enough, after that unwritten novel, which we still hope to get around to writing one of these days.

Once I realized that Octavian would be dimension-hopping with Squire, it occurred to me that many things were possible and strange plans took shape in my brain. Other links began to grow. If Octavian and Squire could co-exist, then couldn't Squire be a link to . . . well, everything else?

Readers who are familiar with my other work might notice references to *Strangewood, Straight on 'til Morning, Joe Golem and the Drowning City*, and others, as well as a tiny cameo or two. Phoenix Cormier is the central protagonist in my novel *Soulless*, in which you will find a much more detailed account of the events she alludes to in these pages. Wayland Smith appears in all three books in my *Veil* trilogy, *The Myth Hunters, The Borderkind,* and *The Lost Ones*. In the books of *The Veil*, all sorts of mythological and legendary people and creatures exist side by side, and if I was going to retire Octavian and his surviving allies, well . . . I think he'll be happy there.

I began writing about Peter Octavian during my senior year at Tufts University, either late 1988 or early 1989. Now, a quarter century later, his story is over.

For now . . .

Thank you for reading.
It means the world.

Christopher Golden
Bradford, Massachusetts
July 2013